The Light and Dark Side of Seventeen

By: Judith Kristen

AuthorHouse™
1663 Liberty Drive, Suite 200
Bloomington, IN 47403
www.authorhouse.com
Phone: 1-800-839-8640

AuthorHouse™ UK Ltd.
500 Avebury Boulevard
Central Milton Keynes, MK9 2BE
www.authorhouse.co.uk
Phone: 08001974150

This book is partially fictionalized. All of the characters' personal circumstances are products of the author's imagination.

© 2007 by Judith Kristen. All rights reserved.

No part of this book may be reproduced, stored in a retrieval system, or transmitted by any means without the written permission of the author.

First published by AuthorHouse 1/16/2007

ISBN: 978-1-4259-9000-8 (sc)

Library of Congress Control Number: 2007901969

Printed in the United States of America

This book is printed on acid-free paper.

Cover design by: Louis Castelli, PhD., of Philadelphia with the assistance of Mr. Tim Litostansky
Cover photographs by: Louis Castelli, PhD.
Cover Models: Samantha Bennett and Morgan Martino

Ms. Kristen's hair style by: Hope Doms of Salon Rouge, Cherry Hill
Ms. Kristen's makeup by: Felicia Green
Ms. Kristen's photo by: Jonathan Reed West

Please visit: www.JudithKristen.com

Acknowledgements:

For Andrew: You are my hero, my husband, my soul mate, my favorite dance partner, my sunshine, and my best friend. Without you... there is no me.

For Dr. Louis Castelli: The Emperor. My dear friend, all purpose genius, and mega-talented artist. Thank you for everything. ...So it is written.

For Kristen Lauren E.: This above all: To thine own self be true.

For the entire West family: Thank you from the bottom of my heart for being the wonderful, kind, loving, and supportive family that you are. I love you all.

For Harris Eckstut: Who taught me that half the game is 90% mental.

For Mallory McDonald-Eckstut: What was that again about posture and pensiveness?

For Betsy Bernhardt: A Flower Child for life. Love ya, Miss Betsy!

For my darling friend, Franny "The Shark" Fredman: For her glorious spirit, great sense of humor, and wonderful friendship.

For Shelly Fredman: Superb author, excellent teacher, terrific friend, fellow Beatlemaniac, *and* chocolate lover. How can ya miss, Shell?

For Taylor Beatty: One of the greatest teenagers on the planet. Thank you for being "you!"

For Aunt Anna and Uncle John Turner: For opening their home and hearts to me every summer of my younger years.

And for the following people who in many different ways helped me see this project through with their love, guidance, memories, friendship, and support:

The Gang at Ark-Media, Matthew Assante, Tony Barger, Francis X. Bell, Glenn Bennett, Robert Bennett, Jim Bernhardt, Big Kitty, Suzie Bird, Dr. Martin Black, Joce and Maxwell Black, Dianne Firth-Blythe, Pam Burns Bosco, Ruth Bowman, Andrew, Theresa and Quenton

Braithewaite, Frankford High Sweethearts - John and Denise Brouse, Raymond Burke, Esq., Carole Burke, Artist Nick Caprari, Gerry Carroll, The Cherry Hill Library, Larry and Beverly Ciletti, Dr. David Cohen, Captain Cramer, Alicia Crawford, "Dalrymple's", Lynn Cummings, Candis Dance, Mary O. Davine, MaryBeth Davis, Magna Diaz, Jennifer Dickson, Hope Doms, Donna Orio, Dr. Jay Dugan, Barbara Durban, Meredith and Burr Eckstut, Henry R. Edmunds School Staff, Carolyn Ellis, Linda Esh, Matthew Fegley, Dudley Fetzer, Richard Floyd, Bernie Foster, Evelyne Freiman, Marsha Galdi, Judy Gangemi, Maureen Grace, Meghan Grace, Sharon Grossman, Liz Guity, John Guthrie, Edna Horko, Helena Hubbard, Glen Hudson, Pete Hunter, Theresa Hunton and family, Akram "Homeslice" Ibrahim, Vishnu 'Joe' Jaglal, Nicole Jones, Kristen Jovi, Adam und Frau Junker, Angie Kelly, Dr. and Mrs. John Kershaw, James Killough, Kristen Kinder, Angela LaPolla, Arthur, Don, and Dustin Laricks, Stanley Leather, The students and staff at Lindenwold High School, Partners in Performance Founder – Sandra Lippman, Kathy Long, Genevieve Lumia, Donna Magliari, Richard Mantell, Bill, Kate and Madison McGinn, Johnny Metal, Dr. Andrea Miller, Angelica Miller, Harry Miller, Dr. Thomas Mills, Mrs. Mitchell, Monti, Lois Moskowitz, Ray Murray, My girls at Costa's, My "Linen Sister" Ona Kalstein, Kat "Kathy" Parsons, Thom Pastor, Pat Petronis, Bobby Phillips, Artist Brion Pizzi, The Darling of West Chester- Dot Plantholt, Dave Pruet, Carol and Cortney Quick, Principal Frank Ranelli, Inez Recupido, Doris Riley, Lloyd Remick, Esq., Captain Robbins, The lovely and talented Corey Rose, Jane M. Saffici, Mrs. Scally, Author Jason Sherman, Milton Hershey School, Maurice Pierre Shellbonte, Jason Sherman, Scott Shields, Annabell Shore, Margaret Siempre, Bernice Silverman, Grace Silverman, Dr. Hester M. Sonder, Lois Spearman, Mike and Marie Stafford, John 'Stag' Stagliano, Francisco Carreno-Stewart, Daisy Carreno-Stewart, Judd Stone, Dr. Sanya Sweeney, The late, great, Doc Turtel, Mike Reitter, The Bitners, The Dark Room Studio, The Tree Spirit on 130, (is anybody really reading this?) The Pennsauken Library, The Teen Writers Guild of Frankford High School, The students at Kiva High School, The Teen Writers Guild of Lindenwold High School, Dr. and Mrs. John Trzesniowski, my angel-connected friend - Dez Veerasawmy, Author Bob Wagner, Bob Sr., Suzie Wagner, Frances (with an 'e') "Mom" Wagner, Norm Washington, Janette Wheeler, Edna Widmaier, Misty Wyatt, Leslie Betts-Woodward, Denise and Jack Yeager, my son, Jonathan Reed West, To Sea Isle City, New Jersey, and, to my beloved Townsends Inlet, and, last but not least, to my wonderful sister and 'Sparkly' friend, Viva Reynolds-Pastor.

Just when the caterpillar thought the world was over
…it became a butterfly

This book is dedicated to the memory of:
Aunt Millie…
Carmela Rose Gioffre

for her kindness, spirit, and inspiration

For Dolly

The Light and **Dark** Side of Seventeen

By: Judith Kristen

1959 Cost of Living

New Home Purchase……..……..……$12,400.00
Average Yearly Income………….....… $6,048.00
New Car…………………….………..… $2,250.00
Gasoline………………..……. 19 cents per gallon
Ice-cream cone………………...…….... 10 cents
Harvard University Tuition….. $1,250.00 per year
Cigarettes………..……………. 21 cents a pack
Movie Ticket…………..…… 25 cents (matinee)
Summer Home Purchase – Beachfront Property
    Townsends Inlet, New Jersey
      $4,500.00

Prologue

June 1st, 1959.

Brenda nervously grabbed my hand and whispered, "Can you believe it?! As soon as Old Man Killough says, 'You are now *graduates* of Frankford High School, The Class of '59,' it's all over, my friend!"

I smiled at Bren and she smiled back at me.

Principal Killough continued speaking, but he was such an old blowhard I wasn't paying one bit of attention to a word he was saying - actually, I never did. So, to tune in to something more pleasant, I focused all of my attention on my parents seated just three rows away from me.

Mom was dabbing her eyes with a beautiful flowery handkerchief she had made the day before, while my Dad sat there with a 1000 Watt smile on his face. Oh, every now and then I could see his lip quiver a bit, the old softy, but, no matter what their reaction, I knew it made them both so proud to see me there - the very first member of our entire family to ever graduate high school!

I blew them each a kiss.

My mother sweetly smiled and then hid her face in her handkerchief. My father's face blushed just a wee bit, and then he grinned so hard I honestly thought his cheeks would burst.

Brenda nudged me, "I think this is it."

"Huh?"

"I said I think…"

Brenda's voice stopped dead in its tracks as a few odd squeals sounded from the microphone. One of the science teachers immediately ran over to the stage to remedy the situation and soon Mr. Killough's voice was booming over the PA system once again, "CLASS… it is my *great* honor to say… as well as my great, and heart-felt *pleasure* to say…"

Cut the drama.

"… that you are *ALL*… *each* and *every* one of you…"

Come on already!

"… graduates *of*…"

For God's sake, just SAY it!

"Frankford High School… The Class of 1959!"

Yippeeeeee!!

Bren and I turned toward each other as we moved our tassels from left to right.

"We did it, Kiddo!" I shouted.

"We sure did!" Brenda tossed her mortarboard high in the air. "UCLA, here we come!!!"

No sooner had Bren finished her sentence when we were swamped! I never saw such a rush of people in my entire life. It seemed as if everyone Brenda and I had ever known had stopped by to congratulate us. And then there was my poor Mom and Dad, struggling valiantly to get through that entire mob - to me. My mother's hand reached out in my direction and I held onto it tightly and pulled her in close. Dad managed to muscle his way in-between the school's star linebackers Johnny Metal and Norm Washington.

Finally, the three of us were all together!

Whew!

Mom wrapped her arms around me and so did my dad. Amid all that happy, jumping up and down, whooping and hollering going on, the three of us stood there in our own little loving cocoon.

"This is the proudest moment of my life," my father's voice started to crack.

I nuzzled my face into his strong, broad shoulders. My eyes started to fill, so did Dad's. "It was a *team* effort, Daddy!" I smiled. "All the way from Kindergarten to here." Immediately I slipped my mortarboard onto my father's head. Then, I gently unfastened the red, blue, and gold tassel from it and hooked it around the top button of my mother's pretty shirtwaist dress. "See? We're *still* a team!" I smiled again.

"Team Townsend, I like the sound of that." My dad grinned.

Just then Brenda's mother and father stopped by to say their congratulations. Mr. Mayberry thought the three of us looked 'pretty spiffy' so he just *had* to snap a picture of us: Dad wearing the mortarboard, me in my long, white graduation gown, and my Mom proudly displaying Frankford High's official 1959 red, blue, and gold graduation tassel on the front of her favorite pale blue eyelet dress.

It was the happiest moment of my life.

"Well, you three sure look super special," Mrs. Mayberry said.

"Congratulations, Pattie!" Walt Mayberry announced in his usual BIG booming voice. "And to you, too, George and Emma. You raised yourselves a mighty fine girl there!"

My mother and father smiled broadly and thanked them both - so did I.

What a terrific night.

I felt *so* grown up.

By now, most of my fellow classmates were heading home to big family parties, but Mom and Dad were all the family I had left except for my Aunt Anna and Uncle John over in New Jersey. Well, they were *really* my great aunt and uncle, both in their early 70's, but they were pretty spry for their age. As Uncle John would always say, "Don't let the snow on the rooftop fool ya!"

We had invited them to come to the commencement, and they were really looking forward to it, but then Uncle John broke his ankle as he walked off one of Captain Cramer's fishing boats. The combination of a rocking boat, a wet pier, and a pair of seventy-three-year-old legs just wasn't to his advantage. So, with his ankle in a cast, and his mobility squelched for a while, Aunt Anna decided it best that she stay home with her darling hubby. We were all more than understanding about it and wished Uncle John a speedy recovery. We also promised that we'd all come down to spend a few days at the shore over the 4th of July weekend. That made Aunt Anna and Uncle John very happy, not to mention me, too.

Mom and Dad had made plans to take me to a nice restaurant to celebrate, but then, upon Brenda's request, The Mayberrys invited us to their house to enjoy a more party-like atmosphere. Mom and Dad thought that was a great idea and so did I.

Brenda Mayberry was my very best friend. In fact, I can't remember a time when she wasn't. Our mothers were both expecting at the same time. I was born on February 26th, 1942, and Bren (as I usually called her) was born a day later. We attended Henry R. Edmunds Elementary School together, sat right next to each other from Kindergarten through eighth grade, and then took the same academic courses all throughout high school. Well, all except one. I studied Latin and German while Bren studied Latin and French.

And, as far as family goes? Well, I always wished I had a little brother or sister, but I had no siblings. Bren had an older brother named Arthur, and a younger sister named Carole, but Brenda and I were closer to each other than she was to either one of them. It was just a natural love and friendship between us from the very beginning.

As we were all filing out of the auditorium, I called to Bren. "We'll be over at your place in about twenty minutes, okay? We're just gonna take some photos here by the front entrance."

"Okaaaaay!" She smiled back, "Bye, Mr. and Mrs. Townsend! Bye, Pat! See ya!"

Mom, Dad, and I waved our goodbyes.

Soon we were standing in front of the beautiful main entrance to Frankford High School. It seemed that all of the 'official' pictures I ever saw of Frankford High took place there. It was a rather majestic area. It had an old world charm to it that attracted every one to that particular entrance.

Dad took photos of me and Mom.

Mom took photos of me and Dad.

I took photos of Mom and Dad, and, lo and behold, good old Mr. Killough came by and offered to take some photos of the three of us together!

Maybe he wasn't such a bad guy after all.

Photo shoot over, Dad neatly packed away his prized Pentax camera, and, without any further delay, we headed straight for our car - the first new one Dad had ever owned. It was a 1959 Chrysler New Yorker 4-door hardtop colored a striking 'Lustre-Bond Spun Yellow.' It made me chuckle every time I thought about the bright color he chose, my parents were such conservatives, but they loved it, they really did, and that was all that mattered.

I immediately hopped in the car and made myself comfortable in the huge back seat while Dad, ever the gentleman, held the door open for my mother.

"Thank you, Sweetheart," she smiled.

"My pleasure, Love," he smiled back.

The minute Dad turned over the engine I asked him, "Daddy, can you put on Wibbage?"

"Put what? What's that again?"

My mother laughed. "George, it's a radio station, W-I-B-G. But the kids all call it Wibbage."

Dad smiled. "Oh, sure... I remember."

No he didn't.

Mom tuned the station in for me and suddenly I heard Hy Lit announce, "For all of tonight's graduates: from Mastbaum, Lincoln, Dobbins, St. Maria-Goretti, Germantown, Frankford..."

"Yaaaaaay," I hollered.

"Roman Catholic and Kensington. This one's for you! Get out on the dance floor and rock and roll one for Hyski!"

The song was, *Get a Job* by The Silhouettes. I thought that was pretty funny, considering most of us were already out there looking for one.

I sang along with it and my parents smiled. In fact, I think I actually saw my mother's toe tapping! Then, *Kansas City* by Wilbert Harrison played followed by *Stagger Lee* by Lloyd Price - both big favorites of mine. By the time Lloyd was finished, we were right outside our house on the 1000 block of Allengrove Street, and, just two doors away, the Mayberry party was going full swing!

I quickly opened the car door, unzipped my graduation gown and there I was, completely dressed for my high school graduation party over at Brenda's house.

Mom had taken me down Frankford Avenue the week before commencement and bought me a beautiful lilac linen dress from Sack's Dress Shoppe. She thought lilac was my color. The dress wasn't anything over the top, but it was really pretty. It looked like something Sandra Dee wore in one of her 'Gidget' movies - sweet, not too mature, but very pretty. I absolutely loved it!

"You look beautiful," my mother said.

"You *look* like a young lady who's ready for UCLA in the fall." My father's eyes seemed a bit watery.

I smiled. "Come on, Mom, Dad... let's go!" I started to pull my parents arms in the direction of Brenda's house. "It's time for a party!"

Suddenly my father stopped me.

"Good grief!"

"What is it, George?" my mother questioned.

"I promised Walt I'd supply the ice! Listen, you two get to the party and I'll run over to The Ice House. I'll be back in a flash." He started to take his car keys out of his pocket.

"That's not right! Team Townsend should go to the party together!" I practically whined.

"No, *you* should be at the party, Sweetheart. This is your day and Brenda's day."

My mother agreed, "Dad's right. You go have fun and we'll be back in a flash."

"But Mom…"

"No 'buts'," she smiled while straightening a ribbon in my hair. "Now you get on in there and have yourself a grand old time. This is the start of a whole new cycle for you, Pattie. Your life is just beginning!"

I hugged my mother. "I love you."

"I love you too, Angel."

Quickly I swung my arms around my father. "Hurry back, Daddy, so I can have the first slow dance with you!"

"That's a promise, Love Bug," my father said with a big, broad smile on his face.

I watched as Dad held the car door open for my mother, and just before he entered his side of the car, he waved at me. "I love you!"

"I love you, too, Daddy!"

Then, off they drove down Allengrove Street in that big beautiful 'Lustre-Bond Spun Yellow' car.

I smiled all the way to Brenda's front door.

* * * * * *

I was a lucky kid.

I really was.

Maybe I didn't have any siblings, but I had wonderful parents who truly loved each other, *and* who also loved *me* unconditionally. Mom was a bit reserved by nature, but she was always very loving toward me - never a day went by that I didn't hear an 'I love you' from her. And, *most* Dads, in 1959, didn't even hug their sons or daughters as I recall. It's not that they didn't love their kids; that was just the way it was back then. But, despite what the times called for, my family showed the emotions they felt quite openly and honestly.

I was blessed and I knew it.

* * * * * *

I ran up to Brenda's door, rang the bell, and was immediately greeted by at least fifty people.

"Congratulations, Pattie!!!"... "YOU DID IT!!!"... "Look out, California, here come Pat and Bren!!!"

Brenda was the first to rush up next to me. "Hey you! Where's your Mom and Dad?"

"They ran over to The Ice House, my Dad forgot to buy some. Give 'em fifteen minutes and they'll be in here doin' the Jitterbug with us," I joked.

Brenda chuckled along with me.

Suddenly I stopped to take a good look around to see just exactly what was going on at this wonderful party. Records were blaring, kids were dancing, and what a spread!

A HUGE cake, ice cream, my mom's homemade potato salad and macaroni salad, potato chips, pretzels, watermelon, and then, outside, there were all kinds of barbequed steaks, chicken, ribs, hot dogs, and hamburgers cooking on the grill. It looked like the Mayberrys were feeding an army!

I made my way through the crowd, thanked Brenda's parents, and then said "Hi" to some of our neighbors who were in attendance: Mrs. Manuzak, The McGonagles, Mrs. Bluett, Dr. and Mrs. Buzby, The Tierce family, Mr. and Mrs. Dilks... There's no other way to put it, the Mayberry house was wall to wall people.

Brenda's brother Arthur was in charge of the records and the selection was Billboard's Top 40 all the way. We all felt like we were on Bandstand! One super tune after another. *At The Hop*, by Danny & The Juniors, *Willie and the Hand Jive*, by Johnny Otis, *Sh-Boom*, by The Crew Cuts, *Little Darlin'*, by The Diamonds, and, one of my all time favorites, *Tutti Frutti*, by Little Richard.

Just as I was running for the punch bowl, Brenda stopped me and said, "Maybe you wanna wait for that."

"Huh?"

"Hold off on the punch for a bit."

"Why?"

"It's gettin' warm. We're holdin' out for your mom and dad to bring the ice."

Mom and Dad?

"What time is it?" I questioned.

"Twenty after six," she answered as she looked at her watch.

"Twenty after six?! My mother and father should have been back here a half an hour ago!" My heart started to race. "God, I hope nothing happened!"

Brenda was her usual comforting self. "Pattie, don't worry, they probably stopped to talk to Chuck at The Ice House. Your dad is probably braggin' again about you gettin' a full scholarship to UCLA!"

"I guess so," I smiled. "He bent the milkman's ear for almost an hour last week."

She smiled back at me.

The records continued to play: *Jailhouse Rock*, by Elvis Presley, *Little Bitty Pretty One*, by Bobby Day, and *Long Tall Sally*, by Little Richard. I *loved* Little Richard!

Just as I was about to take my shoes off and give my dancing feet a rest I noticed some commotion outside. I thought it might have been a few of the guys out there, the non-dancers, you know, playing some touch football or something... but that wasn't it.

I looked out the window again and saw two police cars parked right outside my house and there were four officers talking to Mr. Mayberry. Then I saw Mrs. Mayberry run up to her husband quickly followed by Brenda. I walked out of the front door in what can only be described as a slow motion feeling with something grabbing at my soul... something foreboding.

As I drew near to my home, I could hear Brenda's voice and all I could hear her say over and over again was, "Oh, my God! Oh, my dear God!"

I don't know how long it took me to make it to where everyone was standing, but when I did, I heard Mr. Mayberry say, "This is their only child... her name is Pattie."

Brenda turned and ran back into her house, while Mrs. Mayberry put her arm around my shoulder.

An officer with a shiny badge number that I will never forget - 1017 - moved closer toward me and began to speak, "Pattie, there's been an accident at Harrison and Castor."

"What's that got to do with me?"

"Miss Townsend," he said softly, "your parents were side-swiped by some joy riding graduates who had far too much to drink."

"Side-swiped?"

"Their car was hit and it slammed into the side of the railroad bridge."

"My parent's car?" I could feel my knees start to wobble and my head was spinning. "Where *are* they? What happened to them?!"

"They were taken to Frankford Hospital, Miss and..."

Immediately I turned toward Mr. Mayberry. "Please, you gotta take me there! I *have* to see them! I..."

Mr. Mayberry sighed and I felt his wife's arm tighten around my shoulder. I saw the officer nod at Brenda's dad as if to give him the okay to tell me exactly what had happened.

"Pattie... well..." his voice was unusually raspy, "when your parents hit the side of the old Castor Avenue bridge, they hit pretty hard, Sweetheart, and..." He glanced back at his wife.

"I'll tell her, Walt." Mrs. Mayberry turned and suddenly we were face to face. Her arms were now holding on to both of my shoulders. I saw her lips quiver a bit and her eyes were filled with tears.

"Just take me to the hospital! Mrs. Mayberry, PLEASE!!!"

Her voice was soft and monotone. "Pattie… your mom and dad…" she cleared her throat a bit, "Your mom and dad died in that accident. The rescue squad did all they could and so did these officers, but they had already passed on before they got them to the emergency room."

"You're telling me my parents are DEAD???!!!"

She nodded and tears fell from her eyes. Just then I saw Brenda running toward me. I screamed at her, cringing in pain, "BREN!!! MY MOTHER AND FATHER ARE DEAD!!! BRENDAAAA!!! OH, MY GOD!!! MY MOM, MY DAD!!! BRENDAAAAAAAAA!!!!!!"

She made it to my side just in time to catch me.

Chapter One

It was June 10th, 1959.
Nine days after graduation...
Nine days since my parents died...
Six days since their funeral...
And I was still in a fog...
Fifty feet thick.

I stood in my bedroom, arms folded over one another, staring out the window. I was looking at a huge, green and white, Miller's Moving and Storage truck filled to the brim with all of the things that used to make my now empty house a home.

I could hear Uncle John downstairs, his heavy foot-cast thumping against the oak flooring. "Pat? The movers are done. We'll be leavin' soon."

I turned toward his voice, "Okaaaaay... I'll be down in a little bit!"

Suddenly my Aunt Anna appeared in the doorway. "Pattie?"

"Yes?"

"Uncle John and I will wait for you in the car. Say your goodbyes to the house, Dear."

"I will," I said quietly.

"And take your time... we're in no hurry."

My aunt turned away from me and then, a few moments later, I heard her sturdy low-heeled shoes heading down the back staircase. She started to talk to Uncle John but I couldn't quite make out what they were saying, I guess it was because I was a bit too preoccupied staring out my bedroom window. I watched as one gentleman in dark blue overalls carefully squeezed in the last two boxes on top of Mom's Singer sewing machine. Then, he closed the doors, positioned a large metal fastener across them, and locked up the truck.

"LET'S GO, BILLY!" he hollered. Without delay, three burly men and the man in the overalls hopped into the green and white moving van and drove away – taking everything our happy home had ever held right along with them.

Less than a minute after that I saw my Aunt Anna and Uncle John get into their car and make themselves comfortable. Aunt Anna had to drive because my uncle still had that clunky white cast on his foot. I watched him as he slowly rested his head on the window, knowing full well he'd be asleep in no time at all. If I knew my Uncle John - and I did - he'd end his nap just about the time we were pulling up outside their cute little house on 85th Street, in Townsends Inlet, New Jersey.

I smiled at the thought of it.

From my window I watched as Aunt Anna opened up a Better

Homes and Gardens magazine, I sighed deeply, and then turned to look at my empty room. Don't ask me how I did it, but, by some means, I managed to look beyond the barrenness, and my heart saw it as it used to be. I touched the flowery wallpaper and remembered the weekend my dad put it up for me.

It was three days before my fifteenth birthday.

Mom and I picked out the pattern at Silverman's on Kensington Avenue.

I remembered the nights my mother would tuck me into bed and say my prayers with me. I remembered the story books she would read: Cinderella... Snow White... Black Beauty... I remembered when Dad made me my very own vanity – complete with matching mirror. Mom made a really pretty lilac-colored net skirt to go around it. It made me feel like a movie star.

When I couldn't bear the thought of another memory, I left my room and closed the door behind me.

See ya...

I walked slowly down the hallway and traced my hands along the textured wallpaper. I walked by the main bathroom, my mother's sewing room, the guest room, and then I opened the door to my parents' room. Even empty it was still beautiful. The floors were a rich cherry wood, unlike the golden oak flooring throughout the rest of the house, and there were crown moldings and chair rails, and a beautiful crystal ceiling light that my father bought for Mom on their honeymoon up in New York City. My mother said it was just too gorgeous to pass up, and so, Dad bought it for her right on the spot.

I flipped on the light switch.

It sparkled like the Hope Diamond.

I leaned back up against the wall, cupped my hands over my face, and cried.

How long I stood there is anyone's guess.

When I was all cried out, I wiped my eyes as dry as I could and then took a deep breath.

Time to get goin', Pattie.

Just as I was about to leave my parents' room, for some odd reason, I remembered the hide and seek games I played with my mom and dad when I was a kid. My favorite hiding place was a very long closet directly across from their bed.

To look at it, it just seemed like a regular old closet, but the further you went to the right, toward the windows, well, the closet just kept going and going and going.

It stopped right at the front of the house. I *loved* to hide there.

I decided to open the door and hide there one last time.

I sat in the dim light and softly called out to my mom and dad.

"I wish you could find me." My eyes started to fill. "And I wish all of this was just a bad dream." I sighed. "Remember how much fun I had hiding here when I was little? And remember how sometimes I would just come in here to sit and be quiet with my thoughts? ...It was a nice, safe place." I rubbed my hands across my face, brushing the tears away and then slowly repeated what I had just said. "A nice... safe... place..." I wiped a few more tears away from my eyes and started to stand up in the tallest part of the closet when all of a sudden something fell down on top of me - a box that the movers had obviously missed.

I walked out into the sparkle of my mother's precious ceiling light and noticed that it was a beautifully wrapped gift... for me! There was a pretty pink card attached to it and I opened it immediately.

It read:

Dear Pattie,
Here is a special present from me and Daddy. Now I know it isn't a poodle skirt, or a charm bracelet, but it's a gift that has love written all over it.
XOXO,
Mom and Dad

I lifted the soft ivory-colored tissue paper away from the box and there was my father's Frankford High School sweater, and, pinned right near the top button was my mother's Drama Club pin - a club she joined when she was a student at Frankford - where she first met my dad.

They fell in love 'in seconds flat' as Dad would always tell me, and I believed it. They had hoped to marry right after they graduated, but they both had to leave school in eleventh grade to go to work to help support their families.

Somehow, as tight as things were back then, they still managed to save enough money to buy some plain gold wedding bands and to rent a little apartment on Princeton Avenue. That sweater was a symbol of the beginning of their love. What a beautiful gift to give to me.

I wrapped the sweater around myself, switched off the light, and then walked down the darkened hall on my way to the back steps.

I turned one last time toward my parents' bedroom, and then slowly walked down the sturdy winding oak staircase, and out the back door.

As I approached Aunt Anna and Uncle John's car, I gave a long, sweeping glance at the house: the apple tree in the back yard, the pear tree, the dogwood tree, the grapevines, the perfectly trimmed hedges, and the huge maple tree that had shaded our front yard since the day I was born.

So long, my beautiful Allengrove Street.
...So long.

Chapter Two

I ran up to Aunt Anna and asked her to give me a few more minutes to say goodbye to Brenda - of course, she said yes.

I was barely up the front steps of the Mayberry home, when Brenda flew out the front door and wrapped her arms around me. "Oh, God, I'm just gonna miss you sooooooo much!"

"But you'll be down in two weeks, right?"

"Well, fifteen and a half days, but who's counting?"

I smiled.

"Take good care of yourself, Pattie."

"I will."

"So, when are the renters moving in?"

"July 1st. A lot can happen in a month, Bren."

She sighed and hugged me again. "I'll write to you. *And*, I'll see you in two weeks."

"You mean fifteen and a half days."

We smiled at each other.

"Listen to me. Just get your dad to drop you off at 13th and Filbert at 9:45. Stay on the bus 'til you're in Townsends Inlet. I'll meet you at 12:00 on the corner of 85th and Landis."

"It's a deal."

"I gotta get goin' Bren. Please thank your family again for me, for all their help, you know, since the… since…"

"Don't give it a second thought. That's what friends are for, Pat."

Again she hugged me and I hugged her back tightly. "See you soon."

"Okay. Love you, Pattie!"

"Love you, too, Brenda."

"See ya."

"Yeah… see ya."

* * * * * *

"Ready to go?" Aunt Anna questioned as she adjusted her driving glasses.

"Uh-huh."

Anna Mae Turner was one of the most cautious drivers in America; as well as one of the slowest. But, today wasn't about speed, today I didn't mind the slow drive down Allengrove Street, *or* the 15 mph trip as we passed by Henry R. Edmunds Elementary School, because that slow and easy ride allowed me to take in all of those sights and burn them into my mind - remembering those places, the houses, the people, and all the wonderful memories that were connected to them.

Before I knew it, the old neighborhood was gone and we were driving down Robbins Avenue, approaching the Tacony-Palmyra Bridge.

"John, I need a nickel for the toll."

"Huhhhh?"

"A nickel for the toll, Dear. There's one in that little blue change purse in the glove box."

Sleepy Uncle John leaned over and opened the tiny compartment, handed my aunt five cents, and then we were on our way over 'The Tacony' and into the lovely Garden State of New Jersey.

What I used to think of as just a wonderful trip to have some fun at the shore and get away from city life for a while, was now a drive to my new home, *and* my new life - without my parents.

I was rather quiet along the way, but my mind was spinning with thought after thought.

Was I really doing the right thing holding off college until next year? Would my parents want me to do that? Would the time I thought I needed to heal truly help me? Will I fit in at the Turners? Would I adjust to the long and lonely winter at the Jersey shore? ...So many questions.

As for my Aunt Anna and Uncle John?

Well, Uncle John was snoring and chuckling in his sleep, and Aunt Anna was singing several old songs that she loved: 'You'll Never Know if You Don't Know Now' … 'The Chatanooga Choo-Choo'… and 'Faith of Our Fathers,' her favorite church hymn. I sat there looking out the back window alternating between thoughts about my future, and saying a silent goodbye to the big city I had known and loved all of my life.

Try as I might to hold on to it, Philadelphia slowly faded away from the rear window of the car and the local scenery soon turned into small New Jersey towns and acres of wide-open farmland. I saw horses playing in the fields, farms blooming with flowers, and endless rows of beautiful golden wheat. Along our way we also drove by a number of little roadside farm stands – a given on the highways of New Jersey in the summer time. They were marvelous places, cute little shacks filled with fresh eggs - a penny a piece - fresh milk, cream, and all kinds of delicious fruits and vegetables.

We finally stopped at one - my aunt's favorite - a place called 'Lucky Mary's' right outside a little town called Tuckerton. Aunt Anna and I picked up a few dozen eggs, some fresh bacon, jars of apricot, cherry, and peach preserves, and one deep-dish blueberry pie made just that morning; while Rip Van Turner never lost a minute's sleep.

"How much longer 'til we get to Townsends Inlet?" I questioned while packing the trunk with our newly purchased items.

"Oh, maybe another hour."

"Okay, just askin'." I nodded politely.

"How are you doing, Pattie?"

"I'm doin' good."

"Are you?"
"Sure."
I mean, I think so.

Aunt Anna smiled at me, I smiled back and then we were off and running, roaring along at a mighty twenty-five miles per hour. Uncle John hadn't stirred. He was still sound asleep and obviously enjoying the fresh air and the nice quiet ride in their 1956 Buick Roadmaster 2 Door Hardtop. The Buick was a pretty cool-looking car. It had a really shiny two-tone paint job, a jet black top, with a deep reddish-colored body. I didn't know much about cars, but I knew I loved that one.

I guess some of that fresh air was getting to me too, because the next thing I recall is my Aunt Anna's sweet voice, saying, "Time to wake up, John... Pattie. We're home, Dears!" I slowly stretched my arms out wide, yawned, and then looked around me.

Yup, there we were on the two hundred block of 85th Street, right outside the charming little house they had called their own since 1927. As I exited the car a clean ocean breeze surrounded my face and it felt wonderful. I took a deep breath, grabbed my purse, and then stood by the back of the car waiting for Uncle John to open the trunk. As I waited, I gave a rather detailed and appraising stare at their quaint green and white cottage. Yes, I had to admit it, the Turners had a pretty neat little place.

First off, it was situated on eight-foot stilts. I guess the architect who designed it figured it was a smart idea since they were only about fifty feet away from the bay. Some hurricanes can blow through Townsends Inlet and raise the water level so high that the bay can end up sitting right in your living room. So, stilts were a very good idea.

My summertime friends weren't at the shore just yet, so the cheerful greetings my presence usually garnered was nothing more than a quick smile and a wave from neighbors Jake and Carrie Robinson.

I waved, grabbed my luggage, and then walked up the twelve steps to the front door of the Turner household - my new home.

Aunt Anna's and Uncle John's house was welcoming and comfortable. Flower boxes overflowed from each window, filled with red geraniums, white petunias, purple verbena, and long, lush sweet potato vines. As soon as I entered the small porch I noticed two overstuffed chairs sitting across from each other, and a rather large puzzle of the Grand Canyon spread out all over a well-worn, leather-topped card table.

The dining and living room were combined all into one, making it a nice, open-spaced area. The oak floors were covered with beautiful old woolen rugs, and the sofa was big, plaid, and comfy, 'cause Uncle John liked it that way. My uncle was a slightly large man and he loved to nap there, so it had to be nice and soft and cozy. To the right of the sofa was an overstuffed chair that matched it, and next to that was a rather ornate standing ashtray that always held a few rare Cuban cigars, one cherry wood pipe, and two packs of Lucky Strikes. Across from my uncle's smoking stand was Aunt Anna's own personal piece of heaven, a big, straight-backed rocker with a bag of yarn and knitting needles tucked neatly in-between the rungs. And, as a nice finishing touch, there was an antique brass domed lamp centering itself over a small shiny wooden table, complete with crocheted table cloth, courtesy of the talented hands of Mrs. John Turner.

Then... there was the kitchen.

The biggest room in the entire house.

The table was huge, at most it could comfortably seat twelve. The chairs were unique; they were pretty, rounded Windsors – solid maple - and they weighed a ton! The chair seats were beautifully covered in sturdy white linen, perfectly stitched by Aunt Anna on her old push-pedal Singer sewing machine.

In fact, everything in Aunt Anna's kitchen was totally white with the exception of the little café curtains that were specked with a pretty strawberry blossom pattern here and there, and a bit of light green coloring on her old 1939 porcelain claw foot stove.

And, because the kitchen faced the west, every night, when the sun would begin to set, the entire kitchen took on this magical, golden glow. It was beautiful. And, from the open window above the sink, you could hear the seagulls squawking as the fishing boats came in, hoping for a free handout from some good-hearted fisherman. And then there would always be the glorious aroma of another delicious dinner from my Aunt Anna's kitchen - served precisely at 6:00. What a great place!

Nothing at the shore ever tasted better to me than the fresh flounder she cooked in her special enamel frying pan - always basted and fried in Carrie Robinson's home-churned butter. Then, to top that all off, she'd make home-made French fries and a nice big garden salad. Oh, and maybe an apple pie or a peach cobbler for dessert. Aunt Anna's cakes and pies were a neighborhood specialty, too! She was often asked to make several for local church events, fund raisers at the local elementary school, or bake sales up at The Civic Center, and she was always happy to oblige.

And, to the left of that wonderful kitchen, directly in the back of the house, was a screened-in porch with a small washroom. I loved that room.

I can recall many nights when my mom and I would sit out there, just taking in that wonderful fresh salty shore air, quietly reading a book. It was peaceful and picture perfect. I guess that's why I always slept so well at my Aunt Anna's.

I was hoping that would still be the case since so much had changed in my life. Would I wake up and expect to see my mom there helping Aunt Anna making breakfast? Dad gearing up for another fishing trip in Uncle John's little motor boat?

I knew the adjustments would be hard, but I was willing to do whatever it was that I had to do. My parents lived their lives to bring me joy, a happy family life, and a good education; it would be an insult to their life on this Earth if I were to fail what they started for me.

For certain I would honor their memory, and, to *continue* that honor, I would do whatever I could to grow up and be a good person, too - kind, caring, understanding, and giving.

... Like Mom

... and Dad.

* * * * * *

I carried my luggage up to my second floor bedroom. Aunt Anna and Uncle John had recently remodeled that part of the house and it looked great!

It used to be one big attic area that functioned as their bedroom, but then they decided to turn it into three nice-sized single bedrooms and a bathroom. Aunt Anna gave me the biggest of the two guest rooms. I loved it. It had a nice full-size bed, a built in wall unit, enormous dresser, and a large double-door closet so I was in pretty good shape as far as a place to stay.

Now, all I had to do was figure out where I fit in, and what it would take to forge ahead in the right direction to make a good life for myself. As I took stock of my situation I especially prayed for the strength to move forward on my own, now that I was without the love and guidance I had come to rely upon from my mom and dad.

This would be the first chapter of my life without my parents and the pages were all blank.

So much to fill in...

So many questions...

Chapter Three

Four blocks from the Turner household lived The Dollio family: seventeen-year-old Christine, her father Sean, stepmother Nikki, and two siblings: Apry, age four, and Mack, just nine months old.

Pattie had never met Christine, but she would - and soon.

Christine Dollio was seventeen going on forty.

Like Pattie, she had experienced a hard-to-deal-with death in her early years. Christine's mother had suffered from kidney problems and polio all of her life, and then, when Chris was barely eight years old, her mom was diagnosed with breast cancer. Mrs. Marcia Christine Elizabeth Dollio died on Christmas Eve of 1952, only two years after her diagnosis.

Christine's father turned to alcohol and other women to ease his pain, while Christine - Dolly as she was called by those close to her - was left to deal with her personal loss and agony all alone.

…And it didn't work.

Dolly's schooling suffered, her appearance was neglected, and nothing ever played straight in her head after that.

Nothing.

Dolly was also very angry and bitter that her father could so easily smooth over all of his own pain with a few bottles of Jim Beam or a 'hot one-night stand' as he would so proudly announce, with a big-busted waitress from a local hang-out up in Atlantic City.

Soon, one of those women became a regular at the Dollio house on 89th Street, and, on April 1st, 1954, less than sixteen months after her mother's death, her father married one of his friend's daughters, a twenty-year old dancer named Nikki Margaret Shallto.

Friend and drinking buddy Dave Shallto owned one of the biggest and most popular night clubs in Atlantic City. And, Dave was friends with Sean Dollio even when Dolly's mother, Marcia, was alive. In fact, all three of them went to high school together!

Christine remembered hearing her father make comments to her mother about Nikki for a long time. You know, how pretty she was and what a beautiful woman she'd grow up to be! He was almost salivating. It made Dolly feel very uneasy, and she was certain her mother was embarrassed and hurt by his comments as well.

So, when Nikki Margaret Shallto was just one day short of her 21st birthday, she officially became the stepmother of Christine Dollio, a girl just about eight years her junior.

Nikki was cool about it and even thought it was pretty humorous. "This is my baby girl," she'd say pointing to Dolly in front of her friends… then they'd all laugh.

Somehow Dolly didn't think it was quite so funny.

Would you?

Shortly after the new Dollio marriage began, along came two children - Apry and Mack - and that left Christine out of the loop entirely. Chris soon learned that her world was never going to change *because* not only did she not have the proper tools to cope with her situation, she didn't even know where to look to find them. As for Nikki? She was a nice woman, just not too bright or compassionate. On her best days Nik couldn't even begin to fathom Christine's pain. So, Chris, or Dolly as she usually preferred, continually hid her real feelings from her stepmother.

What was the point in doing otherwise?

Dolly did her best to reach out for help when she could, but she usually wound up empty-handed.

There was the town minister, a wonderful gentleman, the Reverend Donald L. Marshall who prayed with Dolly, but sadly, it just wasn't enough. She spoke to her favorite Sunday School teacher, and Miss Newman would sweetly tell her to: "Hold a good thought for your mother, Dear, and allow the word of the Lord to heal you." And then her father would say, "You just need to move on, Doll. Your mother would want it that way. Let it go."

None of that even made the slightest dent in Dolly's heartache.

And, sadly, she *never* talked to her loving grandparents about it at all, because every time Dolly even mentioned her mother to them, they would cry and sob over the loss of their only child.

So, for all of those reasons, and more, Dolly's real world was quickly taken over by another place... a new, self-created world in which she could live and cope.

Soon the face she showed to others was no longer her own, and the lines of what was real and what was not real, slowly blurred.

And the lines between the truth and a lie?

Well, sometimes there was no line at all.

Chapter Four

I settled into the Turner household more easily that I thought I would and my first night there was quiet and peaceful. My prayers for my parents, my Aunt Anna and Uncle John, and the friends I left behind, were also quiet and peaceful. I felt a small twinge of hope as I sat up in bed and wished upon my very favorite star: "For my parents to rest in peace, for me to be a help to Aunt Anna and Uncle John and… and for my life to be a good one, and a happy one."

What seventeen-year-old girl wouldn't wish for that?

"Pattie?" My aunt called to me from the foot of the stairs.

"Yes, Aunt Anna?"

"Bill Shellum phoned and he said he'd be *delighted* if you would consider a summer job there at the store. How about that?!"

"Really?!"

"He sure did! The hours are 9:00 AM 'til 5:00 and the pay is $1.50 an hour!"

"Wow! $1.50?! Are you sure that's what he said?!"

"Indeed I am! The Shellums know what a fine young lady you are and what a good work ethic you have. I'm sure that's why he wants to give you some extra pay!"

"Should I call him first and then go over there?" I said making a fast appearance in the kitchen.

"I think that would be the order," my Aunt smiled, "but how 'bout some breakfast first?"

I gave her a big hug and immediately sat down to two perfectly poached eggs, three strips of crispy bacon, and a delicious potato pancake.

"Orange juice, coffee, or tea?" she questioned.

"Just tea, Aunt Anna. Thank you." I looked at the beautifully set table and noticed my uncle's plate was missing.

"Where's Uncle John?"

"Oh, Mr. Early Bird caught Captain Cramer's fishing boat about 5:30 this morning. He won't be home until at least 4:00."

"That's a long day."

"Well, John's a Sea Captain in his heart," she chuckled. "It makes me happy to see him enjoy it so. And, we always have great fish dinners when he comes back! You hafta keep that in mind!"

I smiled.

"So, I say, let the salty old sailor go to sea."

I smiled again.

So did Aunt Anna.

Chapter Five

Breakfast was soon over, the dishes were all done, and I rushed to the alcove where a black phone and spiral address book rested on a highly polished mahogany chest.

I picked up the small, well-worn book, and then ran my finger quickly down the 'S' list.

Margaret Saybolt... Seagreen's Pharmacy... Shamrock Knitting Mills... Bill and Millie Shellum...

There you are!

I dialed the number immediately: Sea Isle 7-1964 - on the second ring, the line was answered.

"Good morning, Shellum's!"

"Good morning," my voice smiled. "This is Patricia Townsend. My Aunt Anna told me that Mr. Shellum wanted to speak to me about a job."

"Oh, Pat! This is Millie, sure, Bill's waiting to hear from you! How... how are you doing, Dear? We all loved your family very, very, much, you know. Are you okay?"

"I'm doing as well as can be expected, I guess, Mrs. Shellum. I'm just really blessed that I have Aunt Anna and Uncle John."

"They're good people, Pattie."

"Yes, ma'am, they are."

"Well, hold on for just a sec, lemme give Ole Bill a holler. He'll be right with you."

"Okay, thank you."

I sighed when I thought about how many more times I would be asked how I was doing since my parents died.

It was a hard question to answer.

I wanted to cry and tell them I was angry at God for taking them away from me. I wanted to say I wished that I had died that night, too. I wanted to say how much I missed my home in Philadelphia... the familiar surroundings... my friends...

But no, I did the polite thing and made an awkward situation as pleasant as possible for the kind, inquiring soul who needed an answer. As for my own heartache? Well, I'd deal with it in the best way I knew how - one *very* long day at a time.

Just as my mind was drifting back to Philadelphia, Bill picked up the phone.

"Pattie? It's Bill Shellum."

"Hello, Mr. Shellum!"

"How are you doing, young lady? My deepest sympathy to you for your loss."

"I appreciate your kind thought. I'm fine, thank you."

"Pat?"

"Sir?"

"I have a job for you if you think you're up to it. Or, if you'd like to wait a few weeks, that's okay with me, too. You tell me."

I needed no time at all to mull things over. "I'm ready as soon as you want me. I think it'll be a good thing for me right now. What exactly will I be doing?"

"Well, we're not trying to send a man to the moon over here, just some order taking, stocking shelves, and a little cash register work. But, if you can help with the ice cream dipping, hoagie, and sundae making when the crowd comes in at lunchtime that would be terrific!"

"I can do that! When do I start?"

"Well, if you want to come over later today and fill out some papers, we can welcome you aboard tomorrow at 9:00 AM. How's that sound to you?"

"Sounds great!"

"And, young lady, because I know what a hard worker you'll be, *and* the fact you'll be needing a little extra cash for when you're off to UCLA next year, I'm going to pay you *one* dollar and *fifty* cents an hour!"

I had already been told about my 'forty-cents over minimum wage' salary by Aunt Anna, but I didn't want to burst Bill's bubble by saying I already knew the figures.

"A dollar fifty?! Wow! Thanks, Mr. Shellum, that's the best! I *really* appreciate it!"

"Well, we'll appreciate having you here, young lady. See you today around 3:00?"

"Three it is."

"Okay, well… see you soon, Miss Employee."

"Yup, see you soon, Mr. Employer."

Bill chuckled and then I heard the line disconnect.

I placed the phone back down into its cradle and called for my aunt. "Aunt Anna?!! Aunt Anna?!! I got the job!!! It all worked out!!! I got it!!!" I turned to see her walking in from the back porch.

"Now that is *really* wonderful news! Good for you! When do you start, Dear?"

"Tomorrow at 9:00, but he needs me to sign papers today at 3:00."

I bowed my head for a moment and Aunt Anna immediately picked up on my mood change.

"What is it, Pattie?"

I sighed heavily. "I'm not ungrateful or anything, I'm not. I just…"

"Talk to me, Pat."

"Well, right now I… I should be on the 'B' bus heading to Boulevard Pools with Brenda, or shopping with Mom for my school clothes for UCLA in September, or helping Dad gather up all his fishing gear to come here and… and now look!"

I started to cry and immediately Aunt Anna wrapped her arms around me.

"Sweetheart, I can't even begin to imagine your pain. Your parents were such wonderful people and they loved you more than I ever saw *anyone* love a child."

I held on to my aunt tightly.

"They honored you and your presence on this planet every day of their lives."

I continued to cry.

"This isn't a quick consolation, Pattie… not much can comfort you so soon, I know that."

I sniffled and sighed.

"But in time, the memories of all that was good will overtake the bad turn of events that took your mother and father from you. John and I will do all we can to help you along that path. Always feel free to talk to me. It's what I'm here for, Dear."

I lifted my head away from Aunt Anna's shoulder and I looked into her eyes and saw that they were also filled with tears. It was at that very moment when I realized that my parent's death was not only a huge loss and heartache for me, but for Aunt Anna and Uncle John as well.

How could I forget that?!

I looked into my Aunt's eyes once again. "I know it won't be easy, but I want you to know that I am *so* very grateful that I have you and Uncle John and…" I sniffled again. "And this wonderful house and…"

"We'll all make it, Pattie… you'll see."

I hugged my Aunt once again. "We will, Aunt Anna. We sure will."

Chapter Six

"Dolly? Are you going over to Shellum's to see about that job?"
"Yes, Daddy, I am."
"Today?"
"Yes, today."
"Well, don't go until after Nikki puts the kids down for a nap. Give the woman a break, will ya?"
"When's someone gonna give *me* a break?"
Her father entered the room, totally agitated, adjusting the tie around his neck. "What did you just say?!"
"I said, 'I know she needs the break'."
"Oh. Well, I'm off and running. Let the kids sleep in as long as they like. And when you're cleanin' up around here, be quiet so it doesn't disturb anyone."
"Sure, Dad."
Without a hug, or a peck on the cheek, nonetheless a goodbye, Mr. Sean Dollio was out the front door, into his brand new 1959 red and white Chevy Impala, and off to work. Nikki and the kids would be asleep just long enough for Dolly to do most of the housework and laundry - as usual.

Dolly was definitely looking forward to the job at Shellum's. Last year after she graduated high school, she worked on or near the boardwalk all summer: Dalrymple's, the cotton candy stand, the skee-ball game room, the movie theatre, and the salt water taffy shop. She had plans to attend college but her grades and her ambition suffered and she never made it. There were far too many things wrestling with Dolly's mind, and the thoughts of college life never seemed to win the fight. After her summer boardwalk jobs, her brother Mack was born, and then she worked at Busch's Seafood Restaurant waiting tables on a part-time basis. She really loved it there, but she was always ordered to 'come straight home after work' to help Nikki.

THEY WERE THE RULES!!!

Dolly *hated* 'The Rules.'

It wasn't long before her after work 'work hours' exhausted her and Dolly couldn't juggle both lives. So, she had to quit working at Busch's and stay home. She resented it, but she kept her mouth shut. Her Dad's new family had cost her *all* of her outside jobs, because being the Dollio nanny, cook, housekeeper, laundry girl, etc., *always* came first.

She had no choice.

And, because she had no choice… she also had no life.

None.

As I said, Dolly hated 'The Rules.'

Around 10:00 PM every night, when the house was dark and quiet, and when Nikki and Dolly's dad, her little brother, and sister were all fast asleep, she would go out onto the back porch and play the few 45rpm records that she owned, and sing right along with them.

She could escape from real life so easily - no effort involved. In Dolly's day life, reality meant pain and hard work and apathy - a place where there was no love, no compassion, and no tenderness… at least not for her. So, fantasy became Dolly's best friend, and, on those cool Townsends Inlet nights out there on her back porch, she'd turn the record player on and suddenly she was far away from the drudgery and heartache… standing on a handsome stage in New York City, with hundreds of cameras flashing at her and a crowd roaring with appreciation for her to sing more.

Encore! Encore!

Dolly stood on that stage and sang her heart out night after night… *every* night since her mother had died.

And there, on that stage she found love…

And compassion…

And tenderness…

She wore her broken heart right on her sleeve, but her audience would never know it, because, after all, it's just a song, just a performance…

Isn't it?

When you smile and you sing…
Everything is in tune and it's spring…
And life flows along…
With a smile and a song…

Chapter Seven

It was just about 2:45 when I called to Aunt Anna.
"I'm leaving to go to Shellum's, Nanna! You want me to bring you anything back from the store?"

My aunt walked out of the guest room, where she had been ironing. "No thank you, Dear, I think we have just about everything we need for now. Have a *great* interview. I'm sure you'll be the best employee old Bill Shellum ever had."

I smiled. "Well, I'll sure try! See you around 4:00, I guess."

Aunt Anna walked me to the front door and stood there watching me sprint down the street until I waved one last time and then disappeared from sight as I turned onto Landis Avenue.

Good luck, Pattie.

* * * * * *

Christine 'Dolly' Dollio was dressing for what she hoped would be a successful interview with Bill Shellum. She needed the job *and* she needed a change of pace.

"Nikki?!! I'm leavin'! Wish me luck!"

Dolly could hear her stepmother upstairs playing hide and seek with her children "Okay," Nikki yelled back, "I hope you get the job, Doll!"

"Not half as much as I do," she said softly, closing the front door behind her. "Now let's just hope I can keep it."

Chapter Eight

Within two minutes of leaving the Turner household, I was standing in the entryway of Shellum's-by-the-Sea. As I reached for the door handle I saw a girl approaching, so I allowed her to go in first.

"Sometimes ladies are the best gentlemen." I smiled.

"Yeah, I guess so." The girl seemed kinda fidgety and hyper. "Hey, do you know if I shoulda used the back entrance? I'm... I'm gonna get a job here. I mean, I..."

"Are you?!" I smiled again. "I am, too! I'm Pattie Townsend. I live on 85th Street."

"My name's Christine Dollio, but most people just call me Dolly. I live up on 89th, right on the beach block."

"Nice big houses up there."

"Yeah, they are. I... I coulda driven over here but it was so close, I walked."

"You drive already?

"Yeah. I have my own car, too."

"What kind is it?"

"It's a '59 Impala. Red and white. Pretty cool, huh?"

"I'll say. Your own brand new car!"

"Yup."

"Geez. I still ride my Pink and White Schwinn."

She smiled at me. "I just thought I'd take this job to pass some time."

"Pass some time?"

"Yep. I'll just be here until I figure out what I want to do with my singing career... up in New York."

"I *love* New York."

"Me, too."

"So, *obviously* you're a singer," I smiled.

"Yup."

"That's pretty neat! I can't carry a tune in a bucket." I chuckled.

"I sing every night. You know... practice."

"That's cool. I mean, like you could be another Brenda Lee or Connie Francis!"

She blushed a bit.

"So, I'm in the presence of a future star, maybe?"

"Well, I like Peggy Lee and Ella Fitzgerald better than Connie and Brenda, but Rock and Roll is a big deal in my life, too. I don't know what I wanna do yet, but I've got time and..."

Just then Bill Shellum made his presence known. "Hi, Pattie! How are you? Ready to sign on the dotted line?"

"Yes, Sir, I am!"

"And what can I do for you, young lady?" He said as he turned toward my new found friend.

"She's Christine Dollio, and she's gonna be working here, too."

Dolly suddenly looked a bit embarrassed. "Well, I… "

"*So*," Bill said, "I guess that takes care of my summertime help then! Come on back here with me, ladies, and fill out some forms, and then, how 'bout you both come in tomorrow at 9:00 AM. There's work to be done!"

"I'll be here!" Dolly nodded.

"Me, too!" I was so excited.

We followed Bill back to a little nook crammed with all kinds of papers, two telephones, old magazines, and a typewriter as outdated as I'd ever seen.

"Here ya go, girls." Mr. Shellum smiled as he placed the employment papers in front of us.

Dolly and I immediately signed on the dotted lines making us the official '1959' summer employees of Shellum's-by-the-Sea, in beautiful Townsends Inlet, New Jersey!

Perfect.

Right after a hearty handshake with Bill to seal the deal, his wife, Millie, showed us the simple ins and outs of the operation: where the supply stock came in, how to make a good milk shake, and a reminder that a Shellum's sundae *always* comes complete with two cherries on top.

Millie was pleased. She knew we absorbed all the information we needed, and that both of us also had the excitement and energy it took to do the job well.

"See you in the morning, Mr. and Mrs. Shellum," I waved as I was leaving. "Thank you again!"

"Yes, thank you," Dolly smiled.

"Well, see you at work, Doll. This'll be fun, huh?" I was genuinely happy about the new page in my life that was ready to turn.

"Yeah, and remember… two cherries on those sundaes!" she grinned.

Chapter Nine

I walked in the door of my new home to the delicious aroma of a creamy, buttery, cake baking in the oven.

"That *sure* smells good!" I said as I entered the kitchen.

"Well, I'm making you your favorite coconut cream layer cake. John and I figured this was a special day for you, so we'll celebrate. His end of the bargain was to catch three nice big flounders."

"Flounder?! That's my favorite! Ya think he did?"

"He *sure* did!" my uncle announced as he walked in from the back porch.

"Talk about perfect timing," Aunt Anna said. "Are they clean, John?"

"Yep, cleaned 'em myself right after we docked. So, how's the newly employed Pattie Townsend?" He smiled at me.

"I start tomorrow at 9:00. I'm pretty excited! *And*, I met a girl who's starting with me. Her name is Christine, but she said to call her Dolly."

"Well," Aunt Anna nodded. "A new job *and* a new friend. Today was a good day, Pat."

"And flounder *and* coconut layer cake!" I said as I gave her a nice big hug.

Uncle John walked out of the kitchen and settled into his favorite piece of furniture. "Yup, flounder and coconut layer cake. It's a good day all right!"

Not two minutes had gone by and John Turner was already snoring away on his comfy sofa while I set the table and Aunt Anna breaded the filets.

"Can I help with anything else?" I questioned.

"Well, I guess you could go down to the basement and bring up some ice out of the freezer. I made some lemonade, but it'll need ice."

"Will do."

As I was walking down the steps from the back porch and into the basement, I thought about my day, my new job, my new friend, and *now*, doing my share as part of my new family. I felt a real sense of happiness and accomplishment... and peace.

...And I needed that.

* * * * * *

Long after the flounder was eaten and everyone had a nice big piece of coconut layer cake, I went upstairs, got into my jammies, and pulled the soft, cool sheets over my body. I tossed and turned for the longest time trying to get comfortable. What an awful feeling. Not that it was one of those hot and sticky New Jersey summer nights, or because I ate too much at dinner, it was because of the million thoughts that were running through my head.

How much money can I save before I go to UCLA next year? Why don't I have a driver's license? Dolly has one! Imagine someone so directed in her life that she's already planning a move to New York to become a singer! She's my age! And I don't even know what I want to be yet!

I was still feeling uncomfortable for a little while but then I finally settled in and said my prayers. Praying helped to quiet me down by thinking of the good things that I had in my life. I reminded myself that the future looked bright even though I didn't have a single solitary clue about what was waiting for me.

Let's hear it for the power of optimism!

Chapter Ten

It was close to 11:00 PM and Dolly was on her back porch, looking up at the stars. She sang to her nightly audience of none and then quickly stopped her performance when some thoughts filtered through the music.

How much money will I need to get out of here? Why did I tell that girl I had a driver's license and a car? Why do I keep doing this to myself?! She's going to UCLA next year! She's my age! I don't even know what I wanna be yet!

Dolly sighed and then walked out onto her imaginary stage once more. She blew some kisses toward her make-believe audience and smiled graciously.

"Farewell one and all… 'til we meet again… I'm the opening act for Bill Shellum tomorrow."

Chapter Eleven

I woke up at 7:00 AM to a wondrous fresh bay breeze blowing gently through soft, white chiffon curtains, and the heavenly aroma of a great French toast and sausage breakfast.

I put on my robe and slippers and headed down the staircase to the kitchen.

"That's the way to start a morning out on the right foot!" I said giving Aunt Anna a big hug.

"I had a feeling you'd be up for some French toast!" she smiled.

"Where's Uncle John?"

"He's still sleeping, but I have a feeling he'll be down here any minute now. If anything can wake up old Rip Van Turner, it's sausage and French toast."

No sooner had I poured the orange juice when Uncle John made his appearance.

"Sure smells good, Anna." He smiled and then kissed her twice on the cheek.

"Have a seat, John. What'll it be, Dear? Two slices or three?"

"Four sounds good," he yawned.

I smiled at Aunt Anna.

"He's a growing boy, Patricia," she chuckled, patting me on the shoulder.

"So, today's the big day! Are you nervous?" my uncle questioned.

"No. Well… just a little apprehensive, I guess. I never had a job before except babysitting and mowing lawns and stuff, but I'll be okay once I get into the swing of things."

He nodded as he poured syrup all over his French toast *and* sausage.

"The girl that I'm starting with already worked before, so I know she'll be fine."

"She's worked before?"

"Yup."

"Is she much older than you?" Aunt Anna wanted to know.

"No, I saw her fill out her forms and we're born just a month apart. *I'm* the older one. She lives down here all year, like you do, so it was easy for her to get a job up on the boards."

"What's her name again?" Uncle John asked me.

"Christine Dollio, but everyone calls her Dolly. She graduated last year. I guess she started early."

"The Dollios…" My Aunt seemed to be running the name around in her head. "John? Wasn't that the last name of the man who had the sickly wife? Sean Dollio? Remember them? They had a little girl."

"Oh, Anna, I don't remember that stuff."

"You know her?" I questioned.

"Well, if it's who I think it is, she used to go to our church with her mother before the woman took ill. As I recall, the woman walked with a brace and a cane."

"Why? What was the matter with her?"

"I don't know what was wrong; I just remember the church announced that she had passed away. That was quite a few years ago so I can't quite bring all the details to mind."

"Gee, I wonder if that was Christine's mom? I mean, Dolly's mom."

"Christine... that's right, the little girl's name was Christine. Bless her heart, I heard she was never the same after that - the poor little thing. She was very close to her mother. Carrie Robinson said they adored each other. And, she was about your age, Pattie."

All of a sudden I was losing my appetite.

"Geez, that's awful."

My aunt nodded without adding any more information. "So," Aunt Anna tried to smile. "What time will you be leaving?"

"I think I should go pretty soon."

"So early?"

"Well, I want to get in about a half an hour early today, you know, I have to get my smock on and prepare for whatever comes up. I want to see what I have to do right off the bat, so I'm organized."

"Good thinkin'," Uncle John said.

I managed to finish just one piece of French toast and two pieces of sausage before excusing myself from the table.

"Not hungry, Pattie?" Aunt Anna seemed disappointed that I hadn't eaten much.

"Well, I *am* and I'm not. I... I guess I'm just all revved up about today. But it sure was delicious, Aunt Anna. It really was!"

She smiled at me. "Well, thank you, Sweetheart."

"It was terrific, as always!" Uncle John added, giving his wife a quick kiss on the cheek.

"Well, thank you, too, Sweetheart!" She smiled.

Cute... very cute.

Chapter Twelve

I walked into Shellum's at exactly 8:31 according to the Coca-Cola clock on the far wall. "Goooood mor-ning!" I sang out.

"Good morning to you, too," Mrs. Shellum called back from high atop a nearby ladder.

"Can I help you with anything, Mrs. S?"

"Oh no, Dear, just stacking the new boxes of Rice Krispies that came in. I'm just about finished. You're early!"

"Well, I wanted to make sure I was here in time to get my smock on and set up for whatever you had planned for me."

"An eager worker. What more could we ask for?"

I smiled as I started to settle in.

Shellum's-by-the-Sea was a great store. It was open every day, rain or shine 365 days a year - and they sold everything, well, almost everything: canned goods, lunch meat, butcher shop items, Duncan yo-yo's, light bulbs, pinochle cards, sandwiches, hoagies, and *my* personal favorite, Jane Logan ice cream.

The store did its really big business in the summer months though, you know, selling postcards, water toys, fishing gear, kites, and those famous double-scoop sundaes topped with two cherries.

There was even a tiny post office inside the building with these very ornate brass mailboxes similar to the ones used in fancy old New York Hotels, like The Plaza or The Algonquin. The Turner's box number was 83199. I always thought that was funny 'cause there were only seventy-eight boxes - all earmarked for year-round residents. So, why weren't they just numbered one through seventy-eight?

Who knows?

As I walked out from the small bathroom at the back of the store, I straightened my smock, and checked myself out in the mirror.

Not bad.

No sooner had that thought left my head, when Dolly walked in. It was 8:40 on the dot.

"Hey," she grinned at me, "I thought *I'd* be the early bird this morning. What time did you get here?"

"Just a couple of minutes ago. How are you doin'?"

"Doing excellent, as *always*. Life's good, Pat!"

"That's a great attitude, Miss Dolly." I said as I handed her the official Shellum's-by-the-Sea smock.

"Well, I'm blessed. I guess that makes it easy."

I stood there and sighed thinking about how sad feelings would overtake me sometimes, and how long it took for me to sort them out so they could make some kind of sense to me.

"What are you thinkin' about?" She pointed to my head.

"Well, I just admire your spirit, I guess. Maybe some of that positive stuff'll rub off on me."

"Don't let the world get to you, Pattie. That's what I always say."

I nodded.

"Take no prisoners, Kiddo. You're better off for it in the end."

Somehow when she said that to me, I thought back to what my Aunt Anna said about 'Christine Dollio' and her mother, going to church together, and how ill the poor woman was, and how much Dolly loved her.

Now here's someone who has mastered all the heartache the world has to dish out, I thought to myself. *What a lucky, lucky girl.*

Little did I know.

Chapter Thirteen

The morning went by pretty fast even though there were only a few customers to keep us busy. Dolly and I reorganized the canned goods, opened up five boxes of fishing gear, two boxes of kites and water toys, and then priced all of it. *Then* we made two fried egg sandwiches, lettuce, tomato, and no onion - 'to go' for Reverend Marshall and his wife; seems like they didn't want to miss a beat while finishing up painting the church's new Sunday School room. Soon the official Shellum's-by-the-Sea lunchtime was upon us before we knew it, and things picked up at lightening speed.

The soda fountain was filled with parents and their kids getting a cone or a milkshake or one of those famous Shellum's sundaes to cool down before a day at the beach. Fishermen came by to check out the latest in tackle gear, and then there were the locals who dropped in to pick up their mail or the daily newspaper – or both.

Mr. and Mrs. Shellum were busy making sandwiches and hoagies, Dolly was doing a great job at the soda fountain, and I was selling orange juice, cereal, and other incidentals to the early renters who were down at the shore for a week's vacation.

By the time 5:00 PM rolled around, Dolly and I were ready to hang up our smocks and call it a day.

"It's 5:00, Mrs. Shellum. Would you like me to stay? Is there anything else I can do?" I asked sweetly.

"I'll stay too, if you need me," Dolly added.

"That's very kind of you, girls, but I think things have started to die down and my daughters will be taking over 'til closing time. They should be here any minute."

"Okay," I smiled.

I hate to say it but I was a bit relieved that she didn't want me to stay; I was more than a bit tuckered out from my first day of real work. I sure had a lot to tell Aunt Anna and Uncle John. Shellum's was really fun, but I was *tired*, no point in denying that!

"How are you holding up, Dolly?" I questioned.

"I'm raring to go. I was hoping she'd let us stay!"

"You gotta be kiddin'!" I turned to hang my smock up outside Bill's small office.

"You'll get used to it, Pat," she smiled.

"I guess." I smiled back at her. "See you tomorrow, Doll."

"Okay. Nice working with you, Pattie! See you in the morning!"

* * * * *

The minute I walked in the house I could smell a wonderful ham and sweet potato dinner roasting in the oven, just waiting for me, but I flopped right down on the first chair I could find instead of entering the kitchen as I usually did.

My aunt entered the room and smiled at me. "Rough day, Kiddo?"

"Nanna, I was run ragged, but I guess I'll get used to it. Geez, Dolly was ready to work *overtime*! She wasn't even tired! Dinner sure smells good, though."

Again she smiled. "Well, as soon as you can muscle your way out of that chair, it's waiting for you."

"Okay, I'll be there in a minute."

Man, I'm exhausted! Just absolutely and totally exhausted!

* * * * * *

Four blocks away Dolly entered her house and was greeted by her half-sister, Apry.

"I missed you! How was your new work?" The little redhead grinned.

"Apry," Dolly answered as she flopped down in a nearby chair, "I'm exhausted… just absolutely and totally exhausted!"

Chapter Fourteen

The week seemed to fly by and Dolly and I learned a lot about each other. I told her all about the terrible accident on graduation night that took my parents' lives, she spoke about her mother's illness, her dad's new marriage, and then, right after that, I noticed that we talked an *awful* lot about me and my life, and not much about Dolly and her family at all. But then, I guessed that she was just being a good friend. She, more than anyone else, understood the adjustments and changes going on in my life since my mom and dad died. We'd talk about my old life in Philadelphia, and my *new* life with Aunt Anna and Uncle John in Townsends Inlet. I also told her about my friend, Brenda Mayberry, who'd be visiting me soon. I knew Brenda and Dolly would get along just great and that made me *very* happy. Actually, it made Dolly very happy, too!
Sweet.

* * * * *

The Friday that ended our week was a busy one from the minute we walked into the store.

"It's payday!" Mrs. Shellum smiled.

"Really?!"

I was surprised to find that Shellum's-by-the-Sea didn't hold back a week's pay – as most businesses did. We worked that first week and we got *paid* for that week! Very cool!

And, Shellum's was, along with the fifty million other things they did at the store, also one of those new-fangled check cashing stations.

So, as soon as we were handed our checks at 4:30 PM, Dolly and I cashed them right then and there. I didn't know if she was making the same amount as I was, so I didn't say anything other than I was happy to finally earn some money of my own. When I opened the small white envelope that held my very first paycheck and I saw that I had made sixty-one dollars and sixteen cents for forty-three hours work, I thought I had died and gone to heaven! It might as well have been a million!

"Hey, Doll?"

"What?"

"Don't forget we're going to The Charcoal House to celebrate our first week's pay," I said right as the clock read 5:00 PM.

"How could I forget?" She smiled at me.

"Don't spend it all in one place," Bill joked as we were leaving the front entrance of the store.

"We won't," I chuckled.

As Dolly walked down Landis Avenue to The Charcoal House, she said, "I think I'll have a grilled porterhouse, some onion rings, a coke, and some pie."

"That sounds good to me, too, but, isn't it just a little... expensive?"

"Well, yeah, but this is our big night, so we can afford to spend five dollars, dontcha think?"

"I guess so."

"Pat, do you have to give your aunt and uncle any money for staying there, you know, to help them or anything?"

"No. I'm just saving up for when I go to college next year, remember?"

"Oh, yeah. I remember."

"What about you?"

"Me? No way. I can use this any way I want: clothes, dinner, movies..."

"Your car..."

"My what?"

"Your car," I repeated.

"Oh," she chuckled. "Yeah, my car. I keep forgettin'... I don't see too much of it these days."

We reached the famous little roadside steak house with the wall to wall jalousie windows in about three minutes. Dolly and I took our seats and ordered the porterhouse with onion rings, a large coke, and lemon meringue pie. It was scrumptious! And, I guess dinner tasted extra special to me because I actually earned the money it took to buy it.

I couldn't help but think how proud my mom and dad would be of me at this very moment: my first real job, my first paycheck, and the first meal I ever paid for myself with a good friend whom I had just met.

I could sense that Dolly knew my mind was elsewhere and she shook my arm.

"Hey, daydreamer."

"Sorry, I was thinking about my parents and how... well, how proud they'd be of me. You know, a new job, a real paycheck, a nice new friend..."

She smiled. "It was hard losing my mom, too, Pat. I know what it feels like. But time heals all things. It does."

"I hope you're right." I sighed.

"I am... you'll see."

Doll and I finished up our wonderful meal, left a tip, and then walked out into a nice cool breeze from the Atlantic Ocean.

"It was a great dinner, Dolly. I enjoyed it *and* your company."

"It was great, Pattie. See you Monday, okay?"

"Yup. Monday."

Dolly smiled at me and I watched her walk away. She turned back every now and then and waved and smiled again and again. She had a lively step and, as always, she appeared to be so happy and carefree.

I prayed for the day when I could be so upbeat and capable of handling all the hits life had to give.

"Even a journey of a thousand miles begins with just one step," my mother used to say.

I need to remember that.

As I turned the corner by the church I stopped to wave to Dolly one last time, but she didn't turn around again. In fact, as I saw her making her way up 89th Street, her pace seemed to slow and her head bowed forward just a bit. It seemed odd to me, but I just figured that big meal we had was catching up to her.

I figured wrong.

Chapter Fifteen

"Nikki, I'm home!" Dolly called out. "I worked a little late."

"I wondered where you were. I'm in here fryin' chicken."

Dolly entered the kitchen to see her stepmother cooking a late dinner. There was a large Chef's salad already on the table along with rolls and butter, and the table was set.

"*I* put *all* the dishes out!" Apry sang.

"It looks great, Ap! You did a good job. Where's Dad?"

Nikki put the last of the fried chicken onto a serving platter. "He should be here any minute. He's running late... a new client or something."

"Oh."

"*And*, I meant to ask you, did you get paid today or is it next week?"

"Why?"

"You know your dad said since I'm not working yet 'cause Mack is still so small, you should give us forty dollars a week to help out around here."

Dolly sighed as she resituated her little brother in his high chair.

"Well," Nikki pressed, "did you get paid today or is it next week?"

Without batting an eye, Dolly answered, "It's next week."

Chapter Sixteen

"Well, the working girl is home!" I cheerfully announced. "I got paid today and Dolly and I ate dinner at The Charcoal House!" Uncle John got up from the sofa and Aunt Anna stopped her knitting the minute I walked in the room. "*And*, I'm treating us all at VanSant's Ice Cream Stand tonight. How's that?!"

"Oh, Pattie, you don't have to do that, Sweetheart." My aunt gave me a big hug.

"Ice cream?" Uncle John's eyes lit up. "Does that include milkshakes?"

"Oh John, for heaven's sake," my aunt rolled her eyes at him.

"Sure it does, Uncle John. So, when do you say we go? 7:00?"

"Sounds good to me!"

"Well, that's very sweet of you, Dear, of course, we'd love to go. But don't forget, put as much of your pay away as you can in the big old piggy bank I put up in your room. College will be here before you know it!"

"I promise, Aunt Anna."

* * * * * *

Right around quarter 'til seven, the three of us started our walk up 85th Street to VanSant's.

There was a small crowd waiting to be served and all but one of the outdoor benches was taken. My aunt and uncle immediately walked over to save it for us.

"I'll have a butter almond on a sugar cone, please," Aunt Anna said sweetly.

"And I'll have a…"

"I know, Uncle John," I smiled. "A double chocolate milkshake!"

"That's my girl!"

The line moved swiftly and soon it was my turn. I ordered for Aunt Anna and Uncle John and then, even after all the ice cream dipping I saw all week, I still had a hankering for a nice big double cone filled with a dip of chocolate and a dip of coffee ice cream, topped off with some chocolate jimmies.

The three of us sat there and talked about my day, and about when Uncle John worked at Bromley's Mills in Philadelphia, and the lovely time they had on their honeymoon trip to Atlantic City back in 1911.

"You know, somewhere in the house is that photo we had taken of us in that pretty wicker push chair that we got driven around the boardwalk in. Remember that, John? You wore a straw hat?"

"I remember, Anna, and you were the prettiest girl that boardwalk had ever seen. You still are."

She brushed her hand softly across his cheek. "I need to get a new frame for it and put it back in the bedroom."

I had to smile. What a wonderful thing to hear, even after all those years of marriage they were still so in love with each other. And, representative of that love, my Aunt Anna sported a beautiful diamond ring. She never took it off.

It was a unique design set in platinum with seven stones of various sizes, and it sparkled even in the dimmest of light. It was absolutely the prettiest ring I ever saw in my entire life.

We finished up our ice cream and walked leisurely back to the house, talking about Captain Lawson's new party boat, the mosquito trucks that sprayed the neighborhood every week, and the great sale at Dalrymple's up in Sea Isle City the following Monday.

As soon as I got back home I took a fast shower and hopped right into bed. I said my prayers, thought about how blessed I was to have my Aunt Anna and Uncle John, I thought about my mom and dad… and for some odd reason, I thought about Dolly.

…And then, I said a prayer for her, too.

Chapter Seventeen

The weekend flew by: I cleaned my room, went swimming in the bay, and fished for flounder on Rual's pier with my dear, old Uncle John. Before I knew it my alarm was ringing and it was 7:00 AM on Monday morning. I ate a wonderful breakfast, courtesy of Aunt Anna; I made my bed, got dressed, and then walked over to Shellum's. I was about a half an hour early, as always, so Mrs. Shellum invited me to sit at the green marble-topped soda fountain for a 'cuppa joe' and, of course, I obliged. Just as I took the first sip of my coffee, in walked Dolly.

"Gooooood morning," she said ever so cheerfully.

"Good morning to you, too," I grinned.

"Come on over here and have some coffee with us." Millie Shellum patted the counter top.

"Don't mind if I do," Dolly said as she strolled over in our direction.

"So girls, how was your weekend?" Mrs. Shellum had no sooner asked that question when the first customer of the day walked in.

"You two stay put and enjoy your coffee, you're not on the clock yet." She got up and left us to wait on Mrs. Reed who brought her two kids down to Townsends Inlet for the week. I remembered them from when I was really young and I called out to her, "Hi, Mrs. Reed! Nice to see you!"

"Nice to see you, too, Pattie!" she smiled.

The Reeds visited every year, it was their family tradition and Millie Shellum was quite fond of Martha Reed and her children - in fact, everyone was. They were really nice people.

I soon turned to Dolly to wait for the answer to the question that Mrs. Shellum had asked us.

"Well?"

"Well, what?"

"*Well,* what did you do this weekend?!"

Dolly looked far away for just a moment and then rambled to me, "I took my car out for a drive up to Sea Isle, I stopped in at Pfeiffer's, The Trading Post, and Dalrymple's. I bought some makeup and a new bathing suit, and I practiced my singing and…"

"Wow, and I thought I had a good weekend." I sighed.

"Why? What did you do?"

"Well, I went fishing off the pier with my uncle and I swam in the bay, and I read to prepare for some college work ahead of time and… and… well, I cleaned my room and…"

Dolly chuckled. "YOU are one exciting woman!"

I felt my face start to blush.

"I bet you've never even had a boyfriend either… have you?" she asked as she took a sip of her coffee.

"Me? No. I mean, I have guys that are my friends, and I had a few crushes on some fellas, but…"

"But?"

"But no real boyfriend." I practically hung my head in shame. "I guess you've had one, huh?"

"One?!" She laughed. "If I have my way this summer, the new guy will be number five!"

"What?!"

"Yup. Num-ber fiiiiiive."

"Holy smokes!"

"Scottie, Chuck, Bobby, and Neil."

"You gotta be kidding!" I was just dazzled at how grown up and worldly Dolly was. I had never felt more sheltered and out of the loop in my entire life.

"So, this means you never even had a hickey!"

"You had a *hickey* when you were *sixteen*?! Umm…"

"Umm, what?"

"Ummm…" I felt so embarrassed. "What's a… a hickey?"

Dolly laughed at me again. "My God, Pat. Don't you know *anything*?! It's like a love mark."

"Like a live mark?"

"No, a *love* mark."

"Oh." I'm sure my face looked like I was totally clueless - and I was.

"Pattie, it's when you're necking with a guy, you know, making out and then he kisses your neck and then he bites your neck…"

"What?!"

"Yeah, and then he sucks on your neck for a while and it leaves this… like this big bruise - the size of it depends on how long he sucks your neck."

"Doesn't that hurt?!"

"Well, of course it does, in the beginning and…"

"Well, for God's sake, *why* would you want someone to bite you on your neck so hard that it hurts you?!"

"Well…"

"And worst of all to leave an ugly bruise there?!"

"Be-*cause*," she responded defensively, "it shows *everyone* that you're really cool and that you have a boyfriend and that you were kissing and stuff."

I rolled my eyes at her.

"Pat, it *means* that you're special and cool and that someone likes you!"

"You need a mark on your neck to show people that?! Why can't you just *tell* people you have someone who likes you?"

Immediately her face went blank. "Well, I guess you could… I mean... you *can*, but..."

"Hickeys. Puh-leeze." My turn to laugh. "It's ridiculous." I finished my coffee, washed the cup out and headed toward the place where I left my Shellum's-by-the-Sea smock on Friday, then I turned to Dolly and smiled, "Come on, Mata Hari... time for work." I thought that would give her a really good chuckle, but, for some reason, it just didn't.

Chapter Eighteen

Dolly and I worked really hard that Monday and we even managed to put in an hour of overtime, so we were both pretty eager to get back to our homes for a most welcome dinner.

"See ya tomorrow, Doll!"

"K, see ya, Pat."

The minute I walked in the door, Aunt Anna greeted me. "I'm glad you called me to let me know you'd be late. I made hamburgers, salad, and home made French fries for you, all fresh - no heat-overs."

As always, I gave her a big hug. "You're the best!" I looked around and noticed my uncle was among the missing. "Where's your darling husband?" I smiled.

"Oh, he walked down to The Civic Center to talk to Bill Garrity about running the official Teen Dances. The date's set for Friday, July 3rd, to give a big start to the 4th of July weekend."

"What?!"

"That's what he told me."

"Uncle John is gonna be a disc-jockey?!" I had to laugh. "Aunt Anna, if it isn't a song from before World War Two, Uncle John doesn't know it!"

"Well," she smiled, as we walked into the kitchen, "then I guess he could use a sidekick to help him along."

"You mean me?"

"Sure. You'll be going to the dances anyway. You can tell John all of the new songs that the kids are listening to and he can buy them up at Dalrymple's and then he'll play them for all the kids - thanks to you."

"That would be so cool!"

Aunt Anna walked to the stove and I sat down to a nice big juicy hamburger, a fresh garden salad, picked directly from Aunt Anna's yard, and some of the best homemade French fries I had ever eaten. Just as I had finished my dinner, and Aunt Anna was about to pour some tea and slice us both a piece of chocolate cake, my Uncle John walked in the room.

"Evenin', ladies," he said cheerfully. "How was work, Pat?"

"Work was good. Not as good as this cake is gonna be, but it was good."

He smiled at me.

Aunt Anna added one more plate and cup and saucer to the table and soon all three of us were enjoying a piece of delicious chocolate layer cake.

We talked about Uncle John's new weekend job at The Civic Center and that I was more than willing to pick out the new records for the dances. I also mentioned I saw Mrs. Reed at the store and that she and her kids were down for the week, and then... well, then for some reason, I was thinking about Dolly and the conversation we had earlier that morning. All of a sudden I blurted out, "Aunt Anna? Did Uncle John ever give you a hickey?"

I thought she would choke to death on her food the second I finished that sentence - she spit and sputtered and coughed. "A ... a... hick... a hick-ey?! Good grief, Patricia!" She coughed again and again, and I patted her on the back while directing the same question to my Uncle John.

"Pattie, good heavens, no! Anna and I loved each other and we knew it and that was enough. We weren't a show-and-tell couple. Where did you ever hear such a thing?"

"Well, Dolly told me that..."

"Well, *you* just tell Dolly that there's far more to love than that kind of... well, than that kind of nonsense."

"Yes, Sir."

He turned to my aunt who was still composing herself. "Are you okay, Anna?" he chuckled.

She tried on a smile, "I'm okay, John... I'm okay."

Chapter Nineteen

Another week was moving by faster than a jack rabbit. I shared the letter I received from Brenda with my aunt and uncle and then brought it over to the store to share it with Dolly.

"That's cool. She'll be here next week!" Dolly was really excited and happy about meeting Miss Mayberry.

"Yeah, and then right after she gets here, that's the weekend my Uncle John starts the dances over at The Civic Center. She'll be here for that, too!"

"This'll be fun!"

I was really looking forward to having my old school chum and neighbor meet my new seventeen-going-on-forty-year-old friend.

I had a great week planned for me and Bren and I couldn't wait for it to start. Of course, I'd be working all week, but Brenda was one of those girls who would sleep until noon anyway, so we wouldn't miss too much of each other. She'd get up, have some breakfast, help Aunt Anna around the house, and then walk over to the pier to watch the boats come and go. Then, she'd probably stop by to see me and have a sundae or a soda or something like that. But, *after* work, *that's* when the real fun would begin! We could go up to Sea Isle and walk the boards and play some games or go on some rides, and then there would be those jumpin' Civic Center dances! Brenda and I *loved* to dance. At last I was really looking forward to things instead of backward about my mom and my dad. Not that I didn't think about them, of course I did, but I was doing the right thing by moving in a good direction, into a good place in my head - finally.

Soon Friday night was upon us, and Dolly and I cashed our checks and said our farewells.

"Remember, Doll, Brenda comes in tomorrow at noon. Wanna go to Sea Isle tomorrow night? Can you drive us there?"

"Actually, I think my stepmother needs the car, but…"

"Well, that's okay, we can walk. You wanna come over around 6:00? I'd like you to stop by the house so you can meet my aunt and uncle."

"Sure, I can do that. I'll see you at 6:00."

"Cool. See ya then, Dolly."

"Okay, see ya then, Pat."

* * * * * *

I was so excited when I came home from work that night I could hardly eat my dinner. Aunt Anna and Uncle John were happy to see me looking forward to Brenda's visit and enjoying my old friend's company for two full weeks!

Brenda wanted to wait a whole year to start UCLA, so we could go together as planned, but I wouldn't hear of it, and besides, I'd have a sophomore to watch over me when I got there the following year and I could learn all the ropes - an edge lots of freshmen certainly wouldn't have.

I slept like a rock that evening and daybreak came before I knew it. As usual, breakfast was waiting for me the minute I entered the kitchen. It was delicious - a western omelet with fried onions on top, Canadian bacon and hash brown potatoes. In-between bites, Uncle John and I talked about the records he'd need for The Civic Center dances, the goodies at the concession stand, and, we all enjoyed an extra cup of coffee together.

I felt like a real grown-up.

I sure did.

* * * * * *

"What time is it, Aunt Anna?" I hollered from upstairs. "My clock stopped."

"It's 10:35! Brenda's already on the bus!"

I flew down the steps and grinned at my aunt. "This is so cool, isn't it? I'm just all... well, all happy and... you know..."

She smiled back at me. "I know. John and I are looking forward to seeing her, too. Brenda's a nice girl with a good head on her shoulders - like you. You'll be *wonderful* company for each other."

"Yup, and we'll have Dolly with us tonight, too. I thought we'd walk up to Sea Isle and then go up on the boards for a while. I asked Dolly to come over here around 6:00 so you and Uncle John could officially meet her. I mean, you might remember her from church when she was little, but she's all grown up now."

"Yes," my aunt sighed, "you're all growing up. It seems like only yesterday when your mother and father brought you here and we'd take you down to the beach in your stroller and play in the sand with you. *You*, my dear Patricia, we're a real beach baby. You loved the sand and the water."

"I still do."

She smiled at me again.

"Can I help you do anything?"

"What, Dear?"

"You know, so I can pass the time. I think I should leave here at 11:45, just in case... just in case her bus comes in early."

"Well," my aunt said, "I would appreciate it if you brought the laundry down for me; and then we can cut up some watermelon and cantaloupe for a nice fruit salad tonight. How's that sound?"

"Okay," I said heading toward the staircase.

By the time I took the laundry downstairs to the basement and helped Aunt Anna cut up cantaloupe, watermelon, pineapple, cherries, and a nice big honeydew melon, it was 11:30.

"I think I'd better go upstairs and clean up. It's almost time to meet Brenda!"

"Go right ahead, Pattie. She'll be here before you know it! This is the beginning of a really fun-filled two weeks for the both of you. Your last before you're in college together. Again, I say, *where* has the time gone?"

Barely had those words left my aunt's mouth and I was up in the bathroom putting on some lipstick. A new shade I bought at Pfeiffer's – 'Cotton Candy Pink, Pink, Pink' by Cotey. It was the first lipstick I ever bought with my own money, so this was a really big deal for me. I raced down the steps and bolted out the front door. I called out, "I'll be back in a little bit, with BRENDAAAAA!!!"

Within forty seconds I was standing at the corner of Landis Avenue and 85th Street, staring out toward Sea Isle City and waiting to see a big Greyhound bus pull around from the side of The Coast Guard Station.

I paced the sidewalk, crossed the street to see if I could get a better view, and then crossed the street again.

No Brenda.

I decided I would close my eyes and count to a hundred and see if that worked.

"98... 99... 100."

Still no Brenda.

ARGGHHHHHH!!!

No sooner was I about to walk across the street *again*, when the big silver and blue bus was in sight.

Yaaaaaaaaaay!!!

It got closer and closer and then finally grinded to a halt, making a big whooshing sound as it came to a complete stop right in front of me. The door opened and I waited for what seemed like forever, when in reality it was probably thirty seconds, and then, there she was, Brenda Ethel Mayberry, my very best friend on the entire planet.

She tossed a green duffel bag and a rather large suitcase out of the bus, and then jumped down to the ground from the very top step.

"PATTIEEEEEEEEE!!!"

"BRENDAAAAAAA!!!"

We laughed and hugged each other and laughed and danced the jitterbug and laughed some more.

"Man, am I glad to see you!" I grinned. "Two and a half weeks seemed like two and a half years! Didn't it?"

"It sure did." She smiled at me then suddenly she stopped dead in her tracks and grabbed onto my shoulders. "Listen, before we say another thing…"

"What?"

"Are you *sure* you don't want me to wait so we can go to UCLA

together? I'll hang out another year for you."
"No way! What's the matter with you?!"
"I can get a job in Philly and…"
"No, Bren. You go. I *need* this year. I need to be free to… well, to…"
"I know, Pattie. I understand. It's okay."
"You sure?"
"Yep. Positive."

I smiled at Brenda as I slung her green duffel bag over my shoulder. She picked up the remaining white leather suitcase, and then we started our walk down 85th Street, to the glorious place we both would call home for the next two weeks.

"I love ya, Pat."
"I love you, too, Bren."

Chapter Twenty

Brenda and I walked in the door and straight into the welcoming arms of Aunt Anna and Uncle John, along with a BIG beautiful lunch fit for a queen.

My Uncle John carried Brenda's luggage right upstairs and then the three of us "girls" began to chat.

"Brenda, it's *so* nice to see you!" my aunt said with a smile. "So, how was the ride?"

"It was a long one, but the scenery is so pretty I didn't mind, *and* I finished up my book, so it was good, thanks."

"What book?" I asked

"The Good Earth."

"Pearl S. Buck," my aunt nodded. "A novel *not* to be missed!"

"I really enjoyed it," Brenda smiled.

Just then Uncle John came down the steps and we all walked into the kitchen for lunch.

Believe me; my aunt knew how to make an eye-catching and absolutely delicious lunch.

Beautiful china dishes, bowls, and serving trays filled with assorted lunch meats and sliced cheeses, lettuce, tomatoes, onions, pickles, seafood salad, potato salad and fruit. There was even fresh iced tea and a pot of hot tea sitting under a hand knitted tea-cozy and fresh strawberry shortcake with homemade whipped cream, *and*, a matching vase with flowers picked direct from the side yard - as I said, fit for a queen!

"You know," my uncle grinned, "Pattie sure has been looking forward to you coming down here." He reached for some seafood salad and then continued, "And Anna and I are real happy you're here, too. This is the best time of year as far as I'm concerned."

"Summertime," Aunt Anna nodded in agreement.

"And the livin' is easy," I smiled.

Suddenly, Brenda and I broke out into song together, "Fish are jumpin' and the cotton is high…"

My aunt laughed.

"What was that all about?" Uncle John asked chuckling right along with his wife.

"That was a song from Porgy and Bess called 'Summertime'." I said handing the lunchmeat tray to Brenda.

"Oh, okay. I get it, I get it."

Brenda and I looked at each other and smiled.

"Well gals, you know me, if it's not a song from World War Two or before, then I don't know how it goes."

Again my aunt laughed. "Well, this is why you need some help picking out the new teen records, John."

"That'll be cool," Brenda said. "When do we have to get them, Mr. Turner?"

"Well, if you two are going out tonight, you could pick them up at Dalrymple's."

"Yeah, we're goin' up to Sea Isle after dinner. Dolly's coming over. That'll be great! Can we play them before you take them over to The Civic Center?"

"Well, I guess no harm done." He grinned.

"Neato! I wanna get 'At the Hop' and 'Bird Dog' and that song by The Champs…"

"'Tequila'." Brenda nodded.

"Yeah… and we can get some stuff by Elvis and Buddy Holly and Frankie Lymon and…"

"Whoa, there, how much *are* these records?" My uncle questioned.

"Well, it depends. Some are nineteen cents and some are forty-nine. Dalrymple's always has good deals."

"I suppose that's reasonable," Uncle John looked at my aunt and nodded - she nodded back.

"So, I guess '*And the Caissons Go Rolling Along*' won't be on the list." My uncle made a sad face.

"Caissons?" Brenda asked.

"It's a chest that holds ammunition," Aunt Anna answered.

"Well, lemme tell ya, it was a great song, girls."

Then, as I had a feeling he would, Uncle John started to sing his favorite old Army song, "Over hill, over dale, as we hit the dusty trail, and the caissons go rolling along. In and out, hear them shout, counter march and right about, and the caissons go rolling along."

We all laughed.

"John," my aunt patted his shoulder, "That's lovely, Dear, and a grand old tune to boot, but this is 1959. These girls want Elvis and the Jitterbug, not the stuff we grew up listening to."

"So then I guess no one wants me to sing anything from 'Harry Horlick and the A & P Gypsies' either?"

"Harry Horlick and the *what*?" My eyes widened.

"The A & P Gypsies and…"

Aunt Anna sweetly stopped his sentence. "Never mind girls. Uncle John is done reminiscing for the day."

"But, Anna… I can imitate the horn section and..."

"John Martin Turner!" She gave him 'that look.'

"Well then, how 'bout I sing them something made famous by Sam Lanin and the…"

"Ipana Troubadours?" She raised her eyebrows. "I don't think so, John, I don't think so."

He chuckled and then reached for the potato salad.

Chapter Twenty-One

Brenda and I gave Aunt Anna a night off from the drudgery of cleaning the table, washing pots, pans, dishes, and sweeping the floor. The time flew by as we talked about our trip to Dalrymple's later that evening, UCLA, and my new job at Shellum's.

"Well, that's all done," I said as my eyes made a quick survey of the kitchen.

"We're a good team, Pattie," Brenda nodded.

Both of us walked into the living room and found Aunt Anna in her rocking chair knitting a beautiful cobalt blue shawl while Uncle John snored like a freight train only three feet away. How she could ever tune him out and knit in peace was beyond me.

"Night, Aunt Anna, "I said giving her a big kiss on the cheek. Tell Uncle John I said goodnight when he wakes up, okay?"

"I sure will."

"Goodnight, Mrs. Turner," Brenda added, planting a kiss on my aunt's cheek. "And a pleasant evening to Mr. Turner from me, too."

Aunt Anna chuckled a bit and turned toward my uncle, the window rattler. "I think he's already in the middle of his pleasant evening, don't you think?"

We smiled, said "goodnight" once again, and then left to unpack Brenda's stuff. In no time we had it all put away, I showered, Brenda showered, and then we got ready for our first full day together.

"I think I'll wear these white peddle pushers and my blue and white sleeveless blouse," Brenda said holding them in front of herself. "Whaddya think?"

"I like it. I was going to wear my white ones, too."

"What blouse are you wearing?"

Quickly I rummaged through my closet and found a pink sleeveless blouse with crocheted edging. "How 'bout this one?"

"That's cute! Where'd ya get it?"

"Aunt Anna bought it for me last week up at Pfeiffer's."

"I *love* Pfeiffer's!"

"And she got me this cool black Jantzen bathing suit, too - it's black with a big white button."

"She's a really nice woman, Pattie... thoughtful." Brenda smiled as she plopped down onto my bed.

"I'm lucky, Bren."

"You are... I mean even though..."

"I know. Lots of kids in my situation aren't... well, they aren't nearly as fortunate."

Brenda nodded as I sat down on the bed just about two feet away from her, my back resting up against the headboard.

"So what about this Dolly girl? How's *she* doin'? She lost her parents too, right?"

"No, just her mother. But that's bad enough. She lives with her dad and his new wife and their kids."

"How many kids?"

"Two."

"Man, that's some kinda adjustment. How's she like that deal?"

"I guess they're really good to her."

"You guess?"

"Well, she's got lotsa free *time*, she has her own brand new *car*, she…"

"A new *car*? Isn't she our age?"

"Yep."

"How'd she manage that?"

"I don't know, but I feel so behind the times when I'm around her. I mean, I *like* her, don't get me wrong, but…"

"But?"

"Bren, we've…"

"We've what?"

"We've lived *very* sheltered lives."

"No we haven't."

"Is that right?"

"Yeah. I think we're pretty much up to speed." Brenda's voice sounded extremely confident.

"Oh, *really*?"

"Absolutely."

"Do *we* have a car?"

"Well, no, but…"

"Do *we* even drive?" I nudged her.

"Not yet, Pat, but…"

"Do *we* have a singing career ahead of us?"

"Well, no career just yet, but…"

"Come on! Have we ever had *boyfriends*? Even *one* boyfriend?"

Brenda scratched her head as if to help herself think. "Well, we had prom dates!"

"Bren, that was George and Marty! They went all through school with us. They're buddies, not boyfriends!"

"So, Dolly's got a boyfriend?"

"Well, to be honest with you, she doesn't have one right now, but she will."

"So, she had a boyfriend last year?"

"Brenda, *when*, as Dolly puts it, *when* she nails one again this summer, the new one will be number five!"

"Number five?!" Brenda's eyes widened. "I don't even know five guys I like as *friends*!"

"See? I'm tellin' ya. Dolly is seventeen goin' on forty. She even had a hickey!"

"A hickey?"

"You *know* what a hickey is, right?!"

"Yeah, it's a... well, it's a... I think it's a... a..."

"Oh God, Bren, we're not just sheltered," I started to laugh; "we've been living under a rock for seventeen years!"

Chapter Twenty-Two

Brenda and I woke up right around 9:00 to the wonderful aroma of a late breakfast.

"Mmmm… is that bacon I smell?" Brenda said rubbing her eyes.

"Yup, smells like some coffee too and…"

Before I could get another word out of my mouth, Bren was putting on her robe and pulling slippers onto her feet. "Last one down is a rotten egg!"

I grabbed for my housecoat and quickly put on my slippers, while Brenda made a beeline for the staircase. By the time I made it to the kitchen, Miss Mayberry was already seated at the table.

"So, I guess *I'm* the rotten egg."

"Learn to live with it, Patricia." She said tucking a napkin inside her pajama top.

"How did you sleep, ladies?" Aunt Anna said as she started to serve us breakfast.

"I slept like a baby, Mrs. Turner. There's something about the shore that always gives me a good night's sleep. Umm… can I help you with something?"

"No Dear, I've got everything all done. I enjoy doing this."

"Can't I just pour the juice for you?" I questioned.

"Already done," she said, placing a tall crystal pitcher filled with freshly-squeezed orange juice right next to us.

"You are the best," I smiled.

"I agree," Brenda said as she reached for her toast.

"Where's Uncle John… out fishin'?"

"Yes. He left here around 5:00. He wanted to catch some more flounder for us for dinner."

"He left at 5:00 AM?! That's awfully early!"

"Not when you nap from 7:00 PM until 9:45 and then go back to sleep again at 10:00."

"I guess not." I laughed.

Aunt Anna poured us all some coffee and then asked, "So what are your plans for the day?"

"Well," I answered, "after we eat we'll go to the pier, then go to the beach, walk around, see stuff, you know."

"Then?"

"Then we'll come home and help you get ready for dinner and, after that, Dolly's here and we're off to Sea Isle for the evening."

"Well, that sounds like a fun day!"

Brenda nodded, "I know… I'm *really* looking forward to it!"

I reached for another cup of coffee and then we all sat there chatting away about everything under the sun. *What* a great time we had! Before we knew it, breakfast was over and we were ready to officially start our day. We helped Aunt Anna wash and dry the dishes, and then, of course, we put them back into their proper place inside those pretty white cupboards right across from the stove. Brenda and I quickly dressed in the clothes we had chosen the night before, and soon we were off and running.

First we trekked down the street to the bay, made a left and walked by Suzie Wells' house. Suzie was a nice kid - a little quiet, but a really nice kid. Her mom was out on the side of the house hanging out laundry and Brenda and I waved her a hearty 'hello.' We walked a bit further and then dodged under a few lines of old crab nets that Dungeness Dan O'Dell had for sale, and, before we knew it, there we were, on John's Pier.

The tide wasn't in yet and some of the boats docked there were laying in swampy-looking gray mud amid thousands of clam shells, sturdy reeds, and a few empty minnow boxes.

"Ya think it's too early for an ice cream cone?"

"Pattie," Brenda answered back, "Didn't you used to call me Brenda *Breyer's*? It's never too early for ice cream as far as *I'm* concerned!"

As we were walking up the dock to enter the pier building, two really cute boys were walking toward us. The tallest one slowed down a bit and made eye contact with me.

"Hi." He smiled.

My heart started to race. I thought I recognized him, but how was that possible? "Hi," I answered.

"You don't know who I am, do you?"

"Umm... well, you *look* familiar."

"I'm George Ludlam. I come into Shellum's now and then. I saw you working there. I'm here all summer with my family - on 93rd Street."

"Well, nice to see you... again. And, umm... this is my friend Brenda Breyers. I mean, this is my friend, Brenda *Mayberry*." I'm sure I appeared stunned and nervous although I was trying so hard to be cool and confident.

Brenda nodded her hello.

"And," George smiled, "this is my friend, Clark Lowen. He's here with his family for the summer, too."

"Nice to meet you," Clark was soft spoken and appeared a bit nervous himself.

The four of us stood there for what seemed like an eternity before another word was spoken. "Well," I said, "we have to get goin'. This is Brenda's first full day down here. Maybe we'll see you again sometime."

"I sure hope so. See ya later." George smiled.

"See ya," Clark followed.

Brenda and I turned to look back at them as they were walking away. We giggled like two ten-year-olds and then quickly entered the pier building that housed the soda fountain and the coolest looking Wurlitzer jukebox on earth.

It was just about 11:15, and we opted for an early high calorie lunch - two chocolate nut sundaes with wet walnuts and extra chocolate syrup. As we took our seats, we immediately started to talk.

"My God! He said he *hopes* he *sees* us again! Did you *hear* that?!"

"I heard," Brenda smiled dreamily.

"Like when I said, 'Maybe we'll see you *again* sometime,' George said, 'I sure hope so.' Didja hear that?! He hopes so… he *hopes* so!"

"My God, Pat. And, what were the odds of that happening if they didn't like us? *And*, to top that off George's friend is really cute!"

"Yeah, Clark, that's right. I mean, they coulda just walked on by, right?"

"They coulda."

"Yup, they coulda."

"I mean, most guys do, right, Pat?"

"Well, they do to *us*." I sighed.

"Geez… ya think this is how easy it happens for Dolly?" Brenda asked as she ate the last of the whipped cream off her sundae.

"Well, Dolly never said, but how much *easier* could it possibly get?!"

We both looked at each other and laughed.

Chapter Twenty-Three

The rest of our afternoon was spent walking and talking. It was the usual girly stuff and we loved it. In our Townsends Inlet travels, we stopped at VanSant's for a soda, checked out The Civic Center's dance floor, and then we walked over to Shellum's so I could introduce Brenda to Bill and Millie. After the "hello"s and "nice to meet you"s were said, we trekked up to the beach, sat at the Pavilion for a while, then walked down 85th Street to Landis Avenue, around the tip of the inlet, and then back home.

As we were walking up from the bay area I heard my uncle call to us, "Hold up there, you two!"

Brenda and I walked toward Uncle John and saw the ton of fish he was carrying.

"Good grief," I said, "How many flounders did you catch today?"

"Sixteen." He said proudly. "That was a record for Captain Cramer's boat!"

"Do we have to clean them?" I asked.

"*Please* say we don't have to clean them." Brenda grimaced.

My uncle laughed, "No, I told Anna after I retired that I'd be doin' some extra fishin' so she said if that was the case, I'd either clean them myself or pay some kids on the pier to do it. So…"

"You paid some kids." I smiled.

"Thank *God*." Brenda let out a huge sigh of relief.

"Yup. Bill Wechler's three boys are usually there when we dock, or Bobby Phillips, Billy Rual, and sometimes George Ludlam's son. They're willing and able and I'm happy to let them do it - so is Anna, by the way."

"George Lud-lam?" I said slowly.

Brenda turned toward me and made a silly face.

"Yup, George." My uncle said as we turned up the side yard to the house. "George junior is a pretty good fisherman himself. He's a fine boy. You know him, Pattie?"

"Well, I guess… I guess I saw him at Shellum's. The name just… just sounded familiar."

"Pat, the Ludlam family has been down here for generations. Your paths probably crossed dozens of times. But, I guess with him bein' a boy and you bein' a girl you didn't have enough in common to really get to know each other."

I smiled and Brenda nudged me.

"I guess not, Uncle John."

In no time at all the three of us were walking into the kitchen where Aunt Anna was waiting - cutting tomatoes for our dinner salad.

"Uncle John caught *sixteen* flounders, Aunt Anna!"

She turned, and smiled. "That's *wonderful!* That must be some kind of record!" She hugged Uncle John first, then me, and then Brenda.

"Cramer's record flounder catch for the day!" He grinned.

"Geez, Uncle John, you know, with all the fish you have in the freezer downstairs, plus *this*, you won't have to fish again 'til 1965!" I chuckled.

"Pattie," Aunt Anna said gazing lovingly at her husband, "if we had enough fish to fill Connie Mack Stadium, John would *still* go fishing."

* * * * * *

Dinner was superb, as always, and Brenda went on and on about how good the flounder tasted, how wonderful the cole slaw was, the salad, the onion rings, the peach sponge cake... see, Brenda's mom wasn't much of a cook. Oh, she could whip together a fast dinner of hamburgers or hot dogs or a stew or something, but to create homemade meals like Aunt Anna? Well, that was pretty hard to beat - for *anyone*.

We cleaned the kitchen for our magnificent chef, carried our laundry to the basement, and then readied ourselves for a night out in Sea Isle City with Dolly.

"This is *so* neat! I don't think I was ever up on the boards without adult supervision before," Brenda said as we were nudging each other for space in front of my dresser mirror.

"Pretty cool, huh?" I smiled at her reflection.

"I'm gonna take ten dollars with me. You think that's enough?"

"Bren, at the very least we'll eat a piece of pizza, have some cotton candy and..."

"*And*, some ice cream!"

"Yes, Brenda Breyers, *and* some ice cream. So, what would all that cost, anyway? Eighty cents? Ninety?"

"Yeah. But what about the rides?"

"Well, okay say *ten* rides, that's another buck. That's about two dollars."

"Postcards? A few records for my own collection?"

"Bren, postcards are only a nickel and four records could be a dollar and a half. But, Dalrymple's always has a deal. Last week they had Elvis' 'All Shook Up' for only nineteen cents."

"I guess you're right. Ten dollars is a bit much. Who am I anyway? Mrs. Rockefeller? I'll bring five."

I nodded and reached inside my jewelry box for my own five dollars.

"Hey! Don't forget your Uncle John's record money!" she reminded me.

"Oh, geez, that's all I'd need to forget!" I opened the top drawer to my dresser and took out the white envelope Uncle John had given to me - as a reminder, it read: **'Rock and Roll Civic Center Money.'**

"How much did he give you?" Brenda asked.
"I don't know, lemme look." I carefully unsealed the business size envelope and looked inside.
"WOW!"
"Wow, what?"
"He gave us twenty bucks!"
"You sure it's not a ten?"
I carefully removed the bill from within its safe keeping place and held it out in front of me.
"What's that say?"
"Twenty dollars." Brenda shook her head in amazement. "That's a lotta Rock and Roll."
"You can say that again!"
"*That's* a lotta Rock and Roll!"

* * * * * *

Over at the Dollio household things were a bit different.

Dolly had told Pattie that she always bought new clothes with all of her money and she knew that Pat and Brenda would be expecting to see her all 'dolled' up. The truth was that after she gave Nikki and her Dad forty dollars and bought herself shampoo or toothpaste or some other minor incidental, there wasn't any money left to buy *anything* pretty to wear. She looked in her closet and found a nice pair of peddle pushers that once belonged to Nikki. In fact, as she rummaged through the closet most of the items she did find that were half way decent originally belonged to Nikki. Dolly pulled out blouse after blouse and nothing was up to date; just okay clothes that she could wear to work.

What am I gonna do?!

At that thought Dolly quickly put on one of her old blouses and walked into her father and stepmother's room. Nikki had great clothes - her Dad always saw to that. If it was hot and in style, well, then his darling Nikki would get it. And *now*, his Nikki could be wearing even more stylish clothes thanks to the forty dollars a week they were getting courtesy of the hard work from one Christine Elizabeth Dollio.

Quickly Dolly grabbed a beautiful Indian inspired gauze-like blouse, making sure no one saw her, and then ran it downstairs to the outdoor shed. She walked back into the house, and noticed her little sister, Apry standing in front of her.

"You look pretty, Dolly." She smiled.

"Thanks."

Just then her Dad and Nikki entered the room, her brother Mack was sound asleep on his mother's shoulder.

"Don't you have a better blouse to wear?" Nikki asked.

"This *is* my better blouse. I would have liked to buy a *new* one this week, but…"

"Well, you look okay to me," her father quickly interrupted. "You're only goin' to the boards with a few friends; you're not goin' to the prom!"

Not that I ever went to my prom in the first place.

"Have a nice time," Nikki said as they all started to head upstairs.

"Have BIG fun!" Apry shouted. "We're gonna go out later and get some treats!"

"Well, you have big fun, too, Ap! See ya, everyone!"

The only voice that answered was Apry's. "See ya, Dolly."

Knowing that all of her family was now on the second floor, Dolly ran down to the shed, closed the door behind her, and immediately exchanged her old faded blouse for the beautiful one Nikki had purchased two weeks earlier on a trip to Stone Harbor. She caught a glimpse of herself in an old mirror that had been hanging down there since God knows when. She looked into it and gave herself quite a lengthy, appraising stare and then eventually smiled at her reflection.

As Dolly was leaving the shed and running down the street toward Pattie's house she thought to herself - *You look good, Doll. The rest?… you can fake.*

Chapter Twenty-Four

The doorbell rang.
I knew it was Dolly.
"I'll get it!! I'll get it!!!" I said as I was flying down the staircase with Brenda close behind me.
I opened the door and there she stood. Christine Elizabeth Dollio - 'Dolly.'
"Hi!" She grinned.
Dolly had a great smile.
"Come on in, come on in!" I motioned with my hands. By now my aunt and uncle were also standing in the front porch.
"Dolly, I'd like you to meet my Aunt Anna and Uncle John Turner, and my best friend from Philadelphia, Brenda Mayberry."
"Nice to meet all of you," Dolly said hanging onto that smile.
"Well, it's a pleasure for us to meet you too, Dear." I was hoping Aunt Anna wouldn't say anything about seeing Dolly in church when she was little.
I didn't want Dolly to be reminded of the loss of her mother and have her feel sad on such an otherwise happy night. Aunt Anna never mentioned it and that was a relief to me. Uncle John tipped a make-believe hat and smiled a hello right back to Dolly.
"Well, I have heard so much about you!" You could almost hear the awe in Brenda's voice.
"I've heard lots of good stuff about you, too. I've been lookin' forward to this for two weeks now!"
"Are we driving to Sea Isle in your car?"
"My car? Oh, no, darn it. My dad is... I mean he's taking his wife and kids to a late dinner in Stone Harbor. So he took it. I mean, Dad has his own car, but the kids like mine better, so I said, what the heck... you take it, we can walk... it's not far anyway!"
"That's all right, it'll take us a little longer, but we can talk more!" I nudged Dolly.
We all smiled at each other.
"Sounds good to me," Brenda said.
"Me too," Dolly agreed.
"Well, ladies have a wonderful evening. Be safe and I can expect you when? 9:30? 10:00?"
"Well, I think more like a bit after 11:00, Aunt Anna... the boardwalk closes then."
"Well, John and I will be asleep before that, but as long as you have your key..."
I pulled a small knitted chain from inside my blouse - the house key

was attached to it. "I got it." I smiled and tucked it back inside the shirt.

"That's a cool idea. You'll never lose it that way!" Dolly said.

"Aunt Anna made it for me."

My aunt smiled. "You better get going! Have fun, girls!"

"We sure will," we all seemed to say at the same time.

"And pick out the best records they have. It's important that the kids have a hip disc-jockey, you know," my uncle laughed.

I smiled, waved and blew a kiss to Aunt Anna and Uncle John.

"Now that is one *nice* family," Dolly said in a softer tone than usual.

"We're all so lucky to have such good families, aren't we?" Brenda added.

For a moment Dolly seemed a bit far away, then she answered, "Yeah... real lucky."

"You know, I meant to say something back at the house, but I just *love* your blouse," Brenda smiled at Dolly. "It's *really* beautiful."

I nodded. "It is, Doll... it's *very, very* pretty."

She looked down at her blouse and fussed with one of the small pearl buttons. Again, she seemed far, far away. "Thanks guys."

Chapter Twenty-Five

The walk from 85th Street to the boardwalk took no time at all. We weaved through several backyards, over large and small sand dunes, then on to the beach front, and suddenly, there we were!

What a boardwalk! You could smell the pizza, hot dogs, and buttered popcorn before you even got there! And, the fresh roasted peanuts? Well, they just about called to you. And, some days, when the wind was blowing in the right direction, you could hear the old calliope pumping out carousel music from more than three blocks away. I loved it! Truthfully, the most beautiful carousel animals in the world were inside a big old pavilion that was the centerpiece of the entire boardwalk. All the animals were hand carved in Europe at the turn of the century, and they were, each and every one of them, exquisitely detailed works of art. Ever since I could remember, out of *all* the other animals, the lion was my favorite. He was so regal and so big, with this shiny mane, huge white teeth, and eyes that sparkled like yellow diamonds.

I called him 'Big Kitty.'

"Hey, wanna play some skee ball?" Dolly yelled as she hurried inside a large building housing not only the skee ball games, but also Pokeno and miniature versions of basketball, bowling, and ice hockey. Brenda and I ran into the game room and grabbed a seat right next to Dolly. We played skee ball for about twenty minutes, and never seemed to play a very good game. The six-year-old sitting next to us was doing better than the three of us put together. It made me laugh. "So much for adult coordination," I smiled.

I guess the guy in charge of the game - Fred, according to his name tag - felt bad that we didn't earn enough tickets to win even the smallest of prizes, so he gave all three of us these cute little pink and white stuffed poodles. I thought that was sweet - in fact, we all did. As we walked out of the game room we bought ourselves some cotton candy that perfectly matched our 'prized' poodles and we started to walk down the boards.

"Is that where you used to work, Dolly?" Brenda questioned.

"He sorta winked at you, Doll! Did you see that? Does he know you?"

"Oh, I worked here for a while, but..."

"But?"

"I left."

"You worked there last year?"

"Yeah. I decided to go down the other side of the boards."

"What was the wink all about?"

"I don't even know the guy. But, I guess the wink is to be expected... you know, the old Dollio charm," she grinned.

As we walked down the boards toward Dalrymple's, Dolly pointed out a few places where she used to work over the last two summers. "Let's go in!" Brenda would say, but Dolly always nixed the idea, saying something like, "Oh, no one works there that I used to know. Kids get summer jobs and leave."

"Did they fire you?" Brenda asked playfully.

"Fire *me*?!" Dolly practically laughed in her face. "I was probably the best employee any place up here ever had."

"So, what happened?"

"I left them and went elsewhere. Better pay."

"She's a *very* good worker," I added. "I don't blame her."

"Yup, ya gotta know when to move on with things," Dolly said nonchalantly.

"Do any of your old boyfriends work up here?"

"Brenda, they were summer guys, they come and they go."

At that very moment two girls walked by us and gave Dolly what I would call a dirty look. "Look at *you* all dressed up. Goin' to the prom, Miss Dolly?"

"Screw off, McIllhenney."

The two girls burst into laughter and then walked by us with a significant air of superiority.

"Well, that wasn't very nice," I frowned.

"Why did they say that?" Brenda wanted to know.

"Oh, well… ummm… my last boyfriend, Walt, well, Mary McIllhenney liked him, and… and he didn't like her, and…"

"And so she's mad because he was your boyfriend and not hers?" I asked.

"That's about the size of it."

"Well, that's silly."

"I know," she nodded, "But that's the way it goes sometimes."

Suddenly Brenda was uncharacteristically quiet.

"What's with you?" I asked.

"Nothin'."

"You sure?"

"Yeah." Quickly the subject was changed. "So, are we off to Dalrymple's now?"

"Sure, why not!" I said.

Dolly, Brenda and I ran down the sloping ramp, and then all the way to Dalrymple's just a half a block from the boardwalk.

"Hi, Mr. Dalyrmple," I waved as we entered the store.

"Evenin' Pattie."

"These are my friends, Dolly and Brenda."

"Hi there, Dolly, nice to see you again." He half-smiled. "Doin' okay?"

"Yessir, I am. Thank you."

"And Brenda, a pleasure to meet you!"

"We're headin' toward the back of the store. Uncle John is going to run The Civic Center dances, so we get to pick out the records or the only thing he'd be playing would be 'And the Caissons Go Rolling Along'."

Mr. Dalrymple laughed. "Good old John Turner. Well, there's quite a selection back there, girls. Help yourselves!"

We walked by the summer water toys and kites, the sweatshirts, the new Tiki charm necklaces, books, candy, and then… *then* there they were, racks and racks of the latest rock and roll hits. I was in heaven!

"Start pickin' some songs, ladies." I grinned from ear to ear.

"Look at *these*," Brenda said rifling through a large stack of latest releases. "'All Shook Up,' 'Hound Dog,' 'Don't Be Cruel,' 'Wake Up Little Susie,' Buddy Holly's 'That'll Be The Day'…"

"Oh, poor Buddy. I'll never get over that plane crash." I sighed.

"Yeah, and the Big Bopper, Richie Valens… all gone," Brenda added.

"We have to get *all* of their records," I stated. "It's a tribute to three lost kings of Rock and Roll."

Dolly nodded in agreement as she picked up 'La Bamba' and 'Donna' by Richie Valens, 'Chantilly Lace' by the Big Bopper, and everything Dalrymple's had of Buddy Holly's recordings.

"Look what else I found!" Dolly said, all full of excitement. "'Jailhouse Rock!' Oh, God, Elvis is so yummy! *And*, 'Whole Lot Of Shakin' Goin' On,' I *love* Jerry Lee Lewis," she gushed.

Brenda handed me a few of her choices: 'At the Hop' by Danny & The Juniors, 'Tequila' by The Champs, and 'Turn Me Loose' by Fabian.

"I picked some slow tunes," I said. "'To Know Him Is to Love Him' by The Teddy Bears and 'It's Only Make Believe' by…"

"Conwaaaaaay Twitty," Brenda smiled.

"What a name!" I chuckled. "But a *fabulous* song."

"Speaking of fabulous songs," Dolly said as she clutched the forty-five to her heart, "It's Frankie Avalon!"

"Oh, 'Venus'," Brenda said with an equally dreamy look in her eyes. "And he's from Philadelphia, too. How come we never ran into him, Pat?"

"Bad timing, I guess."

"You know, I sang that song for three weeks straight," Dolly said, still appearing quite enchanted.

"Venus?"

"Yup."

"So, *sing* it for me," I nudged her.

"Yeah, sing it for us. Don't be shy. No one else'll hear you."

Dolly bowed her head and her face blushed a light shade of pink. "Nah, I can't sing that here."

"Why not?" I asked.

"Yeah, do Frankie proud!" Brenda smiled. "Sing, songbird, sing!"
"No, later maybe. I just…"
"You just what?" Brenda pushed.
"Ah, that's okay," I said putting my arm around her, "you can sing it for us some other time."
Dolly smiled at me, and Brenda? Well, Brenda just sorta grumbled.
"Oh, lighten up, Bren," I said to her. "This is a fun night. We didn't expect to be serenaded anyway. Let's get these 45's to the cash register!"
A soft, "Okay," was all Brenda could muster.

Chapter Twenty-Six

"Look at all this!" Mr. Dalrymple laughed, "Do I have any records left back there?!"

"Quite a collection, huh?" I said proudly.

"I'll say! Well, if this doesn't make John Turner the most popular disc-jockey in America, I don't know what will!" Again he laughed.

I opened up the 'Rock and Roll' envelope and waited to hear the total.

"That comes to exactly twelve-fifteen."

"That was a good year," Brenda grumbled.

"It sure was," Dolly chimed in with a smile, "King John signed the Magna Carta in 1215!"

I laughed, and again, Brenda grumbled.

"Hey, you two go on outside. I'll be out in a sec, okay?" Dolly politely requested.

"Ummm... yeah, sure," I said.

Brenda and I said our goodbyes to Mr. Dalrymple and waited by the front door for Dolly.

"What in Sam's Hill is the matter with you?" I asked Brenda. "You're gettin' weird on me. What is it?"

She sighed. "I'll tell you later."

"Tell me now."

"No! I'll tell you *later*."

"Is this... is this something about Dolly?"

"Didn't I just say I'd tell you later?"

"It is, isn't it?"

"I *said*..."

"Okay, okay. Later."

Brenda and I stood there in silence for just a few seconds when Dolly sprung out of the doorway with a huge smile on her face. She handed Brenda and I two small white Dalrymple boxes.

"What's this?" Brenda said, still half-grumpy.

"Dolly," I smiled, as I opened the box, "Dark chocolate fudge with walnuts! It's my favorite! You remembered!"

"Sweet." Brenda added, "No pun intended."

"Open yours, Bren," I nudged.

Brenda opened her candy box and inside it was strawberry and vanilla mint salt water taffy.

"Bren! Your favorite candy in the whole world!"

"I hope you like them. Dalrymple's really gets all the good taffy," Dolly stated.

Brenda looked up at her, "Thanks. That was very thoughtful of you."

I spread my arms wide and rested them over the shoulders of my two dearest friends. "This is such a fabulous night! Two wonderful pals, a night on the boards, all the coolest records in the world, candy and…"

"Three pink and white stuffed poodles," Dolly chuckled.

I started to run toward the boardwalk, "Come on guys! The night is young!"

Dolly made a silly face, clicked her heels together and followed right behind me.

"Come on, Slowpoke!" I hollered to Brenda. "Get up here!"

I watched as she took a piece of taffy from the box, unwrapped it, and then popped it into her mouth. "I'm comin'," she grumbled, "I'm comin'."

Chapter Twenty-Seven

It wasn't long before all three of us were back up on the boardwalk. Once again Dolly pointed out one place after another, "I worked there for six weeks"... "I worked there for two months"...

Brenda just rolled her eyes at me.

"Stop that," I whispered.

Soon we all decided that after too much pizza, popcorn, fudge, and salt water taffy that maybe we should just sit at the pavilion, rest and watch the cool evening ocean water flow up onto the beach. For three seventeen-year-olds, peace and quiet could only be tolerated for about ten minutes, and so, we were off and running again in nothing flat.

Dolly suggested a carousel ride, and Brenda and I were all for it.

"I *always* get the brass ring!" Dolly smiled.

"Of course you do," said Brenda.

No sooner had we entered the circus-tent shaped building and handed Joe Godfrey ten cents a piece when we were all sitting on our favorite carousel animal. Of course I was on Big Kitty, Brenda hopped on her old stand-by, a giraffe she called Spot, and Dolly rode a beautiful black stallion with bright and shiny emerald-green eyes. The calliope started to play and around we went, one turn after another, each of us trying so hard to be the first to get the brass ring. Three minutes later the ride was over and I gave Mr. Godfrey another ten cents for each of us. We were all bound and determined to get that ring!

On my first pass I almost had it. On the third pass I was almost certain Brenda had it in her hand, but she didn't.

"I'll get that thing yet!" I heard her shout.

As the carousel slowed down, ending our second ride Dolly reached out, just in time, and, as luck would have it she pulled out not one ring, but two!

"Oh my God! I got it! I mean, I got *them*! Did you see that? Look! I got *two* brass rings!"

I started to laugh. I could see Mr. Godfrey applauding and heard him say, "Why don't you go around one more time, Dolly, maybe you could get another and you'd all have one!"

Brenda hopped off the giraffe she named Spot and then strolled over toward me and Big Kitty. "That's enough carousel riding for me for one night."

I laughed again. "Can you imagine, she got *two* brass rings! I told you Bren, she's amazing!!"

"So I've heard."

Dolly quickly jumped off the carousel and handed Mr. Godfrey both of her brass rings.

"Now Dolly," he said "Normally you get a prize and a free ride in exchange for the brass ring, but, no one since I've ever worked here, and that's forty-two years mind ya, no one has *ever* pulled two rings at the same time!"

Dolly was all smiles.

"So," he continued, "Tonight is very special! And you get to pick a prize *and* you can all ride again for free when ever you choose, *and,* you get to keep both rings as a souvenir!"

"You gotta be kidding!" she shrieked. "That is *so* cool! Really? I get a prize, we all ride for free *and* I can keep the rings?" She smiled at me and Brenda, then immediately turned toward the prize gallery.

"Wow! Okay, I'd like that... that black and white shaggy dog, please." She giggled.

"One black and white shaggy dog it is!" said Mr. Godfrey.

Dolly turned toward us, hugging the little black and white dog to her heart. "I'm gonna give this dog to Apry, she'll just *love* it!"

"That's really thoughtful of you, Dolly. Isn't it, Bren?" I nudged her.

"Yeah... real sweet."

As we were leaving the pavilion, Dolly was clutching her pink and white poodle and Apry's black and white shaggy dog in one arm and twirling two brass rings on the index finger of the other. "Know what guys?"

"What?" I answered.

She stopped twirling the rings and took them off her finger. "Tonight was a very lucky night for me. *And,* I believe it was such a great night because I had you two with me! So I want to give one of my rings to you, Pattie, and one to you, Brenda."

I didn't know what to say.

Apparently Brenda didn't either.

"Well, say *something* for God's sake!" She smiled again.

"Geez," I said looking at my brass ring, "I never, *ever* thought I would get one of these. I've been riding that carousel since I was a baby! Even my dad couldn't get me one! Thanks Dolly. I mean it... Thanks."

"Yeah. Thanks Dolly." Brenda's voice was soft and... well it was just different.

Before we knew it, the boardwalk stands started to close down, the bright neon lights were turned off, and the music from the calliope had been silenced.

"The end of a perfect day," Dolly said, arms spread wide as we walked down the boards. "Thanks guys, it was really cool."

We saw Mr. and Mrs. Godfrey getting into their old 1948 Plymouth and they asked us if we would like a ride home.

"No thanks," Dolly smiled, "after all that food we ate tonight, we *need* to walk."

They nodded and waved us a goodbye.

The walk down Landis Avenue seemed faster than usual, and before we knew it, we were at 85th Street, just half a block from home.

"How about Brenda and I walk you to your house? There are two of us and, you know, it's kinda late."

"No, no, no," Dolly said. "Don't even give it a second thought; I'll be home in less than two minutes, no big deal. But thanks anyway." Dolly re-adjusted the stuffed animals in her arms and then reached her hand out toward Brenda. "It was really a pleasure to meet you. I can see why Pattie loves you so much."

Brenda nodded.

"That's all you're gonna do? Nod your head?" I leaned into her. "Has it been too long a day for you, Miss Mayberry... and your manners have flown the coop?"

"I'm sorry. Nice to meet you too, Doll. I'm just tired I guess."

I wrapped my arms around Dolly and thanked her for a great night. "We gotta do this again *real* soon," I smiled.

"I'll be lookin' forward to it, I can tell you that!" she smiled back. "Night Pattie... Night, Brenda!"

Bren and I stood at the corner until we saw Dolly make the left onto 89th Street. As we started our walk home I noticed Brenda was unusually quiet - especially considering the great night we all had.

"What's the matter with you?" I asked.

"Funny," she smirked, "I was just about to ask you the same thing."

Chapter Twenty-Eight

It was exactly 11:00 PM when we walked into the house.
"What do you mean what's the matter with me?" I was totally annoyed by her question.
"Listen…"
"I'm listening."
"You know, it's one thing for me and you to be naïve where boys are concerned, BUT… your naiveté toward ordinary human behavior is just totally unacceptable to me. You're smarter than that."
"What?"
"You heard me."
We started to walk up the steps, lowering our voices so we wouldn't disturb Aunt Anna or Uncle John.
"What are you talking about?"
"See, there you go again. I'm *talkin'* about Dolly?!"
We walked into my bedroom, took off our shoes, and then sat on the bed.
"Dolly?! How could you say *anything* bad about Dolly?"
Brenda looked me straight in the eyes. "I didn't say I was gonna say anything bad, unless you consider the facts bad."
"The facts? What are you talkin' about?!"
"Listen, Pat. We both went to Sunday school together and…."
"So?"
"Well, as far as I can recall, only one person ever walked on water."
"Oh, puh-leeze!" I rolled my eyes at her. "What could you *possibly* have to say about… Oh, my God! I know what it is!"
"What *what* is?"
"You're jealous!"
"*Jealous?!*" Brenda thumped me on my shoulder. "I wouldn't be jealous of you if you married Elvis Presley! I'd be *happy* for you!"
I got up from the bed and put my pink and white poodle on the dresser and then quickly turned back toward Brenda. "Bren, she's a nice girl, a *really* nice girl. I don't know *what* your problem is."
"Well if you'd shut up long enough, I'll *explain* some things to you, because apparently you *need* to hear some severe explainin'."
"Okay, okay, she-who-has-all-the-answers… Talk!"
"First of all, I *do* think Dolly is a nice girl. I just think she doesn't have a foothold in reality."
"How can you *say* that?"
"Will you shut up and just listen to me?"
"Okay, okay!"
"All right. Here's how this is gonna work. I'll ask you questions and

you answer me honestly. Can you do that?"

"Of course, I can. Ask."

"First off, have you ever seen Dolly's 1959 red and white Chevy Impala?"

"Well, let me tell you about that..."

"No!" Brenda put her hand out to stop me. "Don't give me an excuse, give me an answer. Again, I repeat. Have you *ever* seen Dolly's 1959 red and white Chevy Impala?"

"No."

"Okay, now. Didn't you think it was a little odd that *every* place she said she used to work, nobody was there who ever worked with her? I mean, it's not like she worked on the boards twenty years ago, Pattie."

"But..."

"Stop! You expect me to believe that in the *seven* places Dolly showed us that she worked, it's just a... a what... a quirk that she didn't want to take us in to any of them? That in just *one* year everyone she ever worked with is somewhere else? I'm not buying it. Doesn't that seem just a little odd? Answer me."

"Yes."

"*And*... she is *such* a wonderful singer... so wonderful that she's gonna study in New York. *Your* Dolly is the Connie Francis of Townsends Inlet, New Jersey and you *never* heard her sing even one note, have you? Not even along with the radio at work... have you?"

"No, but..."

"No buts, Pattie. Yes or no?"

"No."

"And *what* was the deal with those two girls on the boardwalk? Don't you think it's just a little *strange* that Miss Mary Sunshine could have two people that obviously despise her so? What was the *real* story behind that, '*Look-at-you-all-dressed-up-goin'-to-the-prom-Miss-Dolly*' thing, huh? Do you *really* know?"

I hemmed and hawed for a moment, "No."

Brenda got up off the bed and looked out the window. "I'm sorry to be sayin' these things about somebody I just met, Pat... especially someone you like so much, but something just seems *awfully* fishy to me."

"Brenda, listen..."

"*And*," she continued, overriding my interruption, "*because* of the answers that you gave me, whether you're ready to admit it or not, you think somethin's fishy too!"

I crossed my arms over my chest and turned toward the window. "I'm very upset with you right now."

"For what? For the *truth*?"

It was hard for me to get a good breath. "She's been through a lot, Brenda. She lost her mother, you know. See, that's something you can't understand. I can *feel* Dolly's pain, I *can*... or do you forget what happened the night of graduation?"

Brenda dropped her head into her chest and sighed. "Pattie, I'll *never* forget what happened on Graduation night and I miss your parents terribly. I loved them. But losing your parents and being a liar are just two totally different things."

"A *liar*?!" I immediately lowered my voice for fear I would wake my aunt and uncle. "A liar? Dolly was wonderful to us."

"I didn't say she wasn't."

"And she bought *me* my favorite chocolate fudge with walnuts, and bought you your favorite saltwater taffy, *with* her hard earned money, I might add!" My voice was growing louder again.

"That's not my point, Pattie."

"*And*, to top it all off, Brenda, she gave each of us one of her brass rings. I mean, that was really sweet, kind, and unselfish. Admit it."

"So you're saying sweet, kind, and unselfish people don't lie?"

"And she's smart, too!" I was defending Dolly with a vengeance. "I mean, how many people know that King John signed the Magna Carta in 1215. Huh?"

"Anyone who can read the 'Fun Facts' on a Cracker Jack box, Pattie."

I cut my eyes at her. I was so angry I was ready to explode. It scared me a little because I never felt that way in my whole life. Was this some leftover anger I didn't express when my parents died? Was it because I was disappointed in Brenda's quick condemnation of my new friend? Or, was I angry at myself because I truly had to agree with what Brenda was saying to me?

The facts *were* that there were *no* facts at all to substantiate anything Dolly said and it made me feel very displaced, hurt, and upset.

"*So*," Brenda said to me, "What do you have to say for yourself?"

I knew at that moment if I opened my mouth I would say something I'd probably regret, so I grabbed my white beaded sweater from the closet, put my shoes back on my feet, and started to leave the room.

"What are you doing?" she asked, tugging at my arm.

I immediately pulled myself out of her grasp. "I'll be back in a little while. I need to go for a walk and think about a few things."

"This is *crazy*, Pattie."

"Bren, this whole *thing* is crazy," I said as I was closing the bedroom door. "See ya."

"Suit yourself," she huffed. "See ya."

Chapter Twenty-Nine

By the time Dolly reached 89th Street she was exhausted - happy, but exhausted.

As soon as she walked in the house, she sat down at the table and wrote a little note for Apry, then she attached it to the black and white shaggy dog and sat the pooch right next to her sister's breakfast plate. Just as Dolly was about to walk up the steps, the kitchen light went on and there was Nikki, standing right in front of her.

"Hi. What are you doing up?" Dolly asked.

"I'm making Mack a bottle. And what are *you* doing wearing *my* blouse?!"

Dolly had completely forgotten to change back into the old clothes she left in the shed earlier that evening. "Umm… I… Didn't I ask you about borrowing this? Didn't you hear me? I know I *did*."

Nikki shook her head. "Dolly, you don't have to lie to me. And you don't have to steal from me either. All you had to do was ask."

Dolly bowed her head in shame. "Sorry."

Nikki walked to the stove, heated a pre-made bottle from the refrigerator and then started to walk toward the staircase. She turned and looked at Dolly, "And don't worry, I won't tell your father."

"Ummm, okay… thanks, Nik."

Dolly was beyond humiliated. She felt sad, depressed, and angry. She walked down into the shed, exchanged blouses, and then, instead of going back into the house, she decided to take a walk up to the beach, up to a spot where she and her mother would often play - right on top of the highest sand dune on the entire inlet.

At the very same time, I was out walking the darkened streets of the little town as well, and, for some reason, I decided to turn up 89th Street.

Why?

I don't know.

I guess thinking about Brenda grilling me over my naiveté naturally led me in Dolly's direction.

Why would she lie to me about a red and white Chevy Impala?

…about having boyfriends?

…about working on the boardwalk?

Why would she lie about being such a wonderful singer?

What would be the point?

As I walked further up 89th Street, to the very last house before the beach, there sat a beautiful 1959 red and white Chevrolet Impala, right in the driveway. The scripted name on the mailbox read: **The Dollio Family**.

I was so happy to see it, I almost did a little dance right in the middle of the street.

I knew she didn't lie to me!

Then, all of a sudden, as I was about to run home to tell Brenda about my discovery, I heard a noise in the wind, no, it was more than a noise, it was a voice… and, the voice was singing. I walked about twenty feet, stepped over a little wooden fence, and then climbed up one of the sand dunes. As my eyes just about cleared the top of the dune, there, not ten feet away, back facing me, arms spread out wide, was Dolly, singing her heart out to no one but the universe.

It was absolutely the most beautiful voice I had ever heard in my entire life.

*"Once on a high and windy hill…
In the morning mist…
two lovers kissed…
and the world stood still…
Then your fingers touched my silent heart…
and taught it how to sing…
Yes, true love's…
a many splendored thing."*

I wanted to jump up and down and applaud, but it didn't seem right to me - not proper somehow. You know, like how you never want to talk loud in a library, or at church? Well, this too was one of those times where silence was required of me - this time, to allow me the pleasure of hearing one of God's angels sing - and I was awestruck.

As Dolly finished her song, I quickly slipped down the sand dune, climbed back over the fence, and then ran down 89th Street all the way back to the house. I was very careful not to make any noise when I got back home, you know, so I wouldn't wake anyone. I took off my shoes, tiptoed up the steps, and went straight to my room.

Brenda was sound asleep.

Immediately I got into my pajamas, turned the fan speed to medium, and then crawled into bed.

"What time is it?" she said sleepily. "What were you doing?"

"It's after midnight, I guess. Go back to sleep."

"*So,*" Brenda yawned, "Did you make peace with yourself?"

"An angel sang to me, Bren."

"Huh?"

"I said, an *angel* sang to me, Brenda… how could I not be at peace with myself?"

Chapter Thirty

A combination of the early morning sun shining through my bedroom window and the delicious aroma of fresh coffee brewing woke me with a big smile on my face. I got up out of bed, put on my robe and slippers, and then shook Brenda's shoulder. "Wake up and smell the coffee, sister!"

Bren just grumbled and rolled over.

"Hey, it's almost eight o'clock! Aren't you coming down for breakfast?"

She grumbled again, and then pulled the pillow over her face, "Go a-waaaay."

"Okay, suit yourself."

I walked down the stairs and as I reached the kitchen I saw Uncle John all dressed in his Sunday best and Aunt Anna looking absolutely lovely - even her apron matched her outfit. I thought that was pretty cute.

"Good morning, Pat," they both said.

"Mornin'."

"Where's Brenda?" my aunt asked me.

"I think she's got an acute case of Fresh-air-itis," I said seating myself.

"That's city folk for ya," Uncle John smiled as he reached for the toast and strawberry jelly. "They're not used to what real clean air is. It just knocks 'em out."

"You look really pretty," I said to my aunt. "Goin' to an early service?"

"Nine o'clock on the nose" she answered. "I hope you decide to go with us one of these days, Pattie."

"I will, just not now... I'm..."

"No need to explain," she said patting my hand.

"And what about me?" Uncle John chided while straightening himself up in his chair. "Don't I look handsome?"

Actually, he did look handsome, but he also looked like a genuine stuffed shirt - and an uncomfortable one at that! You see, John Martin Turner was the consummate man of leisure. All summer long he'd wear shorts, a nice short-sleeved shirt, an old straw hat and his sneakers. That's who he was, and he was 'comfy.' But then came Sunday, and my Aunt Anna expected them both to look prim and proper. So, he'd wear a light colored summer suit, starched shirt, necktie complete with diamond stickpin, and a pair of shoes so highly polished you could see your face in them.

"Uncle John," I smiled, "You're the Cary Grant of the inlet."

"Now that's what I wanted to hear!" he raised his coffee cup in a toast to my comment.

"So, what are you and Brenda going to be doing today?" my aunt questioned.

"Well, today is beach day! I mean, a full day of swimming and then reading on the beach, talking, getting a bite to eat… just a nice day together."

"I gather the three of you had a wonderful time last night?"

"We really did! OH!!! Wait a second!" I quickly left my chair, ran into the dining room and brought back the Dalrymple's bag that was carrying all of the records for the Civic Center dances. "These are the coolest records in the whole universe! Mr. Dalrymple said you'll be the most popular disc-jockey in America!"

My uncle placed his coffee cup back in the saucer to take a look at what we purchased. "Tutti Frutti?"

"It's a fast song by Little Richard."

"I thought it was an ice cream flavor." He turned toward my aunt. "Isn't that an ice cream flavor, Anna?"

She shook her head and smiled.

"And, 'Bird Dog'?" he said as he was moving through the titles.

"It's The Everly Brothers, Uncle John."

"A song about a bird dog is a hit?"

"A BIG hit," I smiled.

"Bird dogs and some Tutti Frutti? I don't get it, Anna."

"Just play them John, you don't have to understand them. More coffee, Sweetheart?"

"Bird dogs and…" he mumbled to his wife.

"John Turner?!"

"Oh, sure, Anna… more coffee."

"And, Uncle John? The bill was only $12.15! So you've got some big change coming to you!"

"Well, you're a good shopper, Pattie," he said closing up the Dalrymple shopping bag.

"I'll go get your change," I said as I started to leave the table once again.

"No, don't do that, finish your breakfast. *And…* I think because you did so well last night, you and Brenda should keep the change and treat yourselves while you're enjoying your beach day!"

"Really?!"

"Yes, really."

I leaned across the table and hugged my Uncle. "Thank you sooooooo much!"

Aunt Anna got up to leave the table and patted me on the shoulder. "When Brenda wakes up, Dear, her breakfast is right here on a plate on the warming tray."

"I'll tell her. Thank you. And, I'll clean up, Aunt Anna. Don't risk getting a spot on your beautiful outfit."

She smiled at me. "Well, thank you, Pattie. I appreciate that very much."

My Uncle left the table for a brief sit down in his favorite chair to smoke a cigarette while Aunt Anna went upstairs to put on the new hat she bought at Pfeiffer's. The hat was lovely: a pretty little band of white silk with a few delicate moiré violets here and there and a small veil that hung down just a bit onto her forehead. It wasn't my style, but it was absolutely perfect for Aunt Anna.

As she entered the living room I heard Uncle John say to her, "Anna, you look beautiful! But then again, you've looked beautiful to me since you were sixteen-years-old."

"And, you've look handsome to me ever since I *was* sixteen-years-old." I could hear the smile in her voice as she hugged him.

Now that's the way it's supposed to be... yup... that's love.

Chapter Thirty-One

Aunt Anna and Uncle John left the house at 8:45, with plenty of time to make it to church and say hello to all of their friends before the service began.

I said goodbye to them, locked the front door, and watched as they strolled up the street arm in arm.

Sweet.

I had just finished the dishes and was dusting in the living room when Brenda dragged herself down the staircase. "Well, good morning, Miss Bright and Cheerful." I smiled.

"Any coffee?" she said as she walked toward the stove.

I pointed her back in the direction of the kitchen table. "Sit down and I'll get it for you. My Aunt left your breakfast on the warming tray, so you're all set."

Brenda rubbed her eyes and yawned. "Thanks."

I poured myself another cup of coffee and sat down right across from Brenda while she ate breakfast. "Well…" I cocked my head to the right and grinned, "Aren't you going to ask me about last night?"

"What about it? Oh, you mean when you left here in a huff?"

"I didn't leave in a huff. I was hurt."

"Hurt, huff… what's the difference?"

I was just about to explain the difference when I realized it wasn't even necessary. After all, I had an angel on my side.

"Bren?"

"Yeah?"

"You're wrong about Dolly."

"Oh, God, not this again! It's not even nine o'clock!"

I leaned in further and looked right into Brenda's eyes. "Just listen to me."

"What?"

"When I went out last night I thought about everything you said to me."

"As you should have."

"And I had to agree there were no facts to back anything that Dolly said."

"Toldja."

"*But…*" I said as a smile started to wash across my face.

"But what?"

"Well, when I was out, for some reason, I walked up 89th Street."

"Where Dolly lives?"

"Yup."

"And…"

"*And*, right there on the last house before the beach was a brand spanking new 1959 red and white Chevy Impala - parked smack-dab in the middle of the driveway!"

"You don't even know her address. That could be a neighbor's car."

"No, it wasn't. The sign on the mailbox said, 'The Dollio Family'."

Brenda raised her eyebrows a bit and then just grumbled.

"I mean it, Bren, I was so happy I was ready to jump up and down and dance the hootchie-coo in the middle of the street! But you know what stopped me?"

"The voice of sanity?"

"No, wise ass. A *voice*."

"Oh, so *now* you're hearing *voices*?" She started to laugh.

"I don't mean *those* kinds of voices, I mean a *real* voice!"

"Yeah, so..." Brenda seemed bored to death with my story.

"Well, I thought it was a voice from far away...like maybe someone was talking or something, then somehow I turned in the right direction, and the wind favored me..."

"And?"

"And then I realized someone was singing."

"Yeah, so?" She rolled her eyes at me.

"*So*, I followed the voice. I had to hop over this small fence and climb up one of the dunes, but when I got to the top of it, you know, just enough for my eyes to see over it?"

"I know what you mean."

"Well, that's when I saw Dolly."

"*Dolly*?"

"Yep. That must be were she practices. She was singing 'Love Is a Many Splendored Thing', and I mean it, Brenda, she has the voice of an angel. I'm not kidding. I never heard anything like it. Cross my heart."

"So *that* was the angel thing you were talkin' about when you got into bed last night?"

"Exactly!"

Slowly Brenda left her chair, took her plate, cup and saucer to the sink and started to wash them.

"Bren? Hey!"

"Hey, what?"

"Aren't you gonna say anything? You know you owe me a big apology."

"I what?"

"Well, and I guess you owe Dolly one, too, only she doesn't know it."

Brenda glanced over her shoulder at me, but said nothing.

"So, Miss Skeptical and Judgmental, I shall accept *one* nice and neat apology for me *and* Dolly."

Brenda finished drying her dishes, put them away, and then sat down next to me. "Listen, *maybe* the car belongs to the Dollios, but it doesn't mean it's *her* car! And, as far as the singing story goes?"

"The singing story?! *Story*?!!"

"Pattie, puh-leeze."

"What?!"

"Do honestly expect me to think that really happened? Maybe you were dreaming that part."

"So now you don't believe me?!"

"Well, how would it sound to you?"

"It would sound just like it was - the truth!"

"Oh, right. You and I have a… well, not a fight, but a tiff or something about a girl who has trouble within the realm of reality and then you leave the house and find the mysteriously ever-missing 1959 Chevy. *And,* not only that, but you just *happen* to walk up her street close to midnight and Dolly just happens to be outside, *on* the beach, singing her little heart out and YOU were the only lucky listener on planet Earth?! Puh-leeeze!"

"Well, okay, so it sounds a little far fetched, but…"

"Gee, ya think?"

"But, Bren, it's true! I swear to God! I *saw* the car and I *heard* her sing!"

"You know, Pattie, you don't have to fabricate something to make me like her."

"Fabricate?!"

"Just listen to me. I do like her. She just lies for stupid reasons and she doesn't have to! It's nuts. That's all I'm saying. So…"

"So?"

"So, I love ya, Patricia, but I'm just not buyin' it! And that's that."

Brenda patted me on the shoulder in a condescending fashion and started back up the staircase.

"And that's *that*?!" I said following behind her.

"You heard me."

Chapter Thirty-Two

Brenda and I packed a little bag filled with lotsa good stuff to eat, brought a blanket, towels, and some Coppertone to the beach with us. On our way, as we walked by the Civic Center, I remarked, "This weekend is the first dance here!"

"What?"

"Look at the sign!" I said pointing to the rather large poster.

> **Townsends Inlet's First Rock and Roll Summer Dance!!!**
> **Friday Nite, July 3rd !!!**
> **7:00 to 10:00 PM**
> **All Teenagers welcome!!!**
> **50 cents Admission**
> **Refreshments Available**

"Oh, yeah, I remember. Well, at least we know there's gonna be some cool music," she said staring inside The Civic Center window.

"Yeah, considering we're the geniuses behind it!"

I smiled and Brenda smiled back.

Nice.

You know, that was the lightest moment the two of us had together since she walked off that big old Greyhound bus.

In a way, I could see why she was skeptical, but in another way, I had a sense that Brenda just didn't like the place that Dolly had taken in my life. Dolly and I barely knew each other for two weeks and we had become really good friends. That was something that *never* happened to me, and Brenda knew it. But there was a way about Dolly, something that couldn't actually be defined in words that made me gravitate toward her. And I knew that in time, no matter what she was saying now, that Brenda would get over her rough feelings for Miss Dollio and like her as much as I did. Dolly deserved good friends, she was a nice kid, she really was, and no one was ever going to convince me otherwise.

* * * * * *

"Gimme some Coppertone, will ya, please?" Brenda held her hand out toward me.

"It's right next to you."

"Huh?"

"I *said*, it's right next to you!"

"Oh."

Brenda reached for the little brown bottle and started smoothing the coconut smelling liquid all over her arms, legs, and face. "Are you going in the water?" she asked me.

"Of course, I am. You think I'm gonna bake out here all afternoon? No way."

"Well, *I'm* not going."

"What?"

"I *said*... I'm not goin'."

"Why not?"

"I'll feel too icky."

"Gimme a break."

"Pattie, I have *all* this cream on, the sand blows, then it sticks to me, then I get in the water and the salt is all over me. EEE-YUCK!"

"For Pete's sake, Brenda."

"No, seriously, I'm better off in the bay. A quick dip, then a shower at your aunt and uncle's place and I'm done. I hate the ocean thing, I *hate* it!"

"That's crazy! Look at all those great waves rolling in. How can you just wanna stay on the beach?"

"Look, I'm stayin' on dry land and that's that! You go in and then tell me *all* about it when you get back, okay?"

"Of course, Little Miss Coppertone." I playfully tossed my towel in her face.

"That's me, all right," she said, as she smoothed a bit more lotion across her arms. "Now *that's* the smell of summer, dontcha think?"

"Yup."

"Today's a beautiful combination of all the elements, isn't it, Pat? The water, the breeze, the nice sunny day…"

"My Coppertone…"

Brenda smiled at me as she adjusted her big straw hat. "Yeah. But, you know what's missing from the equation?"

"Besides you not wanting to go swimming?"

"Stop it! I'm serious. Know what's missing?"

"What?"

"Guys."

"Guys?"

"I didn't stutter. I said *guys*… men… the opposite sex!"

My eyes quickly started to scan the beach. "You're nuts. There's plenty of guys out here!"

"Pattie," she shook her head, "Take another look. All the cute guys are already *with* girls."

Again my eyes made a sweeping survey. "Hmmm."

"Well?"

"Well, that stinks," I answered.

"You're not kiddin'!"

I sighed deeply and dramatically. "Where art thou, George Ludlam when I *really* need you?"

No sooner had Brenda and I smiled at each other over my comment, when a voice sounded from above us.

"Hey, did someone just mention my name?"

I looked up and put my hand across my eyebrows to block out the sun. "Huh?" I couldn't see *anything* but a silhouette completely surrounded by sunlight.

"Pattie?" the voice spoke once again.

"Yeah?"

"Oh, my God, it's George and Clark!" Brenda quickly whispered.

"George? George L*udlam*? Is that *you*?"

"Uh-huh. It's me, all right. Mind if we sit for a spell? Me and Clark?"

Immediately Brenda and I started to fuss: we straightened out our blanket, I moved the towels to my left, and then Brenda placed the Coppertone back in the little carry-all bag we brought with us.

"Sure," I smiled, "have a seat."

"Hi, Guys," Brenda nodded with an air of nonchalance.

"*So*, I heard my name mentioned. I hope it was for a good reason."

I didn't know what to say.

Think, Pattie THINK!!!

"Pat?" he smiled.

"Well, Brenda and I were talking about the dance that my Uncle John is running at The Civic Center. You know, about the people we thought who might be attending. See, a nice crowd would make it a success, and then maybe we can have one every Friday for every summer to come."

"And?" he smiled again.

"And, we remembered you and Clark, so that's where your name came in."

"Timing is everything," Clark said staring at Brenda.

"Well, that's cool."

"Are you going to the dance, George?"

Please say you're going to the dance!!!

"Yeah. Clark and I, and my friends Dustin, Joe, and Andrew were talking about the dance last night. We're looking forward to going."

"So," I smiled, "Are you a good dancer?"

"Are you?" George asked.

"Well…"

"Pattie's light on her feet. The Ginger Rodgers of Rock and Roll," Brenda chimed in.

I laughed.

"No, seriously, Pat's one of the best dancers in Philly."

"Bren, please…"

Brenda was switched on and nothing was about to stop her.

"Pattie won a trophy at Chez-Vous, one at Concord, and one at

Wagner's. The best dancer award! Well, the best *couple's* dancing award - Pat and a guy named Bruce Schulman."

"Is he your boyfriend?" George asked.

"No, I don't have a boyfriend."

Hear that George Ludlam?! I do NOT have a boyfriend!

"Bruce went to dancing school with me. We used to get partnered up when we were kids, you know, for recitals and stuff, so... we just kept it up. I never see him unless there's a dance."

George grinned.

"But," Brenda continued, "Pat would win even if Bruce wasn't there, I mean it, she's that good!" Brenda was proud of my jitterbugging accomplishments. She had two left feet, but Brenda still took to the dance floor with a vengeance.

"What are Chez-Vous, Concord, and Wagner's?" Clark asked.

"Chez-Vous and Wagner's were old Ballrooms and there's a teen dance there every week, and Concord is really a roller rink on Frankford Avenue up in northeast Philly, but they have dances there, too."

"We go to all of them," I smiled.

"Well," George said, "I guess I'm gonna have to practice a lot to make sure I'm worthy of dancing with you, Pattie."

I could feel my face getting warm. I prayed it was because of the sun and not because I was blushing. "George Ludlam, I think you'll do just fine."

"So, you'll save a dance for me?"

Oh, God... I'd save every dance for you!

"No problem at all," I smiled.

"Hey, wanna go in the water?" Clark asked Brenda.

"In the... in the *water*?" She was almost wincing.

Clark stood up and then reached for Brenda's hand. "Yeah! Come on, this'll be fun!"

"Oh, yeah, sure, this'll be great!" Brenda quickly put an awkward grin on her face. "Umm... sure! Pattie and I were just about ready to go in anyway. I love the water! Don't I Pat?"

I stared at her like a deer in headlights.

"I mean it, Clark, I *love* the water! As soon as I get to the beach I wanna go jump right into the waves! That's me all over! I get here and I'm ready to go swimming quicker than you can say..."

"Quicker than you can say 'a 1959 red and white Chevy Impala'?" I smirked.

"Not funny, Pattie... not funny at all."

Chapter Thirty-Three

Brenda and I had a super day at the beach; in fact, I don't think I ever had a better time at the beach in all of my life than I did that day!

George and I sat on the blanket and talked, trying our best to get to know each other while Brenda and Clark swam and played around in the breakers as soon as they rolled onto the shore.

"So, you're here every summer?" he asked.

"Well, yeah. My mother and father brought me here every year... until this one."

"I heard about what happened to them when I was up on the pier, somebody said something about it. I'm awfully sorry, Pattie."

I sighed. "It's hard to take in sometimes, you know, I mean it's hardly been any time at all since they've been gone. But I know they would want me to move on and do well in school, and do well with my life. I have to think of the good things to pull me through this."

George was kind and sympathetic. "I can't imagine how you do it. I know your Aunt and Uncle are really nice people, so I'm sure that helps some, huh?"

"It helps plenty. And sitting here with you and listening to the kids on the beach and watching Brenda and Clark is good too. I always look for the bright side of things. You know, the silver lining."

He smiled at me. "Well, do you..."

"Do I what, George?"

"Well, do you think you could find a silver lining if I asked you to go to the dance with me on Friday night?"

Stay cool, Pat. STAY COOL!

"Well, Geroge, first you have to tell me..."

"Tell you what?"

"Do you think you can handle the Chez-Vous dancing queen?"

"Yes," his smile widened. "I'm sure I can."

"Well, then George Ludlam. It's a date!"

A DATE!!!! MY FIRST REAL DATE!!!!

Just as my head was about to stop spinning, Clark and Brenda ran up to us from the water. Bren grabbed her beach towel and wrapped it around her body.

"George, we'd better get going." Clark was all out of breath. "The early boats'll be in and if we wanna get some work, we only have ten minutes to get to the pier. We just saw Captain Robbins' boat sail under the bridge!"

George turned to me and grinned. "It was short but sweet, Pattie. Thanks for a nice time. Nice to see you, too, Brenda."

"Thanks, George," she said while steadily towel drying her hair.

"See you Friday night, Pat… and don't forget, bring those Chez-Vous dancin' shoes."

"I'll remember."

"Bye, Clark!" Brenda was all smiles and she practically sang his name.

"See you soon!" he waved.

"Friday!" she called out to him as they ran up the beach toward the pavilion.

"Yup, Friday! See ya!"

We both stood there on the sand waving and smiling until George and Clark were completely out of site.

"Oh, my God… a date!" I shrieked.

"I know! I could hardly believe it!"

"And at a really nice place, at a nice dance… great music… it's perfect!"

"It sure is," Brenda sighed.

"So *you're* still coming to the dance, right?" I asked Brenda.

"What do you mean am *I* still going? Weren't we just talking about me going to the dance with Clark?"

"WHAT?!!! I thought we were talking about ME going to the dance with George!!!"

"You mean?!!"

I started to laugh. "BRENDAAAAAA!!!!! We *both* have dates for Friday night's dance!!! Oh, my God, Bren!! Can you imagine that?!! Me and George, and you and Clark!"

Brenda and I danced on our blanket, and laughed and smiled and then danced some more.

"Our first real dates ever!!! The summer of '59!!! This is one for the old diary! I'm happy for you, Pattie. George seems like a really, really nice guy."

"Well, Clark is no slouch either, Bren. I think we both did pretty good for just a day at the beach, don't you?"

She nodded. "Hey, how about we celebrate by having a nice big chocolate milk shake at VanSant's They're using Jane Logan ice cream this year, Pat… your favorite."

"No twisting my arm, Kiddo," I said as I was packing our things to leave.

Walking up toward the pavilion Brenda turned to me and smiled. "Real dates, Pattie!"

"Yup. *Real* dates. Geez."

We walked on for a few minutes not saying anything at all, just taking in the fun and magic of an absolutely wonderful day. As we turned the corner to walk to VanSant's I pointed to the sky. "See those two clouds up there, Bren?"

She glanced upward. "Yeah."

"They both have silver linings."

She gave me an odd expression. "How do you know that?"
"I just do, Bren," I smiled. "I just do."

Chapter Thirty-Four

Brenda and I walked to VanSant's, bought two delicious chocolate milk shakes, and then headed back to the house. All we could talk about was George and Clark, Clark and George, and George and Clark.

"Do you think your Aunt will allow you to go on a real date?"

"Brenda, for God's sake, it's just a dance and Uncle John'll be right there."

"Hmmm... I forgot about that."

"So, what would *your* Mom and Dad have to say *if* they knew."

"Well, I guess they'd think about it and considering your Uncle is there, I doubt they'd bat an eye."

We smiled at each other and as we were just about reaching our front door, we noticed Captain Cramer's boat coming up the bay.

"Bren? You think George and Clark will stick around and clean the catch from Cramer's boat, too?" I said as started to walk down toward the bay.

"Where are you, going?" she asked.

"Let's just walk down to the water, if they're still on John's Pier we can see them."

"Well... what are we waitin' for?" She smiled.

Brenda and I were at the edge of the bay in less than a minute and both of us immediately noticed Bobby Phillips and Billy Rual - both locals - hauling a few rather large King fish off Captain Robbins' boat.

"They've gotta be there, Bren. They work on that boat!" No sooner had those words left my mouth when we saw George and Clark.

Brenda and I started waving and jumping up and down, but only Bobby and Bill waved back. I kept pointing in George's direction.

"Over there, Bob... get George... over *there*...*THERE!!!!* Ugh!" I don't know why I was even talking, because Bobby couldn't hear me, but... finally he got the hint just the same, and about one second later Clark and George were waving back at us.

Captain Cramer's boat was docking right behind Captain Robbins', so we knew the guys had to go and get their work done, but it was nice to see them one more time. We waved again, they waved back, and then we left to go back to the house.

"What nice guys," Brenda sighed dreamily.

"Yeah," I smiled as I finished the last of my milkshake.

"Are we gonna tell your Aunt when we get home?"

"Sure, why not?" I smiled again.

"Are you gonna tell Dolly tomorrow when you see her at work?"

"Of course, I am. She'll be so happy for us!"

"Yeah, and she'll probably tell you she has three dates for the dance and can't make up her mind which guy to date."

"Brenda... no more nasty stuff about Dolly."

"I wasn't being *nasty*."

I just gave her one of those 'looks.'

"Okay, so I was being nasty. Sorry."

Brenda and I walked around the side of the house, and gave ourselves a quick rinse under the outdoor shower head. Then we took our towels around the back, shook out the sand that was still clinging to the soft terrycloth material, and started to walk up the back steps.

Just as we reached the top step, Aunt Anna opened the door. "Well, hi, girls! How was your day?" she said handing us each a dry towel to cover our wet bathing suits.

"Oh, Aunt Anna," I grinned from ear to ear. "George Ludlam asked to be my date for the dance on Friday! I never had a date before! It's okay if it's a date, isn't it?"

"Okay?" she said with a huge smile on her face. "I think it's terrific!"

I could hear Brenda breathe a sigh of relief. "And, Mrs. Turner? George's friend, Clark Lowen asked if he could escort me to the dance, so, ummm... that's a date, too!"

"Well, then that makes it *doubly* terrific!" she smiled again.

Brenda and I gave each other a big hug and then followed Aunt Anna into the kitchen.

Chapter Thirty-Five

Shortly after we were in the house, Brenda and I went upstairs to bathe and change. Even though I rinsed myself under the shower head outside, I still felt all sticky and salty, so a traditional shower was definitely required.

In just about twenty minutes, Brenda and I were both clean and refreshed and back downstairs helping Aunt Anna with dinner, setting the table, and talking about George and Clark, Clark and George, and The Civic Center dance.

"So, you saw them on the beach?" my aunt asked.

"It was so funny. I was just talking about him, 'cause we saw each other on the pier and then…"

"And then… he a-*pier*-d," Brenda joked.

Aunt Anna chuckled.

"See, you're not the only person around here who can come up with a good pun, Pattie!"

I rolled my eyes. "Well, when you come up with one, let me know, will ya?"

Brenda quickly dismissed my comment with the wave of her hand and continued, "So then all of a sudden George and Clark were there! I thought that was *so* cool. And then I went into the water with Clark and we were swimmin' out past the sand bar, he's a good swimmer. *And,* Pattie and George were talking, he's a good talker, *very* bright, and before we knew it, they had to leave to go up the bay to wait for Captain Robbins' boat, you know to clean the catches and stuff, and, and *then,* well, and *then* we had… well, then we had *real* dates for The Civic Center dance! *Real* dates!!!"

"Say that ten times fast." I smiled.

"This is *very* exciting," Aunt Anna nodded. "I remember my first date with your Uncle John, I was just about sixteen, and I was so thrilled I could barely contain myself. He was so nice and *so* sweet. I couldn't believe he really asked me out!"

"Did you ever date anyone else? Didn't you ever have another?" Brenda questioned.

"No. John Turner was the one, and I knew it."

"True love." I sighed.

"Indeed it was," my aunt said dreamily.

How sweet I thought. Here she is, in her mid-seventies, and she still has that dreamy look in her eyes when she talks about a man she's known for almost sixty years. My Mom and Dad were like that, too. What a wonderful thing. And I knew that kind of love was something that I wanted and needed. I wanted a soul mate. I wouldn't settle for less. And somehow, I knew it would happen to me. I don't know how I knew... I just did. And maybe he wasn't George Ludlam... but I'd find him... someday, somehow.

Absolutely I would.

Brenda noticed the faraway look in my eyes. "Hey, day dreamer," she nudged me. "Hand over the salt and pepper shakers, will ya?"

"Oh... sure."

Aunt Anna stood at the counter carefully carving the pork roast, my personal favorite, when Uncle John walked in the door.

"Hi, girls!" he smiled. "Well, only seven fish today, but seven's a lucky number!"

"Here, Uncle John, I'll take them and put them in the freezer for you."

"If there's any room!" Aunt Anna said as she gave her darling husband a peck on the cheek.

Uncle John took off his straw hat and placed it on the tiny wall rack out in the back porch. "Anna, maybe we can have a big fish-fry for the 4th of July and invite the neighbors! That would take care of some of those fish."

"John, that's a *wonderful* idea!"

My Uncle turned and smiled at me and Brenda. "And maybe you ladies could invite a guest... or *two*. That would be nice."

"A guest?" I said placing the fresh green beans on the table.

"Or two?" Brenda added.

"Sure, I'm certain there's someone that you'd like to invite."

"Someone?" Brenda asked as she sat down at the table.

"Well, you know, maybe two nice boys who like to dance?"

My face started to turn beet red. "How did you know that?! Did George and Clark tell you? Did they?"

"Well, truth be told," my Uncle started, "The minute I walked off Cramer's boat, George and his friend..."

"Clark," Brenda interrupted, "Clark Lowen?"

"Yes, that's right, Clark Lowen," he smiled. "They both came up to me and asked how I was doing, and I told them it was a seven catch day for me. And then I asked them how their day was, and..."

"And they told you...?"

"Well, no...they sort of asked me if it was okay. You know, to take you to the Civic Center dance."

"And...?" I sat there with a fork full of green beans waiting for his answer.

"*And?*" Brenda said anxiously.

"*And*, I said, absolutely not... and then I threw them both into the bay!"

Aunt Anna calmly placed her tea cup back in its saucer and then took a deep breath. I dropped my fork, and Brenda just sat there with her mouth hanging wide open.

My uncle burst into laughter. "I didn't do that! Of course, I said it was okay!"

"John Martin Turner! You old teaser!" my aunt chuckled. "Now just what do you have to say for yourself?"

"Me?" he smiled.

"Yes, you!"

Uncle John looked at all of us and smiled again. "I guess I'll say George and Clark are very nice young men. And…"

"*And?*" I grinned.

"And pass the potatoes, Pattie. I'm starving."

Pass the potatoes, Pattie, I'm starving?!!!

Well, so much for Uncle John's interest in the dating scene for 1959.

Chapter Thirty-Six

Sunday at The Dollio's was quite different from the after-the-church-services life at The Turner household. Dolly, Nikki and the kids drove over to the Acme in Sea Isle for the coming week's groceries. They took the kids to the beach and the rest of the day was spent doing laundry, cleaning, and making dinner. Dolly's father decided to grill some hot dogs and burgers so Dolly made a delicious macaroni salad and Nikki made an attempt at potato salad then sliced up a big watermelon into bite-size cubes for dessert.

Little Mack sat outside in his high chair and Dolly fed him some baby food and tiny pieces of watermelon. Apry had the appetite of a thirteen-year-old and ate two hotdogs and a small hamburger.

"Where does she put it?" Nikki laughed.

"*And* I still have room left for some ice cream!" Apry smiled. "Can we get some later, Daddy?"

Sean Dollio sat down at the small table and placed a napkin into the neckline of his shirt. "I guess we could do that a little later, Ap! Sounds good to me."

"Me too." Dolly smiled back at her little sister.

"So, work tomorrow, Dolly?" her father asked.

"Work all week. Maybe I'll get some overtime in so I can get a new blouse or something."

"Don't waste your money. You got plenty of stuff."

"Sean," Nikki interrupted, "she could use a few new things."

"Well, whatever you make over the forty dollars you owe here, you can do what ever you want with it."

"Just how far can seven dollars go, Dad?" she mumbled.

"What did you say to me?!" He squinted his eyes at her.

"Well, I said... I mean, I wanted something nice 'cause there's a..." she started.

"There's a what, Dolly?" Nikki asked.

"Well, there's a dance on Friday at The Civic Center and I was wondering if I could go with Pattie and her friend, Brenda."

"How much is it?"

"Fifty cents."

"When's it over?"

"Ten o'clock."

"Who's the chaperone?"

"Well, Pattie's Uncle John is playing the records and..."

"And what?"

"Can I go, Dad? I'll have the money to go..."

"Well, I don't see why not," Nikki stated. "Sounds okay to me. What do you think, Sean?"

"As long as you handle your chores, pay your way, and get to work."

"I will. I know what I have to do."

"Did you clean your room?"

"I did."

"And Apry and Mack's rooms?"

"I cleaned them right after I did mine."

"Well then, as long as you took care of your chores, and *continue* to take care of your chores, you can go."

Gimme a break.

"Okay, thanks, Dad."

I don't know what I'm thanking him for.

"You're welcome," he grunted. "Now go clean up your brother and sister so we can go out and get some ice cream. And bring me my hat, and take these utensils back into the house."

"Okay, okaaaay."

"Are you getting an *attitude* with me, young lady?!"

"No, Dad. I was just saying, okay. That's all."

"Well then, do it."

"Yes, Sir."

Chapter Thirty-Seven

"Boy, am *I* glad to see this place!" Dolly said as she strolled into Shellum's.

"Rough weekend, Doll?" Millie asked.

"Well, I had a *great* time with Pattie and Brenda on Saturday. We were up on the boards, ate, bought some records, *and* I got two brass rings at the carousel, but..."

"Two?! I don't think I ever heard of any one who caught two brass rings!"

"Well, *Dolly* did!" I said as I walked toward the back of the store. "And she gave one to me and the other one to Brenda!"

"Now wasn't that a sweet thing to do!" Millie commented.

I nodded in agreement.

"Hi, Pat!" Dolly said as she adjusted her smock. "I was just telling Mrs. S. what a great time we had this weekend."

"Yes, she was, and she was about to tell me something else. What was it, Doll?"

"Oh, nothing. Umm... it was a great weekend. I took it easy, not much to do... just laid around, went swimming. I've got it too good sometimes, I guess."

I smiled at her.

"Well, ladies," Millie said as she looked at her watch, "ten minutes and you're ready to start your day. Why don't you grab a donut and a cup of coffee before the gang's all here."

"Sounds good to me," I said as I walked toward the soda fountain.

"I'm with you," Dolly said following close behind.

"You sit, I'll pour."

"Okay, Pat. Thanks."

"Extra cream, extra sugar, right?"

"Yup."

"And a jelly donut?"

"That's me," she smiled.

"Dolly..."

"What?"

I started to giggle.

"What?! What is it?!"

"Oh, Miss Dolly... have *I* got news for *you*!"

"What *is* it?!" she said leaning in toward me.

"I *actually* have a date for The Civic Center dance!"

"WHAT?!"

"Yeah! And so does Brenda!"

"Oh, my God!"

"It's the first date, I mean the first *real* date either one of us ever had! I'm sooooooo excited! Brenda too! I mean, like we're doin' back flips over this and…"

"Holy cow! That's great! Who is it?"

"George Ludlam asked *me*, and Clark Lowen asked Brenda."

"I know those guys! They come in here a few times a week. Geez, George is *really* cute!"

I was blushing. "I know."

Dolly took a sip of her coffee. "Umm… yeah, I wish I could go to the dance this weekend."

"What?! I thought you were going!"

"Well my stepmother and dad are… well, they're goin' out and I forgot I promised them I'd baby-sit."

"Don't tell me that!"

"Yeah, but maybe next week, Pattie."

Yeah, Dolly thought to herself, *maybe next week… if I can find a date and I don't look like an idiot being the only one of us without one!*

"I wish you were going, Doll." I was *so* disheartened.

"That's okay, no big deal. I'll be there next week."

I watched Dolly take our empty cups and plates and start to wash them in the sink.

"I'm really happy for you, Pat. He's a nice guy and you're a great girl."

"You're a great girl, too, Doll."

She smiled at me. "Ya think so?"

"Think so? I *know* so!"

"Nine o'clock, girls! The magic hour has arrived," Millie Shellum called to us.

"Ready when you are, Dolly," I said as I pinned on my name tag.

"It's ShowTime," she smiled as she placed the door stop at the front entrance.

"Good morning, Dolly," Carrie Robinson said as she walked in the store.

"Mornin', Mrs. Robinson. How's your husband feeling?"

"Oh, old Jake? Just a cold. He'll be fit as a fiddle in no time. He'll live to be a hundred."

"Can I help you with anything?"

"Just a few odds and ends, Dolly," I glanced over Carrie's shoulder and saw a list that had to have at least forty items on it.

Odds and ends?!

Dolly took the list in her hands and started to shop around for Mrs. Robinson. "Have a seat," she told Carrie. "I'll be done this in no time. Would you like some coffee and a Danish while you wait?"

"Well, thank you, Dear," she smiled, "Don't mind if I do."

Dolly quickly poured the coffee - cream, no sugar, *and* she remembered Carrie's favorite Danish was blueberry and cream cheese, and placed it right in front of her.

"Thank you again, Dear."

"You're welcome." Dolly then immediately went back to filling the very long 'just a few odds and ends' shopping list.

"She's a really *lovely* girl," Mrs. Robinson said to me, taking the first sip of her freshly brewed coffee.

"She sure is," I smiled.

Chapter Thirty-Eight

Dolly and I were pretty busy all morning, right up until the usual lunchtime rush. And, even though we always had at least three things going on at once, I could see that Dolly had something else on her mind, something far beyond what was going on at Shellum's by-the-Sea. It was in her eyes, and in a certain look that I'd catch every now and then right there on her face. I mean, it was that obvious. But, just shortly before 1:00 PM, her preoccupied look turned into a happy one the second Brenda walked in the front door.

"Hey, Bren!"

"Hi, Dolly! Where's my partner in crime?" Brenda smiled.

"Right here," I called out. "What's up with you? Ya hungry?"

"Are you *kidding*? After breakfast at the Turner's?"

"So what's up at the house?"

"Not much, I did some dishes, dusted the living room with Aunt Anna, and then I helped Uncle John untangle some old fishing line. I just thought I'd come over to visit."

"Busy girl," I said.

"Sorta. Hey, did you tell Dolly about…"

"George and Clark?" Dolly chimed in from over my shoulder. "Yeah! That is *waaaaay* cool!"

"So, I guess your date can bring you to Pattie's and then we can all walk to The Civic Center together!"

Dolly's happy expression quickly left her face. "Can't happen."

"What?"

"I'm a no show this week, Bren."

"Why?"

"I forgot I had to baby-sit."

"Oh, for Pete's sake! Can't you get out of it?"

"Nah. They won't let anyone but me watch Mack and Apry."

"Well that stinks!"

"I know," Dolly agreed, "but I can go next week!"

"So, you have a date for next week?"

"Well, I…" Just then Dolly saw Dr. Thomas walk in. "Ooops, Doc Thomas is here, lemme get his order. See ya later, Bren."

"Yeah… see ya later, Doll."

Brenda made herself comfortable at the soda fountain and then snapped her fingers at me. "Oh, Miss! Oh, waitress… or whatever you are."

"What do *you* want, Wise-ass?" I tried hard not to smile.

"Wise-ass? Shame on you, you foul beast. I shall have you fired for such profanity."

I rolled my eyes at her. "Hmmm… let's see, might I soften that lousy disposition of yours with a delicious hot fudge sundae, Miss Brenda Breyers?"

"Well, yes. I think that could do it," she smiled back at me.

I opened the freezer to take out a new container of chocolate ice cream and then fixed Brenda one of the best sundaes in the house. While she was enjoying her treat, I cleaned up, refilled the utensil drawer, and made three Black Cows to go for The Bitner Family.

Suddenly Brenda leaned into the counter and whispered to me, "So… what's with 'Little Miss Dolly No Date'?"

"What are you talking about?"

"Pattie, puh-leeeeeze. Just two days ago she was dancin' a jig thinkin' about going to the dance."

"So?"

"So now *we* have dates, she doesn't, and that's why she's lyin' about babysittin' Mack and Apry."

"Stop that! She's *not* going because she has her reasons and that's it. She'll go next weekend. You heard her. Eat your ice cream!"

Brenda dug into her sundae and then stuck her tongue out at me.

"That's a good look for an honor student on her way to UCLA. Too bad I don't have a camera."

"Get back to work," she dismissed me with her hand. "We'll talk about this later."

"Indeed we will."

I wasn't sure if what Brenda and I did could be called playful banter or if we really were just ticked off at each other. Either way, we'd talk about it later. I wasn't really looking forward to it, but I knew it had to be done.

Then, right out of the blue, Millie Shellum called to me and Dolly to make six Italian hoagies for Laricks Real Estate up in Sea Isle. "Make sure you put hot peppers on all of them," she reminded us.

"No problem, Mrs. S."

Dolly and I were a good team in the kitchen. She'd cut the rolls, I'd add the olive oil, she'd put on the lettuce and tomato, I'd add the hot peppers, salt and oregano, then Dolly would add the lunch meat and I'd put on the provolone and then cut the hoagies diagonally, wrap them in white wax paper, bag them, and then we were done!

"Perfecto!" I smiled.

"You know, if this was ever an Olympic event, we'd win the gold," Dolly said as she packed six sodas and a bottle opener into a small box.

"I'd have to agree with you on that one, Miss Dollio."

"All done, girls?" Millie questioned.

"All done," I said, carrying the hoagies and sodas to the front counter.

"Good, Arthur will be here any minute. You two did a good job."

"Thanks," we said in unison.

No sooner had I handed over the Laricks' order to Millie, when Brenda was standing right in front of me.

"You leavin', Bren?"

"Yeah. I think I'll take a walk down the bay area, you never know when my ship might come in. Know what I mean?"

I smiled. "See you after five, Miss Mayberry."

"Okay! Bye, Pat! Bye, Doll! Bye, Mrs. Shellum!"

We all said our goodbye's to Brenda and then within the span of a very short breath, we were all back to work again. Canned goods had to be unboxed, cleaned off, and then shelved. The sugar cone supply was low and we needed to fill both cone holders, and The Philadelphia Evening Bulletin was being delivered, so I took the twenty papers and put them in piles of ten in two spots right in the front of the store where they could easily be found.

"Dolly! Hold the fort down will, ya? I have to clean out this back closet and store the extra Tide boxes and spray starch bottles, okay?"

"Sure, Pat. I can handle the front! No sweat."

What did I get myself into?

It must've taken me about forty-five minutes to complete my job back there. It was hot and humid and I couldn't wait to get back into the air conditioned part of the store.

This is Dolly's job next time!

As I washed my hands and rinsed my face to cool off a bit, I reached for a hand towel and as I did, out of the corner of my eye, I thought I saw Dolly talking to George Ludlam at the soda fountain. Quickly I grabbed some lipstick out of my handbag, ran a comb through my hair, and then straightened my smock. I was going to give him one of those 'Oh, George, I didn't know *you* were here' looks. But as I got closer to the counter I noticed that it wasn't George Ludlam at all, in fact, I didn't know *who* the guy was, but whoever he was, Dolly was certainly turning on the old charm for him.

"Pattie, this is Jack Dawkins. He's here for the summer... like George and Clark! Isn't that just peachy keen?"

"Nice to meet you. Hey... Jack Dawkins! That was the name of The Artful Dodger!" I smiled.

"Who?" Jack looked a bit puzzled.

"You know, The Artful Dodger."

He stared at me.

"From Charles Dickens?"

Another blank stare.

"You know, from Oliver Twist?!"

"Who?"

"The book."

"What?"

"It's *classic* literature, I thought that maybe…" There was that blank look again. "Oh, never mind."

"Yo, I'm more like a non-reader."

"A *non*-reader?"

"Yeah. I'm like out for the adventure of real life. I ain't read no book since I left high school."

"And you freely advertise this fact?"

He smiled. "I'm tellin' *you* free of charge, ain't I?"

"I see. Well Jack, until 5:00 PM, Shellum's is all the adventure we get around here, so it's back to work for me. And you too, Dolly!"

Dolly didn't hear a word I said. She just stood there smiling at him.

"Let's *go*, Doll!"

"Oh… oh, sure! Well, see ya, Jack." She smiled the biggest smile I had ever seen.

"Yeah, okay. See yiz later."

I watched Mr. Dawkins as he left the store and artfully dodged across the street, avoiding one motor cycle, two delivery trucks, and Don Laricks' blue convertible.

"Yiz?" I turned to Dolly. "See *yiz* later?!"

"He's just a little rough around the edges, Pat. Like James Dean was." She sighed. "I think he's a hunk. And he said he's a good dancer, too."

"You have *got* to be kidding! Jack 'the non-reading, see yiz later, Artful Dodger' is going to be your dance partner next week? Is that what you're saying to me?"

"No, Silly, he'll be my dance partner *this* week!"

"This week?! No! You have to baby-sit for Mack and Apryl Remember?"

"Oh, I'm sure I can get out of it. No sweat." With that said, she smiled at me, turned and headed toward the back of the store to make two hamburgers for Mr. Hamil who lived right above Shellum's in a nice, fully furnished, efficiency apartment.

Oh, I'm sure I can get out of it. No sweat? Is that what she just said to me?!

I don't like this.

I don't like this at all.

Chapter Thirty-Nine

The clock read 4:58 and I walked back to the small office area where I could drop off my smock, grab my pocketbook, and sign out for the day.

Dolly was right behind me.

"Wow! Now *that* was a busy day! But that's what made it zoom on by, huh, Pat?"

"I guess."

"It'll be fun tomorrow hanging up the new kite display, *and* better yet, we'll get in some overtime!"

"Yeah."

I started to walk toward the front of the store. "Night, Mrs. Shellum."

"Night, Pattie! See you tomorrow. Bill should be in to help you and Dolly with that kite display. Remember, be in by 8:30!"

"I'll be here."

"I'll be here, too, Mrs. S! G'night!"

"Good night, Dolly. Have a wonderful evening, Dear!"

We waved and smiled as we walked out the door. Normally, Dolly and I would talk for a few minutes, but tonight, well, tonight I just wasn't in the mood for it.

I had already walked about ten feet when Dolly called to me, "Pat! Wait! Stop!"

"What is it?" I sighed.

"What *is* it?! You hardly talked to me all afternoon!"

"Well, just think about it."

"About what?"

"Oh, *please*. You meet this guy, he's a numbskull, and you're all over him. And for what? A date for the dance? For a dance you said you wouldn't be going to anyway because you had to baby-sit?"

"I didn't say I was sealed into it. I mean…"

"Yes, you did! You said your Dad and Stepmother wouldn't allow anyone else but you to watch the kids!"

"Well, yes, but…"

"No need to lie to me, Doll."

"Huh?"

"How would it look to you? You think we're all going to the dance together, just us girls, and you're raring to go. Then, I mention that we were lucky enough to get dates and all of a sudden you can't go."

"Well, I…"

"Dolly, why would you be embarrassed about being dateless? You woulda met someone at The Civic Center and you know it! This is *my first* real date! You've already had *four* boyfriends!"

"I didn't lie, I just…"

"Stop it. If you're trying to impress me and Brenda, this is *not* the way to do it. Look, I gotta go." I turned and walked away.

"Pattie," she called out again, "If… if you don't like Jack, I don't have to go to the dance with him! I don't want you to be mad at me."

I stopped dead in my tracks and walked back to her. "You change gears faster than a 1959 red and white Chevy Impala! You know that?"

She stared at me sheepishly.

"Dolly, didn't you just hear what I said to you? You don't have to do *anything* to please me. You need to learn to do what's right for you. I was just making an obvious statement."

"I know you were."

"Do you?"

She shrugged her shoulders at me. "Kinda."

"So, are you babysitting or not? Can you get out of it or not?"

Dolly bowed her head.

"Well?"

"Pattie, I…"

"Look, even if you *can* get out of it, or you never had to baby-sit in the first place, why lie about it? No dance at any time in your life will be worth taking Jack Dawkins to. You're a smart girl, you know what I mean?"

"Well, he's no George Ludlam, but…"

"Forget George. You're a *great* girl! You deserve better, that's all I'm sayin'."

"You think I deserve better?" Her voice was soft and child-like.

"Of course, I do! Why don't you?!"

Just then I saw a dark-dungareed, dark tee-shirted figure artfully dodging his way across the street. "Dolly! Yo, Dolly!"

She turned toward the voice that called to her and then turned back to face me. "Pattie, I…"

No sooner had she started to speak to me, when Jack 'See yiz later' Dawkins was standing right behind her. He put his arm around her shoulder and Dolly glanced back at him. "Yo, I wuz gonna work on the dock but too many guys wuz up there already, so I thought I'd walk ya home."

Dolly looked at me, and then turned toward Jack. "Well, I don't… I don't think it's a good idea to walk me to the house 'cause…"

"Then I'll walk ya to the corner."

"No, I don't think that's a good idea either and…"

I stood there never saying a word, but I'm sure the look in my eyes said plenty.

"Come on." He started to pull her along by tugging at her blouse.

"No, Jack, I…"

"I said, let's *GO*! See ya, Kathy."
"My *name* is Pattie."
"Whatever."

Dolly shrugged her shoulders as if she had no mind of her own, no choice of her own. I watched the two of them walk up the street together, his arm draped across her shoulder as if he was her lord and master.

And Dolly was allowing it *all* to happen.

For what?

Acceptance?

So she'd have a dance partner at The Civic Center?

So she could say she had nailed boyfriend number five?

As I turned down 85th Street, I asked myself… *What kind of ugly mess could a guy like Jack Dawkins get a poor insecure and lonely kid like Dolly into?*

There were no good answers.

None.

Chapter Forty

By the time I reached my front door I was exhausted. It wasn't because the Shellums worked us hard all day, although they did, it was because I was mentally and emotionally spent over the Dolly and Dawkins situation. I was feeling uneasy about her choice of men, and feeling sad about her constant need to please other people to the point of blurring her own wants, needs, and reality. It made me crazy. It did. I had a headache just thinking about it.

And I was *still* thinking about it the minute I set foot in the house when Brenda greeted me. "Well, don't *you* look like ten miles of bad road!" She laughed. "What happened?"

I plunked myself down into Uncle John's favorite chair, took my shoes off, and played dead.

"Hey, working woman! What's the matter with you?" Brenda said tugging at my pant leg.

"After dinner, Bren, okay?"

"No."

"Leave me alone."

"What's the matter with you?"

"Brenda, puh-leeeze."

"Okay, okaaay. Later."

"So," I sighed, "where's Aunt Anna and Uncle John?"

"They're pickin' greens and tomatoes for salad. I was holdin' the fort down 'til you got home."

Just then, my aunt and uncle walked in the back door.

"Welcome back home, Pat. Looks like you had a rough day, Sweetheart!" My Aunt walked to the fridge, poured some lemonade and then handed me a nice frosted glass of it, filled to the brim.

"Rough day?!" Uncle John nudged her. "Oh Anna, she's young, she probably ran old man Shellum ragged!"

I smiled. "Dinner smells really good. Pork chops?"

"*Stuffed* pork chops," she answered.

"Mmmmm, my favorite." Uncle John smiled and patted his tummy.

"Land sakes, John, everything I cook is your favorite!"

He smiled again. "So true, so true, so true."

"*So,*" I asked my Uncle on our way out to the kitchen table. "Just what *is* your real favorite?"

He thought for a moment and then turned toward his wife. "Anna was right. My favorite is *everything*!"

"It's easy to see why!" Brenda said surveying a table filled with yet another fabulous Anna Turner meal: delicious roasted pork chops filled with fresh herb stuffing, and grilled onions, buttery mashed potatoes and gravy, home made apple sauce, fresh picked green beans cooked in the rich pork drippings, a salad picked right from the garden, plus a perfectly made lattice-topped apple and cranberry pie.

"I'm starved," my Uncle announced.

"Well, starvation will be on hold for just a minute, we have to say grace." My aunt looked at me. "How about your turn tonight, Pat?"

"To say grace?"

She nodded.

"Sure!" I bowed my head and remembered a little prayer that my mother taught me when I was just about three or four. "We thank you for this food. For rest and home and all things good. For wind and rain and sun above. But most of all for those we love."

"Beautiful," my aunt smiled.

Dinner was delicious of course and our conversations went from fishing for flounder off Henny's Pier back in 1948, to a place that used to be called 'The Teen Bar' (which wasn't a bar at all) and the dance at The Civic Center on Friday, to that 'young Kennedy fellow' from Massachusetts and did he have a chance to become our next President.

We touched on many subjects, but I never mentioned Dolly, not once, although I wanted to. No, that could wait until later.

Brenda and I helped Aunt Anna do the dishes and set the table for breakfast, then I suggested a trip to VanSant's for an ice cream cone and a walk to the beach to cap off the evening for me and my best friend.

"Sounds good," Brenda said as the last dish was dried and put away.

"Well, you ladies have fun. It's a beautiful breezy evening, and, if you see any pretty conch shells, will you bring some home for me? I want to put them in the garden."

"Sure, Aunt Anna."

Brenda ran upstairs to get our sweaters. "I'll be right down!"

She was back in the kitchen in nothing flat and handed me my favorite white sweater with the crystal beading, and she draped hers (just like it, but in blue) around her shoulders and then we were off and running.

"Bye, Turners! We'll be home around 9:00 or so!"

"Okay! Bye, girls."

"What a beautiful night," Brenda said as we walked out of the house.

And it was.

The sun was just setting and the water in the bay sparkled back at us like a fifty carat diamond. We could hear the faint cry of seagulls, and a gentle breeze was blowing toward us from the ocean front.

"Whoever says New Jersey isn't a pretty place has never been here on a night like this," I said.

"That's the truth!" Brenda nodded and smiled as we walked up the street.

In less than a minute the two of us were standing in line at VanSant's waiting for our chocolate ice cream.

VanSant's was always crowded on summer nights. Banana splits were their specialty and the talk of ice-cream-loving South Jersey. Not that I didn't think I made a pretty wicked sundae and split over at Shellum's, but, there was just something special about VanSant's. Maybe it had more to do with all those wonderful memories of me and my Mom and Dad walking there for a late evening treat after a lovely dinner at the Turner household. Those times were precious to me even then, and now... even more precious.

"Here ya go, Pat! Have a nice night!" Sally VanSant said as she handed me the cones.

"Thank you, Miss Sally!" I smiled.

I handed her twenty-five cents, she gave me a nickel change and I put it in the SPCA donation tin to the right of the pick-up window.

Brenda and I walked up 85th Street, into the pavilion, and then onto the beach.

As soon as we trekked over two huge sand dunes, I spotted a few really pretty conch shells.

"Looks like King Triton heard Aunt Anna's wish!"

Brenda smiled and nodded.

I took off my sweater and made a make-shift bag out of it to hold the five shells so they wouldn't get broken.

Just what the doctor ordered.

Brenda and I took our sneakers off and left them and my conch shell-filled sweater resting on the sand, and then we headed down toward the water. We were both wearing peddle pushers, so we didn't need to roll up our pants to go wading. The water was cool and felt good on my feet. I was deep in thought, so much so that Brenda had to wave her hand in front of my face a few times to bring me into some form of spoken communication.

"Hey, are you gonna talk to *me* or the voices in your head?!"

"Sorry."

"You weren't thinking about your Mom and Dad again were you?"

"Well, I was thinkin' of them earlier, you know, at VanSant's. It's hard not to."

"Yeah, I remember going there with you and your parents. Your Dad loved those banana splits! Remember he'd always ask for..."

"Extra chocolate syrup," we both said at exactly the same time

I laughed. "Yup, that was my Dad, all right!" We were quiet for just a moment and then I said, "Actually, I was thinking about Dolly."

"Why?"

"It was something that happened at work."

"Ooooooh," Brenda nodded recalling my exhaustion as I walked into the house. "So *that's* what was wrong with you. What happened?"

"Well, you know how thrilled Dolly was about going to the dance?"

"Yeah."

"And she couldn't wait to go."

"Yeah… so?"

"Well, first let me mention that I told her almost as soon as I got in the store that you and I had dates for the dance. That finally, we had *real* dates! I mean, I couldn't wait to tell her!"

"And, what? She wasn't happy about it? She was jealous or something?"

"No, that wasn't it. She was genuinely happy for us, but…"

"But *then*?"

"Then she gave me some story about not being able to go to The Civic Center… that she forgot to tell us she had to baby-sit for her brother and sister."

"Well, Pattie, I *told* you that she…"

I stopped dead in my tracks. "Brenda, no preaching to me or I swear to God I won't say another word about this."

She gave a frustrated groan of sorts, but agreed, "Okay, no preaching. Talk."

"Well, then there was this guy…"

"What guy?"

"Let me finish. When I was walking out of the back room I saw this guy talking to Dolly. He looked like George to me for a second, but as I got closer to the soda fountain I could see that he wasn't."

"Who was he?"

"Some guy named Jack Dawkins."

She laughed. "Like the guy from 'Oliver Twist'!"

At least someone else besides me remembers.

"Yeah, that guy!"

"And?" she prodded.

"Well, to make a long story longer, Dolly was all over him like he was the last guy on the planet. I mean he's *really* cute, but he's such a lame brain!"

Brenda chuckled.

"And *then*, as if by magic, later in the day she tells me that she's going to the dance with this Jack guy!"

"What?!"

"Yup, and I jumped on her because when I told her we had dates, she came up with this 'I have to baby-sit' thing, which was kinda okay until *Jack* came into the store. Then I knew it wasn't about baby-sitting. Dolly just didn't want to go because she felt bad that she didn't have a date! So, she lied to me."

Brenda gave me one of those looks. "Umm… can I get preachy now?"

"No, you can*not*! She's not a bad kid, Bren… she's *not!*"

"She lies and she's screwed up. That's bad enough."

"But you *need* to know *why*! Where's your compassion?"

"My what?"

"Think! Why does anyone tune out real life? Because it's too *painful*... because something went *horribly* wrong that they can't cope with and..."

"And, what, Pattie? We should give *everyone* with a hard luck story a big, fat, pity party?"

"I didn't say that! She just needs some help. It's hard to get real help for certain kinds of pain, Bren... just ask me. It's not like casting a broken arm! This is a broken heart! I *know* that's what it is!"

Brenda was angry and frustrated.

"And Dolly never healed right, Bren. Think about it! Maybe she doesn't have any support at home. Maybe she feels like a fifth wheel over there with her father's new wife and kids, maybe..."

"Yeah Pat, and maybe her need to heal on *your* time will wear you thin... burn you to a crisp. Think about that one!"

"What?"

"She's wearin' you out!"

"Is that what I did to you?"

"Is *what* what you did to me?"

Tears started to fill my eyes. "Did I wear *you* thin after my Mom and Dad died? Were you sick of hearing about my pain and you just never told me the truth?"

"Pattie! For God's sake!"

I kept right on talking, "Did you tolerate me instead of really caring about what I had to say and what I was feeling?!"

"Of course not! I was heartbroken right along with you! I *loved* your parents!"

We reached the end of the inlet; I dried my eyes, and then sat down on the beach, and stared out at the water. "Well then, that was real compassion, Brenda, and I love you and thank you for it."

She smiled at me.

"All I'm sayin' Bren is that compassion and understanding shouldn't just be saved for family and really close friends."

"Pattie..."

"Listen to me, if the world is *ever* gonna be a better place, we need to show that compassionate part of us to everyone. We need to stop judging people, stop breaking hearts, and... and start mending them."

"One at a time?" she sighed.

"Whatever it takes."

"For cryin' out loud, Pattie... we're not Ghandi!"

"You know what I mean, Bren."

"Yeah, well, the day we can get to Avalon by walkin' on water instead of takin' the bridge, maybe it'll happen."

"This may not be your idea of how to deal with someone else's pain, but I'm not…" My voice started to get shaky with emotion.

"You're not what, Pat?"

"I'm not the kind of person to beat a dead horse, you know that."

"Yeah?"

"But this isn't the case with Dolly. She's a good soul; she's got scars no one can see. I won't give up on her. I *can't*…" My eyes started to fill again. "I can't. It's not right! She just needs some help."

Brenda sighed and then leaned in toward me. "Okay."

"Okay, what?"

"I mean, okay… I won't give up on her either."

"Huh?!"

"I won't give up on her, Pat."

"Honest, Bren?"

"Well, yeah. Hey, I'm not that much of a hard ass, am I?"

I smiled at her, "So, it's a deal then."

"That's what I'm sayin'."

"Cross your heart?"

"Honest, Pattie… cross my heart."

Good girl.

Chapter Forty-One

Saturday and Sunday went by faster than either Brenda or I expected. We spent Saturday shopping in Sea Isle at The Trading Post, Dalrymple's, and Pfeiffer's. Brenda bought a few post cards and a roll of three cent stamps and then sent out the standard "Wish you were here" cards to everyone in her address book. We both picked up a new outfit for the dance and then we bought ourselves these cute wooden Tiki charms that hung from a leather shoelace necklace. We also had lunch on the boardwalk - a great combination of pizza, hot dogs, French fries, coke, and cotton candy. Not even close to the delicious nutritional fare we get from Aunt Anna, but it was good just the same. It's hard to explain but there's just somethin' special about Jersey boardwalk food in the summer time.

Saturday evening came and Aunt Anna and Uncle John invited us to The Moonlight Cruise ride on Captain Robbins' boat. "We got four free tickets from Ed down at Garrity's," my Uncle told us.

I thought it was a great idea and a wonderful trip for Brenda, but I felt kind of sad because the last time I was on Captain Robbins' boat it was a moonlight cruise with my mother and father.

I just miss them so much.

But, it didn't take me long to smile. Not five minutes after the cruise started Brenda pointed out several dolphins playing in the water off the inlet. What a glorious sight! And, to top that off, the sunset was beautiful, the ocean was calm, and the full moon had already settled itself into the night sky. Bren and I left Aunt Anna and Uncle John's side and headed toward the front of the boat. There were two little seats where the boat came to a point. Brenda sat of the left side of it and I sat on the right.

"Dontcha ever wonder who's on the other side of this ocean? I mean, maybe someone directly across from us, a few thousand miles away, is wondering who's over here. And it's us! I think that's pretty cool. They'd be English, right?"

"What are you talkin' about?"

"I mean this is the Atlantic Ocean, right?"

"Uh-huh."

"And it stops out there somewhere. There's another shoreline, like this one."

"So?"

"It's gotta be Great Britain, right?"

"Well, I wasn't a geography major, but I'd say that's about it."

"I just think it's romantic, Bren."

She smiled. "You think a lot about romance these days... thanks to one George Ludlam, huh?"

"Oh, stop it, you know I always had romance in my soul."

"Yeah, Pat, but your soul never put a name to it until last week."

I sighed. "He's really a nice guy, isn't he?"

"He sure is," Brenda quickly acknowledged, "and Clark, too. Great guys!"

Again I sighed, "Too bad Dolly's stuck with the likes of Jack Dawkins."

"Pattie, look, I know I said I wouldn't give up on her, but I just wanna say that Dolly isn't stuck with anybody. If Dolly goes out with this creep, that's her choice."

"Yeah, I know."

"*And*," Brenda continued, "remember the deal with choices?"

"What deal?"

"That there are certain consequences that come with that choice - good or bad."

I started to feel sea sick, but I think it was more the conversation about Dolly than the motion of the water. "Well, if Jack's the choice, and apparently he is, the consequences can only be bad." My head started to pound.

Brenda patted me on the back, "Look we've got all week to work on her - two brilliant young ladies against the loathsome Artful Dodger."

"So, you're sayin' the odds should be in our favor, right? I mean two against one and all that."

"'Should be' are the operative words, Pattie, but let's be hopeful."

"Yeah, I will."

"You sure you're up to it?"

"That's what I said."

"Cross your heart?" She nudged me.

"Honest, Bren… cross my heart."

Chapter Forty-Two

Sunday morning at the Turners always meant a great big breakfast followed immediately by 85th Street church services. The routine never wavered. This particular Sunday, Brenda and I decided to go to church with Aunt Anna and Uncle John. Attending services wasn't something Brenda and I did all that often in our later teen years, but this Sunday, it just seemed like the right thing to do. As I walked into the tiny little church on the corner of 85th Street and Landis Avenue, many of my mother's and father's seashore friends came up to me to convey their heartfelt condolences.

It wasn't as sad as it could have been, and I was grateful for that. It wasn't at all like after their funerals, where everyone just hugged me with tear-filled eyes and said, "I'm *so* sorry, Pattie." This time they all told me something they remembered about my mom or dad and it made me smile.

I needed that.

"Ya know, Pat?" Mrs. Bitner said, "I remember when you were little, maybe five or six and there was a huge crab and flounder dinner down at The Civic Center." She started to chuckle. "And one of the big crab baskets tipped over on the floor. There had to be 100 crabs all over the place! I never saw anybody move as fast as your mother. She hopped up on the only empty kitchen counter while the rest of us were scurrying all over the place; and she laughed and laughed. We all must've looked pretty funny! Your mother had a great laugh, Pattie."

She sure did.

Mr. Bernhardt came up and shook my hand. "My wife's singing in the choir today, Patricia. You know, if it wasn't for your mom and dad she would have never had the nerve to sing. They always encouraged everyone to be their best! In fact Sarah's singing 'Amazing Grace' today."

"That was my mother's favorite," I said.

A few more people stopped to talk to me when Aunt Anna politely interrupted, "Excuse us, please. Come, Dears. We have to take our seats now. Services…"

I smiled back at the faces that had come to cheer me and took my place next to Aunt Anna. But, as it is in most Methodist Churches, the minute you sit down, you're standing up again to sing something. Carrie Robinson had no sooner seated herself at the rather large pipe organ to the left of the pulpit when the choir began to sing.

"Amazing grace… how sweet the sound…"

Beautiful…absolutely beautiful.

Unfortunately, things were not sounding as sweet just three blocks away at the Dollio household.

The poor kid.

* * * * * *

"Dolly!!! Help Nikki and take that laundry down to the shed!"
"I just did!"
"Then do the dishes!" her father hollered from his comfortable, overstuffed parlor chair.

Dolly walked to the doorway and spoke to her father, "Dad, I *did* all my chores. And, I did stuff I wasn't even supposed to do."

"Like?" He cracked the newspaper, laid it in his lap, and then stared at her.

"Well, I ironed four of your work shirts. I gave Apry a bath, I hosed down the vegetables in the backyard, and I changed the sheets in Mack's crib."

He nodded. "That's good. You *need* to learn woman's work."

Woman's work?!

"I don't call it woman's work. I just think I'm doing my bit as a part of this family."

"So, are you insinuating I'm not part of the family because I don't do that stuff?"

I can't win.

"I'm just saying it's a family thing, Dad. That's all."

Dolly's father cracked his newspaper back into position. "I do plenty around here. I keep a roof over everyone's head. And that includes yours, in case you've forgotten!"

Just then Nikki entered the room. "Did you tell your father about your date for Friday's dance?"

Oh, brother… not NOW, Nikki!!!

"Umm, no… no, I didn't. But I was going to." She tried her best to smile.

"Date?" Her father glared. "What *date*?!"

"A guy named Jack Dawkins asked me. I met him over at Shellum's."

"I don't care *where* you met him. You're too young to date! The answer is no!"

Nikki rested her arm on my shoulder. "Sean, she's seventeen."

"I know that," Dolly's father continued to grumble, "that's my whole point! She's too young to date!"

"Well," Nikki smiled sweetly, "You asked me out when *I* was seventeen. Remember, Honey?"

He didn't answer her.

"Remember, I…"

Sean dropped the Sports Section onto the floor and stared at his wife. "This conversation is *over*! Now find something to do and take Dolly with you!"

"But, Sweetie, it's just a dance. And, like I said, I was only seventeen when…"

"You *weren't* seventeen!" he interrupted.

"Yes I was. It was when…"

"Not another word!" he yelled. "You were NOT seventeen! Now get the hell outta here!"

Nikki started to cry, and immediately ran up the stairs.

Dolly stayed there in the doorway, staring at her father. She never budged.

Quickly she counted back the years to the point where Nikki would have been seventeen.

Dolly's mother was alive then. She was very sick with cancer at the time, but, the fact was, Dolly's mom was still alive.

No wonder her father exploded on Nikki. I guess he was hoping his anger would wipe out any of those precise mathematical details in his daughter's head - that Dolly wouldn't think about the fact that she *now* knew that even when her poor mother was dying of cancer, and still caring for her *and* her dad, that he was trying to make out and score one with Nikki Shallto… the only *seventeen-year-old* Nikki Shallto.

The man should hang his head in shame, but he wouldn't.

Dolly stood there in the doorway for the longest time, arms folded across her chest.

"What do *you* want?" Her father never even made eye contact with her, he just belted out his words.

"What do *I* want?" Dolly asked quietly.

"Just get upstairs. Go!" He turned toward her but still he didn't look at her.

"I'm seventeen, Dad. I was asked to go to The Civic Center dance. And I want to go."

"You're too young!"

"As I said, Dad… I'm *seventeen*."

Her father's uneasiness was more than evident. He knew instantly that she had figured out why he yelled at Nikki and why he wanted to end their conversation so abruptly.

It made Dolly wonder just how many other women besides Nik her father tried to be with when her mom had cancer. Her thoughts took her back in time, and Dolly recalled a fight her mom and dad had one night. She was barely six-years-old and she didn't know what her dad meant at the time - but she knew now! "You're not even a woman anymore! I HAVE NEEDS!" he screamed at her poor mother.

What an awful man.

Her father's voice broke the silence, "I know how old you are."

"And?"

"All right then. But he comes here to pick you up and he brings you back! And, you'll be home right after the dance is over!"

Dolly smiled in sad victory, and quietly left the room.

Chapter Forty-Three

Monday, Tuesday, Wednesday, and Thursday, Brenda and I did all we could to talk Dolly out of her date with Jack Dawkins, but to no avail.

All we'd hear was, "But he's *so* cute... He's *such* a good dancer... You just don't understand him like I do."

She never heard us when we said, "But he treats you badly... He's controlling... He's mean to your friends... He's rude... He smokes..."

Nope, Jack Dawkins was *cute* and a good dancer, and, as we all know, that's *all* it takes to be someone's Prince Charming.

HAH!

But, on the *other* side of the tracks, there was an up-side for us amid all the Dollio/Dawkins upheaval. Brenda and Clark were now a nice little item and even though Brenda would be leaving soon to go back to Philadelphia, and, a few weeks after that, leaving again for UCLA, they had a great friendship, they *really* liked each other, and that was a pretty cool thing.

George Ludlam, however, was a different story for me. Even during the "off" season, George and I would only be seventy miles away from each other. If things progressed, it would really be possible to have a relationship of sorts with him. It's not like the three thousand mile gap Clark and Brenda had. George was a terrific guy and I really liked him. He'd stop in for coffee and a donut at 9:00 AM every morning. We'd talk about our day, the news, music, or whatever crossed our minds. And, when he and Clark finished their work after the boats came in, somewhere between 2:30 and 4:15, they would both sit at the soda fountain, front and center, for a nice conversation, a hamburger, coke, and French fries.

I was lucky and I knew it.

Jack Dawkins, on the other hand, never really wanted to communicate with anybody. He'd just hang around outside the store, smoking cigarette after cigarette, waiting for five o'clock to roll around so he could tug on Dolly's shirt and walk her up the street. He rarely said Hello to me - just a head nod and a grunt of some sort. What a Neanderthal! Dolly felt bad about all that and I knew it, but it didn't change things.

Although, on Thursday night the scenario *did* change a bit as Dolly and I left work. Not only was Jack outside waiting for Miss Dollio, but Brenda, Clark, and George were walking up the street toward us. Dolly and I smiled and waved to them.

Jack immediately started to walk away, tugging at Dolly's shirt sleeve. Come on, let's go." I gently moved his arm away from Dolly. "Wait, Jack! I want you to meet our friends."

Dawkins stood there with a look of defiance on his face and a chip on his shoulder the size of a football.

Brenda could sense the awkward moment but she was cheerful anyway, and the first to say hello. "Allow me to do the introductions," she smiled, "I'm Pattie's friend, Brenda Mayberry, and to my left are Mr. George Ludlam and Mr. Clark Lowen."

Clark and George immediately extended their hands.

Dolly nudged Jack, "Shake hands, Silly. Hi, George! Hi, Clark!" She grinned.

Jack reluctantly removed his hands from his pockets, "Nice ta meet yiz."

Dolly smiled at me as if his words were some of the most profound in all of the English language.

I rolled my eyes.

When is she ever gonna see this guy for who he really is?

"We've heard a lot about you," George said.

"Who from? Brenda and *Kathy*?" Jack questioned slyly.

"My *name* is Pattie."

"Whatever."

"No," Clark added, "We heard about you *long* before Brenda and Pat came along."

I could sense the uneasiness and I immediately started to diffuse the situation. "Yup, they heard 'Nobody can roll a pack of cigarettes up in their sleeve faster than Jack Dawkins'."

Brenda laughed. "We gotta get goin', Pattie."

"Why?"

"Your Aunt Anna said dinner was at 5:15 and if we didn't get to the dinner table on time the pork chops would be like shoe leather."

"Yeah, we gotta split. So, I guess we'll see you at the dance on Friday, huh, Jack?"

"Yeah, Friday. Come on, Dolly."

"So long." George smiled.

"See you tomorrow," Clark added.

"Yeah, see yiz."

"Yeah. So long, Jerk." I tried hard to hide my smile.

"My *name* is Jack."

"Whatever."

* * * * * *

As the four of us walked back to the Turner household I couldn't help myself and I had to make another comment, "He's a real charmer, isn't he?"

George's voice sounded frustrated, "I'll never understand what girls see in a guy like that."

"Well, he *is* cute. A jerk, but a cute jerk." Brenda smiled.

I added, "Yeah. He's got that James Dean look to him."

"Is that *all* it takes to get the attention of a girl nowadays?"

"Only girls like Dolly, George."

"Didn't *you* just say he was cute, Brenda?"

"Well, he is, but Clark, for heaven's sake, it's about a lot more than just cute for *me*."

"Oh, well, thanks a lot." Clark shook his head and groaned.

"Silly! What I meant was that you're a lot more than just cute to me."

That brought a smile back to Clark's face.

"But Dolly, poor thing, she, well she doesn't seem too concerned about anything else. It's just about having a cute date for the dance."

"Poor thing is right. Thank God Brenda and I were raised by people of substance. We expect more."

"That's not fair, Pattie." George pointed out. "I knew Dolly's mother. She *was* a woman of substance. A real nice lady."

"George, I'm sorry." I cringed for making such a stupid remark.

"Pat, this doesn't have anything to do with parents, this has to do with personal choices. Dolly made this choice, no one else." George said.

Brenda nodded. "Yeah, Pattie and I were talking about choices and consequences on Saturday."

"And?" he asked.

"Well, we were saying that it doesn't matter that we're just seventeen. We could screw up bad this week and… well, it could ruin us for a long, long time!"

My mind drifted back to Dolly and the train wreck of a relationship she'd have with Jack if she didn't put a stop to it and *soon!*

"Ya know, Bren, I told you, guys like Dawkins are bad news." Clark put in his two cents worth.

"He has a nice family," George added, "but he's the bad egg. He dropped out of school, he bums around. I heard the guys on the dock say that his father said if he didn't straighten out and go back to school and learn a trade or something he was going to ship him off to his uncle in upstate New York."

"Uncle Sal… Sol, somethin' like that," Clark said.

"Yeah. He's a retired longshoreman , a welder, or something. He sounds like a pretty tough guy, he'd straighten Jack's ass out."

That was the first time I'd heard an ungentlemanly word out of George's mouth. He could see the surprise on my face and apologized immediately.

"Sorry, Pat. Sorry, Brenda."

"Apology accepted, George."

"That's okay, George."

Right at that point in our conversation we were only two doors away from The Turner household. I looked toward the house and noticed

Aunt Anna standing in the doorway. "Time for dinner, girls! Hello, George! Hello, Clark!"

In unison the boys answered, "Hello, Mrs. Turner!"

"Thanks for walking the girls home."

"You're welcome."

Brenda and I ran up the steps straight into the loving arms of my Aunt Anna.

We turned and waved, "See ya tomorrow, fellas!"

"Bye!" they waved back. "See you tomorrow!"

As the screen door closed behind the three of us my Aunt smiled at me, "Now don't you just wish there were more nice boys out there like George and Clark?"

"Aunt Anna," I sighed, "You have no idea!"

Chapter Forty-Four

The alarm rang on Friday morning at exactly 6:00 AM. I could smell bacon and eggs cooking, so Uncle John was apparently having an early fishing day on Captain Cramer's boat.

I got up out of bed to hop in the shower when I heard Brenda mumble something to me.

"What did you just say, Bren?"

"Huh?"

"I *said*... what did you just *say* to me?"

"Oh," she smiled. "I said... bacon."

"Aha! But even bacon isn't enough to get you out of bed at 6:00 AM, is it, Miss Rip Van Mayberry?"

Bren never answered me, she just grunted and then pulled the covers back over her head.

So much for an early breakfast with Brenda.

The next thought that came into my mind was that it was Friday, not just *any* old Friday, but Civic Center Dance Friday! I started dancing just thinking about it.

By the time I showered, dried my hair, and walked downstairs, Uncle John had already left for his fishing trip.

I was so excited about the evening to come I scarcely ate a bite.

"Pattie? You've hardly touched a thing. Aren't you feeling well, Dear?"

"I feel great, Aunt Anna. I'm just excited about the dance tonight, that's all!"

"Oh, that's right! Tonight's the big night! John said something to me about that this morning! This is his big premiere as a disc-jockey, you know."

I smiled.

"Well, how about I pour you some orange juice and make you a bacon sandwich on toast?"

"Can I modify that order?" I asked sweetly.

"Sure."

"Okay... then how about a glass of milk *and* a peanut butter and bacon sandwich?"

"Pat!" she shook her head at me. "How you and my John can eat that horrid concoction is beyond me, but... if that's what you want," she smiled pouring me a big glass of milk, "well then, that's what you get!"

I watched her as she carefully spread the peanut butter evenly all over the bread, and then, she placed four strips of crispy bacon in a star-like pattern right on top of it. My Aunt handed me the sandwich, my milk, and a napkin. "Here you are, Sweetheart."

"Thanks, Aunt Anna."

I took a bite of my sandwich, it was delicious. The peanut butter was warm and creamy and the crisp bacon on top of it crunched inside my mouth. It was perfect!

"Know what, Aunt Anna?"

"What, Dear?"

My Dad used to like apple butter on his scrapple!"

She smiled at me. "I remember that."

"And Mom used to put coleslaw on her hoagies!"

She chuckled. "I remember that, too. Well, I guess you come by your unique culinary tastes honestly."

I smiled and took another bite of my sandwich.

Just then Brenda walked down the steps. I was shocked! "Well, as I live and breathe! Not even 7:00 AM and Brenda Ethel Mayberry is awake!"

She rubbed her sleepy eyes and had but one word for me.

"Bacon."

Chapter Forty-Five

By the time I got to work, Dolly was already seated at the soda fountain.

"Hey, what time did you get here?" I asked.

"Around 8:30."

"How come?"

"Well, sometimes I just wanna get an early start, ya know?"

"Yeah. And, umm, it couldn't be that you're just a *little* bit excited about the dance tonight, could it?"

She smiled at me.

Just then Mr. Shellum walked behind the counter. "You know, I remember the first dance I ever went to. It was during the holidays in 1931. I met Millie there. It was the best thing that ever happened to me."

Mrs. Shellum strolled by us and smiled. "He only said that because I'm within earshot!"

We all laughed.

"Now, Millie Mae Brooks-Shellum, you know that I was crazy about you from the first time I laid eyes on you!"

Again she smiled. "I know. And I felt the same way about you, Bill."

Sweet.

Right about the time we ladies were ready to dig into a good conversation about dances and dating, in walked five customers. Millie, Dolly, and I were up and running and it didn't end until well after our usual lunch time. Mr. Shellum had to drive to Philadelphia to pick up some supplies, so we were short a pair of hands and we really missed him.

"Wow, lunch break at 2:30 PM," Dolly said as we finally got to sit at the soda fountain for a bite to eat.

"Weekend shoppers, that's a given on Friday," I noted. "Looks like we're not the only ones anticipating a fun weekend."

Dolly patted her heart nervously. "Are George and Clark pickin' you guys up at the house?"

"Yup."

"Yeah. My Dad said Jack has to come to the house to pick me up, too."

"How do you think that'll go over?" I questioned.

"I don't know. Not so good, maybe."

"Doesn't that bother you?"

"Not really."

I knew she was lying to me.

"Dolly…" I was about to start another brief lecture on my concerns about Jack Dawkins, when Millie called out to us.

"Short lunch, girls… sorry. More customers comin' in."

Dolly and I walked to the front counter and saw a station wagon parked right outside the store. Then we saw six children, two parents, and what appeared to be a grandma and grandpop, all piling out of it. The ten of them walked in and headed straight for the soda fountain. Dolly and I immediately manned our stations and took order after order.

"Three cheeseburgers, three plain burgers, four hotdogs, 8 orders of fries... Oh, no! Sorry. Make that *four* cheeseburgers, two plain and... Oh, no... make that..."

Five minutes, and six order changes later we had lunch for ten cooking on the grill. As soon as they were finished lunch, Dolly and I handed out four ice cream cones, five popsicles, and one ice-cream sandwich, and then the happy family was out the door, in the car, and gone.

Whew!

As I turned to get back to work I noticed that the store was really quiet and all I could hear was the sound of Dolly scraping the grill and Mrs. Shellum shuffling receipts around in the cash drawer. Ever dutiful myself, I focused my attention on the messy soda fountain countertop and as I started to wipe it clean I noticed something under one of the saucers. "Hey! Look what I found!" I held a crisp five dollar bill in my hand. "Is this a tip or did they leave it here by accident?"

Dolly gave me a puzzled look. "Geez, Pat, I don't know. Five bucks is a huge tip. What did the bill come to?"

"Lemme add this up again." I re-read the order. "Four burgers, one cheeseburger, two cheesesteaks, a pizza steak, two hot dogs, eight orders of fries, ten sodas, and the ice cream... ummm...$16.68."

"$16.68? And they left five bucks?! Wow!"

Mrs. Shellum overheard our conversation. "Well, girls, that is a really big tip, but the food was great, your service was impeccable, and obviously they thought you two were worth it!"

"Two-fifty a piece. Not too shabby!" I said waving the five dollars in my hand.

"Here's something else that's not too shabby," Millie smiled. "I'm letting you both go early today - 4:00. My daughters will be in to take your places."

My mouth dropped wide open.

"You worked really hard today and you both had a short lunch. Take the extra time to fuss over yourselves for the dance tonight!"

Dolly and I both ran over to Millie to hug her. "Yet another reason why we always say you're theeeeee best, Mrs. S."

Immediately I glanced at the clock and noticed that it was already 3:30!

Only a half an hour to go, I could hardly believe it. So, by the time we swept the store, emptied the trash, opened a new carton of sugar cones, and refilled six ice-cream bins, Dolly and I were ready to hang up our 'Shellum's by-the-Sea' smocks and get ready for the first big dance Townsend Inlet had seen in thirty-four years.

"Well, I guess we'll see you at the dance around 7:00?" I asked Dolly as I put my week's pay into my wallet.

"Yup, we should be there as soon as the doors open." She gave me a half-smile.

Whether Dolly would admit it out loud or not, her face said it all. Jack Dawkins wasn't a good partner for this dance, or, for anything else for that matter. He was a slimy jerk and that was that.

As we were leaving, Millie waved a goodbye. "Have a wonderful evening, ladies. Tell me all about it on Monday!"

"We will," I waved back to her. "And thanks again for the early evening!"

"You are both *very* welcome, Dear!"

Dolly and I stood for a moment just staring at each other until I broke the silence.

"I'm gonna be as polite as I can tonight, Dolly, but you know I don't like Jack."

"I know." Her voice was barely audible.

"And Brenda, George, and Clark aren't crazy about him either."

She nodded.

"I really like you, Doll. I think you're a great person, and…"

"And what?" Again her voice was soft and quiet.

"And you deserve better. I mean, do you think your mom would like Jack?"

Dolly looked at me and her facial expression was a mixture of what could only be described as hurt and confusion. I felt terrible. The minute those words left my mouth I regretted them.

"I'm sorry, Dolly. That was *way* out of line for me to say that."

"That's okay, Pat." She turned and walked away without as much as a goodbye. I waited for her to turn back around, but she didn't.

Me and my big mouth…Ugh!

Chapter Forty-Six

The minute Dolly walked in the door her sister jumped into her arms.
"Doll-leeeeeee! You're home! I'm happy now!" Apry giggled.
Nikki entered the living room with Mack on her hip. "Hi!" She smiled. "How come you're home so early?"
"Well, we worked pretty hard today, we didn't even get a full lunch."
"Yeah?"
"So Millie let us go at 4:00."
"Well, that was nice of her."
"Yeppers," Apry said hugging Dolly's neck, "that was *really* nice of her!"
"Apry," her mother said, "go upstairs, wash your hands and put your toys away."
"Now?"
"Yes, now."
"Okaaaaaaaaay." Apry gave her sister five quick kisses on the cheek and then she practically leapt out of Dolly's arms to run right up the stairs to do as she was told.
Good kid.
Nikki placed Mack in the playpen and then she walked out into the kitchen.
Dolly was unusually quiet and Nik picked up on it.
"As a rule you have a lot more to say after work, Doll. What's the matter? Nervous?"
"Well, it was something Pattie said."
"About?"
"About Jack."
"Your date?"
"Yeah."
Dolly took a good deep breath and continued, "No one likes him Nik, and…"
"And?"
"Well, I don't think you're gonna like him all that much either."
Nikki shook her head and sighed.
"But, I guess it's just a date. I mean it's not like…"
"What did Pat say?"
"Huh? Oh, she asked me if Mom would like me going out with a guy like Jack?"
Nikki turned away from cleaning the evening's vegetables and looked right into Dolly's eyes. "What did you say?"
"Nothing."
Nikki slowly turned back toward the sink while Dolly walked toward

the staircase.

"Doll?" Nik's voice sounded strained.

"What?"

"*Would* your mom like you going out with a guy like Jack?"

Dolly turned to her stepmother and without a moment's hesitation she answered her. "No. She wouldn't like it at all. Wrong guy, wrong time… But, like I said, it's just a date… ya know?"

Nikki gave no answer, just a look of understanding, of genuine compassion, a look as if she knew *exactly* what Dolly meant about the wrong guy… the wrong time.

And she did.

All too well.

Chapter Forty-Seven

The minute I walked in the door Brenda hugged me and started to dance around the porch.

"Our first *real* dates! Our first genuine dance!!!"

Brenda's joy was contagious and we laughed and laughed and then we both danced all the way into the kitchen.

"Well, you're home early, Miss Patricia." Aunt Anna smiled.

"Hey, yeah," Brenda added, looking at the wall clock. "It's not even ten after four!"

I explained the busy day and Mrs. Shellum's act of kindness - letting me and Dolly go early so we could, 'fuss over ourselves before the dance.'

"That was very kind of Millie," my aunt acknowledged.

"I'll say," I smiled. "Aunt Anna?"

"Yes?"

"Can I help with dinner or anything?"

"Well, I think I've got it all under control. John will be in any minute now and since you're home before your usual time maybe we'll eat a little earlier tonight. How's that?"

"Sounds good. What are we having?"

"It's a lighter menu this evening because I know you'll be eating some burgers or fries or something at The Civic Center, so, I'll be making some deviled crabs, asparagus tips, and a garden salad."

"Dee-licious" Brenda said. "I'm gonna miss this cooking when I'm at UCLA, I can tell you that!"

My aunt smiled in her direction. "You're a resourceful college girl now, you'll be just fine. I'll tell you what… I'll give you some of my easier recipes so you can cook for yourself and not eat pizza every day."

Brenda hugged my Aunt. "You're the best, Mrs. T."

The table was already set, courtesy of Brenda Mayberry, so Bren and I decided to go upstairs and select our clothes for the evening. I opened my closet and started to shuffle some outfits around trying to figure out what I was going to wear, when I suddenly spied my father's Frankford High School sweater - the one my mother and father had left to me. It made me stop and think how special this moment would have been for me and Mom and Dad and then I started to cry. Brenda immediately put her arms around me.

"Pattie, what's wrong?!"

I turned away from her and reached for my father's sweater.

"I found this in the closet the day we left to come here."

Brenda sighed.

"Mom and Dad were going to give it to me as a present."

"Oh, Pattie…"

"Dad gave this to Mom, you know, like as a symbol of his love for her."

"That was very sweet."

"Yeah. They were just about our age, Bren. I remember Mom saying she wore it every day… wind, rain, sleet, or snow and…"

"They were the nicest people I ever met, Pattie."

I nodded and wiped my teary eyes across my shirt sleeve.

"I'll never understand what it was, Pat. I mean why they were…"

"I know. I don't understand it either. I do so good for days on end and then something triggers a memory and I just… fall to pieces." I started to cry again.

"Pattie, sometimes a happy memory or a good cry are just what you need."

"And sometimes *both*," I sniffled.

"Yeah, sometimes."

I dried my eyes once more.

"They're watching over you tonight, Pat. I know they are. They wouldn't miss this for *anything*."

I held my father's sweater in my arms and then gently placed it on the bed. "*This* is the finishing touch for my outfit tonight, Bren. Whaddya think?"

She looked at the well cared for Frankford High School sweater with a slightly frayed Junior Varsity Football letter on it, and smiled at me.

"I think it's beautiful, Pattie. Just absolutely beautiful."

Chapter Forty-Eight

Brenda and I devoured dinner in record time and then immediately ran upstairs to shower, dress, and put on our make-up. What fun we had!
"Do you think this shade is good for me?"... "Does this match my outfit?"... "Do you think George'll like what I'm wearing?"... "Where's my charm bracelet?"... "Where's the shoe polish?!"
We were making each other crazy but we laughed all the way through it nonetheless.
Just as I located my charm bracelet, Uncle John called out from the bottom of the staircase.
"I'll see you at The Center, ladies! I have to set up. What song should I play first?"
I thought about it for a second and then Brenda and I both seemed to shout out at the same time, "Tutti Frutti!"
"Tutti Frutti? Isn't that some kind of ice cream flavor?!"
"No, Uncle John" I laughed. "Remember? It's that record by Little Richard! Play that one first!"
"Oh, okay. Will do. See you later, gals."
"Bye, Mr. Disc-jockey." I smiled then turned toward Brenda. "Oh, my God, it's almost 6:30! George and Clark will be here any minute!"
"Deeeeeeep breath, Pattie. We'll make it."
I smiled again.
"Girls! Oh, Girls!" Aunt Anna's voice sang out sweetly.
Brenda quickly ran to the window. "They're here, aren't they! Oh, My GOD!!! That's why she's calling us! How do I look? Is my ponytail straight? Do I have lipstick on my teeth?!!"
"Deeeeeeep breath, Bren. We'll make it." I laughed.
Again Aunt Anna called to us, "Girls! I want to take your pictures before the fellows arrive. Come down and let's have a look at you!"
I heard Brenda breathe a sigh of relief.
"Okaaaaay, be right there!" I said as I took one last look at myself in the mirror above my dresser. "Not bad", I nodded.
Brenda stood by my side and gave herself an appraisal as well. "Yup, not bad at all."
"Girls!"
"Coming, Aunt Anna!"
Brenda and I grabbed our pocketbooks and hurried down the steps. My aunt was waiting for us in the living room.
"My, my, my, now don't you two look pretty!" She smiled.
"You *really* think so?" I asked in all of my teenage insecurity.
"Absolutely! You'll be the hit of The Civic Center!"
She then turned to reach for her small Brownie camera and pointed

it at us. "Now, smile!"

The two of us leaned in to each other and gave a nice big toothy grin to the camera. It was easy to do because we were both so happy and excited. I mean, after all, this was our first real dance with a *real* date. *This* was a BIG deal! A MAJOR event! A FABULOUS evening of unparalleled... well, you know what I mean.

Brenda and I giggled and looked each other over once again.

"Ya know, we look pretty darn good." She smiled at me.

And I guess we did. Well, at least for 1959 we did.

After changing our minds about a dozen times, we opted for full skirts, instead of the peddle pushers we bought at Pfeiffer's earlier in the week. My skirt was black and Brenda's was pale blue. They were both decorated with dazzling sequins and poodle appliqués. We also wore lightly starched white Peter Pan collared blouses that we tucked into our skirts, *and*... under the skirts were crinolines, you know, petticoats, "can-can" petticoats. They were kinda itchy, but you got used to it after a while.

To complete our outfits we both wore a very wide "stretchy" waist cincher belt. Then to top *that,* Brenda wore a twin sweater set, in pale blue, to match her skirt. The set was beaded with tiny pearls and rhinestones. It was really pretty. Of course, *I* was wearing my father's high school sweater. Oh, and both of us wore our hair in ponytails and then, *then* the final touch - freshly polished black and white saddle oxfords.

Now there's some kinda fashion statement, huh?

Who says the 1950's were conservative?!

Just as I was checking myself out in the hallway mirror, the doorbell rang. There was no doubt about it, our time had come, and, right on the other side of that door would be George Ludlam and Clark Lowen.

Another deeeeeep breath, Pattie.

Brenda and I did our best to be calm, cool, and collected, and in fact, we even looked that way. But inside? Well, inside we felt like we just dropped twenty floors in that old Otis elevator at Gimbel's department store.

Aunt Anna walked to the door while we waited a mere ten feet away.

"Good evening to you, George. Evenin', Clark. The girls are waiting right here in the parlor. Won't you please come in?"

"Good evening, Mrs. Turner" they said in unison. I smiled at Brenda and she smiled at me. Then, within the bat of a well-mascara'd eye, there they were, right in front of us - George Nathaniel Ludlam and Clark Matthew Lowen, looking ever so handsome.

Wow!

George was wearing a pair of light gray pants and a crisp white shirt with an open collar, Clark was wearing khaki colored pants and a light blue short sleeved button down shirt, and, *oh, my goodness*, when I looked at their feet!

...Blue Suede Shoes!

I was in Rock and Roll heaven.

Just then George pulled out a small white box with a purple ribbon tied around it - Clark did the same.

And, in well rehearsed albeit slightly nervous chorus they both said, "For the most beautiful girls in Townsends Inlet." Then they handed us the carefully wrapped package and when we opened it...

"A wrist corsage! Oh, George, red roses! They're my favorite! Thank you!"

"Clark, yellow for me! You remembered!"

Since the guys had no clue about the formalities of corsages, Brenda and I put ours on ourselves.

"Look, Aunt Anna!" Brenda and I extended our hands toward her.

My Aunt looked over our beautiful wrist bouquets and then turned to George and Clark. "Well you two gentlemen certainly knew the right thing to choose. The flowers are lovely." The guys seemed less nervous as she continued, "Roses, baby's breath, tiny soft ferns for contrast. Why, I didn't think there was a man in New Jersey but my John who had such fine taste when choosing flowers for a young lady." She smiled at them and they smiled back. "Now how about a few pictures before you go?"

Aunt Anna went right to the server and took her Brownie camera out of its case. "All right now... smile."

First she took pictures of me and George, then of Clark and Brenda, then of all four of us together. Then, we asked George to take one of me and Brenda and Aunt Anna. He obliged, of course.

"I can't wait to get this film over to Shellum's. Do you think we can get them back in a few days, Pattie?"

"I can run them in tomorrow and ask Mrs. S. to put a rush on them, they might be back on Thursday, Aunt Anna!"

"Well, that's super! Now you four better mosey along, the dance will be starting soon and you don't want to miss one minute on the dance floor, *especially* since there's going to be a really... well... how do you say it? A really cool Daddio playing the records for you tonight."

Brenda and I laughed. "Yup, he's the coolest all right. As long as he remembers that Tutti Frutti is a dance record and not an ice cream cone at VanSant's!"

Aunt Anna chuckled.

George opened the door for all of us and we started down the steps, on our way to The Civic Center dance, with our first dates *ever*! I hugged my Aunt and held her close to me.

"Thanks, Aunt Anna."

"For what?" She smiled.

"For everything."

Chapter Forty-Nine

The moment we entered The Civic Center there was magic in the air.
The dance floor was polished and sparkling, there was a huge mirrored ball above our heads that turned ever so slowly while flashing tiny colored lights all over the room, and, last but not least, there was music softly playing in the background. It was one of Brenda's very favorite groups - The Platters.

"Heavenly shades of night are falling, it's twilight time… Out of the mist your voice is calling, it's twilight time…"

A few of the girls I knew from my yearly visits to the shore stopped by and said, "Hi," and some of George's and Clark's friends did, too. We introduced Brenda to everyone: Bobby Phillips, Billy Rual, Don Laricks, Betsy Hubbard, Helena Bernhart… and, just as I was about to comment on how crowded the dance floor was, I heard my Uncle John's voice over the PA system.

"Teenagers of Townsends Inlet, New Jersey… welcome to the first of many Friday night 'At the Hop' dances here at The Civic Center!"

A cheer whooped up from the crowd.

"Now let's get started with a favorite song of mine - thanks to my love of ice cream - that's a joke, I'll tell you about it later – 'Tutti Frutti' by Little Richard!!!"

All four of us got out on the floor and started to jitterbug right away. How could we help ourselves? It was Little Richard!

"A-Wop-bop-a-loo-lop a-lop-bam-boo."

* * * * * *

George was a great dancer, and he knew all of the words to every song that played: "Long Tall Sally", "Venus", "Little Darlin", "At the Hop."

By the time we had danced our fifth dance, the boys went over to the food counter to get us all a coke. I turned to Brenda and said. "Look, I know it's only fifteen minutes since the dance started, but where in God's name is Dolly?"

No sooner had those words left my mouth, when Christine 'Dolly' Dollio walked in with The Artful Dodger - Jack 'see yiz later' Dawkins.

Dolly looked great. She was wearing dungarees rolled up like peddle pushers, bobby sox, saddle oxfords, of course, a white opened collar blouse with a bright red silk scarf tied around her neck, and the traditional ponytail.

Dawkins looked like he always did, straight out of a James Dean movie. Tee shirt, cigarettes rolled up in the sleeve, dark-colored dungarees and motorcycle boots. His hair was so slick it looked like he bathed it in motor oil

Eee-Yuck.

"Where have *you* been?" I said as Brenda and I rushed to see her.

"I'm gettin' a coke." Jack announced and then nudged us aside - his date included - to walk to the snack bar for a soda.

Whatta jerk.

"Soooooo," I asked again, "Where have *you* been?!"

Dolly looked around and then quickly grabbed my arm and Brenda's dragging us both into the Ladies Room. Lois and Ruth Procter were just leaving so we had the bathroom all to ourselves.

"What is it?" Brenda wanted to know.

"I think Jack really likes me!"

"God help you." I shook my head.

"So, why couldn't you say that out on the dance floor? What are we doing in this cramped-up space?" Brenda asked.

"Well, it's not so much what I had to *say* but what I want to show you!"

With that said she immediately untied the bright red silk scarf from her neck to show us four ugly bruises on her neck, each one bigger than the other.

"Oh, my God! Are these..." I started.

"Hickeys?" Brenda finished my sentence.

"Yeah," she smiled dreamily. "We were necking on the beach before we got here. That's why we're late." She unbuttoned her blouse just a bit, and, with one of those rough brown paper towels they always have in public bathrooms, she de-sanded herself.

"You got *sand* in your *bra*?!" I was shocked.

"Well, we were on the beach. It happens."

"Dolly," Brenda's voice was calm and collected. "This guy is trouble with a capital 'T'. If you think this means love, you're in for more than just a few ugly hickeys."

"He's just a little rough around the edges, Bren, but he's really very thoughtful and kind."

"Thoughtful and kind?" I rolled my eyes.

"Yeah. Like George, and Clark."

"Are you nuts?" Brenda huffed.

"Doll," I added immediately, "he left to get *himself* a soda. He never even asked if you wanted *anything*! He never even acknowledged that Bren or I existed! He never..."

Dolly closed her blouse up and then re-tied the scarf around her neck. "Thank God, I had this scarf around my ponytail. It's hiding these things real good." She checked herself out in the mirror once more and smiled.

"You didn't hear a word I said, did you?"

"Yes I did. Pattie, it's… well, I guess it's just gonna take some time for you to see who he really is."

"Who he really *is*?!"

"Is that right?" Brenda was at a slow boil.

"And just how long is it gonna take *you*?" I asked.

"And what's your Dad and Nikki gonna say when they see those ugly things on your neck? Huh?!"

Dolly re-applied her lipstick, and, totally oblivious to what we had just said, she smiled and headed for the door. "Let's just forget about all this and have some fun."

With that said, the door was opened and she was gone. Brenda and I looked at each other and shook our heads. We checked ourselves out in the mirror, I made a minor ponytail adjustment and then we were back out on the dance floor. Not only were George and Clark standing there waiting for us, but The Artful Dodger was as well. Dolly was practically glued to his side.

Sheesh.

"Here ya go," Clark said sweetly handing Brenda a coke.

"Thanks, Clark."

George smiled, "You too, Pattie, you too, Dolly."

"Thanks, George."

"We saw you right after you came in with Dawkins and thought we should get you one, since Jack already bought himself a coke."

George placed the cold soda bottle in my hand and then gave one to Dolly.

"Thanks. You two are *quite* the gentlemen. Aren't they Doll?"

She turned to look at Jack and there he was, chug-a-lugging his own bottle of coke. Dolly lowered her eyes and softly said, "Gentlemen… yes. Thanks, guys."

Wake up, Doll! I thought to myself.

At that very instant 'Breathless' by Jerry Lee Lewis started to play and Jack grabbed Dolly before she barely had a sip of her soda. "Let's dance!" he ordered.

"Hold this!!!!" she said reaching out toward me while Jack was pulling her in another direction.

"Sure." I shook my head in disgust.

Clark and Brenda rested their sodas on a nearby table and then walked out onto the floor.

George turned toward me. "You wanna dance, Pat?"

"No, actually, I wanna throw up."

He laughed. "Pattie, listen to me."

"What?"

"There's nothing you can do about this Dolly and Jack thing. She's making a *huge* mistake, but it's *her* choice."

"I can't help it."

"Yes, you *can*."

"Well, maybe so, but she's like a train wreck that I know is gonna happen. I'm just trying to switch the rail lines for her."

"You're a good friend, Patricia Townsend, but she's gotta see this for herself, you know, she's gotta stop painting this pretty picture of a very ugly man."

I nodded. "You can lead a horse to water..."

"Exactly. Now, come on, let's dance. It'll do you good."

I sighed. "Okay. Why not?"

Amazingly, when the six of us were on the dance floor all the usual thoughts that filled my head were gone and it was a really great night! Jack, for all his shortcomings was a terrific dancer and he and Dolly did the jitterbug and the cha-cha like professionals at an Arthur Murray Dance Studio. George and I, also light on our feet, danced for a while and then sat out for a burger and fries. Then, Brenda and I danced together, *Dolly* and I danced together and then Brenda and Dolly danced together. We were Jitterbuggers extraordinaire - no question about it.

And, as for our disc-jockey? Well, Uncle John played those songs like he'd been a DJ all of his life!

"Johnny B. Good", "Wake-up Little Suzie", "Poor little Fool", and everything Elvis ever sang!

What a night!

I remember the first slow dance I had with George. It was to a song called "To Know Him Is to Love Him", I thought... *how appropriate.*

Then we sat a few numbers out just to talk or watch other kids dance. I recall Dolly's first slow dance with Jack, it was Connie Francis singing, "Who's sorry now?" Again, I thought... *how appropriate.*

More fast songs played, and George and I were back on the crowded floor. We danced and danced and danced. My skirt was in a constant state of whirl and twirl and I don't think my cardiovascular system *ever* had a better workout!

"We're wearin' out the tread on these saddle oxfords" Brenda laughed over the music. I laughed too, and then noticed Dolly dancing with Ruthie Proctor, one of the regulars at Shellum's. In fact, Dolly jitterbugged with all our friends - the girl had energy to spare! She knew how to Bop and Stroll and Cha-cha, she was *amazing*! Dolly really did have a good time, despite the fact that Jack was her date. The only time I really noticed that she was uncomfortable was when that red scarf around her neck would loosen a bit. She would quickly re-tie it and strategically re-adjust it, and then, well, and then she just kept on dancing. I kept thinking to myself... *How is she ever going to hide those marks from her father and stepmother? They'll be there for two weeks!*

Of course there was no tell-tale evidence on Jack, unless that smirk on his face counted for something.

Whatta mess!

For some reason I looked at the big black and white wall clock by the concession stand and I could hardly believe it - it was almost ten o'clock!
Where did the time go?
Uncle John's voice soon boomed over the PA system, "Now here's a *big* favorite of mine, 'Tequila!!!'"
I smiled at Brenda, "I wonder if he meant the song or the drink?"
"Who knows? He's still got that Tutti Frutti thing all mixed up! Anything's possible."
"Come on! COME ON!!!" Dolly yelled over the music, "This is probably the last fast song! LET'S GO CRAZY!!!"
And we did!
The six of us walked out onto the floor and immediately we were dancing, spinning, jumping around, and gyrating, Elvis would be proud!
As Dolly predicted, that *was* the last fast song of the evening and we all let out a collective groan. Uncle John's voice sounded once again over the loud speaker.
"Now, don't be sad. Remember there will be another dance next Friday evening, and the good news about that *is*..."
Uncle John left us hanging briefly.
"IS WHAT??!!" Jack yelled.
"The good news is that *next* week the dance will be a half an hour longer! Next Friday we'll be dancing from 7:00 to 10:30!!!"
You should have heard the noise *that* generated! Hoots, hollers, whistles, applause, it was incredible! Then, for some reason I found myself boldly taking center-floor and announcing, "Now let's *all* give a BIG hand to the best disc-jockey in South Jersey, Mr. John 'Rock and Roll' Turner!!"
Everyone made even more noise than before, stomping their feet and cheering.
I must have been about fifty feet away from my uncle but I could still see him blush.
The final song of the evening was "It's Only Make Believe", by Conway Twitty. That always made me smile to myself. *Conway Twitty? No one's name is Conway Twitty.*
Well, silly name or not, it was a beautiful song, and Conway had a beautiful voice. I guess that moment would have been even more beautiful if I was dancing with someone I was madly in love with, but, still, it was a really nice song to end my first formal evening with George. He was a Prince... not my Prince Charming, but a Prince nonetheless.

"My hopes, my dreams come true
My life, I'd give for you
My heart, a wedding ring, my all, my ev-ery-thing
My heart I can't control; you rule my very soul
My only prayer will be
Some day you'll care for me
But it's ooooo - only make believe."

I sighed to myself, *so romantic.*

As soon as Mr. Twitty sang his last, the bright overhead lights went back on in The Civic Center, and the whole place looked different, but somehow the magic lingered. Maybe that's part of being a teenager, making magic and then holding on to it.

Well, whatever it was, I was grateful for it.

"Wow! What a night!" Dolly smiled. "Wasn't that keen, Jack?"

He shifted his weight from one foot to the other. "It was aw-right."

"Well, I thought it was *really* cool!" Brenda was grinning from ear to ear.

"It sure was." I agreed.

"It was great," George added.

"I thought it was pretty cool, too," Clark smiled.

"Umm... excuse me for a second, okay?" I asked.

"Sure."

I opened the door to the second level of The Civic Center and started to walk up the steps. "Uncle John?" I called out, "Do you need help with anything?"

I saw his smiling face peek around the door jamb. "Well, thank you for asking, Little Miss Jitterbug, but I think I gotta handle on this! You just walk home with Brenda and Dolly and your gentlemen friends."

I nodded, "Well, *two* gentlemen friends anyway." I made a smirky face like the one Jack always wears.

Uncle John chuckled. "I'll see you about 11:00. Tell your Aunt Anna, okay?"

"Will do." I turned and started down then steps and then I called to him once more. "Ummm... Uncle John?"

"Yes?"

"All the kids thought you were the best disc-jockey *ever* - especially me!"

"Thanks, Pattie," he smiled. "That's waaaaaay cool."

We both laughed and I headed down the steps one more time. All five of my friends, well, all four of my friends, plus Jack, were waiting for me.

I looked around. "Wow, this place sure emptied out fast, huh?"

Brenda and Dolly nodded.

"Are we on for next week?" George asked.

"Why George Ludlam," I replied as he held the door open for me. "Is this another date?"

"It will be if you say yes!"

"Then I say, Yes!"

"And *you*, Miss Mayberry?" Clark nudged her.

"Wild horses couldn't drag me away. That'll be two days before I have to leave. I wouldn't miss it for the world!"

By now we were all outside the building heading down 85th Street.

Poor Dolly. I knew she was waiting for Jack to ask her out for another date, but he didn't. We talked about how good the burgers were, the great concession stand people, the kids at the dance, the music, and Uncle John. Before we could start another topic we had reached the point where Brenda, George, Clark, and I would be heading in different directions. "Well, we'll *all* do it again next week!" I beamed. Then I remembered Jack hadn't asked Dolly and I felt embarrassed for her *and* me.

Dolly never missed a beat and took it upon herself to ask Jack. Something I had never heard a lady do before.

"It's a date for us too, huh, Jack? Huh?" She snuggled her head into his shoulder.

Yuck!

"I got nuttin' else ta do."

"Thanks," she gushed.

Again, Yuck!

"See you Monday, Dolly," I tried to smile.

"Yup, see you then," added Brenda.

"Night!" George said.

"It was fun," Clark nodded.

"Let's go," Jack said pulling her along by her shirt sleeve.

As the four of us walked away I turned back to watch as Jack and Dolly strolled down Landis Avenue.

Once again I saw Doll carefully re-tie and re-adjust that bright red silk scarf around her neck.

Heaven help her.

Brenda said her farewell to Clark and gave him one of her million dollar smiles. I also thanked George for the wonderful evening. And, as I was saying my own goodbye, I had such a strong urge to give him a kiss but, well… that would be far too bold. *Then* I even considered a small peck on the cheek, but again, this was my first real date and it wasn't proper. George and Clark smiled and waved us a goodbye and then Brenda and I walked into the house. When we looked around and saw that Aunt Anna hadn't decided to wait up for us, we had to quiet our exuberance. Even though what we said to each other was barely in a whisper, we were still as jazzed as if we were screaming at the top of our lungs!

"Isn't Clark a great dancer?"… "Did you see how attentive George was to me?"… "Didn't we have a blast?"… "We've got dates again for next Friday!"… and the standard mantra for teenage girls everywhere: "WHAT WILL WE WEAR?!!!"

Brenda and I did a little happy dance in the parlor and then we removed our beautifully scuffed saddle oxfords and tip-toed up the steps.

What a great night!

Chapter Fifty

July 4th, 1959

Saturday morning, came unusually early for me, considering the exciting Friday night Brenda and I had. But, the smell of fresh bacon frying in the pan was just too much for me to resist. Even Brenda rolled over and tapped me on the back just as I was about to leave the room. "Bring me up a peanut butter and bacon sandwich, will ya, Pat? I'm exhausted."

"Who died and left me *your* servant? Get up and get your own!"

She grumbled something at me, rolled over, and went back to sleep. *Oh, well... more for me.*

It was barely 8:00 AM but Aunt Anna was fully dressed, complete with lipstick, a strand of pearls, and pretty little shoes. She looked like June Cleaver's older sister.

How does she do it? I thought as I rubbed my still sleepy mascara-caked eyes.

"Gooooood morning, Pattie. I heard the dance was a tremendous success!"

"It was the absolute best!" I said giving her a huge hug.

I proceeded to tell my aunt everything. Well, almost everything. There was no way I was going to mention Dolly's ugly hickeys or that slug of a guy, that sub-human jerk, that selfish son-of-a... well, you know who I mean - Jack Dawkins.

She sat there quietly, for the most part, as I ate and talked and talked and ate. Aunt Anna laughed in the right spots and was thoroughly interested in *everything* I had to say. What a wonderful woman!

"Well, it certainly seems like The Civic Center is the place to be on those otherwise 'what to do' Friday evenings."

I nodded.

"I'm happy you both had such a wonderful time. John did, too. He almost missed Captain Cramer's boat this morning talking about all the fun he had!"

I smiled.

"Then he reminded me to start cooking early so I'd have plenty of time to enjoy the cookout!"

"The cookout! I almost forgot about it. Today's the Fourth of July! Well, Brenda and I can help!"

Just as those words had left my mouth, I heard Miss Mayberry dragging herself down the staircase. I laughed and said to my Aunt in an over-exaggerated tone, "Either that's the Frankenstein monster clopping down those steps or Brenda is willing her sleepy self toward an oversized peanut butter and bacon sandwich."

"I heard that!" She half smiled, entering the kitchen. "Mornin', Mrs. Turner."

"Good morning, Sleepyhead."

I had just rinsed off my plate when I heard the doorbell ring. "I'll get it."

I tied my robe belt around me and walked toward the front door. It was the mailman.

"A good mornin' to ya, Miss Patricia Townsend. Today is special delivery day! " Joe Linkletter smiled at me. "Just sign here, please."

I scribbled the Turner name and then took the package. "Thanks, Joe."

I'd known Mr. Linkletter all of my life. He was a local also. And, he was a great weekend fisherman who was genuinely looking forward to his retirement in 1962 so that he could be a daily commuter to Captain Robbins' or Captain Cramer's boats, like Uncle John was.

"Wish a good mornin' to your aunt and uncle for me, will ya?"

"I sure will. See ya later!"

"Bye, Miss Pattie. Take care now!" He waved and smiled at me and then started his walk down the street and into his neat little red, white, and blue pickup truck.

Nice guy.

I walked back into the kitchen and handed Aunt Anna the small box. She started to open it when she realized it wasn't for her - it was for Brenda.

"I'm sorry, Dear, I just took it for granted that it was for me or John."

"That's okay, Mrs. Turner." Bren placed the peanut butter and bacon sandwich back on her plate and finished the job Aunt Anna had started. With one more rip of the scotch tape, the box was open.

"Oh, look! Pictures!"

"Lemme see… lemme see!!" I scooted my chair next to Brenda and we started rifling through the photographs her mom had sent: Mr. Mayberry and his new power lawn mower, Mrs. Mayberry knitting a sweater on the front porch, a neighborhood bar-b-que, cousin Alicia and her new toy poodle, Fifi.

"I miss those faces." I sighed.

After Bren and I looked at them we passed the photos along to Aunt Anna who put them immediately into a neat little pile. Suddenly I noticed Brenda wasn't handing me another picture.

"Hey… lemme see!"

"No, Pattie," she said softly.

"Brendaaaaa… I *wanna* see them!"

Gingerly Bren handed me the photos.

The second my eyes made contact with the first picture, I understood her hesitation.

They were our graduation photos and my heart sank in my chest.

I moved through them quickly - one right after the other. All pictures of me and Brenda smiling as if we didn't have a care in the world.

And we didn't...

...Not until the night was almost over, that is.

Suddenly Brenda handed me a separate envelope, one marked especially for me. It was in Mrs. Mayberry's handwriting, all it said was: For Pattie.

I opened it and my hands started to shake, I had so many emotions churning inside of me I didn't know *what* I was feeling. There, right in front of my eyes were my own graduation pictures from the film that had been retrieved from our car on the night of the accident. Photos my Dad had taken, photos that I had taken, photos that Mr. Killough took of me and Dad and Mom, some of them less than an hour before they died.

I didn't have to force myself to look at them, I was almost obsessed. I wanted to see every detail. I looked at my father's broad smile as he stood next to my mother - my mortarboard on his head. And Mom... so beautiful, proudly wearing the red, blue, and gold graduation tassel that I had clipped on to her pretty dress.

I relived everything and I could see the entire scene play out before me.

"This is the proudest moment of my life," my father's voice started to crack.

I nuzzled my face into his strong, broad shoulders.

My eyes started to fill - so did Dad's.

"It was a team effort, Daddy!" I looked into my father's eyes and smiled. "All the way from Kindergarten to here." Immediately I slipped my mortarboard onto my father's head. Then I gently unfastened the red, blue, and gold tassel from it and hooked it around the top button of my mother's pretty shirtwaist dress. "See? We're still a team!" I smiled again.

"Team Townsend," my dad grinned. "I like the sound of that."

Just then Brenda's Dad stopped to say Congratulations and he snapped that very picture of us.

The *last* picture of us.

CLICK.

I quickly grabbed the photograph and ran from the table in tears. I cried all the way to my bedroom. I slammed the door behind me and just sat on the bed staring at that picture, that little four by five inch picture.

My God, I knew how much I missed them and that it had only been a little over a month since they'd been gone, but I thought I was on the mend.

I thought that talking to Brenda and Aunt Anna about what happened would help.

I thought that having a good life here would allow me to move passed the awful heartache.

I thought I was ready to be left with only the good memories, the fun times, and the happiness those two beautiful people had brought to my life.

…I thought wrong.

All I could feel was the pain of losing them. I guess initially I didn't have time to grieve because my life was forced to take such an abrupt turn. Then again, perhaps I was just too numb to feel it. But right at that moment?… I ached everywhere.

EVERYWHERE.

I couldn't get past it. I was devastated - in absolute agony - in a pain I didn't even feel at their funeral.

"Time heals," is the first thing people usually say to comfort you… yep, they're the words they use, all right, "Time heals."

But they never say how much time.

Not even once.

Do they?

Chapter Fifty-One

Saturday at The Dollio's went by pretty smoothly, because Dolly managed to keep another strategically placed scarf tied neatly around her neck. Not that it didn't get noticed - it did. But, it was the *style*, she was *seventeen*, and so Dolly's fashion statement went by without much ado. *Thank God.*

Nikki, Doll, Apry, and Mack ran their usual weekend errands, while Sean rested in front of the television watching the Phillies play a double header.

"Remember to get me enough beer for the bar-b-que! And go to Diamond's, it's cheaper!"

Nikki smiled and nodded.

"Dolly? Put the kids in the car for me, will ya? I forgot my wallet."

"Sure, Nik."

In nothing flat, both kids were situated in their seats, Dolly turned the radio on, and Nikki was back in the car.

"All ready, Mommy!" Apry smiled.

"All ready, Ap!"

Mack made a few baby noises, Apry was singing along with Sheb Wooley's 'Purple People Eater', and Nikki turned to speak to Dolly. "Aren't you a bit uncomfortable with that scarf around your neck?" she questioned as she backed out of the driveway.

Ever so nonchalant, Dolly answered her with a smile. "Well, you know Nik, being in style and being seventeen go hand in hand!"

Nikki sighed, "Yeah, I know. I remember."

"Umm... can we stop by Pfeiffer's so I can get a few more, you know, to match some other clothes I have. They're only a quarter a piece."

"Can I get one, too?" Apry chimed in.

"Sure," Dolly said, "We'll get you a pink one to match your outfit."

"Then I'll be in style too, huh?" asked the cute little six-year old.

Nikki had to laugh. "I guess girls are never too young to want some style. Are they, Doll?"

"I guess not." Dolly gave a half-smile as she readjusted her neck scarf in the mirror. "I guess not."

* * * * * *

Uncle John came home early because of the holiday. All the fishing boats were in at Noon. When he stepped foot in the door Brenda and Aunt Anna greeted him and then explained what had happened to me. So, the usual Fourth of July celebration was toned down a bit, but it was still a lovely day. Jake and Carrie Robinson dropped by as did Doc Thomas and his family.

    I managed to enter the kitchen almost as soon as the smell of bar-b-qued ribs made their way through my bedroom window. Dinner was wonderful and so was the company. It was the usual Turner feast: scrumptious shrimp, lobster, flounder, macaroni salad, hamburgers, hot dogs and chicken, and fresh, home-made pies - cherry, blueberry, and banana cream! And the potato salad? Well, it was absolutely the best I had ever eaten.

    The only things missing… were my parents.

    How they loved this holiday.

    Right around sunset, Aunt Anna, Uncle John, Brenda and I walked to the 85th Street pavilion and at 9:00 on the dot we watched the magnificent Townsends Inlet fireworks being shot off over the beautiful blue Atlantic Ocean.

    The combination of the stars, the fireworks, and a pretty crescent moon seemed like magic to me. I remember just a year earlier when I was standing right in the very same spot, with Mom on my left side and Dad on my right. We would Ooooh and Aaah as every new firework was set off - each more beautiful than the other.

    "This is the kind of magic that stays with you," Mom said.

    I remembered how my mother smiled when she said that to me.

    As the memory of last year slowly faded, I looked up into the sky trying not to blink, not even once, so I wouldn't miss any of that magic.

    And when it was over, I was okay.

    Once again, my mother helped me. I was grateful for those kinds of things that mom used to say, for that, too, was a kind of magic that would always stay with me.

Chapter Fifty-Two

Sunday morning was a slow and easy one. The smell of a delicious breakfast woke me but I took my time for a change and didn't rush right down into the kitchen. I combed my hair, brushed my teeth, and then strolled down the steps. Aunt Anna smiled the minute she caught sight of me.

"Good morning, Pat. Did you sleep well?"

I nodded. "Yup. Did you?"

"I sure did. So, how 'bout some breakfast?"

Another nod.

Before I knew it there was a western omelet on my plate and a nice big piece of pork roll with some rye toast with apple butter on the side.

"Thanks, Aunt Anna."

"You're welcome, Dear. Brenda still asleep?"

"Yup. Uncle John?"

"He left with Joe Linkletter for a little crabbing up the road. So, if they do well, it'll be deviled crabs for dinner!"

I smiled. "Well, I'll be sure to keep my fingers crossed!"

She smiled back at me. I sat quietly and ate my breakfast. There were a few thanks you's as Aunt Anna set a glass of orange juice and then a cup of coffee down next to me, but other than that I was unusually quiet. But that was just on the outside; inside my head was another story. I knew I had a wonderful night on Friday at the dance and we had a great bar-b-que for the 4th of July, and the fireworks were a blast (no pun intended.) But I still felt as if I should say something to Aunt Anna. You know, about my abrupt leave from the table when I saw those photos of me and Mom and Dad.

I took one last swallow of my coffee and just as my Aunt was about to leave the room I called to her, "Aunt Anna?"

"Yes, Dear?"

"Can I talk to you for a minute?"

She walked back over to the table and sat down next to me. "Why of course you can."

I took a deep breath, looked down at my empty plate and said, "I'm really sorry I flew upstairs yesterday. You know, I mean… because the pictures… well, they just…" I turned to look in her eyes. "They just made me feel *so* sad."

She nodded.

"And they made me long for those days with my parents. And they made me angry at God because he took them away from me. And they made me feel sick because… because I thought about the way they died… it was *so* awful. And looking at them made me feel heartbroken all over again and I… I just can't shake it. What am I doing *wrong*?!" I started to cry.

    My Aunt patted my hand. "Pattie, you're not doing anything wrong. You reach out to those who understand you. You acknowledge what happened and you deal with it in a positive and reasonable manner, one that will help you heal. You do *all* of the right things, Sweetheart, but it's only been a month. It takes time, Pattie. You know, when people say to you that time heals…"

    "Yeah, I know… they never say how much time."

    "That's right. But you will heal, in *your* time. Not anyone else's."

    I wiped my teary eyes on my napkin and hung on every word she had to say to me.

    "You have so many good memories that you talk and smile about - even now. Don't you?"

    I sniffled and nodded.

    "Well, someday you'll be able to look at those pictures and you won't see what happened that night. You'll just remember that happy moment at graduation."

    "Really?"

    "Yes. You'll look at those photos and see the love you shared with them for seventeen wonderful years."

    "Will I really, Aunt Anna?"

    "Yes, Sweetheart, you will."

    I sighed again.

    "You know, I lost my mother when I was only ten. She died in childbirth. That happened a lot in those days."

    "That's sad." My eyes started to fill.

    "Hold on a second. I'll be right back."

    My Aunt patted me on the shoulder as she got up from her chair, then she walked up the staircase. She came back down just a minute or so later with a beautifully framed picture in her hand.

    "This is me and my mother. The only photo we ever had taken together. I was nine years old."

    I took the beautiful silver frame in my hands and studied the photo. It wasn't like the pictures of me and mom and dad, it was very formal looking and tinted in a kind of beige color, a sepia tone I think they call it. But even in the formality of the late 1800's I could see a slight smile on both of their faces. I could see happiness in their eyes. I could feel the love they had for each other. There was no mistake about it.

    "Now what do you see when you look at *this* photo, Pattie?"

    "Happiness."

    "And so do I, Dear. It took a while, but eventually, I saw happiness, too."

    My eyes filled once again. "I put my pictures back in the envelope Mrs. Mayberry sent to me. I guess I'll keep 'em there until I'm ready to bring them out and... and get my own pretty frame."

She smiled at me. "You'll make it, Pat. It's not going to be easy and you'll have your bad days, but... well, the good days will start to outnumber the bad ones and soon, as if by some sort of divine intervention, you'll find that the bad days have gone, and peace will come."

"So all heartaches go away?"

"I don't think so, Pattie, not for everyone. I think some people wish that the pain would end, but sometimes there are circumstances that just don't seem to allow that kind of peace back into their lives."

"That's awful."

"But it doesn't mean that they can't be productive. It doesn't mean that they won't have good days or happy memories. It's just that some of the fog never seems to lift."

I sighed. "Know what Dad said to me?"

"What's that?"

He said, "Kites rise highest *against* the wind, not with it."

"Do you know what he meant by that?"

"I didn't," I smiled back, "but I do now."

Chapter Fifty-Three

Sunday was another busy day for Dolly. She cleaned off the bar-b-que grill, took all of her father's empty beer bottles and put them back in the case, she did her laundry, took the kids to the beach with Nikki, and helped make dinner. And her Dad? Well, he was resting from a rough 4th of July in front of the grill. Actually it was pretty easy in front of the grill since all he did was flip a few burgers and turn the chicken. Truth be told *his* rough weekend came as a result from a major hangover after polishing off an entire case of Ortlieb's, a few tequilas, and the last of his Johnny Walker Red.

"Is there anything else for me to do?" Dolly asked Nikki.
"Kids in bed, Doll?"
"I just tucked them in."
"Well, that's the last of the daily duties then." Nikki said as she finished some ironing. "Consider yourself free."
Dolly breathed a sigh of relief. "Where's Dad?"
"Sleeping."
"Still?"
"Yup. I'll wake him right before you get up tomorrow. A few cups of coffee and he'll be as right as rain."
"Nik?"
"Yeah?"
"Can I talk to you for a minute?"
"Sure," Nikki said as she plopped down on the nice big sofa. "What is it?"
"This is just between me and you, okay?"
"Sure."
"Ummm…"
"Ummm what?"
"Well… I mean, like…"
"Like?"
"Like how do you get a guy to… to treat you nice?"
She laughed. "You're asking *me*?!"
"Well, Dad's pretty good to you, right?"
"Doll, this is your Dad and I don't want to complain about him, but it was a lot different before I became Mrs. Dollio I can tell you that. It's just the way guys are."
"All guys?"
"Not all guys, Dolly, but… well, *most* guys."
"But if you can show someone how you expect to be treated… wouldn't that help?"
"Well, yeah, maybe, but really, what you *expect* and what you *get*, Doll,

is the difference between fantasy and reality. My mom told me don't expect anything and you won't be disappointed."

Dolly grimaced.

"What did your mom tell *you*?" Nikki questioned.

"I was just little when she died. We never talked about any of this stuff."

"Well, my mother's alive and I still get nowhere with her. It's one of those 'you made your bed you lie in it' situations with me and my mom, so I just don't even bother telling her anything anymore. If it's not one thing, it's your mother." She chuckled.

"Well, my mom and I always talked about *everything*. She was my best friend."

Nikki sighed. "I don't have a clue what that's like, Doll."

"I miss her, Nik. I feel so sad sometimes, I don't handle things well and…"

All of a sudden Nikki became extremely uncomfortable with Dolly's confession. She was turned off and feeling antsy that it would lead to talking about Mrs. Dollio's death, and about feelings and emotions. That was *not* what Nikki was all about. That was *not* how she was raised. Nik had learned to tuck away all her feelings when she was a child and she continued to hide them as the new Mrs. Sean Dollio.

That's just the way it was for her. It was all she ever knew.

Keep it all in.

Stiff upper lip.

Be strong.

Handle that pain.

Move on.

Don't bat an eye.

Never let them see you sweat.

Never let them see you have a weak moment.

Never.

So, in the process of learning all of that, she lost a very precious part of herself.

Nikki got up from the sofa and patted Dolly on the head. "It's late. See you in the morning, Kiddo."

"But can't we talk? I mean…"

"I don't think so, Dolly. I feel bad for you and all that, but I don't even know what to do about my own life. How can I help you with yours?"

Dolly sighed.

"Hey! How 'bout after you get home from work we get Mrs. Molehall to watch the kids and we can get our hair done after dinner. My treat! That'll make you feel better!"

"Sure…" Dolly half-smiled. "That'll be swell."

"See! *Now* you feel better, don't you? Huh?"

Dolly tried on another smile. "I feel fine. G'night, Nik."

"Night, Doll."

Dolly sat in the over-sized rocking chair for about five minutes and allowed all of her thoughts to sift through her head.

Her reality was this:

There was no one in her family she could talk to about BIG emotional issues.

No one in the family who would listen to her pain, her loss.

No one in her family who genuinely cared.

Family? That's not what the word family means.

That, my friends, is what the word *lonely* means.

Dolly walked slowly upstairs into her room, and then opened the bottom drawer of her dresser. She reached for a small 'Capezio' shoebox and opened it. Inside were about three dozen pictures of Dolly and her mother: at church, on Christmas Day, at the beach…

Dolly held the last photo that was ever taken of the two of them together. Her mother's cancer had ravaged her body and she was a very frail ninety pounds. But there was a smile on both of their faces and Dolly could still see the happiness and love in their eyes.

She held her mother's picture close to her heart and softly cried.

"I see happiness when I look at *you*, Mom… but I just can't find it anywhere else."

She reached for a tissue to dry her eyes.

"I don't know who I am. I don't have anyone to talk to. I'm… I'm not even real anymore. I'm just a fake. I'm a…."

Dolly continued to weep; tears fell from her saddened face onto the precious photograph.

"*Please*, Mom…Please help me."

Chapter Fifty-Four

As I walked into Shellum's on Monday morning I saw Dolly sitting at the soda fountain nursing a large cup of coffee and a jelly doughnut. I walked up behind her and tugged on her perfectly placed neck scarf.

"How did things go this weekend?" I questioned.

"Have a seat and I'll tell you about it." Dolly took a long sip of her coffee and stared into my eyes.

"Oh my God! The hickeys! Did your father find out?! Did Nikki?!"

Dolly finished her coffee and sighed. "Nope, I got away with it. And, by the looks of these things another four or five days and I'm home free." She lowered her scarf so I could witness their improved status.

"They still look ugly as far as I'm concerned. I mean, they look *better*, but, my God, Doll what the hell were you thinking?"

She sighed once again, "Apparently I *wasn't* thinking."

"Apparently you're right."

"Pat, can I ask you a question. A serious question and you won't get upset?"

"Of course you can."

"Do you have anyone that you can talk to? I mean, someone that you can really unload your problems to?"

"Since my mom and dad died?"

"Well, yeah."

"Sure. I have Aunt Anna and Uncle John, and, I have Brenda. But…"

"But?"

"But it's Aunt Anna that I usually talk to about what happened to my parents. Not that I couldn't talk to Brenda or Uncle John about it, but Aunt Anna seems to have the coolest head, if you know what I mean."

Dolly nodded and sighed, "Must be a good feeling to have someone like that."

"It is. It's so hard to get rid of some of the pain. You know, that stuff that creeps up on you now and then and…"

"Yeah."

"But I'll tell ya, a big burden like that when you have someone to share it with… it just seems to cut the load in half. At least it does for me."

"Thank God, huh?"

"I'll say."

I picked up on Dolly's need to vent and I put my arm around her shoulder. "So, you have anything you want to talk about? I'm a good listener."

"Umm… not right now, maybe later."

"Whenever you're ready."

Just as I was about to pour myself a cup of coffee, Mrs. Shellum called to us, "Time to crack the whip, girls."

"Be right there," I called out.

"We'll talk later. Okay, Pat?"

"Okay."

* * * * * *

The week seemed to fly by. I guess it was because it was Brenda's last six days here. After work Bren and I went to Pfeiffer's or Dalrymple's, we went to the boardwalk, ate ice cream at VanSant's, and then we dropped in to Busch's Seafood Restaurant for a delicious baked deviled crab and flounder dinner.

Yummy!

It was a good week all in all - it was just too short. Shellum's wasn't as crowded as usual all week long, I don't know why, and so I figured Dolly would open up and tell me what was troubling her, but she never did. Once again, just like the preceding Friday, Mrs. Shellum let us out of work a half and hour early so we could fuss over ourselves before going to the dance.

What a nice woman she is.

As we were leaving the store, Dolly turned to me, "Here's to another great night at The Civic Center, huh?"

"Yeah. Brenda's last night," I sighed. "We'll be there around 7:00."

"How come so early?"

"We promised we'd set up Uncle John's song selection for the night. George and Clark are going to meet us there at 7:30."

"Well, I guess Jack and I'll be there around 7:30, too."

"*Well,* you'll *be* there around 7:30 *if* you don't make another stop at the beach like last week!"

Dolly smiled at me "Hey, I may be crazy, but I'm not stupid. I'll be there at 7:30. See ya, Pat!"

"See ya, Doll."

* * * * * *

Brenda, Uncle John, and I left the house at 6:45. Mrs. Orwatt and Bessie Newell, the concession stand ladies, were already there waiting for us. Uncle John fumbled through his two jacket pockets for the keys.

"Be patient ladies, this might take a while. I'm not as young as I look."

Mrs. Orwatt and Bessie smiled at each other. "That's all right, John," Bessie smiled, "we're not either."

"Ahh, here it is."

One quick turn of a rather ornate silver key and we were all inside The Civic Center. Brenda and I ran up the steps and into Uncle John's private disc-jockey room.

"I think we should play a slow song first," Brenda sighed, "How about something by The Platters?"

I shook my head "No, you've gotta get the joint jumpin' first. It has to be something by Elvis, or Jerry Lee or Little Richard. Know what I mean?"

We both finally agreed that Jerry Lee would be our opening number. A hot and hoppin' little tune called, "Breathless."

Following that was Elvis, the Everly Brothers, Elvis, Elvis, and more Elvis.

By the time Uncle John made it up the steps, Brenda and I had already had his evening hit parade planned out for him and we both got a big smile for our efforts.

"I hope you gals put 'Tutti Frutti' on my play list, you know it's my favorite. Just don't tell Mrs. Orwatt and Bessie Newell, it'll ruin my image."

Chapter Fifty-Five

The dance was fabulous. Forget the fact that Jack Dawkins was there. It was still fabulous.

Brenda danced like there was no tomorrow, Dolly seemed less enraptured with Jack than the previous week, and I was just crazy about George Ludlam. What a great guy! What a dancer! He was just absolutely adorable!

Clark was a sweetheart, too. He was extremely attentive to Brenda. Well, he and George were always gentlemen. Jack Dawkins, as you know, was not.

The night went by quicker than any of us could have anticipated and before we knew it, Uncle John was playing 'Tutti Frutti' again, The Spaniels sang, 'Goodnight Sweetheart', the lights in The Civic Center went back on, and the dance was over.

The six of us wended our way through the crowd and then started our walk down 85th Street.

"That was the best dance in the entire world!" Brenda beamed. "Geez, I wish I was staying here for the rest of the summer!"

I watched as Clark gently took her hand. "I wish you were staying here for the rest of the summer, too, Bren."

How sweet.

As we strolled down the street we were all just a flurry of conversation - except for Jack that is. "You know, I think 'All Shook Up' is the best song that Presley ever sang"… "Aren't those hamburgers delicious"… "Did you notice there were kids from Wildwood who came all the way up here for the dance?"… "Yup, that's how fast word traveled last week!"… "Face it, Townsends Inlet has the best teenage dance in South Jersey!"

By the time we were done yakking. Dolly and Jack were about to leave us and go their separate ways.

"Are you going right home?" I said, tugging at my own neck scarf as a helpful reminder.

Dolly immediately got the hint, "Yeah, I told Jack that Nik wanted me home right away."

He stood there, rolled his eyes, and lit a cigarette. "See yiz later"

I could tell Jack wasn't so thrilled about Dolly's need to go straight home - a hickey-less night for Mr. Jack Dawkins.

What a pity…The Jerk.

The four of us waved our goodbyes to Dolly and the Artful Dodger. Only Dolly waved back.

"He is the *creepiest* guy on earth," Brenda said.

I nodded. "I know there's something just weird about him. He's trouble."

George agreed wholeheartedly, "Ordinarily I wouldn't judge a guy I barely know, but I've heard enough things about him to be scared for Dolly."

"So, what does her father and stepmother think about this guy?" Clark wanted to know.

"That's hard to say. I don't hear much from Dolly about it. I guess Jack can put on a good act when he wants to."

Before we knew it, we were outside The Turner household saying good bye to George and Clark. "What time did you say you were leaving tomorrow Bren? Three o'clock?" Clark *had* to be certain.

"Unfortunately," Brenda sighed.

"Hey! How 'bout we all go to The Charcoal House for lunch? You know, our last time out together until…"

In less then a split second Brenda and I both said, "We'd love to!"

"So how about 11:30 and we'll pick you up here?" George asked.

"11:30 it is! Goodnight George." I smiled and then gave him a quick hug - still no kiss, just a quick hug.

"Goodnight, Pattie."

Brenda quickly followed suit with Clark, a quick hug - still no kiss, just a quick hug.

"Night, Bren."

"G'night, Clark."

Brenda and I took our shoes off as soon as we entered the house and walked up the staircase. We barely got into our pajamas when we both flopped on to the bed and fell sound asleep. So much for all that dynamic seventeen-year-old energy.

Chapter Fifty-Six

I could hardly believe my eyes. Brenda was rustling around the bedroom and according to the clock on my nightstand, it was only 6:16 AM!

"Is the house on fire and I just can't smell it?" I yawned.

"Wise ass." She smiled at me.

"I just wanted to get my stuff packed up so we could spend as much time as possible together. That three o'clock Greyhound'll be here before we know it."

I sighed "I wish you weren't going home, Bren."

"That makes two of us. But…"

"But?"

"But I leave for UCLA in another three and a half weeks. I've got lotsa stuff I have to do."

"Yeah, I know."

Brenda stopped packing and sat down on the bed beside me. "Hey… I'll be home for Christmas, and I'll be home for Easter, *and* when I come home next summer, *you'll* be going back with me!"

The thought of not seeing my best friend for five months made my eyes start to fill. I never spent five days away from Brenda before my parents died, and then and everything changed.

Everything.

"Maybe I oughta say forget the hardship delay and just start college in September with you."

"No way. You're not ready, Pat. You know you're not!"

I sighed. Knowing full well Brenda was right. "Yeah. I wouldn't do well, I know I wouldn't. I mean if they were giving out minus 4.0's I'd probably get one of those, and then I'd really be sunk."

Brenda nodded. "You need this time Pat, and it'll go fast. We'll be together before we know it."

"And you'll write to me and let me know what's happening out there?"

"Cross my heart. I'll write you a detailed letter once a week and fill you in on all the dirt."

I chuckled. "I'm holding you to that, you know."

"The letter writing or the dirt?"

"All of the above," I smiled.

Brenda grabbed my hand and shook it, "It's a deal."

Suddenly there was a knock on my bedroom door.

"Girls, are you awake? It's *awfully* early."

"Come on in, Aunt Anna. We didn't wake you and Uncle John up, did we?" Brenda said with a guilty look on her face.

"Heavens no. John was up at 4:30 this morning. Captain Cramer was sailing off at 5:15. I already made breakfast for two and did all the dishes. I just came up to make the bed."

I smiled "You are a wonderful woman, Aunt Anna."

She smiled back "Well, let me continue being wonderful and make you two gals a nice breakfast. What would you like?"

In unison we said, "Peanut butter and bacon sandwiches!"

My Aunt Anna rolled her eyes at both of us, "Okay ladies, two peanut butter and bacon sandwiches comin' right up."

* * * * * *

Aunt Anna sat at the kitchen table with me and Brenda and drank some hot tea, extra cream, extra sugar, while we devoured not just one peanut butter and bacon sandwich a piece, but two!

We talked about our lunch date at The Charcoal House with Clark and George, Bren's freshman year at UCLA, and how much we would all miss her.

Brenda and I cleaned up our dishes and decided to take one last long walk down the inlet.

The sky was a beautiful periwinkle blue, some sea gulls were arguing over a horseshoe crab on the beach, and I was feeling very melancholy about yet another loss in my life.

"I want to thank you for being such a wonderful friend to me, Bren. And I don't mean just since Mom and Dad died, I mean ever since I knew you."

"Oh, Pat..."

"Nope... hear me out. I want to thank you for, well for sticking up for me when Frannie McManus stole my roller skates and you stole them right back. I want to thank you for being so nice to my mom and dad. I want to thank you for all the times you bought me pretzels on Wednesdays, because I always forgot my pretzel money. And... did I say thank you for being so nice to my mom and dad?"

"Yes you did, Patty... twice."

I smiled. "You're the best friend anyone could ever ask for. I mean, initially you were a real pain-in-the-ass over that Dolly stuff, but I got over it."

She chuckled. "I'm gonna miss you, Patricia Townsend."

"And I'm gonna miss you too, Brenda Mayberry."

Brenda and I walked across two huge sand dunes and found ourselves on 89th Street, just about twenty feet from the Dollio household. As luck would have it, we saw Dolly in the backyard moving a rather large grill over to the picnic bench.

"Dolly! DOLL-EEE!" I called out.

Immediately she ran right over to me and Brenda.

"Hey, nice scarf", I said, tugging at the piece of blue chiffon she had wrapped around her neck.

"Yeah, well this fashion statement is gonna be gone with the wind in a few more days. Know what I mean?"

"Let's hope so."

"You go home today, right Bren?"

"Yeah, I don't want to, but I have to."

"Hey, were goin' over to The Charcoal House around 11:30, it's like a farewell lunch for Brenda. You wanna come?"

"Who's goin'?"

"Just me, Bren, George, and Clark."

"I guess you don't want me to locate Jack so he can tag along?" She made a funny face.

"That would be a fair assessment," I smiled.

"Let me run in and ask Nik. My dad's not home."

Just then Nikki came out with Mack on her hip.

"Nikki, you remember Pattie from, Shellum's, don't you? And her friend, Brenda?"

"I sure do," she smiled.

"Today's Brenda's last day here because she's going to college and they invited me to The Charcoal House for lunch." Quickly Dolly turned to me and asked. "How long are we going to be there?"

"Well I guess from 11:30 to maybe 1:30. Something like that."

"Can I go, Nik? *Please* can I go?"

Nikki readjusted the cute little baby on her hip and smiled. "Sure, why not?"

"Thanks *very* much, Mrs. Dollio." I smiled. "She'll be home before 2:00."

Nik turned and walked into the house and Dolly gave a *huge* sigh of relief.

"Wow, I thought I would *never* get out of the house. I'm always stuck here on Saturdays. Do this, do that."

"But *I* thought…" Brenda started.

I looked at her but quickly shook my head as if telling her not to say anything about how easy Dolly always said her Saturdays were.

"Well okay," Brenda grinned, "we'll see you over at The Charcoal House at 11:30."

"Bye, Dolly," I waved.

"See you later, guys. And thanks!"

We made it back to Aunt Anna's by eleven o'clock just in time to wash up and change into something pretty for a lunch date at the Landis Avenue Charcoal House.

"Come on girls, it's 11:20. George and Clark will be here any minute."

I adjusted my ponytail one more time, tied a pretty purple scarf around my neck, put on just a hint of lipstick, and, at the very moment when I saw near perfection in the mirror, the doorbell rang.

"Girls, they're here!"

Although Brenda and I could have flown down the steps because we were so happy, we took our time instead and entered the parlor with style and grace.

"Hi, George," I smiled.

"Hi, Pat! You look great!"

"Thank you."

"You look great too, Bren," Clark smiled.

"Why thank you, Mr. Lowen."

George took the lead and asked, "Are we ready to go?"

"I guess so. Umm...is there anything we can get you while were out Aunt Anna?"

"No, Dear. Thank you very much, but we're fine. You youngsters just have a good time."

With that said, the four of us walked down 85th Street, made a right onto Landis Avenue, and within three minutes, we were inside The Charcoal House.

Dolly was already holding a table for us. "Hi, Guys!" she said with a huge smile on her face.

"Hi, Doll!"

We all quickly settled ourselves at the table and reached for our menus.

"The treats on me," said Clark. "I've been saving my extra fishing money for *just* such an occasion."

My eyes scanned the menu and the thought of a triple-decker turkey BLT set my mouth watering.

George and Clark each ordered a cheeseburger deluxe, Brenda got an egg salad, lettuce and tomato on rye bread, and Dolly ordered a grilled polish sausage with sauerkraut. And *all* of us ordered onion rings, grilled peppers and onions and iced tea on the side.

The Charcoal House knew how to cook! And it wasn't just their famous steaks that brought people in from all over South Jersey, it was *everything*! It was the friendly waitresses, the sociable atmosphere, and all the scrumptious food they served: the salads, those triple-decker sandwiches, the hamburgers and the hot dogs. It was such a terrific place. In fact, it was the very first place my mom and dad took me when I was old enough to eat "big people food." Memories aside, all five of us were having a really great time. We talked about lots of things: the dance, the shore, fishing, the boardwalk, salt water taffy... Yup, it was fun all right, and the atmosphere seemed an awful lot easier and breezier with out Jack Dawkins on the scene. Dolly brought up the subject of college and we all realized just how much our lives were about to change. Clark would be off to Temple University in 1960. I would be at UCLA and George would be at the University of Pennsylvania. And, next year would make Brenda a sophomore at UCLA.

A sophomore!

Dolly was quite honest about her situation.

"I'd like to go to college to study music, but I didn't even take any tests to know if a college would want me. I play a little piano. I think I'm pretty good. I… I think I might like to be a music teacher."

"Really?" I was so surprised.

"Yeah well, when I graduated last year, I was only sixteen, so I had to be a pretty smart kid *somewhere* along the line. My father just never gives me any credit for anything."

"That's so wrong." Brenda sighed.

"Yeah. So, I guess I just never gave an advanced education much thought. I mean, I *know* Mom always wanted me to go to college, but, as I said, my dad was never encouraging after mom died, and anyway…"

"Anyway…?"

"He had other plans for me." She seemed heartsick.

"What do you mean he had other plans for you?"

"Well, I guess you could say they were unspoken plans. The day after I graduated Dad and Nikki went to South Carolina for a golf tournament and I stayed home with Apry - for ten whole days!"

"That's not right Dolly." Brenda nudged her.

"A lot of things aren't right. But I'll fix them."

Dolly let out a big sigh and then our waitress reappeared. "Cheesecake, anyone?"

"Sounds good to me," George said.

I nodded.

"A day without cheesecake is like a day without sunshine," Brenda smiled.

We all agreed.

"So that's five cheesecakes, right?" our waitress asked.

"Yup, five cheesecakes and five coffees and that'll be it."

No sooner had we placed our order when five huge pieces of thick creamy cheesecake with a rich buttery graham cracker crust were placed in front of us.

Dolly politely asked the waitress if she had any matches.

The woman fumbled through her pocket and took a small box of stick matches out and handed them to Dolly.

Doll took two. She placed one in the middle of Brenda's cheesecake and then lit that with the other one.

"Now you have to make a wish, Bren."

Brenda closed her eyes, inhaled deeply and blew out the candle.

We all applauded.

"Is this like a birthday wish, you know, like you can't tell anyone what your wish was?"

I nodded. "Of course it is! You can't tell someone your wish!"

"Then can I say who I made the wish for?"

"But didn't you make it for yourself?" Dolly asked. "You're supposed to, you know."

"Well, I didn't", Brenda said looking Dolly right in the eye, "I made it for you."

* * * * * *

Lunch was over by 1:45 and we all started to say our goodbyes. I was happy that a new friendship was born between Dolly and Brenda. It did my heart good to see it. We had decided not to let the guys walk us home; Brenda thought it would be a little too emotional and she wanted to avoid it.

"Don't forget to write to me, Mr. Lowen."

"A promise is a promise, Bren. I'll write."

"It was so wonderful to meet you." Brenda gave Clark a quick hug. "Thanks for… well, thanks for everything, Clark."

"Maybe we'll get to do it again next summer."

"Now *there's* something to look forward to!" She smiled.

"So, it's another date, Ms. Brenda. Next July, me and you and Townsends Inlet, New Jersey."

"I'll make a note of it in my diary."

Clark stepped back and I knew he was about to make his exit. I felt sad.

George was the next one to step up to the plate. He gave Brenda a quick little hug, too. He also said how nice it was to meet her and that he was holding her to that diary entry for 1960 – for Clark's sake. In a flash, the two nicest guys I'd ever met were walking down the street waving goodbye to the three of us.

"What wonderful fellas," Dolly said.

"I'll say." Brenda sighed.

"Think you'll find someone like Clark Lowen in sunny Southern California, Bren?"

"I don't know Pattie, but if I don't… there's always the summer of 1960."

Smart thinkin'.

Chapter Fifty-Seven

Before the three of us knew it we were standing outside The Dollio household.

"I'm gonna miss you, Brenda. Write to me, okay?"

"You can count on it!"

Just as Brenda hugged Dolly, a car horn beeped from behind us. It was Dolly's dad.

"Hi, girls."

No smile, no display of affection, just a curt, matter-of-fact, "Hi, girls."

"Hello, Mr. Dollio."

"Hi, Mr. Dollio."

"Hi, Daddy!"

He brushed by us carrying a large brown paper bag quickly followed by the faint smell of alcohol.

Faint smell? I take that back. He reeked of the stuff.

"Get in the house, Christine! You have chores!"

Before the, "Yes, Dad," had left her lips the screen door slammed shut. I felt so bad for Dolly.

As for Brenda? For all her pain in the neck ways, she was really good at making people feel at ease and she hugged Dolly once again.

"You look into that music career. I think you'd be a *wonderful* teacher. You've already proven you're good with kids!" The smile on Brenda's face was genuine.

"I will, Bren. I'll write and keep you updated on my progress."

"Good!"

"Well," I interrupted. "I hate to be the one to break this up, but we have to get goin' so Brenda's on time for her bus."

"I understand," Dolly nodded.

"CHRISTINE! GET IN HERE!!!!" her father shouted.

Dolly lowered her head. "I hate it when he calls me Christine, it always means trouble."

"You just do your best and things will *all* work out. You'll see." Again, Brenda was upbeat and sincere.

"I will, Bren. Write soon, okay?"

"I promise."

Dolly turned and walked away, waving until she reached the old wooden screen door.

"Bye!" she smiled.

"Bye! See ya!"

Quietly the screen door closed behind her, and then… Dolly was gone.

"Now *there's* a kid that's gonna do okay," Brenda said as we started our walk back to 85th Street.

"What?"

"You were right, Pattie. I admit it. She's a good kid and she's gonna make it."

I smiled. "Yup. She's gonna make it."

Chapter Fifty-Eight

Brenda and I walked in the house just as Aunt Anna's faithful mantel clock struck 2:00. My Aunt was out in the kitchen preparing a nice lunch bag for Brenda to eat on the bus for the long, three-hour ride home.

Such a kind and thoughtful woman!

"There's three pieces of chicken in here - a breast and two drumsticks. I packed you two sodas, a bottle opener, *and* there's a nice fresh piece of Angel Food cake in there, too. It's less messy."

Brenda wrapped her arms around my Aunt. "Can I adopt you?"

Aunt Anna smiled.

"Come on, Bren, let's go upstairs and make sure you got all your stuff."

"Okaaaay... I'm comin'." She groaned as she followed me up the stairs

Brenda and I looked around the small room we had shared for the last fourteen days, and everything she brought with her was right in front of us - all neatly packed away inside one big, white Samsonite suitcase and a scruffy old duffle bag.

"Man, that two weeks went quick, didn't it?" I sighed.

"Yeah. It felt more like two days."

Brenda and I sat on the bed and listened to Elvis on the radio, "Jailhouse Rock" was playing.

"He's one cool cat, isn't he?"

"Yep."

Suddenly a nice breeze blew the curtains around.

"Nice and airy today, huh?"

I nodded. "Yeah."

"It's usually like this around this time of year, isn't it?"

Again I nodded. "Yeah, it is."

I looked at Brenda and she looked at me and in that brief less-than-a-second look we both knew what we were doing.

Chit-chat.

Silly, meaningless, chit-chat.

And *why*?!

Because we knew we had less than an hour together before our walk up 85th Street, less than sixty minutes before we had to say goodbye to each other until the Christmas holidays - if we were lucky. Meaningless chit-chat to hide the pain of our loss. I knew it was wrong. I mean, after all of my talks with Aunt Anna I knew that if I felt that I had something to say, then I should just come right on out and say it.

And so I did.

"There isn't much point in trying to pretend that this is an okay moment. Huh, Bren?"

"I guess not, Pattie."

My eyes started to fill. "I'm gonna miss you. I can't even find the right words to tell you just how much."

We both leaned over and hugged each other and then we started to cry. And I mean *cry*! We were sobbing and carrying on so much that our words were all garbled, but we still managed somehow to understand what the other was saying.

"I'll remember this great time that we had together *all* of my life!"

"We're *always* gonna be best friends, no matter how many miles are between us."

"I love you, Pattie."

"I love you, too, Bren."

Then each of us clumsily handed the other a Kleenex. First I poked Brenda in the eye and then she dropped the tissue meant for me, and then handed me another that somehow landed right onto my foot. We laughed and we cried and then we laughed some more.

"Girls! It's 2:45! You'd better get going!"

Brenda and I looked at each other.

"Time to go, Miss Mayberry," I sniffled.

Bren took one last sweeping glance at the pretty little room, then turned to me and sighed, "Yep, time to go, Miss Townsend."

Chapter Fifty-Nine

Aunt Anna and Uncle John hugged Brenda and said their goodbyes. No tears, but you could tell they would miss her.

"Good luck at UCLA!" Uncle John waved.

"Make sure you write to us!" my Aunt smiled.

"I will, and thank you for everything! I had a blast!"

More waves.

More smiles.

Brenda and I walked slowly down the street and took turns carrying her big, heavy suitcase.

"Why doesn't someone put a long handle and some wheels on these things?" I groaned.

Before we knew it, there we were at the corner of 85th and Landis waiting for the Greyhound bus to drive in from Avalon.

"Well, it's been one helluva great two weeks, Bren."

"It sure has, Pattie. Just too fast."

"I'll say."

"I'm thrilled about you goin' to California. I just think that's so cool."

"Yeah."

"A great college, Disneyland, the Pacific Ocean… there's something magical about the whole thing."

"I wish we were going together, Pat."

"Well, the best laid plans… you know."

Brenda sighed. "Yeah, I know."

Just then we heard the sounds of a bus grinding its brakes to a halt just two blocks away from us.

"Maybe that's not the Greyhound," I smiled.

"Yeah, and maybe my name's not Brenda Ethel Mayberry." She smiled back.

Barely had those words left her lips when the big old silver and blue Greyhound opened its doors in front of us.

"Let me help you with that luggage there, young lady!" The driver smiled.

He was an older man with a sweet Santa Claus face, like Uncle John's.

"Thank you." Brenda nodded.

"Well," she sighed as she turned back toward me, "This is it, Kiddo."

"I guess so."

"Thanks for everything, Pattie. I had *such* a wonderful time. Thank Aunt Anna and Uncle John again for me, okay?"

"I will."

"All aboard!" Santa called out.
"And tell Dolly and George and Clark that I'll write as soon as I get settled in."
"Okay."
"But you know I'll write to you before that."
I nodded with tears in my eyes.
"All aboard!" Santa called out once more.
"And enjoy your time here, Pat. Take the time you need to heal and remember all of the good things you *do* have!"
"I will, Bren. I will."
"All..." Santa was just about to make his announcement for the third time.
"Sorry," Brenda answered. "Pattie's my best friend and I'm off to college in California, We won't see each other again for a long while."
He smiled. "Well, gals, I'm about a minute ahead of schedule. You have just enough time for one more goodbye."
Brenda and I quickly hugged each other.
"I love you, Pat."
"I love you too, Bren."
Then, in the blink of an eye, she boarded the bus and the large silver doors closed behind her. Suddenly a window opened and there she was, her whole torso hanging out the window with that great big Mayberry smile on her face
"Bye, Miss UCLA Freshman of 1959!" I waved.
"Bye, Miss UCLA Freshman of 1960!"
The bus took off and I just stood there frozen to my spot on the corner of 85th and Landis, waving and waving until I couldn't see her any longer. But I could still hear the faint sound of the bus rumbling and so I stayed there for a few more seconds, listening to the hum of it, until there was no noise left at all.
No more Greyhound.
No more Santa Claus.
No more Brenda.
After I got back home I moped around the house for a few hours. I just didn't know what to do with myself. I decided to read my Verne novel, but after a few chapters I changed my mind. Then I decided to do some crossword puzzles, and quickly nixed that idea as well. Then, just as I was in the middle of my favorite Teen Magazine, the phone rang.
"Pattie! I'm home safe and sound!"
Brendaaaa!
"How was the ride, Bren?"
"Great! And tell Aunt Anna the food was delicious!"
"I will."
"Well, Mom has eight million things planned for me so, I better get goin'."

"Write soon, okay, Bren?"
"You can count on it!"
"Bye, Miss Mayberry."
"Bye, Miss Townsend."

Then with the sound of a soft click from a telephone far away in Philadelphia my best friend was gone... once again.

Chapter Sixty

Sunday morning.
Without Brenda home with me, I felt lost and alone all over again, as if the progress I'd made since Mom and Dad died had taken a huge step backward.
Ugh!
Aunt Anna left me to my own little world - God bless her. I didn't get dressed until about noon, I picked at my food, listened to some music, and then took a long walk on the beach. My head was on overload.
Where was my life going?
What would life be like for Brenda in California?
Would she find another best friend?
What will Townsends Inlet be like for me in autumn... the winter?
What about George?
What about Dolly?
And what about Jack Dawkins?! YUCK! The mere thought of the guy made me sick.
When I reached the end of the Inlet I turned around and suddenly I remembered what Brenda said to me about all of the good things I *do* have in my life – and it was true. For all of my heartache, I still had so much to live for. I had Aunt Anna and Uncle John, nice new friends, a great school to go to within the coming year, summer dances, fishing with my Uncle, a nice job at Shellum's.
With every one of those thoughts intact, and fully registering, all of a sudden the sky seemed more blue to me... the air, cleaner and fresher, and the laughter from the children on the beach practically sang to me.
I felt good.
When I walked into the house the smell of breaded deviled crabs and a newly baked strawberry pie greeted me.
"Hi, Aunt Anna! Smells wonderful in here!" I smiled as I entered the kitchen.
"Well, thank you, Dear. How are you feeling?"
"Much better, thanks."
"Taking time for yourself is a good thing, Pattie."
I nodded. "Can I help you with anything?"
"As a matter of fact, you can. John is down in the shed hanging up some new fishing poles and some crab nets. Will you go down and tell him dinner's ready?"
"I sure will!"
I walked out into the back porch and opened the door and took the steps two at a time. I made a left at the old crabapple tree and then a right to enter the green and white shed door. I stuck my head in and smiled.

"Oh, Mr. Turner, your dinner is served, Sir."
"Why thank you, m'lady. Deviled crabs?"
"Yup, and strawberry pie."
"I'll race you up the steps, Pat!"

Chapter Sixty-One

Monday morning came and I felt more like my old self. I think knowing I had Shellum's to go to was a plus. One thing I *did* think about was that it was kinda lonely not having Brenda around, but, on the plus side, I did have lots more room in the bed!

Aunt Anna made me French Toast on home made cinnamon bread, some freshly squeezed orange juice, and a nice cup of coffee - extra cream, extra sugar - to start my Monday morning off on the right foot.

It was delicious!

On my way to work I saw Carrie and Jake Robinson sitting on their front porch, I waved, I saw Mr. Linkletter delivering mail, we exchanged hello's, the milkman was making his usual morning rounds and the fruit and vegetable huckster was in full voice.

"VEJ-A-TIBBLES... GETCHER FRESH VEJ-A-TIBBLES... FRESH JER-ZEE TA-MAYTERS... FRESH CORN... COME AND GET IT! TWO BAGS FERA DOLLAH!"

I stopped and asked him, "Do you have any bananas?"

"I do, but we don't grow 'em in Jer-zee."

"Well, I'll have two just the same, okay?"

"Ten cents."

"For two?"

"Yup."

I handed him a dime and he handed me two nice bananas in a small brown paper bag. Just as I was about to say, "Thank you," his voice rang out, "GETCHER FRESH NON-JER-ZEE BANANAS RIGHT HERE! TWO BAGS FERA DOLLAH!"

I smiled.

Within two minutes I was walking up the steps and into Shellum's, brown paper bag in hand.

"Morning, Pat!" Millie grinned.

"Mornin'."

"What's in the bag?"

"Two bananas. I got one for me and one for Dolly. You know... snack time."

She nodded. "Did your friend make it home safely?"

"Yes, she did. Thank you."

"I guess you miss her."

"I missed her before she even left."

"But you still have *me*!" Dolly's voice sang out to me from behind the soda fountain.

I walked in the direction of Dolly's happy voice and then sat down at the counter. "Yup, I still have you!"

168

"So, what'll it be, Miss? A regular? Extra cream, extra sugar?"

"And a glazed donut?" I grinned.

"I think I can arrange that. And, would you like some company to go along with your coffee and glazed?"

"I'd *love* some company!"

Dolly poured us both some coffee and placed a nice big fresh glazed donut from The Sea Isle Bakery on a plate right next to my coffee.

"Here's to Freshman Brenda Ethel Mayberry, UCLA Class of 1963," I said raising my coffee mug.

"Indeed! Brenda, this one's for you!"

Dolly and I took a sip of our coffee, clinked our glazed donuts together, and smiled.

"I only hope I can be half the wonderful friend that she is, Pat."

"Dolly, you're a wonderful friend in your own right."

"But I'm different."

"Yes, you are, and different is good."

Just as we finished our coffee Mrs. Shellum called to us, "It's that time again, ladies."

"Coming, Mrs. S."

The day just flew by. Dolly and I had our fresh huckster banana and a cup of tea at break, and then the rest of the day was a blur. There were so many customers we hardly had time to catch our breath, but, that's what made working at Shellum's not seem like work. I just felt busy and surrounded by friends, that's all. I mean, practically everyone who entered the store knew me since I was a baby, or at least knew Aunt Anna or Uncle John – both longtime fixtures on the Townsends Inlet scene. And now, with Uncle John becoming a popular disc-jockey, well, he was a local celebrity as well. I thought that was pretty cool.

Dolly and I had already made plans about what we were wearing on Friday night. Day after day we spent talking and solidifying our friendship. And, when she walked into work on Thursday without her ever faithful neck scarf, I don't know who was happier, her or me!

"Let's not find the need for more scarves any time soon, okay?"

"You don't have to remind me of that one, Pat!"

Off and on during the week Clark and George would drop by and say hello, talk to Millie and Bill Shellum, pick up some fishing gear, or treat us to a soda and some chips for our afternoon break. Jack Dawkins, The Prince of Darkness (as far as I was concerned) would also drop in now and then. To say Hello? To buy us a coke? Puh-leeze. He'd stop in for a pack of cigarettes; say, "Yo!" and then leave.

What a charmer, huh?

By the time Friday rolled around Dolly and I already made arrangements with her Dad and Nikki for Dolly to spend the weekend with me. Of course, that meant she had oodles of chores to do beforehand, but as Dolly told me, she was more than happy to do it. She was so thrilled that she did all of her chores, all of Nikki's chores, and all of her dad's chores!

To hear Nikki tell it her father was amazed, so much so, that he felt she should ask to spend time away more often.

I think that was Dolly's plan from the get-go.

Friday after work, I walked Miss Dollio home so she could pick up her overnight bag and say goodbye to Apry and Mack. Her dad wasn't home and that was just fine with me and Dolly.

"Have big fun!" Apry said hugging her sister's neck.

"You have big fun, too!" Dolly answered.

"Enjoy your weekend, Doll," Nikki smiled.

"Thanks, Nik, I will. You, too."

"I'll try… you know what I mean."

"Yeah, I know."

Dolly picked up her pocketbook, her sleepover bag, and stuffed poodle and we walked out the front door, onto 89th Street, full of life, fun, and anticipation for another great night at The Civic Center.

"I feel free, Pattie." She sighed.

"Thank God, huh?"

"You can say that again!"

Chapter Sixty-Two

Dolly and I walked into the house at exactly 6:00 PM.
"Aunt Anna? We're home!"
"Come on in, I'm just setting the table."
"Hi, Mrs. Turner," Dolly smiled. "I'll help you with that!"
"No, Sweetheart. You're a guest. You just sit down and enjoy a nice little dinner."
"Did someone say dinner?!" Uncle John entered the kitchen from the back porch.
"Hi, Mr. Turner!"
"Hi there, Dolly. Evenin' Pattie!"
"Sure smells wonderful, Anna."
"Thank you, John."
Before we knew it our 'nice little dinner' was served: mussel, clam, and wild rice chowder with minced garlic and parsley, a fresh garden salad, Halibut in a crispy potato crust, grilled asparagus, home-made breadsticks, and a strawberry shortcake that could have won the National Pillsbury bake-off!
"If this is a nice *little* dinner, Mrs. Turner, I can't even imagine what this table looks like at Thanksgiving!"
"Well, you are more than welcome to come on by and see for yourself! We'd be happy to have you, Dear."
"Pass the soup, please," Uncle John pointed in the direction of a beautiful Wedgwood tureen.
"Uncle John, this is mussel, clam, and wild rice chowder with minced garlic and parsley. This isn't *soup*!"
"My apologies to the chef. Please pass me the mussel, clam, and wild rice chowder with minced garlic and parsley."
"He learns fast," Aunt Anna smiled.

* * * * * *

Dolly and I helped clean up the kitchen; we did dishes, swept the floor and took out the trash. Notice I didn't say we put the leftovers back in the fridge!
Leftovers?
You gotta be kidding!
We flipped a coin to see who got in the shower first - Dolly won. So, I took that time to sort out what I was going to wear. After fourteen different ideas, I finally decided on my black peddle pushers, but then I remembered how much I loved wearing my circle skirt to the dance. It just moved and swished and it looked great when I was dancing!

So, I forgot about the peddle pushers and opted to wear my white circle skirt, complete with black and pink poodle appliqués. My white shirt with the Peter Pan collar, and my black waist-cincher, and of course, my saddle oxfords.

Dolly was also wearing a skirt tonight. She went shopping with Nikki earlier in the week and picked it up at Pfeiffer's. I loved it! It was a red circle skirt that had sequined 45 rpm records sewn on to it. It was so cool. She was wearing a crinoline underneath it that had two inches worth of red lace edging all around the bottom of it. She was also wearing a waist cincher, in black, with a really pretty opened collared blouse. And, best of all, there would be no neck scarf tonight!

Not that Dolly and I didn't think they were really cool to wear, they were. But after the hickey incident, she was happy to have her neck freed up for a change.

"Did I bring my saddle oxfords?" Dolly entered the room wearing her blue terrycloth robe with a matching towel wrapped around her head.

"Yup. There in the closet."

"Whew! I thought I forgot them! I can't move my dancin' feet without my dancin' shoes," she smiled.

I headed into the bathroom while Dolly changed into her Civic Center clothes. By the time I got back she was drying her hair in front of the window fan. It was a lot faster than my clunky old hair-dryer, I'll tell you that!

"You know Jack's not picking me up here, right?"

"I remember. What was the story again?"

"Well, he says he's busy. Basically that's it."

"Busy with what?"

"Who knows?"

Dolly continued to talk to me as she brushed her hair dry in front of the fan. "I see what he is, Pat."

"And that is..."

"He's a jerk."

"I'll say."

"I made a real bad judgment with him. I've... well, I've learned a lot watching you and Brenda."

"You mean, by watching me and Brenda with George and Clark."

"That's what I meant."

"As long as you learn Dolly, it's not a mistake. And as long as you don't backslide. It's all a process to help you grow in the right direction."

"I'm a fast learner. Well, maybe not as fast as Uncle John was with the mussel, clam, and wild rice chowder with minced garlic and parsley, but..."

I chuckled.

"I'm going to tell him tonight that whatever it is that we are. We're over."

"Really?!"
"Really."
"Well, good for you!"
She moved away from the fan and brushed her hair back into a pony tail. "I have some more stuff I want to tell you too, if you don't mind. You know stuff like I said to you the other week... things I need to talk to someone about."
"You can count on me, Doll."
"Thanks, Pattie."
I had just enough time to get a quick shower and get ready for the dance. George and Clark would show up right on time and I didn't want to be late! Poor Clark, I knew that he'd be missing Brenda terribly, but he had lots of friends at the dance to keep his spirits up; not that any of them would ever replace my Brenda Ethel Mayberry, but you know what I mean.
As I readied myself for the dance, Dolly and I shared my dresser mirror. Well, it was a huge makeup mirror as far as I was concerned. Good lighting from the window, nice clean glass, and two pounds of makeup sitting in a bag right in front of it!
Teenage heaven!
"What color is that lipstick. Pat? I like it."
"Hot Pompano Pink from Helena Rubenstein."
"Hot Pompano Pink? I think I've heard of that before."
"All the girls in Philly wear it. I even read that Franny Giordano and Arlene Sullivan from Bandstand wear it. It's their favorite color!"
"Well, if it's good enough for Franny and Arlene, then it's good enough for us!"
"Girls! Oh, Girls!" Aunt Anna's sweet voice called to us. "George and Clark are here!"
"Time to make our grand entrance, Miss Dollio."
"How do I look?" She swished her skirt a bit and I could see a bit of the crinoline with the pretty red lace edging.
"You look like a million bucks."
"Honest?"
"Honest."

Chapter Sixty-Three

We entered The Civic Center just after 7:30 and the place was already packed! I could hardly believe it!

Little Richard's 'Long Tall Sally' was playing and, as they say, the joint was jumpin.'

The VanSants were there, Bobby Phillips, Billy Rual, Luke Cramer, The Bushnells, The Bitner kids, The Garritys, and lots of faces I didn't know.

"Oh... my... GOD!" Dolly gasped.

"What?! What is it?"

"Look over there, in that black pencil skirt, with the pale blue sweater set and the silver circle pin."

Leave it to a teenage girl to go for the full description.

"It's... it's..."

"WHO?"

"It's Franny Giordano!"

"From Bandstand?!"

"YESSSSSS!!! Look... over there!!!"

My eyes made a clean sweep of The Civic Center from left to right, and lo and behold, there right in front of my very eyes, not twenty feet to my left, danced the very blonde and very beautiful sweetheart of American Bandstand... Miss Franny Giordano. And, to top that off, I swear that was Hot Pompano Pink by Helena Rubenstein on those lips!

"Well, would you look at that!" I said with a huge grin on my face, "Are we like the 'in-crowd' now or what?!"

Dolly and I took to the floor with Clark and George and we danced out the rest of Little Richard's song. Then, along came "The Stroll" and we all lined up on the floor and did our best "Strollin'." Dolly and I were in the same line with Franny, so we did our best to be hip.

As I finished my stroll down the floor, Franny smiled at me. Dolly soon followed and Franny gave her a nod.

Over the music, Dolly called to Franny, "It's so cool to have you here!"

"I heard about this place last week, so me and my friend hopped on the bus!"

"How do you like it?"

"It's great!" she smiled.

"I *love* your outfit," Dolly continued.

Franny smiled again.

"And I love your lipstick. What color is it?"

"WHAT?!" Franny hollered over the music.

"I LOVE YOUR LIPSTICK! WHAT COLOR IS IT?"

"OH! IT'S HOT POMPANO PINK!"

Dolly turned toward me with eyes as big as saucers. "Didja hear that?!"

"I sure did!"

"The end to a perfect day, Pattie!" She grinned.

No sooner were those words spoken, the song was over, and Jack Dawkins entered the room.

"Well, almost a perfect day," I sighed.

"Huh?"

"Look who's comin'."

Dolly rolled her eyes. "Oh, brother."

Jack breezed by us with his usual charming, "Yo!" and went to buy himself a soda.

What a swell guy.

"Twilight Time" by The Platters started to play, and George asked me to dance. Clark asked Dolly, she said yes, but then had second thoughts when she saw Jack walking back from the concession stand. "Wait, Clark, I…"

Immediately The Artful Dodger pulled Dolly by her shirt sleeve right out onto the dance floor, and then he pushed himself up against her like a second skin. Dolly pushed him away a bit and then they danced at a safer distance from each other. I'm sure Jack didn't like that too much, but there were too many adults around for him to raise a fuss - so he didn't.

George was thoroughly disgusted by the entire scene but I asked him not to say anything. That's all we'd need, a rumble of sorts in sweet old Townsends Inlet, New Jersey – Oh, nooooo, not with Franny Giordano here! I decided to take the matter into my own hands after the song was over and Dolly moved back into a safety net called Pattie Townsend.

Jack immediately moved over toward Dolly and started on her about pushing him away. That was ALL I could take! "Listen, Jack. If Dolly doesn't want to dance with you like you're simulating sex, that's her right to say no and move away from you."

He looked at me with that stern face of his, eyes trying to pierce through to my very soul.

I didn't budge. "I mean it! Back off!"

A slow smile washed across his face. "I liked that, Pat."

"Liked what?"

"I liked the way you said, 'sex'."

"You're a pig." I turned on my heels as quickly as I could and Dolly and I walked as far away from him as we possibly could without actually leaving the building.

What a slug.

"That's it! I'm tellin' him the minute this dance is over. I'm not his *girlfriend*, I'm not *anything* to him because I don't want to be linked to a jerk like that!"

I patted her on the shoulder. "Good for you."

"I'd do it now but he'd cause a stink and I don't want to ruin it for everyone else."

I nodded.

"He won't be back here at The Civic Center again," Dolly said. "I can tell you that much!"

I was so proud of her.

So was George.

So was Clark.

Our little girl was finally growing up!

Jack asked Dolly to dance on a few other occasions, but she refused. I saw him try to strong arm her once, but she got away and she danced with me. Then she danced with George, Clark, Bobby, Sally VanSant, and... Dolly even jitterbugged once with our 'Hot Pompano Pink' sister, Franny Giordano! Jack apparently easily found some solace in another sweet, ordinary girl, named Dale Harding, another nice kid from Townsends Inlet. She was a senior in the local High school.

Wake up, Dale!
Wake UP!!!

Chapter Sixty-Four

The dance wound down to its last two numbers, a fast one by The Everly Brothers and the usual evening ender, "Goodnight Sweetheart."

Dolly bravely marched over to Jack and told him that she wanted to talk to him. I was happy for her. She was finally realizing the importance of being true to herself. I had a feeling it would be a long hard road, but, she was willing to make the trip, and that's what counted in the end. My eyes followed Jack as he walked out of the building to light up a cigarette.

"Are you gonna be all right?" George asked her as she walked back into our invisible safety net.

"Yep."

You're sure you don't want us there? Clark's concern was etched all over his face.

"I'd feel better if you were, but this is something I have to do by myself."

I nodded my head and sighed.

Just then I heard Uncle John's voice announce the end of our dance, and the lights went back on in The Civic Center.

The four of us walked out the door. We all looked around for Jack but I was the first to spot him.

Lucky me.

There he was, leaning up against the side of the building right across the street from us. The moment he saw me he lit up another cigarette, and then stared in my direction with a look of cool defiance on his face.

Such arrogance.

"Wish me luck, guys." Dolly's voice sounded nervous and apprehensive.

"Please let me go with you," I said softly.

"Pattie, I can handle this guy. I'll be all right."

"Dolly, if…" George started.

"I'll be fine, George."

"If he even lays a *hand* on you…" Clark's voice sounded worried.

"I'll be *okay*, Clark. No sweat." Dolly gave us a well rehearsed smile and crossed the street to meet up with Jack.

"I'll be waiting for you on the back porch!" I called out. "Don't be too long!"

Dolly turned and nodded.

About a hundred kids filed out past us, to include Franny Giordano, but we never even took notice. The three of us had our eyes glued on Jack and Dolly, who were now walking up toward the 85th Street Pavilion.

"DON'T BE TOO LONG!" I shouted one more time. Dolly turned

and waved.

"Why is she walking anywhere with that guy?" George questioned.

"She probably wants to get him away from the crowd, you know, so she can handle this privately."

"Well, it's a bad idea." Clark started to walk up the street to follow them when George pulled his arm back and stopped him.

"I know how you feel. But let her do what she has to do."

Clark grumbled something under his breath.

Within three short minutes, there was no one left outside The Civic Center, except me, George, and Clark. The last streetlight before the Pavilion made it possible to see Jack and Dolly, still making their way toward the end of 85th Street. Suddenly the bright overhead lights outside the Center were turned off and I knew Uncle John would soon be on his way out of the building.

"We better get goin', guys."

"Yeah, okay," George's voice was almost a whisper as his thoughts preoccupied him.

As we walked toward my house, every now and then one of us would turn back, hoping to see Dolly running toward us - but it didn't happen..

"Wanna stay here for a while and wait?" I asked as we reached the front steps.

George and Clark nodded and then... we just sat there. Not too much was said except for a "I wish she'd get back here", and a "Yeah."

That was about it until Uncle John turned down the walkway.

"Well, hello you young rock and rollers!" He smiled. "Where's our Dolly girl?"

"Umm... she's talking to someone... she'll be back here any minute!" I tried to smile.

Uncle John nodded. "Did you all have a good time tonight?"

The three of us engaged in a conversation of sorts with my Uncle about what a great time we all had. I mean, we *did* have a wonderful time, it was just that we had our minds elsewhere.

"Well, you youngsters enjoy the nice evening. I need my beauty sleep."

Uncle John smiled, ruffled the top of my hair, and then disappeared into the house.

"Nice guy." George nodded.

"He sure is."

Clark looked at his watch. "10:50."

"Where *is* she?!" George stood and started to walk back up the street.

"George! She wouldn't want you to do that! Come on back here and sit for a while. Dolly'll be here."

Reluctantly George sat back down on the front steps to the Turner household. The three of us, normally would be talking about everything under the sun, but tonight? Well, the entire conversation consisted of: "What a jerk that guy is!", "Where *is* she?", and "What *time* is it?"

We sat until Clark's watch read 11:30.

"That's it! We have to walk up to the pavilion!" George was adamant.

Clark and I agreed.

Our usual leisurely walk was more like a hard sprint and we made it to the pavilion in record time.

No Dolly.

No Jack.

"Where in the *hell* are they?" George said as he walked past the swing set and over a large sand dune.

Clark walked about fifty feet in the opposite direction. "Well, they aren't here!"

I walked down to the beach and headed toward the inlet. "Not here!" I called back.

The three of us met back at the pavilion.

"What time is it now?"

Clark checked his watch. "Almost midnight."

The three of us decided to walk along the beachfront one more time.

"Maybe she decided it was too late to go to your place and she just walked home," Clark sounded hopeful.

"No, she wouldn't do that… would she?"

"Maybe," George shrugged his shoulders. "You know Dolly. She had to be upset after talking to that creep, and she probably didn't want to show up on your back porch and fall to pieces."

Clark seemed to agree. "She'll come over in the morning, apologize for worrying you, and then tell you what happened."

I stopped for a moment and looked back toward Dolly's house and the far end of the Inlet.

"I guess so."

A soft ocean breeze blew around us and I felt the night air begin to chill.

"Let's go," George said.

"Yeah… okay."

Suddenly the wind from the inlet really started to pick up and some wet seaweed flew right onto my shoes. I picked it up and tossed it haphazardly a few feet behind me.

It landed right next to a torn white crinoline.

…with red lace edging.

Chapter Sixty-Five

"What time is it now?"

Clark looked at his watch once again. "12:20."

"You guys better go."

"Pat?"

George's voice seemed far away and wrapped in a fog.

"PAT!" he called again as I walked toward the back of the house.

"Sorry... what is it?"

"Can you two meet us for dinner at The Charcoal House tomorrow night? Like, seven o'clock?"

"What?"

"Pat, *you* and Dolly. Can you meet us at The Charcoal House tomorrow at seven?"

"Sure... that'll be..." My mind was elsewhere. "I mean..."

"Are you okay?"

"Yeah, George, I'm okay. I just..."

I never finished my sentence. I don't even remember if we said goodnight to each other. I don't even recall how I made it up the steps and into the back porch. I was worried sick about Dolly and I knew I'd have absolutely no peace of mind whatsoever until I saw her again.

I walked into the kitchen and poured myself a soda and then sat out on the porch. I rocked in that old wicker chair until I felt sea sick.

My God... what time is it?!

I walked back into the kitchen and looked at the clock. It was barely visible in the dim light, but I could still read it.

1:16!

I decided the rest of my evening would be spent working on some old crossword puzzles I never got to finish. I wouldn't disturb anyone because out on the back porch was a tiny reading light for just that purpose - Aunt Anna thought of everything.

As I was gathering a pencil or two I heard a noise coming from the backyard. It sounded as if a metal can had fallen over. My first thought was that it could be Mrs. Orwatt's wandering tabby cat, who often visited our fish-boned garbage pail late in the evening.

I scurried to the back door. "Fritz! Get outta here!"

I turned to place my puzzle books on the small end table next to the rocker... again the strange noise disturbed me.

Definitely not a cat.

A small yet piercing sound...

Like a cry of some sort...

Like an injured animal...

I turned on the outside light, and there, lying right at the bottom of the stairs leading up to the back porch was Dolly. I ran down the steps as fast as I could and crouched down beside her.

"My God! What *happened* to you?!" I stretched my arms across her body and she flinched in pain. "Dolly!" my voice trembled, "Answer me!!!"

She turned quickly and grabbed onto my arms as if her life depended on it.

"Talk to me!!!" I cried out.

"He... he..."

"Jack?"

"Yeah..."

"He what?!"

Her hands started to shake violently.

"HE what, Dolly?!! Jack what?!!"

She put her hands over her face and started to cry all over again.

"Talk to me, Doll!

"He... he raped me, Pattie!"

"HE WHAT?!!"

"Jack raped me!!!"

Chapter Sixty-Six

I helped Dolly up the stairs and then sat her in the cushioned love seat right next to the rocker. "Hang on, I'll get you some water."

I ran to the sink as fast as I could and filled a large glass right to the brim. My hands were trembling so much I was afraid I'd drop it. I was an absolute wreck. I walked back onto the porch and Dolly was shaking all over. I quickly covered her with the soft over-sized afghan that Aunt Anna had made.

"Better?"

"Yeah," she answered, still shaking. "B-B-B-Better."

"Take a sip of water."

When she reached for the glass, I didn't know whose hands were trembling more, Dolly's or mine.

"Thanks, Pat." She said softly.

When I sat down on the floor in front of her I noticed some of her blouse buttons were missing, her eye make-up was smeared, and her legs were cut and bruised. "Listen to me. Whatever it takes to help you, I'll do it."

Dolly looked into my eyes and she lost it. Her words came in-between sobs and gasps for air. I never saw anyone in this kind of distress in my entire life and I prayed to the heavens for the strength to help her in the way she needed it.

"I told him I didn't want to see him again, then... then he called me a liar. He... he said the fact... the fact that I wanted to talk to him late at night after the dance was..."

"Was what?"

"Well, like I... like I was giving out a different message. That I..."

She started to cry again.

"That you what?"

"That I was comin' on to him... that I was just playing some stupid chick game and..."

I handed her a handkerchief and she dried her eyes.

"And I was so... so disgusted. I mean... what an arrogant bastard! I said to him, 'You think that you're something worth having?!'"

"Then ?"

"He grabbed my arm and pushed me up against some old pick-up truck and... and he kissed me... real hard... real sloppy..."

Dolly's confession made my head start to pound. I wanted to run up to the medicine cabinet and swallow ten Bayer aspirins, but I didn't want to leave her.

"I told him he was hurting me, then he asked if any of my other boyfriends liked it rough."

"Liked it rough?"

"Yeah. Then he grabbed me again… on my chest. Some buttons ripped off my blouse. I was so scared and I started to run away. I *thought* I was running back toward your house, but… but I was so confused and it was… it was just so dark that I was really running toward the beach."

"You poor thing."

"I tried to yell out to someone, but I could hardly catch my breath. I just remember running and running over the sand. It was so hard to do… you know… the sand…" She buried her head in her hands. "The sand just kept gettin' deeper and it slowed me down." Again she broke down and cried. She wiped her eyes once more and continued, "I finally realized I was near the Inlet and that I could turn up 95th Street. The streetlights were all on and he'd be afraid to bother me in public."

"Then what happened?"

"I fell over a horseshoe crab or something, I remember hearing my crinoline tear… and then my hands were full of sand and seaweed."

"Where was Jack?"

"I thought I was well ahead of him, but… but when I fell he caught up to me. Just when I was getting up again, he tackled me to the ground… and he… he laughed."

"That bastard!"

"God, Pat… it sounded like something out of a real scary movie… his voice… it was… it was frightening."

I dropped my head into my chest and started to cry.

"I'm sorry, I'm so sorry, Pattie! Don't cry. Please don't cry."

"Dolly, for God's sake, don't be sorry for me! Talk!"

"I… I…"

"Talk!"

"I… I remember him ripping at my blouse again and… and I felt his teeth bite into my chest and…"

"His *teeth*?!"

"Uh-huh. And then his hands seemed everywhere."

"That pig."

"And I felt him rip my underwear off and… and then I started to get sick. I tried to scream but he put his hands over my mouth."

"The son-of-a…!"

"He said something like, 'You think you're gonna give it up to all those other guys and leave Jack Dawkins without somethin'? Think again!'"

"Dear God."

"I kept shaking my head trying to move his hand away from my face… I tried to bite him. Then… then when…"

"When what?"

"When he sat up to undo his pants I remember that I was rambling things like… 'I lied, I never had any boyfriends, not ever, you were the first date I ever had. I never had sex with anyone!!! No one!!! I'm a virgin!!! Please get off me!!! PLEASE GET OFF ME!!!!!!!'"

Dolly broke down again and I cried right along with her.

When she found the strength, she continued, "He didn't listen to me, Pat. He didn't care. I remember closing my eyes and praying for someone to help me: God... my mother... Buddha... The Coast Guard... George... Clark... *you*..." She put her hands in front of her face and rocked back and forth, crying. "Then... then I felt this... this really sharp pain up inside me. It felt like I was being cut open."

I quickly shook the visual out of my head.

"Then I heard him make some noises, like... well, some grunting sounds. His smelly sweat was dripping on my face. And then, all of a sudden, I felt all wet and sticky and... and sandy and bruised and sore. Then he stood over me, I remember hearing the zipper noise from his pants... it sounded... it sounded like it was magnified a million times. I felt sick and real dizzy. Then... then he laughed and said he always likes to leave his girls with a nice remembrance of him. 'Beaches are always so romantic', he said to me and then he laughed again... that ugly, horrible laugh."

"The sick son of a..."

"I don't even remember when he left me, Pat. All of a sudden he was gone and I was left on the beach like some... some piece of garbage. I felt so sick that I threw up. I ran to the ocean and I got sick again and then I... I just stood there and screamed and screamed. I kept holding my stomach and... and... I FEEL SO FILTHY!!!! I FEEL SO DIRTY!!!!"

Dolly frantically started to rip at her clothes, she kicked off her shoes, she pulled the tie out of her ponytail.

"Dolly, Dolly!!! Wait, wait!!!" I was beside myself as I watched her start to lose all control. "Let me walk you upstairs, get you a hot shower..." My voice was calm and serene, totally unlike what I was feeling at the moment. "I'll bring your clothes in to you, everything'll be all right. I'll take good care of you. Everything is gonna be all right. I mean it."

"Nothing's ever gonna be right again, Pattie! Nothing!" She dropped to her knees and cried.

"Dolly, just trust me," I said helping her back onto her feet. "I'll make sure everything is okay. I promise."

She pushed her hair away from her face. "And what if..." Again she started to cry.

"What, Doll? What is it?"

"Pattie... what if I'm pregnant?"

Oh, my God! What if she's pregnant?!

Chapter Sixty-Seven

I walked Dolly to the bathroom and sat her down on the little chair by the linen closet.
"I'll be right back, okay?"
"Okay," she nodded.
I ran into my room and took her pajamas out of her sleep-over bag. Then, as I started to run back toward the bathroom, I stopped. I realized I had forgotten her robe and slippers. Once again I headed toward my bedroom. My heart was racing a mile a minute as I retrieved the needed items. I took a deep breath and then hurried back to the bathroom. As I passed by Aunt Anna's and Uncle John's bedroom door I thought how grateful I was that they finally bought an air conditioner. Uncle John picked it up in Sea Isle early in '58. Their door was closed and the mind-numbing hum of that big General Electric cooler kept them from hearing any of the ruckus. Thank heaven for that!

I walked back into the bathroom and started the shower for Dolly. I figured it would be best if she rinsed herself off first and then she could unwind afterward in a nice hot bubble bath. I was certain that every muscle in her body was tied up in knots. I handed her a face cloth and a body sponge and then turned my back to her as she undressed.

I heard the shower curtain open and then close again.
"Is that warm enough for you?" I asked taking a seat on the small chair Dolly had previously occupied.
"It's... it's very nice. Thanks, Pat."

I sat there and the water ran and ran and ran. Dolly took the longest shower I have ever known anyone to take. But then, she was washing away Jack Dawkins. I wouldn't have blamed her if she stayed in there for a month!

Suddenly, the shower was turned off and I heard the bath begin to fill. The sweet perfume of some Yardley Bubble Bath took over the room.
"How are you feeling, Doll?"
"Better, Pattie. Thanks."
"Want me to get you something to drink and then we can talk when you're done?"
"A coke, please?"
"One Coca-Cola comin' right up!"

I walked down the steps and quickly rummaged through the dining room for one of Aunt Anna's breakfast trays. I found exactly what I wanted and then filled it with a few cookies, two stray brownies, peanut butter crackers, two bottles of coke, a bottle opener, two glasses, and some ice.

Just as I had turned down the bed, and placed the tray in a sitting position, Dolly walked into the room. The first thing I noticed about her were some teeth marks about three inches below her neck.

I felt sick.

Dolly was still shaking as she reached for her soda and a few crackers.

I sat there and said nothing, but my mind was on overdrive.

After she'd eaten her crackers and drank half of her Coke, she sighed and looked me straight in the eye. "What do I do, Pat?"

I moved the tray and all its goodies to the dresser and then answered her, "I don't know." I thought for a second and then said, "Maybe you should go to the hospital."

"Then they'd call Dad and Nikki. I don't want that!"

"How 'bout the police?"

"Same thing," she sighed. "Dad... Nikki..."

"Then whadda we do? Go over to this jerk's house and beat the crap out of him?"

"Hold that thought." She sighed again.

"Doll, I don't know what to tell you. I mean..."

"What?"

"I mean I never knew anyone who was... you know... I was never told what to do when... when someone gets..."

"I know. I wasn't either. You think they'd tell us something about this in Health Class, wouldn't you?"

"People don't think this stuff'll ever happen. You know, the old, if you don't talk about it, it'll just go away all on its own."

"Well, surprise, surprise." Dolly shook her head.

"Yeah, I'll say."

I left the room briefly to gather Dolly's clothes from the bathroom and straighten up a bit, when I came back, and she saw those dirty, sandy clothes in my hands, it triggered the evening all over again.

"It was my fault!" she cried.

"No! It was *not* your fault!"

"But, he thought I did it before... That I had sex because of..."

"Dolly, stop!"

"Because I lied about it!"

"Please, just stop that!"

"No, Pattie, I... I mean... I..."

"What?"

"I never had five boyfriends. I never even had *one* boyfriend before Jack. I lied to you. And I..."

"Don't torture yourself with this, it's just..."

"No, Pat. Listen, I *never* had a hickey before either! I just wanted to feel cool and be liked and popular, so I told you all that stuff." Dolly rambled and rambled, "I don't *own* that Chevy Impala. It's Dad's car!"

"Forget about all that!"

186

"I don't even have a driver's license!" She started to cry all over again. "Since my Mom died, I go off into this… this stupid fantasy land where I can be happy because…"

She so desperately needed to vent, and so I finally helped her along.

"Because why, Doll?"

"Because real life is *so* awful, Pattie! I *hate* it! I can't… I can't deal with the pain… I just *can't* deal with anything!" Again she sobbed. Her heartache was tearing her soul apart and I could feel it right along with her. "I'm not crazy, Pat. It might seem that way but…"

"Dolly…"

"My mom was wonderful. I was *happy*! I felt *safe*… *loved*… Know what I mean?" She wiped her hands across her eyes.

"Yes."

"I wish you coulda met her, Pat."

"I do, too, Doll."

Dolly took a deep breath to calm herself. "And my dad…"

"Yeah?"

"He was always a… what's the word? A… a womanizer! That's what he is. He was always a jerk - just like Dawkins. How do you think he got Nikki?"

I held my hands to the side of my head as if I could push my headache away.

"You think Nik just appeared out of the blue a month after mom died? I'm not that naive, Pat… and neither are you."

"Dolly, pleeeease, don't *do* this to yourself! You need to vent, but this isn't your fault. None of this is. I'm serious."

"No, Pat. If I had my feet on the ground like you did, tonight would have never happened." She started to cry again. "I never had all of those jobs on the boardwalk. Well, yeah, I had a few, but the hours I had to keep taking care of the house and the kids tired me out so much that I had a hard time doing a good job, and I got fired!"

"Fired?"

"Fired from every one of them… every single one. And I *needed* to work to have money to buy clothes for myself. I really don't have *anything*. Dad's money goes to the house, Apry and Mack, Nikki, the car, and alcohol. Remember those girls on the boardwalk when me and you and Brenda were out together? When they said something about my clothes, and I really looked nice?"

My eyes were beginning to fill. "Yeah."

"Well, that was 'cause I never looked nice in school. I was like some ragamuffin. I was always in leftovers from Nikki or old stuff of mine that I had to let the hem down on. I looked nice that night on the boardwalk 'cause I stole that new blouse out of Nikki's closet. And then she caught me when I came home!"

I wiped the tears from my eyes.

"I'm a liar and a fake, Pat."
"Dolly..."
"I am. I'm whatever the situation calls for. And look where it got me?! Look what *happened* to me?!!" Again she sobbed.
"Dolly..."
"I don't have a life! And I don't have any chance of gettin' one either. My Dad..."
"What about him?"
"He... he takes forty dollars from me *every* week. I never have any money for myself. And I work like a dog around that house."
"Forty dollars?!"
"I'll *never* be able to save for school... for a car... for anything! I'm trapped. And that's just the way they want it! And the first week I was at Shellum's?"
"Yeah?"
"I even lied to them and told Dad and Nik that Shellum's held a week's pay so that I could have a good time with you and Brenda, so... so I could treat you guys and look important so I'd fit in. God, I'm such a mess! I just wanna die! I JUST WANNA DIE!!!" She grabbed a pillow from behind her and cried into it. "How can you *like* me, Pattie? How can you ever *trust* me? I've ruined *everything!*" She pulled the pillow to her face and again she cried. "And what if I'm pregnant? What if I'm *pregnant?!*"

"Don't even think about that right now, okay? We'll cross that bridge if and when we come to it." I looked over toward my clock radio and the time read 3:45! I repositioned a few pillows for my friend and made her as comfortable as possible. "Get some rest. We got plenty of time to talk all weekend."

"Do you hate me, Pattie?" She sniffled. "I'll understand if you do."

"I don't hate you," I answered softly. "You're my friend. You'll *always* be my friend."

"Will I?"

"Yes, you will. Now get some sleep."

I heard her whimper a few more times and then somehow, sleep overtook her. I was praying that she would sleep well and that tonight with Jack Dawkins wouldn't be a nightmare she couldn't shake - once again.

Truly, my heart went out to her. I didn't hate Dolly because she lied to me and to Brenda and Nikki. Dolly was the product of many unhappy endings.

Too many.

She was an accident waiting to happen. She watched her mother suffer from breast cancer when she was barely in grade school. And certainly her Mom's struggle to live day by day by day took its toll on both of them. Her Mom put on many a brave face as she tried to shield Dolly from the physical pain her breast cancer caused. She never hid the disease from her, that would have been impossible anyway... but she constantly hid the pain.

"*Does it hurt you, Mommy?*"
"*No, Dolly. I'm just fine.*"
"*You'll wake up tomorrow... won't you Mommy?*"
"*Of course, I will, Sweetheart... of course, I will.*"

To make matters worse, Dolly never had a chance to talk to anyone about how her mother's illness affected her. It was all hush-hush within the family. And then, right after her mother's death, well... the Dollio's just closed the book on that one. The family stopped talking about it, her dad easily moved on, and Dolly was ordered to do the same.

How wrong is that?!

How could anyone dismiss the affect of such heartache on a young child?

How could anyone not acknowledge the pain she suffered when she lost her mother?

How could they not see the long term damage that their apathy was causing?

How?

Who knows...

But they did.

Chapter Sixty-Eight

I guess Aunt Anna knew we had a really late evening. I'm sure Uncle John told her I was sitting out front with George and Clark, waiting for Dolly, so she let us sleep.

When I managed to eyeball my clock radio, it was already 11:00.

Dolly was all snuggled up in bed, snoring away, so I tiptoed out of the room. I got dressed, walked down into the kitchen, poured myself a glass of orange juice and then reached for a freshly-made blueberry muffin.

There was a note on the table for me.

Pattie,
If you need me, I'm out in the garden!
Love,
Aunt Anna.
P.S. And your favorite disc-jockey went fishing. Surprised?

I walked out onto the back porch, down the steps, and into the garden. And there, right in front of me, was Aunt Anna cutting off some roses for the dinner table.

"You're a regular romantic, Mrs. Turner," I smiled.

"Aren't these lovely?" She stood there and took in the beautiful aroma from some lovely orangey-pink colored roses.

"They sure are!"

"Is Dolly awake?"

"No, but pretty soon."

"Well, I guess with two young children in the house it's a rare treat for her to sleep in late."

I nodded.

"Well, let her enjoy her rest."

If she only knew.

After we came back into the house I helped Aunt Anna dust the living room and fold some laundry. Just about the time we were setting up for lunch, Dolly walked down the steps.

"Geez. I'm so sorry I slept so late. I never…"

"Don't give it a second thought," my Aunt smiled. "Now sit down here and let's get you a nice, yummy, breakfast."

In nothing flat Aunt Anna served up three fresh waffles, orange juice, and a hot cup of tea. Dolly was a tea drinker, and so was my aunt. Aunt Anna had the prettiest teapots; I guess that was her hobby. Not that she had hundreds all over the house, but she had a big china cabinet filled with about two dozen of the most beautiful tea pots any one had ever made - five from England, three from France and others from Sweden and Germany and Ireland. And, Mrs. Turner was no tea bag user, either… nope, not my Aunt Anna! She'd buy special tea leaves up in Sea Isle City, and put them inside a little silver perforated ball and then, when the water would boil, she'd pour it into the tea pot, drop in the little tea ball, put the lid on it, then she'd cover the whole pot with something they call a Tea Cozy - kinda like a big mitten for a tea pot. It kept the tea nice and hot and, well, it looked pretty, too. Aunt Anna had dozens of different tea cozies, all for different seasons and occasions. And, of course, she knitted or crocheted every single one of them herself. You would be hard-pressed to find a handier, sweeter, or more talented woman on the planet!

"Breakfast is delicious, Mrs. Turner. I usually just eat cereal when I'm home."

"Well, enjoy!" Aunt Anna smiled. "Would you like some more waffles, Dear?"

"No, thank you. Three is plenty!"

I sat down next to Dolly and drank a little more orange juice.

"Wanna go to John's Pier after you eat? We can talk up there."

"Okay."

"Aunt Anna?"

"What is it, Pat?"

"Can I skip lunch with you today? I wanted to go up the pier with Dolly."

"Sure, that's okay. Will you be home for dinner?"

"What time do you want us home?"

"Well, I wanted to eat earlier today because of your Charcoal House gathering."

"Then we'll be back around three-thirty or so, okay?"

My Aunt smiled. "Sounds good. I'll see you girls then." Aunt Anna put her gardening gloves back on, smiled at us, and then headed out the back door.

"What a wonderful woman," Dolly said.

"I'll say!"

Doll and I cleaned off the table and did the few dishes that were there from breakfast, then we left out the front door, and walked down the street to take the shortcut to John's Pier. We walked passed Susie Wells' house, and waved to her Mom as she was rocking on the porch, said "Hi" to Bobby Phillips on his way to the beach, and before we knew it, we were walking up the boards to the pier.

"Wanna ice cream cone?" I asked.

"I'd love one - chocolate."

"You want jimmies on it, Doll?"

"Please."

We stood at the small walk-up window and our orders were taken.

"Two chocolates with jimmies on a sugar cone comin' right up!"

In the bat of an eye two Jane Logan chocolate ice cream cones with jimmies were being handed out to us.

"That'll be twenty cents, please, Pat."

I handed Katie Hudson a quarter and then she handed me back my change.

"Thanks, K."

"You're welcome, Pat!"

Cones in hand, Dolly and I walked by several fisherman about to take their boats out for an afternoon catch. We also noticed some of the local crabbers' little rowboats heading to shallow waters, and a few families who were taking their kids out for a joy ride around the inlet. It looked like fun. John's Pier was always hustling and bustling, but in a laid back way. Know what I mean?

Dolly and I took a seat on the left hand side of the pier - facing Avalon.

"It's pretty here, isn't it?"

I nodded. "I love this place."

"You think it'll stay like this?"

"You mean will progress ever meet Sleepy Town, U.S.A.?"

"Yeah."

"If you'd ask me, and you just did... big buildings and glamorous homes belong in the city. This is laid back and easy."

"Yeah, nice."

Dolly and I sat there and finished our ice cream without much mention of what happened the night before. I was worried if I initiated anything it would trigger a panic attack or some uncontrollable crying. So, we talked about the fisherman, the boats, the people on water skis, and then Dolly said, "I need to talk to you. You know, to finish what I started last night."

"You're ready for that?"

"Yeah."

She took in a breath so deep I thought her lungs would burst. "Pat? I'm so sorry I lied to you. I'm sorry I've... well, I'm just all screwed up."

"Doll, I lost my Mom and Dad not even two months ago. I understand how it hurts."

"But you never lost *you*, Pat. You never lied. You talk about your parents, you have Aunt Anna... you get it all out of your system. I wasn't allowed to reach out to anybody."

I nodded. "That's a shame."

"You know what my Dad said to me the day after mom's funeral?"

"What?"

"He said 'If anyone starts to talk about your mother, say you don't want to hear it.'"

"What?"

"Yep. Then I said, 'But I *want* to talk about Mommy!' And then my father said, 'She's dead and leave her dead. Move on, it's what she would want.'"

"Man, what a guilt trip that must've put on you."

"Yeah, 'cause I felt that Dad knew her better than I did. And if he said she'd want me to move on then I should. But I couldn't, Pattie. I had so many questions. I missed her. I wanted to hear her voice. I wanted her to tuck me in bed at night."

My eyes slowly filled with tears.

"I wanted to talk to someone about the good times I had with her. I wanted my memories to live. But it never happened. She died, and all of a sudden it was like she never existed… like I never even had a mother. Her pictures were removed, her clothes went to the Salvation Army, and then Dad started to bar-hop."

This poor girl.

"And I was left to make my own breakfast, lunch and dinner, do the dishes, wash and iron my clothes… and… and tuck my own self in at night." Dolly started to cry. "I was so lonely, Pattie. And I… I was only ten years old. What did he expect from me?"

I nodded, tears still welling in my eyes.

"So, since I couldn't be my real self, I decided I'd be who I needed to be." She bowed her head and I heard her whisper, "So stupid, huh?" Then Dolly looked me right in the eye. "I mean, I could've risen above it all. *You* did! I coulda talked to myself in a way that would have healed me. Couldn't I?"

I sniffled. "That would've been pretty hard work for a ten-year-old, dontcha think?"

She shrugged her shoulders.

"You just needed a real friend, Doll… and you didn't have one."

Dolly wiped some tears from her eyes. "Pat?"

"Yeah?"

"Even if you didn't have Brenda, wouldn't you have been able to be your own best friend? I mean, people *can* be their own best friend, can't they?"

I nodded again. "Sure they can. Actually, they should be."

"I *have* to get my life together. If last night wasn't enough reason to see where I'm headed, then…"

"I'll help you."

Dolly ran her hands across her eyes to wipe the tears away.

"It's all about one step at a time, Doll. One day at a time. Deal with it right away as it comes in. And as for those miserable s.o.b.'s in your past, like those creepy girls on the boardwalk, or Jack Dawkins… you hold your head high. Re-invent yourself."

"Re-invent?"

"Yep. Believe that life is worth living and your belief will help create the fact."

She smiled at me. "Brilliant!"

"Actually, I can't take the credit for that. The 'Belief that life is worth living' thing was a quote from William James, but it gets my point across."

"I'll say."

"Think, Doll. Go back to the person you once were. Remember her?"

"Yeah." Dolly's voice sounded small and faraway.

"What were you like back then?"

"Well… umm, I guess I was pretty smart. My mom taught me how to read before I was in Kindergarten."

"Really?"

"Yup. And I was funny, I laughed a lot. And… and Mom taught me how to play piano… and I liked to read and write stories. I sang a lot. I'm really a good singer, Pattie. I didn't lie to you about that!"

I smiled knowingly. "More, Dolly… think back."

"Well, I was always sensitive and kind. I always stuck up for people."

"That's a good quality." I smiled again.

"You know, my mom wore a leg brace for as long as I could remember and sometimes kids would stare at her 'cause she walked funny. I remember one kid at Dalrymple's who kept peeking around the corner of the bookstand, looking at Mom. I went right up to him and said, 'It's a pretty cool brace, isn't it? Mom keeps it nice and shiny!'"

"What did he say?"

"Nothin'. He just looked at me and sorta smiled."

"How did you feel?"

"I felt good. I let him know that this was my mom, she's got a brace, and so what?"

"This is what you need to do with your own life, Doll."

"I know."

"You're human. We *all* make mistakes now and then. But you're also a person who learned from them and you're moving on in a positive way. You're a kind-hearted, smart, sweet, and compassionate soul. Any person who wouldn't want to be your friend will be the one on the short end of things. I can tell you that!"

She looked out toward the inlet. "But what do I do if…"

"If that time comes, we'll talk about it. Don't worry about something until there's something to worry about."

"What about my Dad?"

"About how he treats you?"

"Yeah, and about me wanting to go to school and about having more of what I earn for myself."

"You need to talk to him and be truthful."

She sighed deeply. The word 'truthful' still seemed to give her the jitters.

"And listen to me," I said looking straight into her eyes, "if things ever get so bad that you feel you can't take it there, I'm a million percent certain that my Aunt Anna and Uncle John would help you in any way they could. That's who they are. They'd take you in. And you'll be eighteen on your next birthday anyway. Your freedom calls, Miss Dollio."

"But what about Mack and Apry?"

"What about them?"

"How can I leave them?"

I shook my head in disbelief. "Here's a better question. How can you not grow up?"

"What?"

"I mean, what are you gonna do, Doll? Wait until Mack is eighteen and on his own so you can feel deserving to leave? You're not their mother. You're their half-sister. Do you think staying there is the answer to happiness? You already know it isn't."

"But, they'll miss me."

"Do you think you're the only older sister on earth? You moved on without your own mother, Dolly! These kids can move on when their half-sister goes to college, gets her own place, and makes new friends. They'll be *proud* of you. On the other hand, how do you think they'll feel about you if they see you used as a doormat all of your life? I'll tell you what! They'll grow up and treat you the same way."

Dolly hid her face in her hands.

"Don't let fear control you, Doll. You'll get into a rut you'll never get out of."

She nodded. and wiped a few tears from her eyes.

"Listen, we *teach* people how to treat us, whether the words are spoken or not. It's… well, it's in the way we value ourselves that others learn how to value us back."

"William James?"

"No, actually, that was me."

Dolly smiled. "How did you ever get to be so smart, Pattie?"

"I learned to be my own best friend, Doll. It was as easy as that!"

Chapter Sixty-Nine

3:30 rolled around before we knew it, and we headed back home.
"What do I say if I see Jack again? What if he comes into the store?"
"I don't think we're gonna see 'The Prince of Darkness' hanging around the usual spots any time soon, Doll."
"But, what if...?"
"We'll do what has to be done. Remember?"
"I remember."
We walked about twenty steps and then suddenly Dolly turned to me and said, "Pat, do you think... ummm... that..."
"What is it?"
"Well, do you think someone like me could really go to college?"
"Of course, I do!"
"I mean, to study music and maybe be a music teacher or something like that?"
"You know I do! Why ask?"
"But how will I do it? How will I get tested to enter a good college? How will I get the money to go?"
"Tell ya what... we'll make this our pet project, okay? I have lots of stuff to do to get ready for school next year, anyway. We can do this together."
"So, do you think I can get into UCLA?"
"Why not?"
"Or maybe some other schools like Colorado or Texas or..."
"Dolly, I think you'll be able to do *anything* and go anywhere you want now that you're your own best friend."
"That's right!" she smiled at me, "Of course, I can!"
Atta girl!

* * * * * *

The minute we walked in the door the aroma of another dinner extraordinaire filled our senses.
"This woman should have her own cooking show!" Dolly took in the aroma wafting into the living room. "Wow, what's that she's making?"
Aunt Anna overheard Dolly's question and answered her straight away as we entered the kitchen.
"Hello, ladies! We're having an early dinner this evening, and, on our menu we have a Garden salad, fresh from our own garden I might add, and a Tenderloin of Beef with Horseradish Sauce, Shrimp Creole, shrimp courtesy of John Turner, creole courtesy of Anna Turner, some white rice, steamed Asparagus with toasted almonds, and fresh

buttermilk biscuits. *And*, since it's in season… peach cobbler with homemade vanilla ice cream. How's that sound?"

"It sounds like dinner at The Plaza Hotel, Mrs. Turner. How do you do it?"

"Well, Dolly, it's my passion. I *love* to cook. It's creative, it's nutritious, and it makes my family happy. We all sit around the table and have a good meal and good conversation. There's nothing like it!"

"Can I adopt you?"

I had to laugh. "There's a lot of that goin' around these days, Aunt Anna," I said recalling Brenda's similar compliment the previous week.

Aunt Anna smiled. "When you find your passion it isn't work. It's just fun! This dinner would seem like way too much fuss for lots of women, but not for me."

Dolly sighed. "I need a passion, Mrs. Turner."

"Well, what is it you like to do, Dear?"

"I like to play piano and I like to sing! I was just telling Pattie that I'd like to go to college next year to study music."

"Then do what it takes to make your dream come true. Think of all the children who would benefit from your love of music. Why, you could pass on that magic to hundreds, maybe thousands of children in your lifetime. And then those children would pass it along to their children, and so on and so on. Your love of music would outlast you! How about that?"

Dolly seemed rather pensive. "Geez, I never thought of it that way."

I smiled. "Are the lights goin' on in your head yet?"

"Like a night game at Fenway!"

* * * * * *

Dolly and I couldn't wait to get over to The Charcoal House. We were still kinda full from Aunt Anna's meal, but by the time we got to see George and Clark, we knew we'd be hungry again. Let's face it, there's no appetite like a teenage appetite.

Thinking about seeing the guys caused my mind to pick up speed and I asked Dolly, "Just *how* are you going to explain last night to the fellas? They're gonna ask!"

"I know."

"Well?"

"I'll give them part of the details. I can't tell anyone what really happened, Pat. And it's not because I'm in denial or that I wanna lie to them."

"Well, they were worried sick about you, the two of them stayed with me last night 'til… geez, 'til well after midnight."

Dolly shook her head. "I can't tell them the whole thing, Pattie. I just can't."

I looked at my clock once again and noticed that it was just about

6:45. "We better get goin'."

"Pat! I *can't* tell them everything!"

"Don't sweat it. No one's gonna make you say anything you don't want to say! Come on, we gotta go."

Quickly Dolly buttoned up her sweater, as I did mine, and then we left the house.

Not much was said on the way to meet George and Clark but that was okay. We both knew what the other was thinking, so… who needed to talk?

* * * * * *

The minute we walked into The Charcoal House, we saw that George and Clark were already being seated.

"Hi, guys!" I smiled as Dolly and I took our places directly across from them.

"Hi to you, too!" George grinned at me. Then he turned toward Dolly. "And just where were you until the wee hours, young lady? We were worried sick!"

"You can say that again!" Clark added.

Now this is where I realized that Dolly's years of denial and fantasy had paid off for her. As I sat there still seething over the horrid violation Jack Dawkins had committed upon my friend, I watched her talk with total nonchalance about her 'late evening.'

"Well, we walked up to the pavilion and I told him I wasn't comfortable with our relationship, or whatever it was and…"

"He got pissed off?" Clark asked.

"I mean it, if he even laid a *hand* on you…" George started.

"Well, of course he got pissed, that's part of who the creep is, but he didn't mess with me."

George and Clark both breathed a sigh of relief.

I wished I could have.

"Then," she continued, "I went back home to pick up a few more things for the weekend, and right after that I went over to Pattie's. I know it was late, but I remembered she said she'd wait up for me on the back porch, so I came over about…" She paused for a moment. "What time did I get there, Pat?"

"About 12:45."

"Yeah, I guess that was it. I'm sorry I worried you guys." She smiled.

How can she smile like that?!

"Sooooo," Dolly continued, "enough about *that* subject, we'd better order, here comes Barb."

I put my disruptive thoughts aside as Barbara approached our table.

Barbara Slavinski - Di Pietro had been a waitress in Townsends Inlet since way before World War Two. She had to be at least seventy-five. She only worked weekends, but everyone knew her and loved her. She was widowed at age twenty-seven, and she raised all four of her children alone on her small waitress salary. Andrew, William, Robert, and Alicia grew up to be wonderful people. Not only was Barb a terrific Mom, she was a well-respected member of our Townsends Inlet community as well. She was an 85th Street church member, a volunteer for the American Red Cross, a Girl Scout Troop Leader, *and* she was funny, charming, and, quite the character.

"Well, as I live and breathe," Barb smiled. "If it isn't the four nicest teenagers on the Inlet."

We all smiled back at her.

"What'll it be, kids?"

"What do you recommend?" George asked Barb.

"Oh, you know me; I like all the stuff here. I got no opinion one way or the other."

"Well, then I guess I'll have the New England clam chowder and…"

Barb shook her head no. "The Manhattan is better."

"Okay, Manhattan then."

"Soup or salad for you other three?"

"I'll have a garden salad, please."

"Get the Chef's salad, Pattie, the turkey and ham were just sliced."

"All right. Chef Salad for me."

"Dolly? Clark?"

"Well," Clark said looking at Dolly, "We were thinking we could share some fried clams for an appetizer and then…"

Barb shook her head once again. "Get the deviled crab roll-ups, you get a better bargain for your money."

"All right. Crab roll-ups sound good."

"Now," Barb said as she finished our starter order, "What would you all like for your main course?"

"What do you recommend?" George asked.

"Oh, you know me," she smiled. "I like all the stuff here. I got no opinion one way or the other."

We all ordered our dinner, with a little help from Barb, and totally enjoyed our evening. We discussed John Kennedy, the inlet's best place to go crabbing, missing Brenda, and the dance the following Friday. It was marvelous!

"I think Kennedy'll get elected and get two full terms and then…"

"I think so too, George," Clark stopped him in mid-sentence, "and then Bobby will get eight years, then Teddy'll get eight years…"

"The Kennedy Dynasty," Dolly smiled.

"But, if John wins, don't you think Richard Nixon will try to slip in there somewhere? I mean, later on?" I questioned.

"Pattie," George shook his head at me. "Nixon won't win next year and no one in their right mind would ever vote for Dick Nixon after that, not after Kennedy."

"Well," I said, "I'm not real crazy about the guy either, I was just sayin' he might try again, that's all. Frankly, I think even if he did get in there, he'd get booted out anyway."

Clark laughed, "Nixon isn't even elected and Pattie has him impeached."

Dolly nudged me. "And I thought *I* had a good imagination."

Barb brought all four if us a nice hot cup of coffee - decaf - because she thought it was too late for us to have caffeine. And then, although we all decided on cheesecake, somehow we all ended up with a nice warm piece of blueberry pie.

George pushed his chair out a bit and patted his stomach. "Man, am I full!"

Clark agreed.

"I love this place," I smiled as I finished my cup of decaf.

"Yep. I'll have good memories of The Charcoal House if I live to be a hundred," Dolly added.

"So, are you two lovely ladies ready for a nice walk home?"

Clark pulled out the chair for Dolly. "Thanks. Yeah, I guess it's about time."

"Got plans for the evening?" George asked me as we were leaving.

Actually we had no real plans, but I knew Dolly and I needed more time to talk about what just happened. We needed time for answers, for some kind of solution... a plan.

"We do, George. Some girl stuff, you know."

He smiled at me. "I have no idea what that means, but, okay."

"Then how 'bout a dinner date for next Saturday?" Clark said as he paid the check.

"Sounds good to me," Dolly answered.

"Sounds good to me, too!" I nodded.

"It's a date then."

"You kids have a wonderful evening!" Barb called out.

"You have a great night, too, Miss Barbara!"

"I really like her," Dolly said as she turned and waved.

"What's not to like?" I smiled.

George held the door open for an older couple, and then for a husband and wife and their little girl, after that we were outside and on our way back home.

"Thanks Clark, it was a great treat!" Dolly said.

"You're the best!" I nudged him.

"You're very welcome."

"See," George added, "nice guys don't necessarily finish last."

"Nice guys will *never* finish last, as far as I'm concerned," Dolly stated as a matter of fact. "Trust me on that one."

Chapter Seventy

George and Clark walked us home and the moment we entered the house Aunt Anna greeted us. "How was your dinner, girls?"

"Not half as good as yours, Mrs. Turner, but it was pretty darn good!"

"I agree with Dolly," I smiled.

"Plans for the evening?" Uncle John asked.

"We're just gonna hang out in my room and play some records."

"Sounds good."

My Aunt turned to sit down on her rocking chair and then reached for her knitting needles and yarn.

"Night, Aunt Anna. Night, Uncle John." Dolly and I kissed them both on the cheek.

"Night, girls." Uncle John smiled.

"Goodnight, Dears," Aunt Anna said as she proceeded to knit one… purl two.

* * * * * *

Dolly and I got an early shower, listened to a few of our favorite 45s, and then the conversation moved to Jack Dawkins.

"This man *has* to be punished," I said with all the disgust my voice could muster.

"What can we do, Pat? Go to his house and confront him? He'd only deny it and we'd look like idiots."

"We could tell his father."

"It'll still be Jack's word against mine."

"What if we tell Nikki and your Dad?"

"Are you out of your mind?!! My father would lose it and go to Jack's house and… and then the news would be all over the inlet." Dolly was almost in tears. "Then we'd have to move."

"Why?"

"You think we'd be able to stay here? Everywhere my family would turn, we'd be the talk of the town."

I sighed heavily. "Well, there has to be something we can do."

"I'll tell you what, if you can think of something that won't get me mortified, killed, or crucified, you can do it."

"I *can*?"

"Yes. You can!"

* * * * * *

It was somewhere around midnight when those all-too-common teenage hunger pangs took over and Dolly and I tiptoed down the steps and into the kitchen.

There was a note on the table.

Dear Pattie and Dolly,

There are some brownies in the ice box. I put them in there because there's chocolate icing on them and I wanted them to stay fresh and pretty for you.

Enjoy your snack.

Love,

Aunt Anna

"Ya gotta love her," I said as I reached inside the refrigerator for the plateful of Brownies.

"I mean it, Pattie," Dolly said as she took her first bite from the delicious confection. "I *really* want to adopt this woman."

* * * * * *

Sunday morning came all too soon. I heard Aunt Anna and Uncle John readying to go to church. I felt kinda guilty that I wasn't going with them, so I said a small prayer for Dolly and Brenda and then rolled over again and fell asleep.

God forgive me.

By the time it was 10:00 AM, the delicious aroma of fried potatoes, pork roll, and cheese omelets were calling to me.

"Dolly, wake up, it's…"

"Fried potatoes, pork roll, and cheese omelets," she yawned.

"Exactly. Hey, Doll?"

"Yeah?" she answered as she tied her robe belt around her waist.

"You wanna start going to church with me on Sunday?"

"Church?"

"Yeah. I used to go all the time when… well, you know when my parents were…"

"I know, Pat. My mother and I never missed a Sunday."

"So?"

"We really should carry on our family tradition."

"Ya think so?"

"You're the one who mentioned it."

"Yeah. Let's go."

Dolly and I walked down the steps and Aunt Anna was still dressed in her 'goin' to church' finery - all except for her hat, that is. As for Uncle John? Well, he was already in his usual everyday wear: a short-sleeved plaid shirt, old khaki shorts, straw hat, and his worn out 'fishin' shoes.'

Someone call the fashion police!

We shared our news about attending church and my Aunt and Uncle were very happy about it. I guess they knew we both needed that comforting sense of the spiritual along with a strong and friendly supportive community, and Townsends Inlet was all that and then some.

We also talked about how delicious breakfast was. Let's put it this way: to say breakfast was delicious would be like saying Babe Ruth was just your average baseball player.

After we ate, Dolly and I volunteered to do the dishes and clean up while Aunt Anna walked over to visit Carrie to show off her latest knitting creation - a new afghan for the back porch in a beautiful pastel green.

Uncle John decided to go down to the basement to mend a broken door on one of his crab traps.

Again Dolly and I talked about Jack.

"What if I'm…"

"If you're what?"

"You know, if I'm…"

"Oh, geez."

"Pat, I'll kill him with my bare hands, I swear it!"

"You'll be in line after me, I can tell you that much!"

"Do you think I am?"

Now that's a loaded question if I ever heard one.

"I want to say you're not, Doll, but we just have to wait. When are you supposed to get your… you know…"

"Oh. Next week, maybe next Sunday."

"Well, we'll know soon enough then. Let's get our minds on other things, like getting you into a great college next year."

"I don't think that's in the cards for me, Pattie."

"Stop talking like that. Is it what you really want?" I asked her.

"With all of my heart."

"Well, then," I patted her on the back. "It's in the cards."

Chapter Seventy-One

Dolly and I decided to walk to the pier right after we cleaned up in the kitchen. Somehow the lure of the beach front wasn't exactly something either one of us wanted to experience at the moment. When we arrived only Hank Garrity was on the pier and it seemed like he just stopped by to check out his boat and to see how many minnows got caught in his 'minny box.' Dolly and I sat in the same spot where we had rested our bones just a day earlier. Doll turned toward me and sighed.

"I ain't the way you found me, am I, Pat?"

"You could say that."

"And you're not upset because of all those stupid lies and..."

"We went all through this before. I understand why you were who you were."

She nodded.

"But I can also see who you are now, and I'm *really* proud of you."

Dolly got up and walked over to a pretty little sea shell that had somehow found its way to the pier. She stood on the very edge of the dock and turned toward me. "Know what I'm gonna do?"

"You're not gonna jump, are you?"

"No, silly. I'm making a vow to... well, I guess to myself and the universe."

"Don't let me stop you." I smiled.

Now color me, Patricia Anne Townsend, dense, but I would have thought that those kind of special words would remain silent, hidden in her soul for only Dolly and God to know... but somehow, Dolly felt free and open and alive and she shared all of her thoughts with me, two seagulls, and that pretty conch shell.

"This is the moment I vow to change my life. From here on I am *me*. Not the me who becomes whatever's called for, but the me I was meant to be. I'm gonna go to college. I'm *going* to make a good life for myself. I'm going to be real and face things as they come - head on. I'm going to be strong, and when some sad thing comes along... some tragedy, I'll acknowledge the pain and then get whatever help I need to pull myself through it in the right way. I will *never* again allow another person to mold me into their idea of who I should be, or what I should think, or how I should feel. I'm the wind beneath my own wings from here on in! Just stand behind me and watch me *fly!*"

Then Dolly's arm reached back and she threw that conch shell out into the bay with the arm of a National League pitcher. All of a sudden one of the witnessing seagulls swooped down before it hit the water and flew off with it. I stood up in amazement.

"They... they *never* do that! I mean it was just an empty shell."

Dolly turned toward me and smiled. "Well then, I guess he's delivering my prayer."

We both watched as the seagull flew down the bay, still clutching that tiny shell in his beak.

"I guess he is, Doll," I said as I watched him fly out of sight. "I guess he is."

Chapter Seventy-Two

Dolly and I walked back to the house, set the table for dinner, and then decided we'd both write Brenda a letter. I really missed Brenda and I knew she missed me, and letters would keep us connected. Our lives weren't really going in opposite directions; I was just lagging behind a year. Sometimes it was hard to imagine that she would be in California in less than three weeks - and without me! But, we were always 98% on the same wavelength, and a geographical difference, even a big one of over three thousand miles could never put a dent in our friendship.

Letter writing complete, Dolly and I placed a four-cent stamp on each of our envelopes and walked downstairs, all ready for dinner.

Aunt Anna cooked up some of Uncle John's flounder, she made macaroni and cheese - with a few of her own secret ingredients, and grilled the green beans that Dolly and I had picked from the garden when we came back from the pier. Dessert was a scrumptious lemon meringue pie.

No one made a meringue pie like Aunt Anna.

Nobody.

Dolly and I gladly accepted the after-dinner duties. For a dinner like that? We would have washed five hundred dishes!

All too soon it was time for Dolly to pack her overnight bag and head back home.

"I had a great weekend with you, Pattie. Thanks for everything," she said as she gave me a HUGE hug. "And I mean *everything*."

"Things'll all work out, Doll."

"I know."

"You're not just saying that, are you?"

"Patricia Townsend! This is the new me! I'm sayin' it 'cause I mean it!"

I smiled. "Atta girl!"

My clock radio read 7:15, and we promised Nik and Mr. Dollio that she'd be back home by 7:30.

We walked downstairs and Dolly said her goodbyes to my aunt and uncle.

"Thank you a million times over for such a wonderful weekend," she said hugging Aunt Anna.

"Well, you're more than welcome, Dear. Come back anytime. We really enjoyed your company."

"And thank you, too, Mr. Turner. I just love it here. I feel so at home." She gave Uncle John a quick peck on the cheek. "*And,* you're not only the best disc-jockey in New Jersey; you catch the best flounder, too!"

Now it was Uncle John's turn to smile. "Why, thank you, Dolly.

Come back again for a visit. The next flounder I catch'll have your name on it!"

She smiled.

"Time to go," I sighed.

Miss Dollio picked up her overnight bag and waved a final goodbye. "Thanks again!"

I closed the door behind us and then we walked down the steps, down the street, and then down toward the end of the inlet - to Dolly's house.

"It really was a great weekend, Pat."

"If you don't count Friday night."

"Yeah."

"But he'll get his."

Dolly sighed. "If there's any justice in the world, he will."

Before we knew it we were standing outside of her house. "Come in with me, okay?"

"Sure."

The minute we opened the screen door Apry came running toward us. "DOLLY!!!!"

"Hi, Ap! How's my girl! Where's Nik, Mack, and Dad?"

"I'm right here," Nikki smiled entering the room with Mack in his usual position on her hip. "Didja have fun?"

"I had a great weekend with Pattie! And Mr. and Mrs. Turner are such wonderful people."

Nik smiled again.

Dolly gave Mack a kiss on his pudgy little cheek. "Hi, Mackey! How's the boy?"

Mack laughed and gurgled.

Little kids are so cute.

"Where's Dad?" Dolly asked.

"Oh, he went out a while ago."

"Where to?"

"The Dawkins' house."

"Jack Dawkins' house?!" We said in unison.

I could almost hear Dolly praying.

Please don't let him find out anything. Please don't let the whole world know what happened to me on Friday night! Please… Please… Please!!!

Just then the famous red and white 1959 Chevy Impala roared up the driveway. Mr. Dollio slammed the car door, walked down the sidewalk, and straight into the house.

Dolly and I stood there with frozen smiles on our faces.

"What's the matter with you two?" he asked.

"Well, I was… I was…" Dolly voice was nervous and erratic, so I stepped up to the plate.

"She was just disappointed that you weren't here, 'cause…'cause she missed you."

"Well, I had to talk to Bill Dawkins."

"About?" Dolly asked.

"I saw a notice in Shellum's that he had a '57 T-Bird for sale. The price was a little steep - nine-hundred and fifty dollars - but I said I'd take it anyway."

Dolly and I looked at each other, our shoulders dropped and we breathed a huge sigh of relief. Then, all of a sudden we both started to laugh.

"What's so funny about a good deal on a '57 T-Bird?" he wanted to know.

Dolly and I said nothing for a moment and then I spoke up. "Oh, nothin' I guess. It's just a guy thing. We women never understand that stuff. Do we, Doll?"

"Nope. We sure don't."

"Well, I'm gonna watch some TV. Get a beer out for me, Nik. And make sure it's nice and cold! And get me some pretzels!" With that said he walked out of the room. Not a hello to his wife, only an order he barked at her, not a word to either one of his children; just off to drink some beer, eat some pretzels, and watch the TV.

It was *always* about him.

"Pattie," Nikki said, "Now that the car's back, I can give you a ride home after I…"

"Thanks, Nik, but I'll enjoy the walk. And, thanks for letting Dolly spend the weekend. It was great to have her stay with us."

"You're welcome."

Mack started to fuss and Nikki and Apry made their exit. "Bye, Pattie." Apry smiled.

"Bye, Ap!"

That left just me and Dolly standing by the old wooden screen door.

"See you tomorrow."

"Yep, back to the old grind."

"You're gonna be okay?" I asked as I hugged her goodbye.

"Pattie, I'm gonna be just fine."

Chapter Seventy-Three

I got to Shellum's about a half an hour early. Millie and Bill had barely opened the store when I strolled inside the building.

"You're an early bird!" Mrs. Shellum smiled. "Relax, Pattie. Have some coffee and a donut."

"Thanks, Mrs. S."

Actually, the main reason I was an 'early bird' because the minute I got up all I could think about was Dolly. *Would Jack be waiting for her at the corner when she left for work? Would she make it in if he did? What would he say? What would he do?* I was totally consumed by all of the things that I told Dolly not to worry about. Truthfully, I was a little ashamed of myself for losing my usual cool and conventional thought patterns. Just as I had poured myself a second cup of coffee, in walked Dolly.

Whew!

"Hi, Everyone!"

"Mornin', Dolly!" The Shellum's voices rang out.

"You're early!" she smiled at me.

"You are, too."

"Yeah, well, I just wanted to get out of the house, my Dad's such a pain in the..."

"I know."

I poured Dolly a cup of coffee, she grabbed a chocolate frosted cruller, and then we sat and talked until it was time to get to work. Maybe it was the bonding that Doll and I had between us this weekend that was bringing us closer, because now, we were even finishing each other's sentences!

"Did you see...?"

"No. Like you said, he wouldn't dare show his face."

"Ya think he'll go to..."

"The dance? Nah. Unless he..."

"Decides he can pick up some other sweet, naïve female like..."

"Dale Harding?"

I nodded. "Yeah. I was thinkin' about her 'cause he was giving her the old James Dean routine at the dance on Friday and..."

"And let's hope Dale gets wise... and fast!"

"I'll say!"

"Ladies!" Millie called out. "Time to start the work week!"

"Okay, Mrs. S!"

I quickly wiped down the fountain counter while Dolly washed and dried our cups and saucers.

"It's a nice cool day," Bill noted as he walked past me. "Looks like I can turn the air conditioner off and use the fan for a change."

I smiled.

As I watched Bill reposition the huge standing fan, I heard him say to Millie. "Let's hope it stays like this the rest of the summer. I don't want another ten dollar electric bill!"

Millie walked by me and said, "Bill swears if the monthly bill ever hits twenty dollars the whole family is moving to Alaska."

"Alaska's nice, so is Canada," I said as I priced and sorted some new cereal boxes.

"Don't give him any more ideas than he already has," she smiled.

After I straightened out the cereal shelves, I looked around and saw Dolly waiting on a new customer and she seemed as if she didn't have a care in the world. After *all* Dolly had been through in her life, Friday night in particular, I was happy to see her in such a good frame of mind.

And me?

I was still fighting off the demons in my head.

...Each and every one of them named Jack Dawkins.

Chapter Seventy-Four

All week long we worked like crazy, but, that was a good thing. Another good thing was that the weather stayed a constant seventy-five degrees, so the Shellum family wouldn't be buying tickets to Anchorage any time soon.

George and Clark dropped by on a daily basis and we were always happy to see them. The four of us made plans to meet at The Turner household at 7:00 on Friday night so we could walk over to The Civic Center with the famous disc-jockey to give him a hand selecting the order of the evening's songs.

George told us that he heard Jack Dawkins was now working at Henny's Pier, and his usual afternoon lunch was no longer at VanSants, but instead he was stopping over to Wiley's Deli for a sandwich and coke.

I wasn't surprised.

Neither was Dolly.

"Why do you think he's doing that?" George asked me.

"I guess he's avoiding us," Dolly chimed in.

"Yeah, well, he's doin' us all a favor," I said.

"Seems like he feels guilty about something. I mean to go that far out of his way and everything," Clark added.

"There isn't a guilty bone in Jack's body," I quickly answered.

"Nope," Dolly nodded. "Snakes don't have bones."

* * * * * *

Friday came and Mrs. Shellum let us go home early, as usual.

What a nice woman.

"Don't forget, Doll. Clark and George are coming to get you first," I said as we were leaving. "Be ready by 6:30."

"I will, Pat! See ya!"

"See ya."

Dolly and I had decided earlier in the week that we would both be wearing our blue denim peddle pushers, a white open collared blouse, and our red waist cinchers - but no neck scarf! And of course, our bobby socks and saddle oxfords. As I was putting the finishing touches on my makeup, Aunt Anna came into my room.

"You look lovely, Dear."

"Thanks, Aunt Anna."

"I just wanted to say that I'm looking forward to having you and Dolly come to church with us this weekend."

I smiled. "I think Dolly is going to join the choir."

"Well, what about you?"

"Aunt Anna, I can't carry a tune in a bucket, but Dolly? She sings like an angel."

My Aunt smiled. "Well, we can all use an angel now and then can't we?"

"Yep," I smiled back. "So, I guess that explains why I have you!"

* * * * * *

George, Clark, and Dolly rang the doorbell and I ran to welcome them!

"Come on in, guys!"

"Hi, Mrs. Turner! Hi, Mr. Turner!" three voices rang out.

My Aunt greeted them and chit-chatted for a few minutes until Uncle John walked down the steps.

"Here comes the oldest teenager in America." She looked lovingly at her husband.

"And here's the most beautiful wife in America," he said as he kissed her on the cheek.

She sighed contentedly.

"Well, kids. Ready to go?"

"All set, Mr. Turner."

Aunt Anna walked us to the front door and waved goodbye to us as we walked down the street toward The Civic Center.

"Have fun, kids!" She chuckled.

"We will!"

As we were waiting to cross Landis Avenue, Uncle John asked, "Who do you think we should open with tonight?"

"How about Elvis?" Dolly answered immediately.

"I like 'Chantilly Lace' by The Big Bopper," Clark said.

"Nah, Jerry Lee." George smiled adding his two cents.

"Any suggestions, Pattie?" my uncle asked.

"How about 'Rock Around the Clock!' Bill Haley and The Comets!"

Dolly shook her head no. So did George. So did Clark.

"Hey!" I said defending my choice, "It's a great tune! I mean, everyone likes it. It could even be a lead in song for a TV show or something. I mean it's that well liked!"

Dolly rolled her eyes at me as I started to sing, "One, two, three o'clock, four o'clock rock..."

"Pattie, *please*." George patted my shoulder, "Bill Haley's day has come and gone."

"It has, Pat," Clark nodded.

"Okay, forget it. You guys win. Pick from Jerry, Elvis, or The Big Bopper. I don't care."

As I heard the three of them giving their own specific reasons for Uncle John to play their song first, I walked ahead and continued singing,

"Five, six, seven o'clock, eight o'clock rock... nine, ten, eleven o'clock, twelve o'clock rock... we're gonna rock... around... the clock tonight! Put you're glad rags on..."

"Change the channel, Pattie," Dolly laughed. "Please, c*hange* the channel!"

Uncle John opened the doors to The Civic Center and then he walked right upstairs. Before we knew it he was back down on the dance floor with three records in his hands: one Elvis, one Big Bopper, and one Jerry Lee Lewis.

"Pat, since you don't have a record request..."

"Through no fault of my own," I said making a face at my three friends.

"You pick the winner of the first song for the night."

"Okay."

Uncle John held them out in front of him and I closed my eyes and picked.

"It's Elvis!"

Dolly squealed with delight. "Which one?"

"Jailhouse Rock!"

She leaned in toward me and whispered in my ear, "Jack's theme song."

"With any luck," I answered.

Chapter Seventy-Five

The dance was fabulous - need I say?!
Dolly and I jitterbugged, cha-cha'd, strolled, and bopped all over the dance floor.

George and Clark were wonderful, as always, and the four of us sat by the concession stand and we ate burgers, and devoured quite a few french fries, and sodas while we were at it.

As Dolly took off to 'stroll' with two dance lines filled with Sea Isle teens, my eyes swept the entire building.

No Jack Dawkins anywhere.

Good.

What really worried me was that the sweet and unassuming Dale Harding was also missing.

Not so good.

For the rest of the evening I appeared pre-occupied and Dolly, Clark, and George couldn't help but notice.

"You okay, Pattie?" Clark nudged me.

"Feelin' all right? George added.

"Yeah, I'm fine."

Then... there was Dolly.

"Pat? What's with you? What's wrong?"

Her face had concern written all over it.

What could I tell her? That I was thinking about what happened to her just seven days ago? That although it might be a blessing not to find that skuzzy jerk here this week, it was a worry for me to see Dale among the missing! UGH! What Dolly admired most about me - my honesty - was about to go flying right out the window. The truth teller was about to lie to one of her dearest friends. "I just feel a little..."

"Crampy?"

"Yeah... *real* crampy."

"You want me to get you an aspirin, Pat?"

"No, thanks. I'll be okay."

"You sure?"

"Yeah, I'm sure."

She smiled at me.

I lied... I lied... I lied!!! I have to talk to the guys. I can't keep doing this.

Not a moment after that thought came into my head I saw George and Clark talking to Bobby Phillips and Billy Rual. I knew it had to be football talk so it was best for me to stay out of it. So, with nowhere else to turn, I decided to watch Dolly dance and have fun while *I* tried very hard not to think about what Jack might be up to... with Dale Harding.

Ten-thirty rolled around all too fast, as it did every week, and, before we all knew it, Uncle John was playing, 'Goodnight, Sweetheart.' George and I danced to the last song of the evening while Dolly and Clark got us all a Hershey bar and a coke for the walk back home.

The lights went back on and I looked up to the booth where Uncle John performed his DJ duties. I smiled and waved at him and he smiled and waved back to me.

"See you at home!"

"K! See ya!"

Clark and Dolly joined the crowd in the mad dash out the door, while George and I just took it easy. A few minutes later we saw them standing on the opposite side of the street.

"Over here, guys!" Dolly called out.

George and I crossed the street and Dolly handed me a soda and a candy bar.

"You got the Hershey bar with almonds, Pat."

I smiled at her. "You're a good girl!"

"You wanna walk down the beach to Dolly's? You know, somethin' different for a change?" George suggested.

"Not the beach," Dolly said quietly.

"No. Not the beach," I added.

"Anything wrong?" Clark noticed how quiet we had become.

"Nothin's wrong. It's just too chilly for the beach tonight, that's all."

George nodded an okay to me, but when he looked in my eyes, somehow I knew he could see that I had just lied to him.

I've got to stop this!

* * * * * *

Within five minutes we were outside Dolly's house. Nikki was waiting at the door, we all said 'goodnight,' and waved our goodbyes.

"See ya Monday, Pat!"

"Monday it is. G'night!"

I took a deep breath and then started to walk down the street.

I had no idea I was being spoken to.

I also had no idea that I missed our usual right hand turn onto Landis Avenue.

And, I had *no* idea just how easy it could be to just tune everything and everyone out but my own thoughts and feelings.

My mind drifted back to a conversation I had with Dolly the weekend before and it stayed there.

"Well, there has to be something we can do!"

"I'll tell you what… if you can think of something that won't get me mortified, killed, or crucified, you can do it."

"I can?"

"Yes. You can!"

Just then I felt George's hand on my shoulder. "Pattie? For God's sake, where are you?"

The voices fought for space in my head.

I can?...Yes. You can!

I can?...Yes. You can!

"Pattie... For God's sake! PATTIE!!!"

I stopped dead in my tracks and answered him, "I'm sorry."

"Sorry?!"

"I guess my mind was elsewhere."

"Well, so is your body!"

"Huh?"

"Pat, we're on 93rd Street!"

"We are?!"

"Look for yourself," Clark said pointing to the road sign.

"Oh, Geez."

"What's the matter with you?!" George placed both of his hands on my shoulders as if to softly shake me back to reality.

Still, the past haunted me.

"I'll tell you what... if you can think of something that won't get me mortified, killed, or crucified, you can do it."

I can?

Yes. You can!

"George..." I started.

"What is it?!"

Again, I heard Dolly's voice. *"I'll tell you what... if you can think of something that won't..."*

Suddenly I was done wrestling with the thoughts in my head. "We have to talk, George."

"*Now* we're gettin' somewhere!"

"Well, do you wanna talk now or do you have plans to walk all the way to Cape May?"

For the first time in hours I had a genuine smile on my face.

"I wanna talk now, and I wanna go home."

"We can do that," Clark smiled as he pointed me in the right direction.

I walked a few more feet and then I stopped and turned toward the two best male friends I had ever had in my entire life. I was scared. I wasn't even sure how to start out a conversation like this. But, as my mother used to say, "When in doubt, cut to the chase."

So I did.

"Jack raped Dolly last week."

"What?!" The look on George's face was almost as if I had spoken that sentence in some kind of foreign language.

"Jack raped Dolly... on the beach... last Friday night."

"Raped?!" The color all but drained from Clark's face.

"Yes!" I started to cry in frustration. "Yes! YES!!! Aren't you listening to me?!!!"

George put his arms around me and I cried into those big strong shoulders of his for what seemed like an eternity. "She… she came back to… to my house around 1:30. She was hysterical. She was bruised, he bit her, the buttons were torn off her blouse, her crinoline was ripped…"

"Bastard," I heard Clark mutter.

"What did you do?"

"Do?! What could we do? Who else could she tell, George? She only has *me*!"

"Couldn't she go to the hospital?"

"So they could do what?"

"Okay, then, how about the police?" Clark added.

"It would be his word against hers."

"Well, her parents could… Oh, forget that!" George caught his thought mid-sentence.

"Jack was a barbarian. She went with an honest heart to cleanse herself of this crud and he thought it was a come-on!"

"What?!"

"You heard me."

"And…" I started to cry again. "She begged him and begged him not to touch her. She fought, she did, she fought like hell but…"

"I'm sure she would, Pat," Clark said softly.

"All I could think about tonight was what happened last week. If you could have *seen* her! If you could have *heard* her! That cry, that pain!!!" I wiped the tears from my eyes and then started to sob all over again.

"So that's why he wasn't at the dance tonight!"

"We should be so lucky," I sniffled.

"What are you talkin' about?" George looked straight into my eyes.

"Guys, not only was Jack missing tonight, but so was Dale Harding."

"Oh, my God," Clark's head was spinning, "the girl he was talking to at last week's dance."

"Yeah, the one he was playing James Dean to, like the number he played on Dolly."

"This guy has to be stopped," George was quiet and matter-of-fact.

Clark nodded. "You can say that again."

Right about that time we had reached 85th Street and we walked the last twenty or so feet to my front steps.

"There's nothing *anyone* can do. And he knew that! He *knew* he'd get away with it! " I started to cry again. "And what if she's pregnant? She's so worried that she's pregnant!"

"Pregnant?" Clark's voice was barely a whisper.

I can't even find the words to tell you the look on my friends' faces when I said that word. "She fought hard, George, she did. She really, really did!"

George reached for me and gave me a gentle hug. "Pattie, Jack Dawkins will get his. I can assure you of that."

"You mean like…" I sniffled once again. "you reap what you sow?"

"Something like that."

"So do you…"

George looked deep into my eyes. "Like I said, Jack Dawkins will get his."

Chapter Seventy-Six

When I woke up on Saturday morning the first thought that came into my head wasn't the usual, "how fast can I get downstairs for breakfast," no… my first thought was about Dolly. Should I let her know I told Clark and George? Would she be afraid they would tell someone, who would tell someone else, who would… well, you know what I mean.

Ugh! Not even 9:00 AM and already I had a headache.

Just as I was heading toward the bathroom I heard the phone ring.

Aunt Anna called to me, "Pat! It's Dolly!"

Oh, God… George called her… or Clark called her… She's gonna kill me!!!!

"Coming, Aunt Anna!"

I lumbered down the steps as if I was walking to my execution at Alcatraz.

I was *not* my usual chipper self as I said hello.

"What's wrong, Pattie? Aren't you feeling well?"

"I'm fine, Doll." My voice was now about 60% normal.

"You sound like something's wrong! Are you okay?"

"The question is are *you* okay!?"

"Me?" Dolly questioned, "Sure, I'm fine. I just wanted to let you know that I called the church and asked about the choir."

"And?"

"And, I told Mrs. Buck, she's the choir leader, that I also play piano and she was *so* thrilled that she asked me to stop by for an audition at 10:30. I just wanted you to come with me!"

"And that's why you called?"

"Sure! Isn't that great news?!"

Whew!

"Doll, it's *really* great news! I'll meet you there at 10:15 okay?"

"Cool! Bye, Pat!"

"Bye, Dolly."

What a relief that was! But I knew right then and there I had to tell Dolly that George and Clark knew exactly what happened. I couldn't live the lie and then be worried every time I saw her or spoke to her on the phone that she would have found out from someone else. I opened my big mouth, I shared her secret, and I was responsible for that.

Aunt Anna fixed me some pancakes and sausage, and then I ran upstairs for a quick shower, put my hair in a ponytail, dressed, and then flew out the door. It was 10:10.

Just in time.

Dolly was sitting on the church steps waiting for me.

"How come you didn't go in?"

"'Cause I was waitin' for you."

"Well, I'm here. Let's get to that audition of yours."

We opened the side entryway to the church and found Mrs. Buck already seated at the piano waiting for us.

"Welcome, girls!"

"Hi, Mrs. Buck!" We smiled.

"Are you ready to start your audition?"

Dolly's voice seemed small and uncertain. "Yes, Ma'am. I mean... I *think* so."

Mrs. Buck moved from her seat at the piano so that Dolly could sit there.

"Sing into the microphone, Dear."

Dolly took her seat at the piano and wiggled around a bit to make herself comfortable. She adjusted the mike, and then cleared her throat a few times. Her hands struck a chord and the sound echoed throughout the church.

"What will you play, Dear?" Mrs. Buck asked her.

"Well, umm..." Dolly spoke softly into the microphone. "I thought I'd do 'Amazing Grace,' because it was my Mom's favorite."

"A lovely choice. Please play and sing for us."

I knew Dolly was a nervous wreck. She never sang for anyone in public before this. Well, *I* heard her sing late one night, remember? But she never knew it. Actually, this moment in time was more than an audition, it was a turning point in her life. Dolly glanced over at me, then, without hesitation, she looked down at the piano keys, and *then* the music began. I was amazed at how well she played the intro, but when she started to sing, her nervousness caught up with her.

"Amaaazin..." She cleared her throat. "Aaa-may-zing graaaa..." Again she cleared her throat. "I'm sorry, Mrs. Buck."

"That's all right, Dear. Everyone's a little nervous when they first audition."

All of a sudden I spoke up. "Doll, just pretend that you're out on the beach, late at night, arms stretched out wide singin' to the heavens."

She looked at me in a strange fashion. "Okaaay. I can do that."

Again she started to sing, "Aaa-maaay-zing Graaaa..." and just as quickly she stopped again. "I'm sorry, I just can't..."

Immediately I stood up from the pew. "Yes you can! Close your eyes and forget we're here. Sing for your Mom, Doll. Sing for her!"

Dolly re-adjusted herself on the piano bench, smoothing her skirt down under her. She took a very deep breath, closed her eyes, and once again her hands moved over the black and white ivory keys. The intro was perfect. And then... well, and then she sang. And I mean she *sang*!!!

"Aaa-maaay-zing Grace, how sweet the sound,
That saved a wretch like me,
I once was lost but now am found,
Was blind, but now, I see."

I listened in amazement. The angel voice I had heard on the beach just a few weeks earlier was singing to me once again.

Mrs. Buck sat mesmerized as Dolly continued,
"Through many dangers, toils and snares,
we have already come,
T'was Grace that brought us safe thus far,
and Grace will lead us home."

I listened to Dolly and tears filled my eyes. I don't even remember if I was breathing or not. I was in absolute awe. It was like seeing the Sistine chapel for the first time, viewing the aurora borealis, like… well, like hearing a real angel sing.

When Dolly finished, she turned toward us. Mrs. Buck stood immediately and applauded. "You *must* sing that in church tomorrow!"

"Tomorrow?!!"

I smiled. "You heard the lady!"

"Well… okay. I mean… when do I…"

"Just be here at 8:15."

"Yes, Mrs. Buck."

"You can play piano for a little while to relax yourself until our members start to come in around 8:45."

"So, I passed the audition?"

"Dolly," Mrs. Buck smiled. "You have a natural talent, the likes of which I have never heard before in my entire life."

"Really?!"

"Yes, really. This is a talent that the heavens gifted you with, I'm certain of it! So, see you tomorrow morning?"

"Yes. Yes, Ma'am!" Dolly smiled. "8:15!"

As we walked toward the front doors of the little church, we said our thank you's and goodbye's to Mrs. Buck. And, when we stepped outside into the soft ocean breeze, Dolly turned to me and said, "Thank you for having such faith in me, Pat. How did you know what to say? I mean, those words just triggered something inside of me."

"I don't even remember what I said."

"You *said,* 'Doll, just pretend that you're out on the beach, late at night, arms stretched out wide singin' to the heavens.'"

"Oh yeah, now I remember."

"And then you said, 'Yes you can! Close your eyes and forget we're here. Sing for your Mom, Doll. Sing for her.'"

I chuckled nervously, "Yeah… oh, well I guess I…"

"I sing out on the beach like that sometimes, it just seems right to me somehow… so peaceful and free."

"And how did singing to me and Mrs. Buck feel to you? And the thought of singing in front of all those church members tomorrow?"

She thought for a second and then smiled. "Peaceful and free, Pattie."

"Really?"
"Yup. Peaceful and free."

Chapter Seventy-Seven

Word always spread around the inlet with lightening speed - always - and, whether it was about a new baby born into the community, or a record catch at John's Pier, the word of it moved fast in Townsends Inlet. After the audition Dolly and I walked down the street to Busch's Seafood restaurant for a celebration brunch. Mrs. Phillips, the owner, walked right up to us as we were being seated. Anna Busch-Phillips was *also* the lady who sewed all the church choir gowns.

"I just got a call from Mary Ludwig, she said you're our lead singer tomorrow, Dolly!"

"Yes, Ma'am."

"Well, that's just fantastic! Your mother would be *so* proud." Quickly she turned toward our waitress. "Ellie! Brunch is on the house!"

"Thanks, Mrs. Phillips!" we said in unison.

"Don't even mention it! It was my pleasure. And come see me on Monday, Dolly, for a proper gown fitting. See you tomorrow, girls."

"Okay! Thanks again."

Dolly and I sat at our table and smiled at each other.

"Mary Ludwig told Mrs. Phillips?"

"Yeah," I said. "Mary's the church bookkeeper."

"Word gets around."

"Well, at least it's a good word," I said as I munched on some breadsticks.

"Yeah, thank heaven."

"You can say that again."

Within five minutes of finishing our celebration brunch we were walking back toward the Turner household so Dolly could share the good news with my Aunt and Uncle.

No sooner had we walked in the door when Aunt Anna came to greet us. She threw her arms around Dolly and smiled. "Well, aren't you just a blessing to this community! Mrs. Bitner just called me and told me that you're singing and playing piano in church tomorrow."

Mrs. Bitner called?

I had to smile.

"Yes, Ma'am," Dolly said still wrapped in Aunt Anna's embrace. "I'll be singing 'Amazing Grace.' It was my Mom's favorite."

"Well, come on in here you two, and have a nice big piece of hot fresh apple pie and a cold glass of milk to celebrate!"

Now right after a piece of seafood heaven at Busch's, we were kinda full, to say the least, but, as it is for most seventeen-year-olds, there's always a little more room for a nice hot fresh apple pie and a cold glass of milk.

My Aunt Anna saw food as a lovely way to express herself, a great way to communicate at the table, as a reward, as a treat, a comfort... you name it and food was the answer. Now you'd think my Aunt Anna would weigh two hundred pounds from all that good cooking and good eating, but if she weighed ninety five pounds soaking wet, she was lucky!

As we sat at the table I smiled at my aunt and said, "So, how did Mrs. Bitner find out?"

"Well, I think she said Mrs. Thomas called her."

"Mrs. Thomas," I smiled. "Who I guess was called by, Mrs. Googer, who was called by Minnie Molehall..."

Dolly laughed, "Who was called by Emma Orwatt, who was called by Bessie Newell..."

Aunt Anna laughed right along with us. "Who was called by Mrs. Phillips, who was called by Mary Ludwig, who was called by..."

"Mrs. Buck!" We all said together.

My Aunt smiled. "This is a *wonderful* community that shares all its good news, its brotherhood, and sisterhood. We're all so very proud of you, Dolly."

"So, Miss Dollio, howsabout a little preview for Aunt Anna?" I nudged my friend.

"Huh?"

"You know, what you sang this morning."

"Oh, sure!"

Then without any of the angst she normally felt, or the shyness that kept her talent hidden since her mother's death, Dolly began to sing... right there at the kitchen table.

"A-maaay-zing Grace, how sweet the sound,
That saved a wretch like me..."

As she continued Aunt Anna leaned in toward me and said, "My goodness, she sounds just like an angel."

I just nodded and smiled.

* * * * * *

After our delicious hot apple pie treat, I walked Dolly back to her house.

Her Dad, of course, wasn't home, but Nikki was, and she too, had already heard the good news from the happy Townsends Inlet grapevine. Apry was thrilled and had already decided what she was going to wear to church in the morning.

I didn't stick around too long because I had some laundry to do and I also needed to iron my blouses for the upcoming week. As soon as I started walking down the sidewalk of Dolly's house, her father pulled up in the driveway.

"Hi, Mr. Dollio."

"Hello, Pat." His voice was that usual dull monotone.

"Didja hear the good news?"

As he was reaching for a case of beer from the back seat of his car, he turned his head and answered me, "What good news?"

"Dolly auditioned for church choir and not only is she gonna be in the choir, Mrs. Buck told her that she'll play piano and sing 'Amazing Grace' as soon as church starts tomorrow."

He turned back around and took the case into his hands and started to walk away from me.

"She's a beautiful singer, Mr. Dollio!" I called out.

He never answered me; he just kept walking toward the house, clutching his case of twenty-four Ortlieb's beer bottles.

"I guess we'll be seeing all of you in church tomorrow!" By the time I got that sentence out of my mouth, Mr. Dollio was long gone, but somehow I kept right on talking just the same. "And she sings like an *angel!* And she plays the piano like a real musician would! She's gonna make one fine music teacher someday!"

I smiled to myself and then turned away and headed down the street - back toward 85th Street. I knew Mr. Dollio didn't hear a word I said, but it felt good to say it anyway. I felt genuinely positive about what was happening, even in the face of all the darkness that had gone on lately, the light was somehow, almost miraculously, shining through.

Not only had Dolly's life altered over the last week… mine had as well.

Chapter Seventy-Eight

Sunday morning came and I was dressed and ready for church by 7:00 AM.

Talk about fired up!

I helped Aunt Anna make breakfast: Fresh eggs-over medium, fried apples, a hash brown casserole with gravy, and homemade buttermilk biscuits. Even Uncle John put the coffee on and poured all of us some orange juice.

I reminded my Aunt and Uncle that Dolly would be at the church around 8:10 and asked if we could leave a little early to hear her rehearse. Needless to say, that wasn't a problem and all three of us walked in the 85th Street church door, right around 8:15, to hear the beautiful sounds of Dolly singing and playing the piano.

By 8:30, the church was almost full.

By 8:45 it *was* full.

By 9:00?

It was standing room only.

I looked around to see Nikki and Mack and Apry. Apry was all smiles and she waved to me and I waved back.

And Mr. Dollio?

...He was no where to be found.

But I did see George and his family, Clark and his family, The Shellums, The VanSants, The Ruals, The Bitner family, The Pfeiffers, The Benders, The Dalrymples, The Phillips',The Thomas family, The Laricks'...

I'm sure Dolly saw everyone too. I mean this wasn't a huge cathedral; it was just a tiny little church that seated about a hundred people - with standing room for maybe another fifty. But she didn't look nervous at all.

I was nervous!

Dolly looked calm and serene, 'Peaceful and free' just like she told me the morning of her audition.

As she took her seat at the piano once again, Reverend Marshall took *his* place at the pulpit.

"Good morning members and non-members. Today we are blessed with the presence of Christine Dollio - Dolly to most of us. Dolly is bringing her talent for all to *hear*, for all to *enjoy* and for all to feel the peace and beauty of the old, traditional American Hymn - 'Amazing Grace.' Dolly... if you please."

With that said, I watched as she took a deep relaxing breath. Dolly adjusted the microphone slightly, looked down at her hands, and then started to play.

You could have heard a pin drop in that place.

I'm certain everyone expected something phenomenal. I mean, after all, Mrs. Buck was a hard-nosed teacher, and for her to tell everyone about how magnificent Dolly played and sang, she *had* to be good. Still, everyone was awestruck. There's just no other way to put it.

I can remember the times I would sit in church with my parents, and listen to a full choir sing, yet, as beautiful as it was, it couldn't compare to one tiny upright piano and the voice of my dear friend, Dolly.

* * * * * *

When our Sunday worship service was over, the standard practice was to stop at the door so the pastor could shake your hand, you'd say a few words, and then off you'd go.

Well, *this* Sunday I think more people wanted to shake Dolly's hand than Reverend and Mrs. Marshall's. As Dolly, Nikki, Apry, and Mack made their way through the crowd, I could hear the accolades she was receiving, right and left. I was so proud of her… so happy for her.

"Well, Dolly, you certainly are a blessing to our church", "I never knew you could sing like that!", "Where did you learn to play piano?", "Your voice is absolutely beautiful!"

Uncle John, Aunt Anna, and I had just said our goodbye's to The Marshall's when Dolly called to me. "Wait for us, okay?"

I waved to her, "Okay!"

In the process of waiting, George and his family stopped to talk to us, as did Clark and the rest of the Lowen family. Of course, we all said that the service was wonderful, but what really bonded us all together that morning, was Dolly. That song just spoke to us, especially to me and George and Clark, who knew what this poor kid had been through in the last ten days.

"I once was lost… but now I'm found… was blind… but now I see."

Dolly eventually made her way over to us. And, of course, the conversation was filled with awe, admiration, and congratulations. But, somehow, among all the kudos, I managed to sneak her away for a moment.

"I *have* to talk to you."

"Sure."

"Can you ask Nik if you can stay at my house for dinner or something? It'll give us the time we need."

"Yeah, I guess. What's the matter?"

"Well, I…"

Just then Nikki called to her, "Come on, Doll! I have to get home to feed the kids!"

Dolly leaned into me, and then whispered, "Gimme a second." I watched as she said a few quick goodbyes to George, Clark, and their families before meeting up with Nik and the kids in that infamous 1959

Chevy Impala.

I knew I was in luck when I saw Dolly give Mack and Apry a kiss and a wave to Nikki!

Thank heaven!

In the wink of an eye Dolly was back standing next to me. And, in even less time than that, Aunt Anna and Uncle John appeared.

"Well, Miss Beautiful Singer, your presence certainly filled our lovely little church this morning." My aunt smiled.

Uncle John nodded.

"Will you sing every week, Dear?"

"I think so. I mean... I *hope* so."

"Well good for all of us!" She smiled again.

"Ummm, Aunt Anna? Can Doll and I go up the pier?"

"Sure you can! I've got some stuff for John to do anyway."

My uncle started to walk away v-e-r-y slowly.

"John Martin Turner, just *where* do you think you're going?"

"To the pier with the girls?"

"No." She shook her head.

"To the pier with*out* the girls?"

"Guess again."

"Back to the house with you to put up the new curtain rods?"

"Why, John Turner! What a good guesser you are!" she teased.

"Anna, I'm about fishin' rods, not curtain rods."

"I know you are, Dear, but not this morning." Aunt Anna winked at me, then, off they went down the street - hand in hand.

"They are just sooooooo cute!" Dolly grinned.

"They sure are."

"So, we're goin' to the pier?"

"Yeah. Let's sit and talk, okay?"

"Okay, but, umm..."

"What, Doll?"

"Can we start now? I mean, why wait?"

"Sure."

We walked down Landis, walked by Shellum's, and then made a right toward John's Pier before I managed to say anything.

"Doll?"

"About time."

"Remember when you said to me, 'I'll tell you what... if you can think of something that won't get me mortified, killed, or crucified, you can do it?'"

"And?"

I was so worried that she'd be upset with me; and it seemed like forever before I managed to spill the beans.

"And..."

"Come on, Pat. I mean what did you do? Feed Jack to the seagulls?"

"No, but…"

"TELL ME!!!!"

"I… well…"

Dolly heaved a tremendous sigh of frustration and then I just spilled out every word as fast as I could possibly say it, "ItoldGeorgeandClark whathappenedtoyoudownonthebeach!" As soon as I said that I stopped dead in my tracks, covered my eyes with my hands, and waited for the ultimate in retribution.

"It's okay," Dolly answered softly.

I removed my hands from my face. "Huh?"

"I said, it's o-*kay*."

"It's okay?!"

"Isn't that what I just said?"

"You mean, you're not…"

"Pat, is this what you were sweatin' over?"

I nodded.

"For God's sake! I *trust* George and Clark with all of my heart! They could only *help* the situation. They'd never tell anyone!"

"Well, I know that and…"

"They're the two nicest guys I've ever known!"

"Sure, well that's why I…"

"And if *anyone* can come up with a way to help me, I mean, *us*, to resolve this mess, it's George and Clark."

I quickly sat down on the small bench outside Wiley's Deli and breathed a huge sigh of relief. Dolly sat down right next to me. "We're all gonna be okay, Pat. You'll see."

I gave her a smile. "Yeah. We will."

Just then we heard the sound of the small bell that rang out at Wiley's when anybody entered or exited the store. We both automatically turned toward the sound, and there he was - Jack Dawkins.

Dolly appeared visibly shaken… and who could blame her?

In all his arrogant swagger he walked up to us as we stood to leave.

"Excited to see me, Doll?" He lit a cigarette.

"Get bent, you slimy jerk." She turned away from him and started to walk toward John's Pier.

"Yeah, GET BENT!" I yelled at him, poking my finger at his chest.

"What?" he gave me a sly half-smile.

"You heard me. I said, GET BENT!!!"

He chuckled a bit at my out-of-character self. "Yo, Pat, does that hot little temper make ya hot anywheres else?"

"Excuse me?!!"

"You heard what I said." He smiled at me again. "Well, does it? Does it make ya hot anywheres else?"

"Let's go, Pattie. Don't waste your time!" Dolly called to me.

"Be right there, Doll!" I stared into his face with all the contempt I could muster, and then, just before I turned to walk away, he moved his hand slowly done the front of his tight black dungarees.

"Hey, Pat, you in for some-a this?"

"You're a grody, disgusting excuse for a human being, and..." I took a deep breath.

"And *what?!*" he sneered at me.

"And you'll get yours, Jack Dawkins!" I turned and walked away. My heart was racing a mile a minute and there was no spit left in my mouth.

"ARE YOUSE THREAT'NIN' ME?!!" He hollered.

I never turned back, but I did call out one last time.

"YOU HEARD ME! YOU'LL GET YOURS, JACK DAWKINS!!!"

Dolly and I didn't say a word to each other right after that, we just kept on walking to the pier. When we got to the bench where we usually sit, she was the first to speak. "I thought I would pee in my pants, I was just so scared when I saw him."

"God, he makes me so angry! I never felt such rage in my life!! What a slime ball."

"But I didn't stay scared, Pat."

"Huh?"

"I said I didn't *stay* scared."

"Good for you." I took a deep breath to try to calm myself down.

"Yup, when I hollered, 'Let's go, don't waste your time!' I meant it. And whether he gets '*his*' from us or not, Pattie, a guy like that will pay for what he did somewhere down the line."

I sighed, "I know, but..."

"But what?"

"Well, I know he'll get what's coming to him. I'm just sayin' that I'd like to be around to hear about it when it happens."

Dolly nodded. "We can't change that Friday night, Pat."

"I know."

"Here's how I'm thinking about all this."

"How's that?"

"Well, if I allow this to haunt me for the rest of my life, he'll be raping my soul, *and* my heart, *and* my mind. What happened to my body was bad enough. I have to let it go, and what ever happens to this slug, happens."

I nodded.

"I'm not in denial. I know what happened, but I'd be a victim twice if I keep holding on to the pain."

My eyes filled with tears as I turned to hug her. "You're my hero, Doll."

"I am?"

"Yes, you are!"

Chapter Seventy-Nine

Dolly and I left John's Pier, walked down to the end of the Inlet and just sat there watching a few big fishing boats slowly sail under the Townsend's Inlet/Avalon bridge.

"The ocean has a soothing quality to it, don't you think?"

I nodded. "Yep. Maybe when I'm big I'll get a house down here. You know, carry on the family tradition."

Dolly smiled at me, "Maybe I'll stay down here, too. Wouldn't that be cool if our kids could play together?"

"Very cool!"

"And wouldn't it be *really* cool if one of us could cook like Aunt Anna?!"

"Dolly, if one of us ever cooks like Aunt Anna, it won't be just cool, it'll be an act of divine intervention."

She laughed at me.

"So," I nudged her, "until divine intervention comes along, how about we go back to the house for some of heaven on earth food."

"You don't have to ask me twice!" She smiled.

Within ten minutes Dolly and I were back home, helping Aunt Anna prepare an early Sunday dinner. Need I say it was another feast?

Southern fried chicken, mashed potatoes and gravy, hot buttered Jersey sweet corn, fresh biscuits and a delicious peach cobbler!

How does this woman do it?

After dinner, Dolly and I washed and dried the dishes, cleaned off the table and then swept the floor. Aunt Anna took a well-deserved break and decided she'd finish knitting the afghan she started while listening to her husband snoring away on the couch beside her. And Uncle John wasn't just any snorer; this man was a window rattler. But, somehow my Aunt enjoyed listening to him. How? I don't know, but she did.

Our kitchen duties complete, Dolly and I sat out on the back porch and talked for a while. It was nice out there after dinner. The sun was just setting, a soft wind blew the fronds of the huge weeping willow tree around my old swing set, and you could hear sea gulls squawking as they flew to their homes for the evening. Dolly and I just sat there for a while taking in the peace of it all.

"It was a good day, Pat."

"All in all, I'll have to agree with you."

She smiled at me.

"Think we'll hear from Brenda soon?"

"Yeah. I know she's in a tizzy gettin' her stuff ready for school and all, but she'll write. She'll wanna know what's been goin' on."

"Should we tell her about…"

I turned and looked at Dolly. "Do you want to?"
"Maybe later."
"Okay then, later."

Chapter Eighty

Monday morning was upon me before I knew it. I quickly dressed, brushed my teeth, drank some orange juice, and then rushed over to Shellum's. I was winded by the time I got there.

"Whoa!" Mrs. Shellum smiled. "Where's the fire?"

"Sorry," I said, trying to catch my breath, "I was afraid I'd be late."

"Well, Pattie, you've got three minutes to spare! Have a seat over there, grab yourself one of those fresh Danishes and have a cup of coffee. Relax a little before you start your day, Dear."

"Thanks, Mrs. S.," I sighed. "Where's Doll?"

"Cast an eyeball over here," Dolly smiled as she adjusted her smock.

"Oh, *there* you are!"

"Yeah, I was in the back re-doing my ponytail. The rubber band broke, so Mrs. Shellum gave me another one."

With a mouth full of cherry Danish, I nodded.

Dolly poured herself a half a cup of coffee and then sat down next to me. "They good?"

"*These* are the best! No one makes cherry Danish like The Sea Isle Bakery! You know that!"

Dolly lifted the large glass lid from the cake plate and took one. She immediately bit into it. "The way to start a perfect day," she smiled.

And it *was* a pretty good day. All morning long we were busy, and that was a good thing. Nice customers came and went, we got a new supply of tackle boxes, so naturally Uncle John and Mr. Linkletter stopped by, some of the local kids we knew from The Civic Center dances dropped in for one thing or the other. Then, right after our lunch break, George and Clark walked in the front door and right over to the soda fountain.

"Two hamburgers with fried onions and two orders of fries, please," Clark was his usual polite self.

"And a chocolate milk shake and a coke, please." George smiled at me.

"Comin' right up, fellas."

As I was setting out the ketchup, relish, and napkins for their late lunch, George spoke to me, "How are you guys doing?"

"Today was a good day, but…"

"But what?"

"I'll tell you later."

"This isn't a Jack Dawkins thing again, is it?" Clark shook his head.

"Unfortunately."

George straightened up in his seat. "Was he in here? He hassled you guys in public?!"

"Well, in public, yes… but not here."

Just then Dolly walked up behind me to make two strawberry milk shakes 'to go.'

"You told them about the pass Creepo made on you?"

"The what?!" George's eyes widened.

"Well, not yet, but I guess I'll have to *now*."

"Sorry, Pat."

"That's okay. I was gonna tell him anyway."

"Tell me what? What happened?"

I leaned in over the counter so no one would hear me. "Dolly and I saw Jack coming out of Wiley's and he started his stuff and Dolly managed to rise above it, but I just got angry. Then he asked me if that hot temper of mine made me hot 'anywheres else.'"

"He what?!" George wasn't really surprised at Jack's lack of respect for women, it just totally grossed him out.

"That's what he said to me, George."

"Did you walk away?" Clark interrupted.

"He didn't touch you, did he?" George's voice was at a slow boil.

"No. But…"

"But what?"

"He moved his grimy hand down the front of his dungarees, and sort of fondled himself, then asked me, 'Hey, you in for some-a this?'"

"What?!!"

"Then I called him a grody, disgusting excuse for a human being, and then I said, 'you'll get yours, Jack Dawkins!'"

Clark pushed his plate away, so did George.

"Are you okay, Pat? Is Dolly okay?"

"Yeah. We're all right."

I didn't know George and Clark all that long, but I could tell by the looks on their faces that something was brewing.

"You're not gonna do anything to him, are you? He's not worth it. He's not!"

They didn't answer me.

"I mean it! Don't get yourselves into trouble over this. He'd get off scot-free and you two would be hung out to dry."

Still no answer.

"Hey! Did you hear me? Please, I mean it, don't do *anything*. Nothing can change this situation. He'll be gone soon anyway. Summer's almost over."

"Not soon enough, Pattie," George said looking me straight in the eye.

"And even when he does go," he added, "If he isn't stopped now, wherever he goes, there'll be another Dolly. It could happen to Dale Harding. If it hasn't already."

I sighed. "My God, what are we gonna do?"

"*We* are not going to do *anything*," he stated.
"We aren't?!"
"No, Pat. *We* aren't."
My head was spinning. I had no idea what was going on. Quietly George and Clark got up from their seats at the fountain without touching a bite of their food. George paid the bill and Clark left a nice tip for me and then placed a dollar in the S.P.C.A donation tin. I walked them to the front door.

"I mean it. You're not gonna do anything crazy are you?"

"No," George said as he exited the store.

As I watched George and Clark walk away toward the pier, I wondered what that word "No" really meant. Did that mean they were going to do nothing at all? Or, did that mean they *were*, but nothing really crazy?

What could be going on here? Think, Pattie.

As I walked back to the soda fountain to clean it off for the next customer, I laid it all out straight in my head.

One: George and Clark were gentlemen from good families.

Two: They knew that the system would turn on Dolly if she talked to them.

Three: It was Dolly's word against Jack's.

Four: They knew if this town ever got wind of what happened, Dolly would never be looked at in the same way again, and then the public *and* the system would make her a victim all over again.

Five: There was no way out for us. No way out at all.

Yup, George and Clark's hands were just as tied as mine and Dolly's.

And they knew it.

Didn't they?

Chapter Eighty-One

By the time Tuesday afternoon rolled around Dolly and I had already talked about the conversation I had with George and Clark at least a dozen times. We both agreed that while we all knew that Dawkins had to be stopped, short of hiring The Mafia, it wasn't going to happen. The system of 1959 wasn't geared that way. So, we decided to hold our heads up high, give Dale Harding the tip on Jack without spilling all the beans, and then just move away from this horrible experience entirely.

One HUGE move away from that horrible experience came to me in a brief phone call from Dolly that very night.

"Pat?"
"Hi, Doll"
"I got it."
"Huh?"
"You know, I got... IT!"
"It? Oh... IT!!! Well, thank God for that!"
"I'll say!" She sighed. "So, see ya tomorrow, Pattie."
"Okay, Doll. See ya."

What a load off of both of our shoulders; Dolly's in particular. Can you *imagine* if she was... Ugh! I don't even wanna think about it!

* * * * * *

Wednesday and Thursday seemed like normal old times back at Shellum's. Doll and I had our hands full, but it was a really great place to work. George and Clark dropped by faithfully every day on their way to work on the pier when the fishing boats came in, and Dolly and I talked about what we'd wear to the dance on Friday every chance we got. *And,* right after lunch on Thursday, Aunt Anna dropped by with mail for both of us, from Brenda! I guess Bren figured it would be safer to send Dolly's mail to my address. Mrs. Shellum gave us a few minutes off so we could read her letters.

Brenda was a busy little bee, I can tell you that! She went shopping for school clothes, then she bought LOTS of stationary, she went to the post office to get stamps, and then to the store to buy a new typewriter. Bren also painted her soon-to-be old bedroom a really bright hot pink! She said it was a cool idea. Personally, I think she painted it 'a really bright hot pink' so no one else would even want to go in there and mess with her old stuff. I mean, come on... hot pink???!!

Well, *then*, on the humanitarian side of things, Brenda also went through everything in her room and got rid of lots of stuff she didn't need, couldn't use, or just didn't want anymore, and then she and Mr.

Mayberry took them to The Salvation Army. Brenda always had nice clothes and shoes, so I'm sure they were thrilled to get them. The day before she wrote her letter to me, Bren went with her mom to the travel agency to get her plane tickets to Los Angeles! She'd be leaving on August 14th. Brenda said she didn't want a farewell party; she just wanted to drop by and see her family and friends. This was not to be a sad and soppy visit, just a light and breezy fun one. Brenda also told me she stopped and visited my mom and dad's gravesite and that the headstone was already in place. She said a prayer for them, and me. I thought that was awfully sweet. She's such a good person and I'm proud and honored to call her my friend.

And, last but not least, Brenda asked me what was new in Townsends Inlet, you know, did anything exciting happen since she left…???

What a question!

Of course, I wrote back to her and told her about work, Aunt Anna and Uncle John, Clark, George, the dance, Bandstand's own, Franny Giordano's appearance at The Civic Center, and that Dolly was singing and playing piano at church now! You know, all the local news.

…Well, almost all of it.

* * * * * *

By the time we left for home on Thursday evening we were just buzzing with chatter about the dance!

"Another fabulous Friday night dance, Pattie!" Dolly smiled at me.

"Man, the week really flew by fast, didn't it?"

"This is a good thing." She smiled again.

"And you're wearing your pale blue circle skirt?"

"Yup. Complete with white Peter Pan collared blouse and this really cool waist cincher that Nikki gave to me. She can't wear it anymore since Mack was born. It's too small."

"Lucky for you."

"I'll say!"

"See you tomorrow, Doll!"

"Okay! Have a good night, Pat! Say Hi to your Aunt Anna and Uncle John for me."

"Will do! See ya."

We waved at each other off and on until I turned down 85th Street.

I felt good… like… like something had shifted in the universe and everything was going to be all right. Maybe it was Brenda's letter that helped me feel that way, or Dolly's good news that she wasn't pregnant, or, maybe it was just, well, maybe it was just one of those unexplainable things that happens, with no rhyme or reason, that makes the road ahead look clear and bright.

After another delicious dinner I decided to write Brenda a letter while listening to some music. I wrote six pages in about ten minutes. The words practically flew onto the paper. Then, I finished reading my wonderful Nancy Drew book, "The Clue in the Diary." In brief, it's a story about helping an innocent victim find justice.

How appropriate, huh?

By the time I looked over at my clock radio it read 11:15! I couldn't believe it was so late! I had to get some sleep. Shellum's was getting in a huge food order in the morning and Dolly and I promised we'd be there by 7:30. In the bat of an eye, I turned off the small lamp on my nightstand, said my prayers, and went right to sleep.

...For a while anyway.

Chapter Eighty-Two

The sound of sirens woke me.
Sirens...
Sirens...
And more sirens...
I looked at the clock. It was 4:35.
I got up out of bed and looked out my window. I was too far away from the corner to see anything, but I did hear the whooshing sounds of several speeding police cars on Landis Avenue, and then those awful sirens again. What a racket!
I hoped no one was hurt, but with all that commotion going on, I'm sure something terrible had happened. See, back in the early 1950s, Landis Avenue after 3:00 AM, on any given night, was a hot spot for drag racers. You know, like something straight out of an old Marlon Brando film - some cool souped-up cars, owned by rebels who thought they had a cause.
Well, whatever they were doing, it all ended on Saturday, August 31st, 1953, when four local kids were killed right there on that makeshift hot rod strip at Landis Avenue and 92nd Street.
Suddenly I heard more sirens and I prayed that it wasn't happening again.
I stood by my window in silent reverie until the last of the police cars and the screaming sirens of the Sea Isle City Ambulance Company were gone.
A cool breeze blew my hair around my face as I looked at the clock.
5:00 AM?!
If I was lucky I could get another hour and a half of sleep.
I crawled in-between the clean, soft covers and then quickly pulled them up over my head... as one more ambulance roared up Landis Avenue.

Chapter Eighty-Three

I woke up around 6:15 and felt like I had no sleep at all. I got dressed, dragged myself into the bathroom, brushed my teeth, and then headed down to the kitchen table.

"Mornin' Aunt Anna. Sure looks good."

"Why thank you, Pattie. Sleep well?"

I sighed as I reached for my orange juice. "I'd like to say yes, but with…"

"All that noise?"

"Yeah."

"It woke me up, too."

"I wonder what happened?"

"I don't know. John went fishing about an hour ago, so I guess if I find out it'll be because Carrie calls and tells me."

"Geez, I hope it wasn't that drag racing stuff again."

"Oh, Lord," my aunt said softly, "I hope not."

* * * * * *

I walked into Shellum's and Dolly was already at the soda fountain drinking her morning coffee.

"Hi, Pat!"

"Hi, Doll! Where's Mrs. S.?"

"Out back watering the tomatoes."

"Oh."

"And Mr. Shellum drove up to Sea Isle."

"Why?"

"He said he wanted to talk to one of the cops up there, you know, to see what all the commotion was last night."

"Did you hear that?! It woke me up out of a sound sleep!"

"Did I *hear* it? I coulda been in Hoboken and I woulda heard it!"

Just then Mrs. Shellum entered with a few delivery men loaded to the gills with boxes of supplies. "The cereals go here," she said. "And the detergent goes there, the canned goods go here…"

Dolly and I immediately started to open boxes and separate the canned goods, Tide, Cheerios, Coppertone, etcetera and put them where they belonged. We didn't have to price anything because now the prices were already marked on the shelves, so all we had to do was re-stock them. There must have been at least forty cartons to empty, but Dolly and I were a good team and we got it done it what I would consider record time. Mrs. Shellum re-supplied the soda fountain while we worked. So, by the time 8:30 rolled around we are all done, and we still had a half an hour left before our official work day began.

Millie smiled, "That was excellent! I didn't think you'd be done so fast!"

"We work well together." I smiled back at her.

"Yep, Pattie and I know our teamwork, all right!"

"Well, your teamwork has paid off. You don't have to work until 9:00, but I'm going to pay you for it just the same."

"Really?!"

"Yes, really," she smiled again. "Now go make yourselves some coffee, grab a Danish, and relax until then."

"Mrs. S. You're the greatest!" I said heading toward the soda fountain.

"Can we get you some coffee?" Dolly asked.

"No, thank you, Dear. Bill and I had some at home. Two cups is my limit!"

We watched her walk back toward the small office. She reached for her smock and then sat down to do some paperwork.

Nice lady.

And so, that left me and Dolly all alone at the counter with two nice big cups of coffee and two cherry Danishes! As I sat at the counter my thoughts immediately turned toward the dance at The Civic Center.

"What time are you comin' over tonight?"

"Around seven, I guess."

"Good. George and Clark will be over around 7:15 and then we can get going. Got a choice for the opening song this week?"

Dolly smiled as a list of her favorite songs filtered through her head. "Well, how about…"

Just then Bill Shellum burst through the front door.

"MILLIE! MILLIE!!!"

Dolly and I both stood up and watched with widened eyes as Mr. Shellum made his way toward the back of the store. He was in a total fog and he rushed by us as if we didn't even exist. Just about five feet away from where *we* stood, Mrs. Shellum was standing there to meet her husband.

"What's the matter, Bill?!

"Dear God, they… they found a kid…"

"What kid?"

"Jack Dawkins!"

"JACK DAWKINS?!!

"Found him? What do you mean they found him?!"

"That's what all those sirens were about last night."

Dolly and I looked at each other with our mouths wide open.

"What about the sirens?" Millie asked.

"They were tons of police cars and two of the ambulances from up in Sea Isle."

"What happened?"

"They… they found the poor kid buried in the sand about fifty feet away from the bridge!"

"Buried?!" The words left my mouth and Dolly's at the very same time.

"Oh, my God, Bill! Here? *Here* in Townsends Inlet?!"

"Right *here*! It's beyond my comprehension. Even the police said they never saw anything like it!"

"My God… how could this happen?"

"That's what *I* said!"

Just then Millie turned toward Dolly. "Oh, you poor Dear! Aren't you dating that young man?"

"Umm… Well, yes, I… I mean, I…"

Dolly and I must've looked like the living dead because the next thing I remember Millie saying to us was, "Why don't both of you go out for a walk to get some fresh air, I think you might need it."

I'm not so sure if Dolly or I said, "Thanks" or "Okay" but the first thing I remember was that we were both standing outside the store, staring at each other in total shock and disbelief.

"Did Bill say…?"

"Yep." My voice was barely a whisper.

"I mean, he *said* that…"

"Dolly… he *said* that they found Jack buried in the…" I gasped for a decent breath, "in the sand by the bridge."

"Oh, my God!"

I thought she was going to fall over, so I carefully sat her down on Shellum's front steps. "Cool it, Doll. Just try to cool it. Take a deeeeeeep breath!"

"My God, Pattie… Jack's DEAD!!!"

Her words pierced right through my head and the reality of it all finally hit me. I sat down next to her and stared out into space.

I didn't even give a second thought as to how it could have happened.

I already knew.

I put my head between my knees and started to feel sick. My head felt light and tingly and I could see these little white dots floating around every time I opened my eyes. I was hoping it was all just a bad dream, but it wasn't.

Jack Dawkins was dead.
Dead.
Dead.
Dead.
…And I knew who killed him.

Chapter Eighty-Four

By the time Dolly and I got up off the steps and re-entered Shellum's it was just about 9:00 AM. The store seemed to flood with people the minute we walked into the place. Dolly and I returned to our normal routine even though we were still shaking in our shoes about the disaster on the beach at 97th Street. Store patrons walked in buzzing about the Dawkins incident. Carrie Robinson, Emma Orwatt, Jessie Epp, Linny Googer, and Delia Ruggles were one big coffee klatch at the soda fountain. And, as much as I tried to tune them out, I heard just about everything they were saying because I had to wait on them - lucky me.

"Can you imagine someone actually buried that poor boy alive?" Carrie's voice was trembling.

Buried alive?

"What could he have ever done to deserve that?!" Jessie asked.

Deserve? That's a tough call.

"The police said he must've been out there for hours," Emma added.

Police?! Oh, God... the police.

"Well, I heard that the police said Mrs. Minnick was letting her cat back in around 4:00 AM when she heard screaming, and she was the one who called."

Screaming?

"That poor boy's throat must've been stripped dry from all that noise he was making to get some attention... and then..."

"Wait! Jack was screaming?" I interrupted. "So then what? Like did he die right after that?"

All four of them looked at me as if I was an alien with six heads.

"Pattie!" Linny looked at me. "Jack didn't die."

"WHAT?!"

"Jack didn't *die!*"

"But... but Mr. Shellum said he was buried in the sand."

"Buried up to his neck, the poor thing," Carrie added.

"Yup. Buried right up to his neck," Jessie repeated.

Dolly rushed up to the counter. "So he didn't *die*?!"

All four women knew Dolly had dated Jack, and I guess they thought she still was, so they asked her to sit down so they could fill her in so she wouldn't worry unnecessarily.

I kept the coffee coming and re-filling the cake plate with Danishes and donuts. For five tiny little ladies, they had appetites like linebackers. Fourteen cups of coffee, a dozen Danishes, three cream donuts, and two glazed later, the story was complete.

Carrie, Emma, Jessie, Linny, and Delia walked out of Shellum's together and Dolly and I were left with the rest of the day pretending to be cool, calm, and collected, while personally sorting out the ugly happenings of 4:00 AM that morning. If ever the two of us wanted and needed time to fly by… well, you know what I mean. But, work had to be done, it was our job, and so we did it.

Ugh.

The one plus was that it was Friday and Mrs. Shellum *always* let us leave early because of the dance.

"Girls!" Millie called out, "I'm letting you go at 3:00 today!"

"Three?!"

"Yes. And you'll still get your full eight hours for the day, plus the overtime hour from this morning."

"Really?!"

"Absolutely. You've been troopers under some pretty difficult circumstances. You could use a break."

Dolly and I ran over to Millie and each of us gave her a big hug.

"Well, as I said, Bill and I feel as if you need the time so, just take it and enjoy!"

I looked at the clock, it was already 2:30!

Only another half hour to go. Thank God!

By the time Dolly rang out Mrs. Bender's food order and I made five Italian hoagies for the Thomas family, we were down to about fifteen minutes.

Hallelujah!

Just then Mrs. O'Reilly and her five children walked in and they all ordered milkshakes. They'd just come back from the beach and this was a special treat from their mom. The O'Reilly's were a nice family, and this was a familiar order for me, so I took it.

"One vanilla for Mrs. O., a strawberry for Kathleen and Maureen, one banana shake for Joe Junior, a chocolate for Irene, and a black and white for Teddy."

Mrs. O'Reilly smiled at me. "That's some memory there, Pattie."

Dolly helped me make the shakes, we gave all the kids a free pretzel stick, and then, it was 3:00!

"Time to call it quits, girls!" Millie called to us.

Yaaaaaaaay!

Dolly and I immediately walked back to the office to take off our smocks and then we picked up our paychecks. Mr. Shellum cashed them right there for us, and, inside of each of our envelopes was a nice crisp new five dollar bill - for the overtime.

As Bill handed me my weekly pay I thanked him for being such a nice boss. Dolly also thanked him for all that he and Millie had done for us. They really were wonderful people.

As soon as we grabbed our handbags and filled our wallets with a week's pay *plus* overtime, Doll and I were waving our goodbyes to the

Shellums and heading out the front door.

Dolly patted my shoulder as we reached the sidewalk. "Hey, we've got an extra five bucks and an extra hour."

"Yeah?"

"So, I say this is an opportunity to get a cone and talk. How 'bout it?"

"Works for me."

We crossed Landis Avenue and the second we hit the opposite side of the street we started to talk non-stop.

"Did you hear the whole story, Pat?"

"Did I? I felt like my feet were glued to the floor, I just stayed there and listened. I mean I mighta missed something, 'cause I was filling their orders, but I heard plenty!"

"Didja hear that Jack said he was sitting up on the beach by the pavilion, around 1:00 AM - *alone*?"

"He's lying. He wasn't up there by himself."

"Then who was he with?"

"I dunno… Dale Harding, maybe?"

"Well, according to the report he was alone."

"Okay," I sighed, "let's go by the police report we both know he faked."

Dolly rolled her eyes at me while I continued, "So, he's on the beach, *alone*… and then two or possibly three guys come up to rob him."

She nodded. "Yeah. And then Jack said he didn't have any money so they roughed him up to see if he was lying."

I thought back to what I heard Carrie say and then I repeated my own version of it, "So when he didn't have any cash, they got ticked off, took him down to the end of the inlet, and buried him up to his neck in sand…"

"Yeah, and Jack said the guys had been drinking, didn't he, Pat?"

"That's what he said."

He lied. George and Clark don't drink.

"And then the report said that the guys put some old fish heads real close to his face. Can you imagine that?"

"Yep! Up to his rotten neck in sand and flounder."

"Pattie, that's not nice."

"Oh, please. It was too good for him if you ask me."

"Pat! For God's sake!"

"It was just a few stinkin' old fish heads. Hey, ya think the crabs that come up on the beach at night got a nice little bite to eat."

"That's an ugly thought." Dolly shook the visual out of her head.

"Wonder if Jack is missing any small facial parts?" I smiled.

"Stop that!"

"Too bad they didn't stake him to the ground or something, then the crabs could've gone for some more vital parts, you know crawled right up onto his crotch and..."

"PATTIE!!!"

"Okay, okay... then what?"

"Well, then Carrie said she heard that the guys just sat there with Jack and talked to him for a while. Like for about a half an hour."

"Did Carrie say what they talked about? I missed that part."

"No. Jack just said he was told to be quiet, or they'd come back and that would be that!"

"Well, if that happened around 1:00 AM, then Jack was quiet for almost three hours? Man, they scared the pants off of that guy!"

"And, Pat..."

"What?"

"Emma said that when the police found Jack his head was about six inches from the incoming tide."

"Six inches?"

"Yup, and that whoever buried him must've known the waters pretty good, 'cause the tide would never have gotten any closer, it was on its way back out."

"Is that right..." My voice slowed down a bit as I took in Dolly's words. It didn't take long for me to figure out that she was drawing the same conclusion I had.

"Yup. *And* that whoever did it just really wanted to scare the Bejeezus out of him."

"Well, they certainly did that!"

Dolly looked lost in thought for a moment and then she said, "They didn't beat him up. There weren't... there weren't even any bruises – not one. I mean he... he wasn't hurt in any way at *all*. ...Pat?"

"What, Doll?"

"This was an act of revenge, wasn't it?"

I didn't answer her.

"George and..."

"Don't even think it."

"But who else would..."

"Not another word."

"But, *Pat*..."

"*Not* another word."

Chapter Eighty-Five

Dolly and I walked to John's Pier and bought ourselves two double-dipped chocolate ice cream cones with jimmies. No matter what we did or what else we *tried* to talk about, somehow the conversation would always drift back to Jack Dawkins.

"Wonder where he is now?" She asked me.

"I don't know. But I bet where ever he is he's not eating a nice seafood dinner. He'll never be able to look a flounder in the eye again."

Dolly chuckled and then immediately stopped herself. "I should be ashamed of myself, laughing at the poor man's misery."

"Puh-leeze. He got what he deserved."

"But look what happened to him?!"

"To him?!! You were sweating it for two weeks that you were pregnant, and he never gave a second thought to what he did to *you*. And what he *did* was rape you!! THEN, right in front of you, at the dance, he zooms in on Dale Harding…"

Dolly's voice was quiet, "Yeah, I know."

"And then, to top it all off, he makes that sickening pass at me, and then he fondles himself, and he thought it was *funny!*"

Dolly bowed her head. She looked sad and disgusted.

"Look Doll, I'm not standin' here with pom-poms in my hands cheering about what happened to him, but my heart isn't broken over it either. He's a pathetic, abusive, self-centered, slimy jerk who got *exactly* what he deserved."

Dolly stood there taking in my words for a moment or two.

"I'm sorry. You're absolutely right. He's a pathetic, abusive, self-centered, slimy jerk who got *exactly* what he deserved."

"Amen, sister!"

* * * * * *

I walked Dolly to the corner of her street and told her I'd see her around seven. She waved, I waved and then off I went, back to the quiet and peaceful Turner household.

Thank God!

"You're early," my Aunt said as she gave me a kiss on my cheek.

"Well, it was a long day, we were busy at work and then… well, I'm sure you know the place was buzzing about what happened to Jack Dawkins. Carrie and the coffee klatch came in and told me and Dolly all about it while we waited on them."

My aunt nodded, "She called me just shortly after you left for work this morning. What a terrible thing. And he was a friend of yours and

Dolly's?"

I so wanted to come clean with my Aunt, but I just couldn't. So, I told her as much as I possibly could without betraying myself or Dolly.

"Aunt Anna?"

"Yes, Dear?"

"Jack wasn't a very nice guy."

"He wasn't?"

"No. He wasn't. And he treated Dolly badly."

"He did? Oh, my heavens."

"He had a history of treating girls like that, I think."

"A *history*?" My Aunt shook her head and sighed.

"My guess is that someone wanted to scare him enough that he'd think twice before violating another member of the opposite sex ever again."

"Well, I would think that what just happened would scare him enough to last a few lifetimes."

"I sure hope so, Aunt Anna. I *sure* hope so."

* * * * * *

Uncle John walked in the house about fifteen minutes later and we discussed the 'Dawkins' thing all over again. Uncle John was such a gentleman, and he truly respected women. It was shocking for him to hear that Jack was so abusive when it came to the fairer sex. It *really* disturbed him.

Imagine if he knew the whole story!

… He probably would've supplied the fish heads himself!

* * * * * *

Despite a day filled with Jack Dawkins chat, dinner was put together easily and it was delicious - as always. I helped Aunt Anna clean up before I went upstairs to get ready for the dance.

"Are you all right, Dear?" she asked me as I was about to make my exit.

"I'm fine, Aunt Anna."

As I entered my room I remembered that I promised Dolly I'd wear my new circle skirt this week, so I took it out and then went rummaging through my closet for a blouse that matched. I set out my bobby sox and saddle oxfords, and my pretty charm bracelet that Mom and Dad gave to me for my 16th birthday. And *no* outfit was ever complete back in 1959 without a cool waist cincher belt. Tonight I was wearing a white one with a bright silver buckle. It was pretty cool.

I tried hard not to think about George and Clark coming over here to pick us up for the dance, but it ran through my mind every thirty seconds just the same.

I'd have to mention *something*! It was the talk of the entire inlet. And I *knew* they did it! I mean, from the moment I heard what happened, I knew it was George and Clark! Well, I was r-e-a-l-l-y shocked when I thought Jack was dead! In my heart they weren't capable of that, but still... I was worried. Who else *could* it have been? But when I heard all the details at Shellum's? I felt it was, well, an act of chivalry, I guess. You know, scaring off the black knight to protect the fair maiden.

Before I knew it Aunt Anna called to me to say that Dolly had arrived. Doll immediately ran upstairs to join me while I put on my finishing touches. As I was adjusting my ponytail, Aunt Anna called again to tell us George and Clark were downstairs waiting for us.

Dolly and I looked at each other as soon as their names were mentioned and then we slowly descended the staircase in total silence.

As we entered the parlor there stood George and Clark looking just as handsome, sweet, and serene as they did every Friday night.

"Hi, Pat," George smiled. "You look terrific!"

"Thanks."

"You too, Dolly," Clark added.

"Thanks, Clark!"

"Well, you kids have fun! John will be following you within a few minutes, he's upstairs sprucing up."

Dolly and I gave my aunt a hug, we all said our goodbyes, and then off we went down 85th Street - again in total silence.

Chapter Eighty-Six

We had almost reached The Civic Center. I couldn't stand the quiet any longer and I tugged Mr. Ludlam's arm. "Can we talk about..." I started.

"About?" George answered.

"About what happened to Jack?" Dolly was quick with a reply.

I couldn't believe she was so upfront about it, but the words just came out that way.

"Let's walk up to the pavilion," George said softly.

"Okay."

We walked on for a moment or two and then Dolly said, "I'm worried."

"About what?"

"The boomerang could come flying back in our faces, I guess."

"Why would that happen to us?" Clark asked.

"Well, you know... because..."

We were only a few steps away from the pavilion benches so we walked up the small, stone sidewalk and then took our seats at the back of the jumbo-sized gazebo.

"Because why, Doll?" Clark asked leaning back on the bench.

I took a giant stabilizing breath and then blurted out, "Because you two did that to Jack. That's why!"

"Pattie..." George started.

"What?"

The guys looked at each other and then Clark gave a nod to his friend as if to say, 'You tell them.'

George cleared his throat and spoke in a voice that was clear, strong, and heart-felt. I trusted every one of his words even before he said them.

"Listen..."

"We're listenin'. Go on."

"Last night around 12:30 Clark and I left Wally Garrity's house. We were playin' poker over there."

"Not for any big bucks, just nickels and dimes," Clark added.

"We walked about twenty feet outside Wally's door and we saw this girl running from the pavilion.

"*This* pavilion?" Dolly asked.

"Yeah."

"Who was it?"

"Well, at first I couldn't tell, and then she ran by one of the streetlights and I saw it was Dale Harding."

"I toldja it was Dale," I whispered to Dolly.

"We thought we heard her crying or something, so it wasn't too hard to figure out that possibly Jack Dawkins wasn't too far behind."

"And?"

"Clark and I ran up the steps and there was Jack… lightin' up a cigarette."

"What did you say to him?"

"Well, Clark sat on one side of him and I sat on the other. He looked kinda uncomfortable and that was just fine with me."

Clark smiled.

"I asked him if he was the reason Dale had run away from the pavilion."

"He said he didn't know what I was talking about."

"Then?"

"Then I told him, it better not be for the same reason Dolly ran to Pattie's house a few Fridays ago."

Dolly hid her face in her hands. "Oh, God."

"Then?!" My blood pressure was rising.

"Then that famous arrogant side showed up. There were some words exchanged that you two ladies don't need to hear and then…" George looked at Clark.

"Then we just warned him to stay clear of our hometown girls, and maybe he'd be better off elsewhere."

"What did he have to say about that?"

"Well, some more words were exchanged and…"

Again George looked at Clark and Clark spoke up, "And then we left."

"And then you *what*?!

"We left."

"You *left*?! Do you think I'm *stupid*?! You didn't *leave*!"

"I said we left, Pat."

"NO! You walked that slug down the beach, buried him up to his neck in sand, and then covered him with the fish heads you took there a few days earlier."

Dolly nodded.

"You guys would have plenty of fish parts from cleaning all that stuff at the pier."

Again Dolly nodded.

"*And*," I continued to ramble, "the cops said, who ever buried him there knew the tides, because he really didn't start to scream until he thought the tide would come in and drown him! You *knew* he wouldn't drown, George! You know those tides like the back of your hand!"

"Pattie… I'm telling you, we left him."

"You're lying!"

"Well, that's my story and I'm stickin' to it. So, whoever followed Jack after we left, well…"

"Well, what?"

"Go find them and thank those guys."

"George Ludlam, don't *lie* to me! We're not going to tell anyone what you did!"

"What's to tell?"

"Here's somethin' to tell," Clark added.

"What is it?"

"My father heard that Jack's dad sent for his brother, you know that guy from up in New York?"

"His Uncle Sal?" Dolly asked.

"Yeah. He came down here and picked him up."

"Picked him up?"

"Yeah. They said Jack was so scared that he never even left the police station. His dad packed his bags, and took them to the cops."

George finished the story. "Then Jack's uncle drove down to get him and the two of them split for New York with a police escort out of the city."

"So he's *really* gone?" Dolly breathed a sigh of relief.

"Oh, yeah… he's gone."

"For good?" I asked George.

"I'm absolutely certain of it."

"One hundred percent?"

"One thousand percent."

Dolly, George, Clark, and I left the pavilion and never really mentioned the incident again. You'd think it would crop up every now and then, but it didn't. The case was closed. Jack told police he never saw who it was, he never even recognized their voices, so he couldn't press charges against anyone if he (supposedly) didn't know who they were. Could he?

So, adios, Jack Dawkins. You slimy, lying, arrogant… you… you… cold, cruel, unfeeling, vicious, brutal, inhuman… pathetic, merciless, stupid… self-absorbed, hard-hearted, ignorant, nasty, sneaky, evil, criminal jerk!

There…

I said it, and I'm glad!

Chapter Eighty-Seven

We entered the dance and the atmosphere was out of this world. The Center was filled with great kids, terrific food, and the music? It was fabulous - as always. *And*, to top that off, Dolly and I felt quite safe and secure in the company of Messrs. Ludlam and Lowen. After five fast dances in a row the four of us walked over to the concession stand for a coke. We had barely taken a sip of our soda, when Dolly and I spied Dale Harding entering the Ladies Room.

"We'll be right back!" we said scurrying quickly away from George and Clark.

I opened the door and immediately saw Suzie VanSant in there fixing her ponytail. We exchanged hellos and then she was gone. That left me and Dolly in there all alone with Dale. She exited the small booth and was washing her hands when I said, "Did you hear about Dawkins?"

She looked up at me briefly and kept washing her hands.

"He's gone and he's not comin' back."

"He's gone?" Her voice wasn't more than a whisper.

"Dale, we were worried about you 'cause…" Dolly's voice started to crack, "because we knew he was making a pass at you and well, when I dated him… he… "

"He what?"

Dolly took a deep breath. "He attacked me. It was really scary and…"

"And," I continued, "we wanted you to know it's gonna be okay now."

Dale dried her hands and gave us a small smile. She started to leave, but then suddenly turned back toward us. "I never had a guy even look twice at me before Jack." Her eyes started to fill. "When I left for the dance that night my mother said, 'Don't compare yourself to anyone else. You're a nice girl, and you'll get a nice fella to dance with you.' You know how Moms are."

I sighed.

"But no one did, Pat. I was here for two hours and no one even asked me to dance. No one ever does." She adjusted her glasses. "Then Jack came over to me and he was all kinds of charming and…"

"And?" Dolly asked softly.

"And I felt special. So I started to see him, and then a few days later he asked me to go to the pavilion to see the stars and the full moon and I thought it would be so romantic and…"

"And then?"

"He was all over me… I was scared to death."

"He didn't…" Dolly started.

"No, he never really touched me, but he tried. He ripped my blouse open and I got up and I kicked him in his... well, you know, and then I ran away as fast as I could."

"That slimeball."

"I know I was crying hysterically while I was running away, but I was so scared. I mean, I was *petrified*. And who could I tell?"

"That's the problem," Dolly answered.

"My sister would've squealed to everyone and my Mom would have had a heart attack! And my *father*?! Oh, God! He woulda killed him! So I just stayed away from Jack and places I knew he'd be and then, you know, it happened."

"You mean when he got buried on the beach?"

"Yeah."

I nodded.

"I hate to say it, but I'm glad it happened," she continued, "whoever did that to Jack, well..." she paused briefly, "Well, I guess knights in shining armor do exist." Dale managed a smile once again.

Just then Carole Bierman, Kathy McGee, and Phyllis Molloy walked into the bathroom, we all said Hello, and then Dolly, Dale, and I left.

I waved to George and Clark still sitting at the concession stand.

"How about coming over and sitting with us for a while?" Dolly asked Dale.

"Well, I'm here with my sister and..."

"So, bring her along!"

Dale's younger sister, Barbara was just sixteen and a really nice kid - like Dale.

We sat together, danced together, and had a really good time all evening.

It was a genuinely great night for all of us.

...For many reasons.

After the dance ended we all helped fold The Civic Center chairs and then made our exit for the evening. George and Clark walked me home first, then Dolly, and then Dale and Barbara.

What wonderful guys.

...For *many* reasons.

Chapter Eighty-Eight

When I walked into work that Monday morning, Mrs. Shellum was already putting Labor Day Sale signs all over the summer shore items.

"Having these beach balls and kites hanging around all winter takes up too much space," she said to me.

Despite the usual hectic work day and the push, push, push, to sell our summer supply stock, Dolly and I enjoyed ourselves. Well, actually, we enjoyed our entire work week! Of course, the town was still buzzing about the Jack Dawkins incident, but we never gave it much thought. He was gone, and we both knew that he'd be looking over his shoulder for a long, long time. And that was good enough for us.

Both Dolly and I hoped that Jack's new life would allow him room to grow up and realize the error of his ways. There's hope enough out there for everyone, but the decision to jump over the line to be real with yourself and others, to clean up your act, to make a difference in your life so that it improves the quality of living for you and also for those around you… well, that takes a real leap of faith, and a lot of work. Maybe that's why most people don't do it – too much pain in the soul search, too much work, too much effort.

So, 'To be, or not to be'… well, that would *be* Jack's decision.

If he chose to remain a creep, a control freak, and an abuser all of his life, then he'd continue to get what he deserved. I personally wasn't going to lose any sleep over it.

I remember my mother telling me that change is the hardest thing for people to do. She said that they get stuck in ruts and ugly patterns and they can talk themselves into believing that anything they've done was the right thing and, that they did it for all the right reasons. Dolly used to be like that too, but look how a reality check turned *her* life around! She made a genuine conscious effort to rid herself of her past, and become who she really was - deep down inside.

It was the best move of her life.

No question about it.

Life was good these days for Dale Harding and her sister Barbara, too. We were all becoming fast friends. They'd stop by Shellum's during the week to say "Hi" to us and have a coke or a sundae, we'd go to the dance together, and then of course, there were our knights in shining armor, Sir George and Sir Clark who dropped by once a day to see how we were doing.

Dolly and I were blessed not only to have each other, but to have so many other good people in our lives: The Harding girls, Clark, George, Bill and Millie, and of course, Aunt Anna and Uncle John, and Brenda.

"Water seeks its own level," my parents used to say.
…I guess that's true.

* * * * * *

Before we knew it another weekend was upon us. Another super-duper dance, another beautiful Sunday in church hearing a great sermon by Reverend Marshall, *and* another chance to listen to Miss Dollio play piano and sing.

Honestly, I never remembered the church being so crowded. I mean, never once in all the years I went there with Mom and Dad did I ever see the church so full that people had to stand in the back because there were no seats left. Then Dolly turned her life around, and so many wonderful things happened. One little seventeen-year-old girl managed to put a smile on the face of the entire inlet every Sunday.

And all because she learned to believe in herself.

* * * * * *

As August was coming to a close I found myself feeling rather melancholy. I knew George and Clark would be going back to Philadelphia, to their normal non-summer lives. They'd work until the middle of next June and then come back to Townsends Inlet, for one last summer before college. *And*, next year would be *my* last summer before I went to college, too.

Geez, where does the time go?!

* * * * * *

When I got home from work that night, Uncle John was just finishing up a big black and white sign for The Civic Center, it read:

ATTENTION TEENS!!!!
Last Dance of the 1959 Summer Season.
Friday, August 28! 7:00 PM until 10:30PM
Come One! Come All!

Wow, the last dance, I thought to myself.
Again…
Where does the time go?

Chapter Eighty-Nine

Dolly had a new routine going on at her house. She'd wake up at 5:30 AM to do all of her daily chores so that she'd be allowed to come over to my house after work. The plan was to pull out all the stops and brainstorm ways of getting her into a good college the following September. Dolly didn't want to say anything to her family until she felt she was close to being locked in somewhere, and I couldn't blame her.

So, by the time Dolly walked into Shellum's at 9:00 AM, she had already done two or three loads of laundry, hung the clothes out to dry, washed up any left over snack dishes from the night before, dusted the furniture, cleaned the bathroom, made her bed, straightened up her room and showered. Dolly never ate breakfast at home like I did. She always had some coffee and a donut or something as soon as she got to Shellum's. As she said, "The less time spent inside the Dollio household, the better!"

That evening right after dinner, Doll and I sat at the dining room table writing letter after letter to schools that hopefully could test her readiness for college. We also mailed letters to colleges and universities to see if she was a likely candidate, letters to her old teachers, to her High School for a copy of her records, you name it and we were writing it and then mailing it! We just didn't have plan "A", we had plan A,B,C,D,E,F, *and* G!

Dolly sat back after she sealed the last envelope of the night.

"Well, that makes twenty-one for today, huh?"

"Twenty-three."

"Really?"

"Yep."

"That was a lotta work, Pattie. I wish there was a faster way to do this, but…"

"Hey, maybe someday we'll be able to write a letter and then there'll be some little magic box attached to the typewriter that'll mail it off for you. *And*, even send copies to as many people as you'd like – instantly!"

"Pat, *instant* messages?" she smiled, "you've read waaaaay too many Science Fiction books in your life. But it's a nice idea, Kiddo."

"I guess."

* * * * * *

During the next few weeks the two of us became so much closer to our new found friends. And it was, well… it's what they call a bittersweet thing. Soon they'd be gone, and all Dolly and I would have left would be the memories of our days on the inlet, those wonderful days when we were all together.

Not that it would be a bad thing to remember all the fun, it would just be kinda sad that they wouldn't be here with us. I think because of the tragedies in our lives, Dolly and I had an awareness of just how precious time is that most kids our age didn't.

Soon August 28th was upon us and Dolly and I were beyond excited about the dance.

This was the last one of the summer.

The summer of '59.

Yes, the summer of 1959...

I sighed at the thought of it.

I graduated High School, and then that very same night, my wonderful parents were killed in that horrible car accident, I moved down to Townsends Inlet, I got a job, met Dolly, George and Clark... and Jack. Brenda came down for a visit, then about two weeks later Bren left for home and jetted off to California. And then... well, then there was that awful night on the beach for Dolly. Many lives changed after that. And now, all we had was just one more night together before we parted ways.

...One more evening before our friends headed home.

* * * * * *

Dale, Barb, and Dolly arrived at the Turner's at 6:15. We were all gussied up in our 1959 Rock and Roll finery. After work on Tuesday the four of us went to Pfeiffer's to get a new outfit. It was a riot! Poor Mrs. Pfeiffer!

"Do you have this in pink?"

"Mrs. Pfeiffer, do you have another crinoline that doesn't scratch so much?"

"Should I wear a white blouse or a pale blue one?"

"Should I buy the red waist cincher or the navy blue one?"

I don't know how she did it, but Mrs. Pfeiffer had us all outfitted from top to bottom in less than an hour!

I couldn't believe I spent twenty-six dollars, but I did.

A half a week's pay on my outfit!

Yikes!

* * * * * *

As we were putting on our lipstick, Aunt Anna called to us, "Ladies! Two nice young gentlemen are here for you!"

We giggled. Aunt Anna was just too cute.

"Coming! Coming!"

Down the steps the four of us flew, straight into the living room to greet our two nice young gentlemen.

"Evenin' George." I smiled.

He tipped an imaginary hat to me. "Evenin' Miss Pattie."

"Hello, ladies," Clark nodded.

"Hi Clark!" we all answered.

"Well, time to get to the last dance of the season," I said with a pout on my face.

"Pat," George said. "We'll have such a great time tonight, we'll remember it until next summer when we can do it all over again!"

Ya gotta love this guy.

"You look just darling, girls." Aunt Anna smiled.

"Thanks!" Dolly and I answered in unison. "Tell Uncle John we'll meet him up at The Center!"

"Will do! Have fun, kids!"

We all smiled and waved.

Kids…

Uncle John must have been sprinting right behind us because as soon as we arrived at the door, greeted by Emma Orwatt and Bessie Newell, up walked Mr. Turner. He gave us all a big grin and headed right upstairs to his own little D. J. booth. I could have sworn he was humming "Heartbreak Hotel."

Never too old to rock and roll, I guess.

From the first song to the very last I don't think I left the dance floor. I didn't want to miss out on one single moment. Dolly felt the same way. If we weren't jitterbugging with each other, we were doing the stroll with The Civic Center regulars, or slow dancing with George and Clark. Bobby Phillips even asked me to dance and Dolly danced a few slow dances with Luke Cramer, Jim Russak, and Steve Daroff - all really nice guys.

From Elvis to Little Richard, from Ricky Nelson to David Seville and The Chipmunks, we were out there rockin' and rollin' our little hearts out.

I never once looked at the clock or my watch, but I knew 10:30 was fast approaching when Uncle John announced the last two fast songs of the evening – 'Stagger Lee' by Lloyd Price and 'Tallahassee Lassie', by Freddie "Boom Boom" Cannon.

The very last song played was, as always, 'Goodnight Sweetheart' by Pookie Hudson and The Spaniels. George took my hand and then led me out to the middle of the dance floor.

"Well, this is the last time we get to dance together until next summer, Pat."

I nodded, "Yeah, I know."

I closed my eyes and we swayed to the music. It felt good in George's arms - comfortable, safe. I knew it wasn't love, but it was nice just the same.

Dolly tapped my shoulder and smiled at me as she danced by us with

Clark. They had a wonderful night together. Dale and her sister had a great time, too. Dale spent lots of time dancing with Bobby, and Barb danced almost every slow dance with Steve.

It was a great night.

The end to a... well, not a *perfect* summer, but a good end... a happy end to the summer of '59.

The magic continued, the music played on, and then came its final refrain:

Goodnight, sweetheart, well, it's time to go,
Goodnight, sweetheart, well, it's time to go,
I hate to leave you, but I really must say,
Goodnight, sweetheart, goodnight.

And then... it was over.

The lights came back on in and we heard Uncle John's voice speak from his little DJ booth directly above us, "Tonight ends the Summer of '59 Civic Center Dances, and I want to thank each and every one of your for making it such a huge success. I also want to thank Mrs. Emma Orwatt and Miss Bessie Newell, our lovely concession ladies for providing all of us with fantastic refreshments, and, at a reasonable price. How about a nice round of applause for Em and Bess!"

We all cheered like crazy and even though I was about twenty-five feet away from the concession stand, I could still see that they were blushing.

"*And*," Uncle John continued, "Here's a special thanks from me personally. To my darling niece, Pattie Townsend and her friends, Brenda Mayberry, not here with us tonight, and Christine Dollio, known to most of us as, Dolly, for selecting the great records you've been dancing to all summer long. I want to thank them from the bottom of my heart for allowing this old man to tune into this crazy new world of rock and roll music. I want you all to know that I'm proud to be even a small part of it, but, even more than that, I'm proud to be here with such a really great bunch of kids! Good night! Have a wonderful Fall, Winter, and Spring, and remember to come back and see us next summer! I'll be lookin' for ya!"

Whoops, hollers, and applause sounded from the dance floor, as if Uncle John had just won a landslide Presidential election. I saw him stand and then wave to all of us, he was smiling... happy. It was a great night for Uncle John. As if he didn't have enough fishing buddies who loved the guy, he now had over a hundred teenagers who thought he was the absolute coolest.

And you know what?

He was.

Chapter Ninety

As we exited The Civic Center with dozens and dozens of other kids, we saw Barb, Dale, Steve, and Bob walking down 85th Street.

"Pat! Dolly! Don't forget to come by and see us before we go. My mom said we'll be leavin' around ten!"

"You can count on it!" I waved.

George smiled. "They're nice girls."

"Looks like we'll be waving goodbye to lots of nice people." Dolly's voice was soft and quiet.

I tried not to allow my head to get trapped in an unhappy place. So, as upbeat as I could be, I said, "Doll, they'll all be back before we know it!"

She gave me a faint smile, and then turned toward Clark. "Your family leaves on Sunday?"

"Yeah. Dad said right after breakfast we'd be on the road."

"So like when? Nine O'clock?"

"Yeah."

"Okay, we'll stop over before church to see you."

"All right." Clark's voice was barely audible.

"What about you, George?" Dolly questioned.

"We're leavin' after lunch on Sunday… probably 12:30."

I draped my arm over George's shoulder. "I'm gonna miss you, big guy."

"I'm gonna miss you too, Pattie. But we can write to each other, and if you get up to Philly, come on over! That invitation goes for you too, Miss Dolly."

"Cool. Thanks."

"Well, the same goes for me," Clark added. "George and I only live five blocks from each other, so if you two make it up to the city, stop and see both of us!"

"It's a done deal," I said shaking Clark's hand.

For the last time that summer the four of us stood outside The Turner household and talked.

"Well, here we are," I said nervously shuffling my feet.

"Yeah… here we are," Dolly nodded.

I was feeling very misty-eyed about leaving George and Clark. What girl wouldn't? I reached for Clark and gave him a big hug. "See you on Sunday, okay?"

"Bright and early."

I smiled. "Thanks for being a big part of a really wonderful summer for me."

He nodded.

"I mean, it coulda been so…"

Again he nodded.

Then Dolly reached over and hugged him close to her. "You're the best, Mr. Lowen. Thank you for everything."

"My pleasure, Doll."

"And *you*," I smiled at George, "I feel like Dorothy in the Wizard of Oz."

"Huh?"

"You know, when she looks at the Scarecrow and says, 'I think I'll miss you most of all.'"

George's eyes started to fill.

"And I will, George," I whispered as I wrapped my arms around him. "I'll miss you most of all."

Very few words were spoken after that.

Dolly and I stood on the front steps waving goodbye to George and Clark as they walked back up 85th Street.

"Goodnight, sweet Princes," I heard Dolly say softly, "and thank you."

* * * * * *

It was just about 10:00 when we got to Dale and Barbara's house.

Mr. Harding was handing over the keys of their pretty summer rental cottage to the owner, Dale and Barb were bringing out their luggage, and Mrs. Harding was trying to persuade the family dog to get into the back of the car.

"You're right on time!" Dale smiled.

"Can we help you with anything?" I asked.

"I think we've got just about everything, Pattie," Mrs. Harding said. "But it's very sweet of you to offer."

One handshake between Dale and Barb's father and Bob Cleeland, the owner, and the Harding family was ready to trek back to Yardley, Pennsylvania.

"Have a great ride home and be safe!" Dolly said. "And don't forget to write to us!" she added.

"We'll write. We promise!"

"See you in the new decade!" I called out. "1960 here we come!"

"Let's go, girls!" Mr. Harding said.

Dale and Barb jumped in the back seat next to Farfel, their faithful dachshund, and off they went.

"Bye, Pat! Bye, Dolly!" they called to us.

"Bye, Dale! See ya, Barb!"

Within less than a minute their car turned the corner, heading toward Sea Isle, and then… home.

I sighed. "Well, there gone."

Dolly nudged me. "Yeah, but…"
"But what?"
"Aw, Come on, cheer up! How about a chocolate ice cream cone?"
"It's not even 10:30!"
"So, like what are you sayin' to me?"
"I don't know what I'm sayin'. Let's go get some ice cream."

Chapter Ninety-One

As if saying goodbye to Dale and Barbara Harding wasn't bad enough, our next two farewells were for Clark and George.

Dolly and I woke up that Sunday around 7:00 AM to get ready for church. We told Aunt Anna we'd meet her and Uncle John at the service, because we first had to say bon voyage to our dear friend, Mr. Clark Lowen.

The Lowens were a really great family. Well, what can you expect when they had a son like Clark! We walked up to 89th Street, and again, there were all the tell-tale signs of a family leaving their summer life behind. Suitcases in the trunk, two bicycles strapped to the roof of the wagon, and the family dog jumping in and out of the front seat.

"Blondie!" Clark called to the beautiful golden retriever. "Come on girl, get in the back!"

"Need any help?" Dolly asked.

"Nope, looks like we're all ready to go. Mom started packing our clothes a few days ago."

"You know Mom," Mr. Lowen smiled. "She washed them and as they came off the clothesline, she folded everything and in the suitcases they went."

"Talk about efficiency!" I smiled back.

Just then Mrs. Lowen came out after checking the house just one more time. "Well, I think that's about it. We're ready to go."

Dolly and I sighed.

"Have a wonderful, peaceful off season, girls. We'll see you soon, I hope. You are always welcome in our home."

"We hope so, too, Mrs. Lowen. And thank you for the invitation!"

"Clark?" his father called. "Time to go, son."

"In a minute, Dad!"

Dolly moved closer to him and gave him a huge hug. "You don't have to say anything, but I know you helped me. You did all you could to make a horrible wrong into a right."

"No, Doll... we..."

"I just want you to know, you're a wonderful friend, and I'll never forget you... even if I live to be a hundred."

Clark smiled.

"That goes for me, too," I said trying hard to hold back the tears.

"Clark! Let's go, son!"

"Coming, Dad!"

Dolly and I gave him another quick hug and watched him walk away, and then finally step into that big Chevy wagon.

"Bye, Lowens! Bye, Clark!"

We waved and waved until they turned the corner onto Landis Avenue.
We could still hear Blondie barking.
"I'm gonna miss that guy, Pat."
"Dolly" I sighed. "I miss him already."

* * * * * *

Not too much was said on our walk to church, I guess it was because we knew that right after services, we'd have to say our very last goodbye - to George.
As we approached the little church on the corner, Aunt Anna and Uncle John were waiting on the steps along with Jake and Carrie, Nikki, Apry and Mack. Dolly gave the kids a kiss and Nikki a big hug the moment she laid eyes on them.
No need to ask where Mr. Dollio was.
"Are you singin' all by yourself again, Dolly?" Apry had to know.
"Yep."
"Aren't ya scared?"
Dolly smiled. "Actually, I'm lookin' forward to it."
"Well, Dear," Aunt Anna added, "you'd better get in there and get your choir gown on."
"Yes, ma'am." Dolly saluted. "See you guys after services."
We all filed into church, and ever since Dolly had decided to share her talents with the congregation, attendance was 100% every week. It did *all* of us a world of good, it really did - especially Dolly.
This week's service was called, "In celebration of Angels."
And when I heard Dolly sing, all I could think was that her voice alone was celebration enough.
And by the looks on the smiling faces of the one hundred and fifty people in attendance - so did they.

* * * * * *

After services, Dolly and I walked back to the house with Aunt Anna and Uncle John, picked some flowers for the dinner table - direct from the back yard, and then changed clothes before we went over to George's house for our final goodbye of the summer.
My feet were dragging as Dolly and I walked down 85th Street.
"You know, Pat, walking slow isn't going to make any difference."
I grumbled.
"He's leavin' no matter what we do. Let's just get to it."
"Since when did you get so smart?"
"Hey, I had a good teacher." Dolly patted me on the back. "You created your own monster, Kiddo."

"You know you've made more changes in your life this summer than most people make in a lifetime."

She smiled at me.

"I can't tell you how proud I am of you."

"Well, it wasn't easy, Pattie, but… but it wasn't too hard either."

"You think so?"

"Yeah. It was just a matter of making up my mind to be real with myself. And if people can't accept me for who I am and the feelings that I have, well, who needs them?"

I nodded.

"Notice Nikki is pretty supportive of me these days? I mean the kids come to church and everything… and she's not even related to me."

"I like Nik."

"I do, too. But my Dad? He sees I'm becoming my own person. He's losing that hold on me and he doesn't like it. Now I'm smarter than the fear he helped put into my head. I'm winning this race, Pat, and he knows it."

"I'll say."

"So now, he treats me even worse, and then doesn't come to church to hear me sing. I think it's to make me crawl to him or something, you know, 'Daddy, *please* come to church and listen to me sing, *please* chaperone the dance'… Baloney!"

"Good for you!"

"I'm not crawling for anyone anymore. And, if my own father can't be genuinely happy for the life that I managed to pull out of the ashes that were left to me, well, he doesn't have to be in my life. I'm not begging anyone for company, Pat."

"That's the way it has to be if you wanna be your own girl, Doll."

"Yup. It's the best lesson I ever learned."

"You know, by the time you're thirty or somethin', I bet you could have your own TV show."

"What?"

"Yeah, you know, a studio filled with people and you could have special guests on and then you'd discuss people's problems and issues, and give them help, guidance and answers and…"

"Pat, what television network would ever do something like that?! Airing people's misery and dirty laundry on TV? And I would be expected to what? Fix them all in a half an hour or an *hour* of TV time?" She smiled.

"Well…"

"I'm happy you have such faith in me, Pattie but that's just a bit of a stretch, dontcha think?"

"But…"

"Come on, Pat!" She chuckled. "Who's got the big imagination now? That's just plain old silly."

I smiled at her. "Yeah, I guess so."

Chapter Ninety-Two

By the time Dolly and I reached George's house, it was a scene that looked all too familiar to us. The big, gray, Pontiac Bonneville was sitting in the driveway, all four doors open, trunk filled to the max, its roof topped off with three bikes, a large trunk and some fishing gear. And then, there was George, staring at us from the front porch with a forlorn look on his face.

"Two families down and one to go," Dolly said with an equally sad look.

As we walked toward George I did my very best to put on a brave front. "All ready to go, Mr. Ludlam?"

"Well," he said as he entered out into the sunlight, "We're all packed, but to answer your question? No, I am *not* ready to go."

"Georgie!" his mother called from the front door, "There's just one more suitcase, would you please come in and get it,, Dear?"

"Sure, Mom."

"Hi, Mrs. Ludlam!"

"Hi, girls! How are you? ...Be right back!"

We smiled at her.

Just then, George's dad walked around from the back of the house carrying a fishing rod in his hands. "Can't forget 'Ole Betsy'" he smiled.

"Oh, I know what you mean. My Uncle John calls his fishing rods his babies. He's got a name for every one of them."

Mr. Ludlam laughed.

George and his mom exited the house at that very moment and Dolly and I watched as she turned the key, locking away their beautiful summer home until next year.

"One of these days you girls will be married and you'll be doing all this moving and packing!" Mrs. Ludlam chuckled. "But it's all worth it." She gave a loving glance toward her husband.

What a nice thing to see.

"Say your goodbyes, son," Mrs. L. said as she situated herself in the huge Pontiac.

"Okay... I will."

I looked at George, and made a silly sad face. "I don't wanna do this."

"Well, join the club. That makes two of us."

"Hey! Did everyone forget I'm standing here? That would make *three* of us."

George immediately reached for Dolly and gave her a hug. "How could I forget you, Angel Face?" He smiled.

"And don't forget to write to us!"

"Doll, I'll write to you guys the minute I unpack my stuff."

"Well, good, 'cause it'll be gettin' pretty lonely here in Retirementville, U.S.A. after you're gone."

He smiled at her one more time and then turned toward me.

"Was what that line from the Wizard of Oz, Pattie?"

"Huh? Oh... you mean the one Dorothy says to the Scarecrow?"

"Yeah."

The words were hard to say, and my eyes started to fill, but I managed to speak them just the same. "I think I'll miss you most of all."

George's strong arms surrounded me and the scent of 'English Leather' filled my senses as I heard him repeat my words, "I think I'll miss you most of all."

Just then his father called, "Time to go, George! Bye, Girls! God bless you!"

"Bye, Pat! Bye, Dolly!" Mrs. Ludlam waved.

Suddenly I found myself out of George's embrace. Dolly and I watched as he slowly walked away from us and into the beautiful new Pontiac that would take his family back to Philadelphia. We heard the engine turn over and watched as it slowly rolled out of the driveway. Dolly and I waved to George and he waved back, until the car turned onto Landis Avenue.

Dolly turned to me and sighed, "And then there were two."

Chapter Ninety-Three

Thank God Dolly and I had each other. I would have gone totally buggy if I had to live in Townsends Inlet during the off season. I mean, it is, as Dolly puts it, "Retirementville, U.S.A." *And*, if it weren't for Miss Dollio coming over to visit, the person on my block closest to my age was Mame Sheehan - and she was sixty-four!

September flew by because we helped Bill and Millie rearrange their store for the usual winter clientele. The remaining kites, pool toys, and water pistols were put away, replaced by large containers of Quaker Oatmeal, soup stock, woolen blankets, and Ovaltine.

We also spent lots of our free time writing to our friends back in Philadelphia and to Brenda, the college freshman - par excellence - out in California

By October we were decorating for Halloween, then came November and Dolly and her family were invited to Nikki's Dad's home for Thanksgiving dinner. Doll asked if she could spend the holiday with me, and although her father gave her a rough time about it, Nikki persuaded him, and we got to spend the Thanksgiving weekend together. It was great! AND, Mrs. Mitchell, the local high school principal set some special time aside to test Dolly for college. Doll was afraid she wouldn't do too well, because she was so nervous, but she did exceedingly well! I was so proud of her! The weekend was a good one. We wrote letters to Brenda, George, Clark, Dale and Barbara, to tell them the good news, we watched Bandstand and learned a few new dance steps, *and*, we helped Aunt Anna prepare her 'Holiday Feast.'

You know, there should be a better word for feast than feast. I mean if the people who write the Daniel Webster's Dictionary ever sat down to a holiday dinner prepared by Anna Turner, they would be compelled to find a bigger and better word than feast!

Our Thanksgiving table looked as if it was set for the eye of a 'Better Homes and Gardens' camera: White linen tablecloth, with matching napkins, festive napkin rings, Fine Dresden China, Reed and Barton Silverware, and Waterford Crystal drinking glasses. Then, there was a twenty-four pound turkey- butter roasted, with sausage, onion, and herb stuffing, Aunt Anna's famous mashed potatoes with a hint of garlic, lots of fresh-churned butter, and just a dollop of sour cream blended in, there was homemade cranberry sauce, mixed vegetables with hazelnut butter, candied sweet potatoes, cheddar and chive buttermilk biscuits, two pumpkin pies, a to-die-for pumpkin crème brulle, and one scrumptious sweet potato pecan pie.

See what I mean about a new word for 'feast?!'

Dolly and I really cherished this holiday because we knew it wouldn't be possible for us to spend Christmas together, not with Apry and Mack still believing in Santa Claus and all that. So, we took our nice four day weekend and totally enjoyed it. It was quite different for us walking on John's pier in late November when we were so used to all those warm summer trips to the bay. But, like it or not, long gone were our peddle-pushers and short-sleeved tops. The holiday season was upon us and we were decked out in winter gear from our heads to our toes.

It was always colder right off the ocean and believe me, it was *colder*. Twenty degrees was the predicted high for the entire week!

Dolly and I sat on the pier, taking in the serenity of the soft silver gray day.

Suddenly, out of nowhere, a large flock of all-weather birds flew by us. We watched as they soared straight up to the clouds and then, within seconds, flew low enough just to skim the top of the bay's icy blue water. Our eyes never left them until they disappeared into the mist at the base of the inlet.

"Pat?" Dolly nudged me.

"What?"

"If you could have one special power what would it be?"

"I'd fly."

"Yeah… me, too."

Chapter Ninety-Four

My first Thanksgiving without my parents was rough, but my first Christmas?
…It was even rougher.

Aunt Anna, Uncle John and Dolly were extremely kind to me and I was so grateful that they were in my life, but as everyone knows, when you lose someone you love, the first everything is always the most difficult; the first Thanksgiving, the first Christmas, *their* birthday, *your* birthday… the anniversary of their death. I know it's something that has to be dealt with, and it *is* part of the healing process, but it's still awfully, awfully hard.

As I sat there on Christmas morning opening one nice gift after another, I realized just how much effort my Aunt and Uncle went through to make this a happy holiday for me. Aunt Anna made me a gorgeous amethyst-colored sweater, I don't know how I ever missed her knitting it, but I guess she did it when I was at work so it would be a surprise for me. I got some Heaven Scent perfume from Brenda, a pretty jewelry box from George, cards and monogrammed stationary from Clark, and the latest Little Richard album from Barb and Dale. And, also from the Turners, two nice pairs of winter jammies, complete with robe and matching slippers. Oh, and Uncle John gave me my own fishing pole, tackle gear, and minnow box. I thought that was so sweet! The last present under the tree had a tag on it that read, "Open me last!" and it was from Dolly. The box was small and flat, wrapped in beautiful paper, the nicest that Shellum's had to offer, complete with a big red bow - my favorite color.

When I opened it, my eyes immediately filled and I started to cry - but they were happy tears. There inside a beautiful silver frame was a picture of Dolly at age six. She was hugging her mom in front of their Christmas tree.

The note that Dolly enclosed said this:

Dear Pattie,

This is my very favorite picture in the whole world.

I took the original over to Mr. Shellum and he sent it out and had an exact copy made of it so that I could share it with you.

Before you came into my life, I'd always look at this photo and be sad.

After Mom was gone, looking at it never made me feel happy. Never. I just always felt the loss.

But, because of the series of events that went on in my life this summer, and because I had you to lean on, and to talk to, and to be real with, my whole life and outlook has changed.

I realize now that my Mom wouldn't want me to be sad.

I would be doing her love for me such an injustice if I couldn't feel real joy or happiness again.

And, I'd be doing myself and everyone I ever met an injustice by not dealing with the reality of my life... good, bad or indifferent.

You not only helped me see the light, Miss Patricia Anne Townsend... you gave my life back to me. And for that, I assure you, both my mother and I are eternally grateful.

Love, your friend,
Dolly

What a beautiful letter. I was so touched by all the effort that went in to making my Christmas as happy and normal as possible. I thanked my Aunt and Uncle for all of the wonderful gifts, folded the wrapping paper so Aunt Anna could 'use it again sometime' and then I went up to my room. I took a new pair of pj's with me, my new robe and slippers, and Dolly's silver-framed photograph. I placed it right on my dresser, then I changed into my pajamas, and, instead of wearing my new robe, I put on my Dad's old Frankford High school sweater, the one I had found in my mother's and father's closet, the day I was moving from my old home on Allengrove Street back up in Philadelphia.

It seemed like a lifetime ago.

I sat on my bed, re-read Dolly's letter, and then I took out some of my new stationary, and wrote a letter back to Dolly.

* * * * * *

Over at the Dollio household, chaos reigned. And why not? Santa Claus had just left trains, teddy bears, trucks, dolls, and candy for Apry and Mack. Dolly remembered with a smile her own joy when she was that age, and the happy picture that was taken to record the event. Dolly had a pretty good Christmas as well - a gold charm bracelet from Nikki and her Dad, some new jammies from Apry and Mack, a pale blue angora sweater set, a new winter coat, new boots, some stationary from Clark, Barb and Dale, perfume from Brenda and some Elvis records from George!

Ya gotta love that guy!

And, although not intended to be that way, my gift to Dolly was the last one that she got to open.

Inside a small, flat box, wrapped in festive holiday paper, the nicest that Shellum's had to offer, *and* tied up with a nice, big, red bow, was my gift.

It was a photo inside a silver trimmed frame that I had purchased at The Trading Post - a photo of me, and my mom and my dad, taken at my graduation from Frankford High School just a half a year earlier.

Along with it came this letter:

Dear Dolly,

As you know, this picture is very precious to me. I asked Mr. Shellum to send out the original one and have a copy made of it so I could share it with you. Remember when Mrs. Mayberry sent those photos here? And how I cried and was in a funk for a while over it? Well, because of you, I can now look at it up on my dresser and smile at the happy moment we shared when Mr. Killough took that photo, and I don't even think about what happened after it was taken. I just remember the joy of the moment.

I hold that happiness inside of me. And although I know my darling aunt and uncle had a great deal to do with making much of my pain subside, it was your friendship and the strength to overcome so many horrible things in your life, that made it possible for me to move on into a happier place that would honor not only my life, but my parents love for me as well.

May the angels guide you through a happy, healthy, and prosperous life, Dolly, for you are truly worthy of such a guard.

Merry Christmas.

Love, your friend,

Pattie

Chapter Ninety-Five

New Years Eve was soon upon us and Dolly and I decided we would bring it in with a bang! Of course, in Townsends Inlet, you have to take that literally. No one gives those loud noisy parties, everyone usually sits in front of their TV or they just go to sleep and start the New Year off the same as any other day.

But *this* was 1960!

This was the beginning of a new decade. So... out came the pots and pans, two party hats from Shellum's basement, one kazoo, and off we went to John's Pier right before midnight.

Dolly and I came equipped with our new Timex watches, a gift from the Shellum's so we were quite prepared for the New Year and the new decade.

At the stroke of midnight, we banged the pots and pans together, we cheered and hollered, and Dolly and I took turns playing 'Old Lang Syne' on the kazoo.

Then we decided to give one last chorus on our own. Not that my voice was any match for Dolly's but I sang my little heart out anyway.

"Should auld acquaintance be forgot...
And never brought to mind?
Should auld acquaintance be forgot...
And days of auld lang syne?
And days of auld lang syne, my dear...
And days of auld lang syne.
We'll take a cup of kindness yet...
For auld lang syne."

We laughed ourselves silly when we finished singing and then, as all great artists are known to do, we took a bow to our appreciative audience: Two sea gulls, a box of minnows, and one totally unrecognizable all-weather bird.

By the time we got back to the Turner's everyone was asleep, and Dolly and I sat at the kitchen table and drank some hot chocolate.

"Wow! 1960! The *sixties*, Pattie!"

"Amazing, huh?"

"What do you think will change?"

"Everything, silly! Look what happened in the '50s!"

"Well, Kennedy will be in for eight years, right?"

"Let's hope so." I smiled.

"And, rock and roll will still be around, right?"

"Dolly, rock and roll is here to stay! Are you kidding?"

"Well, I dunno."

"Oh, puh-leeze."

"No seriously, Pat, with Frankie Avalon, Fabian, and Bobby Rydell singing all those 'safe' songs. Where's the old rock and roll?"

"Don't sweat it. We're in an ugly transitional period, that's all."

"But, Pat, Buddy Holly's dead, so's Ritchie Valens. This could be the beginning of the end."

I rolled my eyes.

"I mean, come on, Pat. How many times can Frankie sing 'Venus' before we all fall asleep?"

I had to laugh. "Yeah, well it doesn't rock you like Little Richard's stuff, that's for sure."

Dolly smiled. "So, you think this looks like a good decade for us, The Kennedys, *and* Rock and Roll?"

"I think it'll be a powerful time in our lives. I can feel it."

"Well, I sure hope so."

"And, listen here, Miss Dollio we're really due for a new revelation in rock and roll music anyway. I mean, that's what rock and roll was all about in the first place. Yes?"

"A new revelation or a new *revolution*?" Dolly asked.

"Both, maybe. You say you wanna revolution?"

"Enlighten me," she smiled.

"Oh, you know what I mean… like how the history books say about the British? Maybe a total revolt, something way out of left field, some new wave of music."

"What are you talkin' about? Like the British are going to invade us with Rock and Roll music?!" She laughed so hard I thought she'd wake up Aunt Anna and Uncle John.

"Well, that isn't exactly what I meant, but, sure, why not?"

Again she laughed. "You cannot *possibly* expect those mild mannered and perfect English souls to make a difference in our home grown rock and roll! That's insane!"

"Why not? Who cares where it comes from?"

She rolled her eyes at me. "Yeah, yeah, yeah…"

* * * * * *

We cleaned out our hot chocolate mugs, dried them and put them away leaving Aunt Anna's kitchen clean and sparkly once again.

"Ready to go to sleep?" I asked my friend.

"Yeah," she yawned, "I'm tired. Let's get some Z's . Tell you what… I'll sleep peacefully and you can be the dreamer of things to come, okay, Swami?"

I smiled at her. "You may say I'm a dreamer… but I'm not the only one."

"I know, Pattie" she smiled back at me, "I know."

Chapter Ninety-Six

January moved by with the speed of a Daytona race car, and with it came the best news of the year.

"Oh, my God!!!" Dolly shouted over the phone line to me. "Pattie! Pattie! I got... I got..."

"Speak up, girl spit it out! What is it?!"

"I got accepted to The University of Colorado!"

"You what?!"

"I got ac-cept-ted to the University of Colorado!"

"Oh, My GOD, DOLL!!! That is like the best news EVER!!!!"

Dolly and I worked so hard to get her paperwork started. She'd taken all the necessary tests, and heaven knows we sent off enough letters, and then, thanks to a very generous someone, who preferred to remain anonymous, Dolly was actually going to be a college freshman in September of 1960, like I was! Tuition PAID IN FULL!

"What did Nikki and your Dad say?"

"Nik thought it was super! She was just so happy for me. She said I need to get out of here and make a life for myself."

"Good for Nikki. And your Dad?"

"He thinks music is a waste of time and that if I was going to go to college it should be for accounting or something useful. But he really thinks I'm more suited to be a manicurist or a restaurant hostess."

"More suited?"

"Yup."

"Well, that's not his decision, now is it?"

"Nope, it's mine. And I'm stickin' to my guns, Pat."

"Good for you!"

"He said, 'Don't expect us to fly out there *if* and when you graduate.'"

"IF?" I huffed.

"Yeah. What a supportive father, eh?"

"Well, you're on your way and you're standing on your own two feet, that's what counts."

"I think Dad would have been happier if I'd just been an uncooperative run of the mill teen rebel."

I smiled. "I think so too."

"I'm sorta rebelling, Pattie, but, I'd say it's more liberation than rebellion."

"Well, Kiddo, whatever it is, you're on your way! I am thrilled for you! YOU DID IT, GIRL!!!"

Actually, we were *all* thrilled: Aunt Anna and Uncle John, Millie and Bill Shellum, Carrie and Jake, Emma Orwatt, Bessie Newell... the list goes on and on. In fact, we didn't even wait to write the news to our friends, we called them all on the telephone! Now that was *something*! Needless to say they were as happy as we were and we all promised each other that this Summer of 1960 would be the best one of our lives!

And it was.

Dolly and I still worked at Shellum's, but Mrs. S. changed her hours, so we started at 7:00 AM but we were done at 2:00 when her daughters took over, So, the new work hours made it possible to spend more time with our friends, and the nice little raise that Bill and Millie gave to us, kept us making the same money with less hours! That was the best!

By the time Spring rolled around, Dolly played a more active roll at the little church on 85th Street. And, because of her, the Easter season was even more special, the choir voices even more lovely. Miss Dollio had proven herself a positive force in the community - a survivor, a young lady of integrity and gentle spirit. She was quite the dynamo when left to be her true self.

Dolly soon became secure enough to write to Brenda about the happenings in late July. She came clean with her about everything, and, as I expected, Brenda was proud of Dolly for surviving not only the tragedy of the Dawkins incident, but for coming to grips with her past as well. Brenda had become a genuine champion of Dolly's, quite like I had.

By mid-May, Aunt Anna was tending to her garden on a daily basis, and Uncle John's fishing trips on Captain Robbins' and Captain Cramer's boats were once again in full swing. Captain Cramer's son, Luke 'The Hunk of Townsends Inlet', was working with his Dad while on summer break from The University of Southern California. And speaking of full swing, The Civic Center was advertising locally about their 2nd annual Sock Hop and opening night would once again be the first Friday in July. All of our friends would be back in town by then so we'd all be together for the grand celebration!

June 1st came around... it was the first anniversary of my parents' death. Aunt Anna and Uncle John asked me if I wanted to go visit their grave site, but I said no. I decided instead to pick some roses from Aunt Anna's garden, and place them in two vases I bought from Mrs. Shellum and place them near the altar at church that Sunday. A rose garden, I might add, that my mother helped start the very year I was born. I had my sad moments that day, I was reflective and quiet, but along with the quiet and the memories came peace. I had gone full circle. I was moving forward. And by doing so, not only did I honor my parents, but I honored the life that was out there waiting for me.

By mid-June, Dolly and I were anticipating the arrival of our dear friends, and, one carload at a time, the old gang started to re-appear.

Dale and Barbara Harding's family drove down for a six week stay starting on June 11th! They stopped in to see me and Dolly as soon as they unpacked. We took our lunch break to spend time with them at the soda fountain and had fun catching up on all the news that happened since our last letters to each other.

"Barb stopped dating Randy," Dale noted.

"Dale stopped dating Dustin," Barb *had* to let us know.

"Isn't this new pearl nail polish a neat color?"

"How do you like Roy Orbison's new song?"

It was such a chicky conversation and I *know* Mrs. Shellum was getting a smile out of it, but, that's who we were and we were glad to see each other and we were just having fun!

Clark was the next to arrive, on June 14th. He joked and wrote to us saying he wouldn't be in until after the 4th of July and then gave us a HUGE surprise by stopping in to see us at Shellum's right after his arrival.

"Umm... excuse me," he said upon entering the store, "but I heard the two best employees in the state of New Jersey work here!"

"CLARK!!!!" Dolly and I rushed over to him so fast we almost knocked the poor guy over! He showed up right at the end of our work day, so we had plenty of time left to sit and chat. *And...* we treated him to our absolute best hot fudge sundae, which of course he appreciated tremendously. Who wouldn't?

George was next in town on June 16th. Dolly and I found out from Clark exactly when they'd be in, and we left a nice big basket of fruit and Tastykakes on the Ludlam's doorstep complete with a welcome back banner!

When he walked in the door just in time for our noon lunch break eating the last of his chocolate Tastykake, Dolly and I whooped and hollered and cheered.

"This is like... like *Elvis* just entered the building!" She smiled. George laughed and gave Dolly a hug. On his way toward me he said hello to Mrs. Shellum and Carrie Robinson who was paying for her weekly grocery bill.

"Pattie! God, I'm *so* glad to see you!" he said giving me a huge bear hug.

"Well, I'm pretty happy to see you too, Mr. Ludlam. Geez, you look terrific!"

And he did. Dolly and I didn't get to go to Philly as we promised but the calls and letters made us all feel connected. We didn't exchange any photos either so, all we had were our memories of each other. George was always a nice looking guy, but it seemed as if over the last ten months he had grown about two inches taller, his hair was a little longer, and his body seemed a lot leaner.

His strong arms surrounded me once again, and I boldly kissed him on the cheek - a nice big smacker.

"What was that for?!" he grinned in surprise.

"Cause I missed you and I wanted to."

"Both *very* good reasons," he nodded. George then brushed the back of his hand slowly down the side of my face. "Gotta run. See you later." With that said, he turned away from me, put his sunglasses back on, and then made his exit.

"Wow!" Dolly sighed. "Is he dreamy or what?!"

"Yep," I nodded in agreement, "Elvis has left the building."

Chapter Ninety-Seven

Last but not least was the much anticipated arrival of Miss Brenda Ethel Mayberry on Monday, June 19th.

George, Clark, Dale, Barbara, Dolly, and I stood at the corner of Landis and 85th waiting for Brenda's bus to arrive.

"A watched pot never boils," Clark mumbled staring out toward Sea Isle City.

"Clark's right. We shouldn't be here." Dolly paced the sidewalk. "We shoulda come by at the last minute. *Then* she'd be here!"

George nudged me and pointed to my left... I smiled. "A watched pot boils if you wait long enough, Clark. Here she comes!"

Dolly and I were jumping up and down long before the bus even came to a full stop.

By the time the Greyhound doors were wide open, all six of us were chanting, "Bren-daaa, Bren-daaa, Bren-daaa!!!!"

Then, there she was... Miss California 1960!

Bren stood at the top of the silver and blue Greyhound steps and posed for a second and then burst out laughing. "I'm soooooo happy to be back here!" she shrieked as she practically leaped out of the bus. George and Clark helped the driver with two rather large suitcases while Dolly, Dale, Barb, and I just jumped around all giggly and silly, *thrilled* to be a full team once again.

"My God, Bren, you look fabulous! You got a tan *already*?!"

"Pat, I had a *tan* in January. I live in Sunshine City, USA!"

I laughed.

She really looked great. College life was definitely agreeing with her.

Her hair was a bit shorter, and it looked as if she was just letting it fall into its own naturally curly state. Less fuss for a freshman who had more things to concern herself with, I'd say. Her clothes were madras and khaki, and very... well, very California.

"I lost ten pounds. My mother said I'm probably not eating right."

Dolly smiled, "Well, two weeks with Aunt Anna in front of the stove and that problem'll be solved."

"Hey!" Clark nudged her, "How long do I have to wait for my hug?"

In less time than it would take you to count to one, Brenda was in Clark's arms.

"I missed you." He smiled.

"I missed you, too."

"And *me*?"

Bren looked toward George. "And *you*? How could I not miss *you!*" She reached out and gave George a big hug as well.

Brenda didn't really know Dale and Barb too well in person, but they had been close because of regular correspondence.

Bren hugged Dale, then Barb, then me and then Dolly and then me again and Dolly again. We laughed and cried and cried and laughed. This kind of silliness is something only girls really understand, it's sort of that bonding thing we do. And, I might add, foreign to most members of the opposite sex. But, George and Clark were used to that kinda chicky stuff from being around me and Dolly, so they just went along with the program and humored us.

By the time we made it into the Turner household, Aunt Anna had prepared us a 'The Gang's All Here Luncheon.' Even Uncle John was in front of the stove!

Whatta guy!

Once again hugs all around for everyone's favorite Aunt and Uncle.

"Brenda, Dear. Welcome back!" Aunt Anna smiled.

"How's college treatin' ya?" My Uncle had to know.

"Everything's great. But I'm just so happy to be here! I'm home!"

I noticed Mr. Ludlam and Mr. Lowen just staring at the kitchen table - eyes as big as saucers.

I had to chuckle.

"So *this* is the The Famous Turner Feast I've always heard about! Holy cow!" George smiled.

"Amazing, huh?" Dolly nudged him.

"Mr. and Mrs. Turner, this looks delicious!" Clark added.

And delicious it was.

The table was set with fine Spring linens, delicate dishes, saucers, cups, bread and dessert plates and my Aunt Anna's favorite glassware - a wedding gift from her sister, Martha.

Food? Well, that was equally exquisite: Shrimp and lobster bisque (shellfish courtesy of Mr. Turner), a beautiful fresh garden salad with home made dressing, fried green tomatoes with sweet onions, chicken salad sandwiches, roasted pork sandwiches, and a slightly blackened flounder sandwich on pumpernickel bread, complete with a peach/pear glaze, and lettuce, tomatoes and red onions - all fruits and vegetables direct from Aunt Anna's garden. There was lemonade, chocolate milk, and iced tea, and… to top that all off, one scrumptious triple-layered strawberry shortcake!

Why this woman never opened up her own restaurant is beyond me.

We sat at that beautiful table for over two hours, talking, laughing, and catching up on all the news. We were so wrapped up with each other that we never even took Brenda's suitcases upstairs to unpack. We just sat down and ate and talked and talked and ate, and… well, you get the picture.

Brenda was filling me in on all of the things that she didn't have the chance to write to me about, you know, school, being a Freshman, and southern California life in general. Naturally we all wanted to hear about

Disneyland. Brenda had been there twice and she fell totally in love with the place.

"Walt Disney calls it, 'The happiest place on earth,'" she said.

"Well," smiled Dolly, "Walt's never been here!"

We all laughed, but you know, at that very moment, as I looked around the table at my friends and my Aunt Anna and Uncle John, all sharing their stories in that cozy little kitchen, seagulls outside calling to one another, sunshine streaming in through those beautiful chiffon café curtains... I had to admit that it was one of the most perfect moments in my life.

To me, *this* was the happiest place on earth.

Chapter Ninety-Eight

Summer was now officially here as far as Dolly and I were concerned because the old gang was back! Hallelujah! Oddly enough, no one ever mentioned Jack Dawkins' absence… none of *us* anyway. I did overhear Carrie say to Aunt Anna that she heard Jack was working on Long Beach Island for the summer.

Silently I said a prayer for every female on L.B.I.

On the home front, things couldn't be better. Dolly and I had even earlier hours than we expected, 6:00 to 2:00 sometimes 6:30 to 2:30 since the Shellums decided to serve a full breakfast, you know, the usual seashore/Philadelphia fare: eggs, bacon, scrapple, pork roll, home fries - the works. I loved to cook breakfast and so did Dolly, so, it was all coming together nicely for the two of us. And, another good thing was that I was always home in plenty of time to still spend a good part of the afternoon with Brenda.

Life was good.

The few days we had before the first dance were filled with anticipation: what to wear, what new records could we buy for Uncle John, and polishing our new penny loafers to perfection.

Life was good. I just said that, didn't I? But it *was* good… it was very, very good.

When Friday finally rolled around I think I had a smile on my face all day long.

At exactly 2:30 PM Dolly and I hung up our 'Shellum's by-the-Sea' smocks in the small office by the time clock, and out the door we went.

"Bye, Mrs. Shellum!" we sang out together.

"Bye, gals! Have a wonderful time tonight! I want to hear all about it on Monday!"

As Dolly and I were about to part ways she turned to me, "Black straight skirts, white blouse, red waist cincher, and penny loafers, right?"

"Yup. Well, a red cincher for you, I'm wearin' a purple one, Brenda's wearing a light blue one, Dale is wearing pink, and Barb's wearing one in some kind of gold color. Cool huh? We're all the same except for the belts."

"Yeah, I think it's pretty cool, too."

"See ya over the house around 6:30, okay?"

"You can count on it! See ya, Pattie!"

As I was walking away I turned again and called out to Dolly, "Oh, my God! I'm so excited! I can hardly wait!"

Dolly smiled at me, did a little dance step and laughed. "That makes two of us, Kiddo! See you in a couple of hours!"

I waved to her. "Yeah. See ya!"

The minute I walked into the kitchen, Aunt Anna, Uncle John, and Brenda were all sitting at the table talking about the Robinson's new car.

"That car is like the coolest!" I heard Brenda say.

My Aunt chuckled, "Who would have thought Jake Robinson would ever buy a new car? And a splashy one at that!"

I walked into the kitchen. "What's all this? Jake and Carrie bought a new car? What happened to their '48 Ford?"

"He still has it," Uncle John answered. "But the new one is *really* something."

"What kind is it, Bren?"

"It's a convertible and..."

I started to laugh. "Jake Robinson? Jake Robinson bought himself a convertible?"

"Not just *any* old convertible," Uncle John added. "But a snazzy Buick Electra 225 convertible."

"You gotta be kidding?! Isn't Jake like eighty-years-old?"

"Eighty-three," Aunt Anna said quietly.

"It's a doozy, Pat," Uncle John said wistfully, "Tampico red, white top, automatic transmission, V8, 401, and 325 horsepower."

"John Martin Turner," Aunt Anna shook her finger at him playfully, "Don't you go getting any funny ideas. There's no way we're going to pay almost three thousand dollars for a brand new car no matter *how* much of a doozy it is. That's just way too much money."

"Whatever made him buy it? What did Carrie say?"

"Well," Aunt Anna smiled, "Carrie's happy whenever Jake is happy. She thought it was a bit extravagant, but it *is* a pretty car and the grandkids will love it, so... it's okay with her."

"Cool," I smiled.

"Man, I hope I can get a car like that someday," Brenda sighed.

"We will, Bren. It just takes time." Then I turned toward my Uncle. "I know three thousand dollars is an *awful* lot of money, but you sure would look spiffy behind the wheel of a Tampico red convertible."

Uncle John smiled at his darling wife, "You hear that Anna? I'd look *spiffy!*"

"No, Dear," she smiled back, "I didn't hear a thing. Coffee anyone?"

* * * * * *

Brenda and I had a piece of orange sponge cake and a cup of coffee with Aunt Anna and Uncle John, then we cleaned off the table, helped prepare for dinner, and then the two of us headed up to Dalrymple's in Sea Isle for some new lipstick. We decided on 'Sizzling Pink Candy Delight' by Helena Rubenstein, with nail polish to match. It was bee-yoo-tee-full!

By the time we got back to the house, dinner was ready to be served and we breezed right on through the meal, talking and laughing, all excited about the first dance of the 1960 summer season. We helped Aunt Anna clean the kitchen and then rushed upstairs to get ready. Brenda and I flipped a coin to see who got the bathroom first.

She won.

Well, that was okay, it gave me time to pick out what jewelry I would wear and to polish my penny loafers one more time. Just as I slipped a brand new one cent piece in my left shoe, Brenda walked into the bedroom.

"Your turn, Patricia!"

"You don't have to tell me twice," I smiled as I made a beeline for the bathroom. I showered, I sang, I dried my hair and sang some more. It was great to be alive!

"Come on, songbird," Brenda hollered, "it's almost time for Dolly to be here!"

"COMING!!!"

No sooner had I clipped on my purple waist cincher and slipped into my penny loafers, the doorbell rang. I rushed down the steps. "It's Dolly, Aunt Anna! I'll get it!"

I made it to the door in record time, quickly opened it, and there was Miss Dollio doing an imitation of Elvis Presley - dancing. "Ready to Rock and Roll, Pattie?"

"Doll, I was born ready!"

Just then Uncle John and Aunt Anna walked into the living room with Brenda trailing a few steps behind them.

"Well, look at the three of you! You look like sisters! All matching outfits with different colored belts! That looks lovely," she noted.

"Dale and Barb are wearing the same outfits too; just the waist cinchers are another color."

"Well, you all look absolutely darling."

Uncle John made an early exit to open The Civic Center and the four of us, me, Brenda, Dolly, and Aunt Anna waited for George and Clark to make their appearance.

Any minute now…

No sooner had Dolly craned her neck to check the time on a wall clock in the dining room when the doorbell rang once again. Brenda rushed to the door and opened it. Aunt Anna, Dolly and I stood to her left.

"Evenin' Ladies!" George grinned while Clark sweetly nodded a hello.

"Well, if it isn't the two nicest and best looking guys in Southern New Jersey," Brenda said as they walked into the house.

George turned back toward the front door. "Did someone just walk in behind us?"

"Oh, Mr. Ludlam," I said nudging him on the elbow, "you know she meant you guys!"

George smiled again. And Clark? Well, it looked to me as if he was blushing. How cute is that?!

"You certainly look all grown-up." Aunt Anna's eyes started to fill. "Gee, it seems like just yesterday you all were just a bunch of little kids playing on the old swing set up at the pavilion." She dabbed at her eyes with a beautiful, hand-crocheted handkerchief.

I hugged her. "The years that went by since then only gave me more time to love you," I whispered.

My Aunt sighed, quietly composed herself, and looked in my eyes. "You've turned into such a wonderful young lady, Pattie."

I smiled. "Thanks, Aunt Anna."

"Now, go on… all of you, if you hang around much longer you'll miss the first dance of the evening. I think John said he was playing, 'Don't Be… Don't Be…'"

"Don't Be *Cruel*?! Elvis Presley?!" Dolly jumped for joy.

"That's right. That's what it was. 'Don't Be Cruel.'"

"Yippee!!!! Let's go guys, we can't miss Elvis! That's almost sacrilegious!"

I heard my aunt chuckle as we all hurried down the front steps.

"Bye, Aunt Anna! See you around 11:00!"

"Bye, Mrs. Turner!"

"So long, kids."

We all ran like the wind up the block and a half to The Civic Center, as the doors swung wide-open, I could hear Uncle John announcing the first song of the night, and indeed it was, 'Don't be Cruel,' by Elvis himself. Everyone hit the dance floor. Dale and Barb waved to us while jitterbugging from the other side of The Civic Center, Dolly and Brenda danced together, George and I danced, and Clark made a beeline to the concession stand to order all of us some French fries and a coke.

Good old Clark.

By the time Elvis had sung the last few bars, I had jitterbugged enough that I was already breaking into a sweat! Those ice cold cokes Clark had waiting for all of us were sure a welcome sight!

Just as I had reached to take a refreshing sip, Uncle John played 'Ready Teddy', by Little Richard and Dolly grabbed my arm, "Come on, Pat! Dance with me! I *love* this song!"

Truth be known, there wasn't a tune that 'The Songbird of Townsends Inlet' didn't like.

"But, Dolly… my soda!" I quickly took another sip.

"Soda, schmoda! Let's dance!"

Our other four friends were a bit more sensible and sat that one out. As I whirled and twirled on the dance floor with Dolly, our friends George, Clark, Dale, and Barb sat and drank their sodas, ate their French fries, and smiled at the two penny-loafered jitterbugs rocking away with

Little Richard. As for Brenda? She lucked out. It seemed to all of us that Luke Cramer had taken a fancy to her. Every time I looked around they were dancing together. Slow song, fast song, it didn't matter. I thought that was pretty interesting.

Three Little Richard songs in a row and I had decided to sit and rest my dancing feet for a while, but my friends had other plans for me. So, with the exception of a few French fries here and there, and the occasional sip of coke, I was on the dance floor all night long! But I didn't regret it one bit!

I danced with everyone. Well, George reserved all the slow dances for me, but when it came to the stroll or the bop or a good cha-cha, I think I danced with every teenager in Townsends Inlet! All of my friends were having a great time, too! I even saw Emma Orwatt and Bessie Newell tapping their feet along with the music! That made me smile. Uncle John had certainly come into his own in 1960. He had fine tuned his disc-jockey act and he was terrific! Every once in a while he'd call out, "Are ya havin' fun?" and the whole crowd at The Civic Center would let out a HUGE holler, letting him know we were not only having fun, we were having the time of our lives! The music rolled by, one top hit after another and we danced and danced and danced: "Rock Around The Clock," by Bill Haley & The Comets, "I Only Have Eyes For You," by The Flamingos, "Ain't That A Shame," by Fats Domino, "Love Is Strange," by Mickey and Silvia, "Earth Angel," by The Penguins, and one of my personal favorites, "In The Still Of The Night," by The Five Satins. Of course, Uncle John played every Jerry Lee, Elvis, *and* Little Richard record he had up in his DJ booth, too! It was Rock and Roll heaven as far as I was concerned. And… well, it was more than just the music, it was the whole atmosphere: the kids, their wild energy, and the sparkling, mirrored globe that flashed brilliant fragments of light all over the room. Sometimes when I was slow dancing with George I would really look at what was going on, sensing the magic of it all, and reeling in the joy of my teenage life. It was a moment in time that I knew I would never forget - even if I lived to be a hundred.

All too soon it came to an end, and as always, the last song of the night was, "Good night Sweetheart," by The Spaniels.

Goodnight, sweetheart
Well, it's time to go
I hate to leave you, but I really must say…
Goodnight, sweetheart, goodnight.

Dale was dancing with Billy Rual, Barb with Bobby Phillips, Dolly danced with Clark, and lo and behold, there was Brenda Ethel Mayberry still dancing dreamily with hunky Luke Cramer. The Cramers had lived on the shoreline for decades and were one of the most well-liked and well-respected families on the inlet. Brenda couldn't have done better if she tried.

Just as the song ended, I felt Dale's hand brush across my shoulder. "Billy and Bobby are gonna walk us home tonight."

I smiled at her. "How cool is that?!"

"Way cool," she smiled back at me.

The usual gang started to gather, and we all watched as the Harding sisters were escorted out of the building by Messrs. Phillips and Rual.

"Now that's a pretty sight!" Dolly said dreamily.

"They're nice girls." I nodded.

"Bill and Bob are cool guys, too," George added.

"It's a good summer," Brenda sighed looking over her shoulder to smile at Luke Cramer.

"Is The Luke-ster walking you home?" I asked.

"He didn't ask me, but I wish he would. God, he's just so nice, so sweet and so…"

"Gorgeous?"

Again she looked over her shoulder and sighed, "Yup, and gorgeous."

Just then Uncle John announced next week's dance and the normal house lights were turned back on. Out of the corner of my eye I noticed Luke Cramer making his way through the crowd, eventually ending up standing right next to Brenda.

"Hi," he smiled at all of us.

"Hey, Luke."

"Would you mind if I walked Brenda home after a treat at VanSants?" He turned toward her, "That's okay with you, isn't it. Bren?"

I knew her heart was racing a mile a minute, but she stayed cool, gave a pretty smile, and nodded. "Sure, that would be fine. Thanks."

"See ya at home, Brenda! Have fun, you two!"

"See ya!" She grinned that silly 'overly happy' grin of hers, then I watched as Bren walked out of The Civic Center, arm in arm with Luke Cramer.

"Now, how cute is *that?!*" I smiled at the remaining members of our gang.

"As cute as a button," Dolly answered.

"It's gonna be an amazing summer, Pattie," George said loosening his tie just a bit. "It'll go by fast, but it'll be a great one, that's for sure!"

"I hear ya, George."

As I turned to say something to Clark, I noticed he was gone. "Hey, where…" Just as I was about to ask everyone where he was, Clark magically appeared with four ice cold cokes in his hands.

Bless his heart.

I smiled, thanked him, and then immediately raised mine in a toast. "Here's to good friendships that last a lifetime and to the glorious Summer of 1960!"

"To good friendships that last a lifetime and to the glorious Summer of 1960," Dolly, George, and Clark echoed.

Our glass bottles clinked together, we took a sip, and then the four of us walked out of The Civic Center into the cool night air of that very glorious summer.

And was it ever glorious!

The earlier hours at Shellum's were a blessing! Dolly and I were out of work before mid-day so that left plenty of time to go shopping, swimming, fishing, crabbing, and just hanging out with our friends, either at VanSant's or over at The Charcoal House. Brenda and Luke would hang around with us for a little while, but they'd always manage to slip away for some private time together.

Dolly and I made regular trips to Sea Isle to buy a few things to wear at school: a shirt here, a pair of shoes there, it all started to add up, so we knew our Freshman wardrobe would be complete by the time we both had to leave for college in late August.

As for Brenda? She extended her stay with us because, well, sure, she extended it because she loved it in Townsends Inlet, *and* it had been a long time since we all saw each other, BUT, let's be honest here, the main reason for the lengthy stay was because there was a genuine romance blossoming between her and Luke Cramer. And, to make things even better, Luke was attending college at USC. He'd be a sophomore in the fall of 1960 just like Brenda. *The ideal California couple!* I thought to myself.

"Pattie?" Brenda said as she carefully applied some 'Sizzling Pink Candy Delight' nail polish, "Ya know how many miles it is from where I live at UCLA to where Luke lives at the University of Southern California?"

"Noooooo, but I have a feeling *you* do," I teased.

"Well…"

"Oh, Brenda, please. Remember who you're talkin' to? How far is it?"

"Okay." Bren smiled at me and then rambled off facts as if she were a walking, talking Rand McNally. "It's 11.9 miles as the crow flies, and 14.2 miles by car, it takes twenty minutes on the bus, *if* you catch it early in the morning, it takes closer to thirty when you ride it later in the day, *and* if we walked and met each other half way it would take somewhere between 45 and 55 minutes, depending on traffic, weather, time of day, and other extenuating circumstances and then…"

I had to laugh. "And then? Well, what if you took a cab? Rode a bike? Went on horseback? Roller skated? Used a hang-glider? Come on college girl, calculate! Calculate!"

Brenda laughed right along with me. But it was plain to see just how head over heels in love she was with Luke Cramer. And you know what the best thing about that was? Luke felt exactly the same way about Brenda.

Sweet.

And, speaking of sweet...

Well, I wish I could say that things were that sweet and yummy between me and George or Dolly and Clark, but it just wasn't in the cards for us. George was a wonderful guy, charming, smart, and need I say... handsome, but George and I had a best friend thing going on, a very precious trust between a male and a female and I think that maybe... just maybe we both decided it was better to lean on the safe side of the line and stay friends. As for Dolly, well, she was just coming into her own, and after that horrific experience with slimy Jack Dawkins in the summer of '59, she wasn't feeling that pressing need to have a boyfriend, just to be one of the crowd, like most girls do. Dolly had a good friend in both Clark and George and she was learning about the opposite sex in a safe way. Learning the importance of being a good friend first... learning to trust and be trusted. Most romances (unfortunately) tend to fade after a while, and those good old heart-fluttering moments don't last forever, so, when the rose colored glasses of first love come off, and there is nothing there but sex... you're in for long term trouble. But, if you love a man who loves you back and, he's also your best friend, well then, you have a happiness that doesn't last for just a few weeks, a few months, or even a few years... you have a love to last a lifetime.

And that's what Dolly wanted.
And that's what I wanted.
And would it be worth the wait?
You better believe it!

Chapter Ninety-Nine

In the bat of an eye the Fourth of July celebration was upon us. Captain Cramer and Captain Robbins advertised a late evening cruise for the holiday so the sea-faring vacation crowd could view the Sea Isle/Townsends Inlet Fireworks from aboard ship. Brenda, of course, was the first to tell us about it and so, because Luke's father was Captain Cramer, we all got to sail off on his beautiful new boat with free tickets for everyone!

And, everyone of us had dates! Well, actually four of us had real dates, Dolly and I went with George and Clark, but, well, you know… it was a different kind of date.

But for Dale Harding? It was a night with Billy Rual. Bill was a great kid. His family owned a tiny pier that rented spots to small boat owners so they could secure a safe place for their rowboat, canoe, or tiny motor boat for the summer. Bill's grandparents were year-round residents and really lovely people. And, to top that off, Bill was cute. Definitely cute. And, he was always the kid who got the first tan of the season. Two days in the sun and he was as brown as a berry. He looked like a walking, talking Coppertone Ad. Dale was crazy about him. Love was in the air between the two of them, and, although not as much romance as I saw between Luke and Bren, there was magic just the same.

As for Dale's sister, Barb? Well, Bobby Phillips was just totally enamored with her. Bobby's family lived two doors down from Aunt Anna and Uncle John. I knew Bobby before I was even in grade school. The Phillips' family owned a cute little green and white bungalow and spent every summer, Memorial Day to Labor Day, in Townsends Inlet.

Bobby was adorable. He had a smile that could knock your socks off. He was also thin and wiry, and quite the athlete. He was the first kid I ever knew who could water-ski. Somehow that was one shore experience I never mastered. I was kinda klutzy on water-skis, but I could out fish Mr. Phillips any day of the week! If Bobby and I went fishing on the pier when we were kids and there was only one flounder to be found, well, I was to one to hook it!

Speaking of flounder, Brenda, Dolly and I enjoyed a lovely Turner bar-b-que earlier in the day, a huge fish fry with the works! Well, of course it was 'the works' because Aunt Anna was cooking! Our mega meal was over around 4:00 so we all had plenty of time to fuss over ourselves for our evening cruise dates. We needed to wear some extra clothing that night because, even as lovely as it was out there on the water at sunset it could get kinda chilly on the ride back home. Dolly and Brenda opted for their beaded sweater-sets over top of their peddle pusher pants and peter pan collared blouses. I thought the peddle pushers were a good idea, too, but instead of wearing one of my sweater sets, I opted for my dad's old Frankford High sweater that my mother and father left to me. Not only would it keep me warm... it would keep me connected.

Know what I mean?

While the three of us sat in the parlor waiting on George, Clark and Luke, Aunt Anna and Uncle John entered the room.

Uncle John put his tan jacket on and then wrapped a soft, wool sweater around my Aunt's shoulders.

"Where are you two going?" I asked.

"I'm takin' my best girl out for a moonlight cruise," Uncle John answered.

"Captain Cramer's boat?" Brenda needed to know.

"No, Sweetheart," Aunt Anna said, "John and I are going on Captain Robbins' boat. But we'll wave to you as we sail by."

Brenda smiled.

"You all have a wonderful night! See you when we get back, ladies!" Uncle John tipped his straw hat, and then escorted his best girl down the front steps.

* * * * * *

"What *time* is it?" Dolly said squinting her eyes, trying to read the wall clock in the kitchen.

I leaned in that direction. "8:15."

"Geez, where are the *guys*?!"

No sooner had those words left Dolly's mouth than the doorbell rang.

"Talk about timing," I smiled.

"Ready to go, Angel?" Luke said as soon as he stepped into the porch area.

Brenda walked right over to him and gave him a kiss - ON THE LIPS!

I thought I would faint. Meek and mild-mannered Brenda Ethel Mayberry actually kissed a boy first!

Luke returned the kiss and then gave her a nice hug. I was so happy for her and Luke. Luke Cramer was a wonderful fellow and quite a handsome guy. He had sandy blonde hair and these steely blue-grey eyes. If he hadn't opted for life as a Marine Biologist, for certain he could have graced a magazine cover or two. I'm not kidding. He *was*, as the girls on the inlet would say, "A Wow!"

George and Clark were their usual dashing selves as well. And then, just as Uncle John had escorted Aunt Anna down the front steps, our charming gentleman friends did the same for us.

By the time we got to the pier, Captain Robbins boat was just leaving. We saw my Aunt and Uncle on the very back of the boat, snuggled up next to each other. We waved, they waved, and then off they went… into the sunset.

Our turn was next.

On the opposite end of the pier Captain Cramer welcomed us all aboard. There were ten of us so we took up most of the front of the boat, but that was okay, everyone along for the ride, thirty one of us all together, had a great seat and we were all nice and comfortable.

It was a beautiful night, the sky couldn't have looked more glorious if Michaelangelo himself had painted it. The soft cries from some nearby seagulls, that delicious bar-b-que aroma from neighboring backyards, and the exhilarating summer air filled my senses. In just a few minutes the ropes that secured the boat were untied from the dock and we were on our way. It was a nice well-paced trip down the inlet, past the T.I. Yacht Club, Henny's Pier, and all the quaint little cottages that dotted the bay area. Before we knew it we were sailing under the bridge that connects Townsends Inlet to Avalon, and then, well, we were out into the beautiful deep blue Atlantic Ocean. We saw a school of silvery fish swim near the boat, their shiny bodies catching the last rays of the fragmented sunlight. No sooner had they passed us by when a pod of dolphins decided to play in the water. What an amazing sight that was! Like a bunch of kids, one after the other they seemed to be playing leap frog with the waves that Captain Cramer's boat had created. Besides all the marine life activity, many daytime boaters and skiers were coming home for the evening, some of them even waved a "hello" as they sailed by us. I was just starting to talk to George about the dolphin experience when I heard Dolly say something and then I watched as she quickly covered her face with her hands.

"What's the matter with you? Seasick?"

She didn't answer me, but as she raised her head once again, I studied her gaze and followed it with my own eyes.

There, coming up on our starboard side, in the snazzy Grady-White boat he had recently purchased from Mr. Garrity, was Dolly's father. And, riding right along with him, as close as two people can sit next to each other, was some strange woman - a flashy redhead, in a bikini, with these big glamorous Hollywood sunglasses on her face.

It was *definitely* not Nikki.

I could hardly believe my eyes. The nerve of this man! Was it *really* Mr. Dollio? I wanted desperately to believe it wasn't - for Dolly's sake.

We both looked in the direction of the boat until it drove under the bridge and then faded from sight as it made a left toward the bay in Avalon.

I *had* to say something. "Dolly," I whispered, "Maybe that wasn't…"
She cut me off in mid-sentence, "No, Pat. That was my father."
"Are you okay?"
"Yeah. I can't say I'm surprised."

I sighed.

"I can't even say it hurts."

I nodded.

"He's numbed any feelings I used to have for him."

I sighed again.

"The way he treated Mom… the way he treats me. Now I just feel bad for Nik and the kids."

Nik and the kids.

"Don't let this louse up your evening, Pattie. It's not gonna ruin mine," she stated as a matter of fact.

"I don't know *how* you do it," I said as I hugged her to my side.

"Well, it helps to know first hand, that the bad guys *eventually* get theirs. Know what I mean?"

Again I nodded.

"So, let the chips fall where they may, Pat. He'll get his."

* * * * * *

Within fifteen minutes we were in the perfect position to witness the famous Townsends Inlet/Sea Isle City Fireworks display for 1960! With every huge burst of color that seemed to fly right over our heads, we'd all oooh and aaah! It was magnificent!

"Look at that one! It's like blue diamonds!"

"Here's my favorite, silver and gold together!!"

"Wow! The whole sky is lit up!!!"

I turned around to make a comment to Brenda, when I noticed that she and Luke had slipped away to the other side of the boat. There they were, silhouetted against the sparkling blue ocean, fireworks crashing above their heads, snuggled together under a beautiful full moon. It looked like a scene in a love story to me. I could almost hear the soundtrack.

Soon the final blast of a few hundred, multi-colored rockets were sent soaring into the sky indicating the end of the evening's festivities.

Every Crayola color you could imagine was set off together. It was amazing! I mean it, if the heavens themselves had opened up and sprinkled some magic our way, it couldn't have been any more spectacular than it was that night.

It was… "a wow!"

Just ask Luke and Brenda.

* * * * * *

By the time we sailed on back to John's Pier, it was close to 10:00 PM. Captain Robbins' boat had recently docked, so I knew Aunt Anna and Uncle John were already home.

Dale, Barb, Billy and Bobby said their goodbyes to us and then left to walk up to their end of the inlet. George, Clark, Luke, Brenda, Dolly and I were all heading toward 85th Street, when Luke announced, "Brenda and I will be over a little later, we're just going for some coffee at The Charcoal House."

Bren smiled at me. "And then I'll be right home, okay?"

"Sure," I smiled back. "See you guys later."

The four of us kinda moved a bit to the left as Luke and Brenda walked by us on their way down the pier and over to The Charcoal House. None of us said anything right away, we just watched the two of them. They were walking close together, Brenda's head slightly resting on Luke's shoulder, arms entwined, softly speaking to each other.

"She's gonna marry that guy," I sighed.

George turned and smiled at me. "You think so?"

Dolly and Clark echoed George's sentiment. "You really think they will, Pat?"

"Take another look."

Luke and Brenda were now about fifty feet away from us and they were holding hands, swinging them in the breeze, then Brenda would laugh, and Luke would grab onto her and dance her around, right there on the sidewalk. And then, he pulled her in close to him and he kissed her. I could tell by the way he held her that it wasn't your typical guy 'wanting something else later' kiss. There was romance to it, there was tenderness and magic.

"Wowee," Dolly sighed.

George and Clark nodded in agreement.

"Toldja," I smiled.

Chapter One Hundred

We walked along leisurely, talking about the lovely fireworks and Luke and Brenda's connection, and how fast the summer was flying by us.

"Another six weeks and we'll all be ready to leave here," I noted.

"Well, Dale and Barb will be gone before that. Barb said they leave on July 25th. That's just three weeks away."

"Geez."

"What's the matter, Pattie?" George nudged me.

"That's not a lot of time for all of us, is it?"

"It is what it is. And we'll make the best of it."

Clark nodded. "True, Pat. It is what it is."

"I guess. No use pining away for something that's still here to be enjoyed, huh?"

"We have each other and that's what counts," Dolly added.

Just as those words had left Dolly's lips we were right outside the quaint little cottage that I called home for just over a year.

"Thanks, guys," I said as I gave George a big hug, and then turned to hug Clark.

"It was a really great night." Dolly smiled as she gave our two wonderful friends a hug of her own.

"See you ladies, tomorrow."

"Okay!"

We waved.

They waved.

And then we entered the house.

"Pat?"

"What, Doll?"

"I think I'm gonna go home tonight. Is that okay?"

"Tonight?!"

I started to reach for the door to call George and Clark back to walk Dolly home, but she stopped me. "No, I can make it by myself."

"Why aren't you going to stay? Don't you wanna wait 'til Bren gets back? Why do you…"

"Pat, I wanna talk to my father."

My mind flashed back to earlier in the evening: Sean Dollio, the red-head in the skimpy green and white bikini… and I understood completely.

"You're actually gonna tell him what we saw?"

"I don't know what I'm gonna say but I can't stay here and have these thoughts gnawing away at me until late tomorrow when he gets home from work. I have to go home."

"Let me walk you."

"No, Pat."

"How 'bout half way then?"

"No, Pattie. Thanks, but I'll need that time to myself before I see my Dad. Know what I mean?"

I nodded. "If you need me, just call."

"I will." With that said, Dolly gave me a tiny smile, opened the front door, and then quietly stepped out into the darkness.

* * * * * *

"It's quarter 'til eleven! What the *hell* are you doing parading in the house at this hour?" Dolly's father had already consumed quite a few drinks and he was looking for a fight.

"Where's Nikki?" Dolly asked.

"In the shower."

"Where're the kids?"

"In bed. Answer my question! Where the hell have you been?!"

Dolly eyed the half a dozen or so beer bottles on the table. She knew her father was a miserable drunk, but she was loaded with ammunition, and she didn't care what he had to say about her late hours. He had questions of his own to answer.

"I was gonna stay at Pattie's tonight after the fireworks cruise, but I thought I should come home."

"At *this* hour?!"

"Yes, at this hour. Did *you* see the fireworks tonight?"

"As a matter of fact, I did. Even though I had to work all day today, I managed to make it home at the last minute to drive my wife and kids to Sea Isle to see them." He took a huge chug of his beer and finished it, quickly opening another. "See, Doll, if you would put your priorities with your family *first*, you would have been there with us instead of flittin' off with your summertime friends."

That was all Dolly needed.

"Flitting off with my summertime friends?! I never *abandon* my family. I take care of my housework, I *pay* to stay here, and I take good care of the kids, *and* I work my fanny off at Shellum's! I deserve time with my friends."

"Watch that tone of voice young lady."

"My tone was appropriate." She stood her ground.

"So, what's this? You're insinuating I flit away my time when *I'm* the one who put a roof over your ungrateful head for the last seventeen years?"

"I didn't say that! *You* did!"

Her father stood with both hands grasping the sides of the kitchen table, staring his daughter right in the face, doing his best to intimidate her.

She never flinched.

She was going in for the kill.

"And maybe flitting isn't the right word for you anyway, Dad. Maybe lying is."

Mr. Dollio reached for his daughter, and grabbed her sweater, but Dolly was too fast for him and she pulled away, sending her father collapsing back onto the old vinyl and chrome kitchen chair.

"LYING?!" he roared.

"Don't you *ever* touch me again! And you heard what I said! I *saw* you tonight. So did Pattie. Don't even try to deny it!"

Her father straightened himself up in the chair. "What the *hell* are you talking about?"

"We saw you cruising around the inlet with... well... that *wasn't* Nikki! Was it?!"

"Dolly, Dolly, Dolly." He shook his head in pity toward her. "Still livin' in your little fantasy world, aren't you?"

"Nikki isn't a redhead, Dad! That's not a fantasy. That's reality."

Her father took a few swigs of his drink and never answered her.

"And, reality is *also* a woman sitting so close to you she was practically on your lap! Is this ringing a bell? Red-head... Rita Hayworth sunglasses... skimpy green and white bikini?"

Sean's face lost all color as Nikki walked into the room.

"Hi, Doll! What are you doin' here?"

"Well, I..."

"I thought you'd be at Pattie's after the cruise. What happened?"

"Umm... I just needed to come home for something."

"And what's all this about a green and white bikini?"

Dolly turned toward her father's ashen face and smiled. "Yeah, what was it again, Dad? What about that green and white bikini?"

"Oh, Dolly." Nikki shook her head. "You didn't ask your father if you could get a two-piece again did you? Remember we said when you're eighteen you could wear one? That rule still holds, young lady."

"I gotta go," Dolly said hurriedly walking toward the screen door. "We'll finish our talk tomorrow, Dad."

Her father slowly got up from the table and staggered his way into the living room.

"Bye, Doll."

"Bye, Nik."

Nikki walked to the window and her eyes followed Dolly as she sprinted down the driveway and then back into the direction of Pattie's house. Nik removed the empty beer bottles from the table, straightened out the chair placement, and then entered the living room.

"Sean?"

He grumbled under his breath.

"You let your daughter just walk on outta here? It's almost eleven!

That's *so* not like you!"

No response.

Nikki sighed. "Well, I'm happy to see you're finally giving her the breathing room she needs."

Still no answer.

Nikki leaned over her husband, now resting on the sofa, and gave him a kiss on the forehead. "You're a good father. It's tough with a teenager in the house sometimes, but you're really doing a good job!" She kissed his forehead once again. "And you're a wonderful husband, too. Working hard all day long and still taking me and the kids to see the fireworks!"

Still no answer.

Nikki slowly traced her finger nails around his face. "Come to bed, honey… I'll be waiting for you." she smiled.

Sean managed to get up from the sofa, but he never made it to bed. Instead he stumbled back into the kitchen and drank the last of the Jim Beam he had hidden under the silverware drawer. Sean sat there and thought about what Dolly had said. Not because he had a conscience, but because he knew that his cover had been blown wide open.

Now what would he do?

Yeah… now what?

Chapter One Hundred and One

It was just about midnight and Brenda and I were sitting on the back porch talking about Luke Cramer and their 'love bird' plans for the rest of the summer.

"I want him to meet my family."

"Geez, Brenda, so soon?"

"Does it feel like so soon to you, Pat?"

I had to be honest with her. "No, it doesn't Bren, it seems like you've been around him all of your life. You're like... well, like..."

"Soul mates?"

"Yeah, that's what I was thinking."

"That's just what Luke said tonight."

"Well, your Mom and Dad will be crazy about him, that's for sure."

"I think so too, and he can stay in my brother's room, and then we can both fly out together since we have to be back in California on the same day for school anyway."

"Talk about perfect timing!" I smiled.

"You're not upset we won't be flying out together, are you, Pat?"

"Bren, please. I have to be out there ten days before you, remember. I'm just a lowly Freshman."

She smiled back at me. "I love him, Pat."

She didn't have to tell me, I already knew. Luke Cramer was meant for Brenda and I couldn't have been happier.

"I know, Bren. And he's one helluva lucky guy!"

"Ya think so?"

"You've been my best friend since I knew what the words best friend meant! If anyone knows what an ace you are, Bren, it's me!"

"You're the greatest, Pattie."

I smiled at her once again. "I know."

Then, just as we were about to head upstairs for the night, I heard someone walking up the porch steps.

"Pssssssst... Pattie? ...Brenda?"

I walked toward the screen door and opened it. "Dolly? What are you doin' back here?"

She finished her walk up the steps and stood right next to me. "I had to get out of there."

"Oh, God. Did you tell your father what we saw?"

"Yup."

"And?!!"

Just then Brenda interrupted. "What did you guys see? What are you talkin' about?"

"You didn't tell her?"

"Well, no, we were talking about Luke and school, you know so I…"

"So, tell me!"

Well, it took us about five minutes to explain what actually took Dolly and I less than thirty seconds to see. By the time we were done, Brenda's head was reeling. "Oh, my God! And when you confronted him he had the *nerve* to deny it?"

"He sure did."

"How can he *do* that?!"

"Pretty easy, I guess," Dolly sighed.

"Well, at least Nikki was oblivious to it," I added.

"For now," Dolly said.

"You're not gonna tell her, are you?"

"I don't know."

"Do you realize what'll happen? I mean, that whole family will blow apart."

"My father exploded that family already, Pattie. The minute he decided to cheat on Nikki, he lit the fuse."

"But, imagine how crushed she'll be. Her whole life revolves around that man."

Dolly looked straight into Brenda's eyes. "If Luke was cheating on you, would you want to know it and get rid of the jerk, or be blinded by his lies, while everyone else knew what he was doing."

Brenda sighed. "I'd want to know."

"Well, then."

"Well, then what, Doll?"

"Well, I guess there *has* to be a way to let her know."

I pushed my hands against the sides of my face. "I gotta headache."

Dolly gave me a half smile. "Join the club, sister."

I walked to the cabinet in the kitchen and took out some aspirin for me, Dolly, and Brenda. All three of us had an excruciating headache that had Sean Dollio's name written all over it.

"Thank God we don't have to be in until noon tomorrow," I said as we all started up the staircase.

"This is no walk in the park, Doll," I shook my head, "but we're here for you. You know that."

"It'll be a rough day for you tomorrow, Dolly," Brenda patted our friend on the shoulder. "Whatever you need, just ask."

"Do you want me to go with you to see Nik? I mean, I was a witness!"

"Pat," Dolly said as we entered my room, "if those aspirins are ever gonna have a chance to work, let's not talk about this again until we have to, okay?"

"Okay."

"It's not gonna be easy, Doll," Brenda said as she adjusted the window fan.

"I've had worse. G'night ladies."

Dolly quickly slipped into her jammies and then scrunched herself up against the wall at the edge of the bed. It was a little tight with the three of us sleeping there, but we managed.

When we were all situated as well as possible, we all once again said our goodnights to each other. Brenda and Dolly were asleep almost immediately, but I just kept seeing that visual, you know, Mr. Dollio and that redhead. I kept thinking about what would happen to Nikki and the kids? How Dolly would handle things? I felt so helpless because I couldn't do anything to change the situation.

It was what it was.

I rolled over and punched my pillow down a few times to make it more fluffy and when I was finally positioned in a comfy spot where I knew I could fall asleep, I said a small prayer for my friend - to her mom.

"Mrs. Dollio… I've never asked for a prayer from anyone I didn't know, just usually I pray to God or my mom and dad, you know, but, your daughter's my friend and she needs some help. Please do what you can to guide her to do the right thing, okay? She's a wonderful girl and she loves you and misses you. If you could give us some kind of sign, we'll be happy to take it and do the best we can with what's left to us. G'night Mrs. Dollio… and God bless you."

It seemed as if I had just fallen sleep, when all of a sudden I heard a car horn beep, a doorbell ring, and then Aunt Anna called to me, "Pattie, Dear, would you please wake Dolly. Her father is here."

Quickly Dolly and Brenda sat straight up in bed.

"My father's here?"

Brenda wiped her sleepy eyes. "Holy cow! What are you gonna do?"

Dolly inched her way off the bed and quickly dressed. "I'm gonna do whatever it takes." As she was tying her shoes, she looked up at me. "This is a sign of some kind, Pat. My Dad would never come here even if the house was on fire! He's the King of denial."

A sign…

I quickly thought back to my prayer to Mrs. Dollio.

A sign?

ABSOLUTELY.

* * * * *

As we were all walking down the back staircase, we heard the charming Mr. Dollio talking to Aunt Anna.

"Sure, I'm thrilled that she's going to college. Colorado is a beautiful state. The University is one of the best in the country. That's my girl!"

Just then all of us walked into the living room.

"Mornin', Doll." Her father reached out to give his daughter a hug but Dolly pulled back a bit.

"I know Mrs. Turner had breakfast all ready for you, but since I didn't see much of you for the holiday I thought we could have breakfast together, you know, up in Ocean City, or Brigantine… wherever you want."

Dolly stared at him. She knew this wasn't a nice father and daughter breakfast. Why would it be? They never had one before this. She knew what was up, and so did Brenda, and so did I.

"I'll get my sweater," was her only response.

I could sense Mr. Dollio's nervousness. He knew that I was aware of the redhead in the green and white bikini, too.

"So," I said. "Dolly told us you made it home in time to take Nik and the kids to see the fireworks last night. That was nice."

"Yeah, we had a great time."

"Good thing you made it home from working all day. It would have been a shame to have your family miss that."

"Yes, it would have."

He couldn't even look me in the eye when he talked to me. He sort of shuffled his right foot and kept looking over my right shoulder to see when Dolly would reappear.

Just as I was about to fire off another round, his daughter entered the living room. She turned and gave us all a hug. "I'll be back in a little bit. Please save me some coffee and one of your blueberry muffins, okay, Mrs. Turner?"

"I sure will, Dolly. Have fun!"

Mr. Dollio was out the door without a word said to any of us, except some muttering that sounded like a goodbye. Dolly was about to close the front door when she looked back at us one last time. "I'll be okay, guys. Don't sweat it. It's all right."

Brenda and I nodded.

Then she was gone.

As Aunt Anna was walking back toward the kitchen she turned to me and asked, "Why did Dolly seem so concerned about your worrying over her?"

Brenda and I looked at each other.

Just then I heard the roar of a red and white 1959 Chevy Impala speed up the street.

"Well, ummm…" Brenda started. "I guess she was worried 'cause lately her father has been a bit… a bit…"

"A bit reckless," I finished.

Brenda nodded. "Yeah, reckless."

Aunt Anna entered the kitchen and poured some coffee. "Men get those jazzy new cars and they just think they can drive like they're on a race track. Shame on them."

I sighed and shook my head.

If it was only that simple.

* * * * * *

Dolly's father drove like a mad man up Landis Avenue and pulled over to a spot where many locals go crabbing late in the afternoon.

"GET OUT OF THE CAR!!!" he ordered.

Dolly opened the door and stood there staring at her father, arms folded in defiance across her chest.

"About *yesterday*, Miss Know-it-all…" he said as he slammed his door shut.

"What about it?" she answered in a voice as tough as nails.

"Her husband's a client of mine."

"What?!"

"Are you deaf?! The *redhead*. Her husband…"

Dolly laughed right in his face. "Do you think I'm that stupid? I *know* what I saw."

"Don't run your mouth when you don't know the full story."

"The full story?"

"Val and I had dropped her old man off to pick up his new boat and I was driving her back to Avalon."

"Val?"

"The redhead – Valerie."

"I see. So, what's the name of your client?"

"What?"

"What's the name of your *client*? The name of this woman's husband?"

"That's none of your business."

"Well, it didn't *used* to be my business, but it is *now*! You've made it my business. What's his name?"

"Joe."

"Does Joe have a last name?"

Her father paused for a moment. "It's… it's…wait, let me look in the glove box. I have his card in there. He's a *huge* client… HUGE."

Puh-leeze.

Dolly still stood next to the car, hands now on her hips, knowing full well her father had no client named Joe on the 4th of July, or *any* client on the 4th of July for that matter.

Mr. Dollio continued to search his glove box. "I know I had it in here."

Dolly was beyond fed up with her father's pathetic attempts to save his own neck. "You're a liar and a cheat."

Her father started to say something, but, for some reason, he stopped himself.

"You cheated on Mom with Nikki and now you're cheating on Nikki. You're only angry with me because I caught you! Admit you cheated on Mom with Nikki! ADMIT IT!"

Mr. Dollio closed the glove box, paused for a moment, and then slowly turned toward his daughter. "If I…"

"If you *what*?!"

"If I tell you… will you keep quiet about Valerie?"

Dolly's hands dropped from her hips. "So, you really cheated on…"

"I didn't want to Dolly, but I'm a man. I have my needs."

"She was *dying* for God's sake!"

"Your mother wasn't holding up her end of the marital bargain. She *forced* me to go elsewhere. I didn't want to, but…"

"SHE *forced* you?!"

"You heard me."

"*Nobody* had a gun to your head, you did it 'cause you wanted to."

"I *didn't* want to! I loved your mother."

"Oh, puh-leeze. Love? The woman was on her deathbed!"

"I didn't know that!"

"Yes you did!!! *Everybody* did!!!"

"You know *nothing* about my marriage to your mother."

"Yeah? Well, I know enough to remember you screaming that she wasn't a woman anymore. Remember that?"

"That's not true."

"Yes it is. Those words stuck in my head 'cause I heard Mom cry so hard after you said that I thought her heart would break. You *owe* Mom, and it's too late for her. But you owe *me, too* - and I'm still here."

"You want *money*?!"

"I DON'T WANT YOUR GODDAMN MONEY!!! I WANT **RESPECT**!!!" Dolly screamed at him 'til her throat was stripped dry. "I want OUT of that house!!! I want AWAY from you!!!"

"I *never* cheated on Nik before this. Not once."

"Once a cheater, *always* a cheater."

Mr. Dollio lit a cigarette and took a long, hard drag. "So, are you…"

"Gonna tell her?"

"Are you?"

"No."

Her father gave a huge sigh of relief.

"Your past'll catch up with you soon enough. You'll get yours." Dolly turned away from her father and started to walk down Landis Avenue.

"Get back in the car! This conversation isn't over, young lady!"

"Oh, yes it is!"

"GET IN THE CAR!!!"

"NO!" By now Dolly was sprinting down Landis Avenue.

"GET BACK HERE!!!"

"I said, NO!!!"

"DOLLY!!!!"

"YOU REAP WHAT YOU SOW, DAD!!!"
"DOLLY!!!"
"LEAVE ME ALONE!!!"

Dolly picked up speed and never looked back. Her father was beside himself. He lit another cigarette and paced the asphalt for a minute or so before getting back into his car. He made a fast U-turn, roared past Dolly, and then drove off in the direction of Avalon's bay area.

To blow off some more steam?
To work?
To Valerie?
To drive off the Townsends Inlet/Avalon bridge?
It really didn't matter.
...Did it?

Chapter One Hundred and Two

Brenda and I had eaten our breakfast, helped Aunt Anna clean up in the kitchen, and then carried our laundry out into the shed. I had already dressed for work and Bren and I were anxiously waiting for Dolly to come driving down the street with her father. *Instead*, we saw Miss Dollio walking down 85th Street all alone, looking a little worse for wear than when she left here, but, she still had a smile on her face as she waved to us.

Bren and I ran to meet her and immediately the questions were flying.

"Where's your father?", "Did he tell you the truth?", "What are you gonna do?", "Who *was* that woman?", "Does Nikki know?"

Dolly quickly answered all of our questions and neither Brenda nor I could blame her one bit for leaving her dad up in Sea Isle and walking back to us on her own two feet.

Dolly's eyes started to fill a bit. "Pat?"

"What, Doll?"

"Do you think it would be okay if I stayed here until we have to leave for school? I can't go back there and I can't…"

"Of course it's okay. Aunt Anna and Uncle John adore you!"

"It's not that I don't want to see Nik and the kids, but they can come over to the store and I can always drop by before my father gets home from work."

I nodded.

"I know they'll miss me, but I'll be off to college anyway and…"

"Consider yourself home, Doll," I smiled.

She sighed as if the weight of the world had just left her shoulders.

"Thanks, Pattie."

Brenda added, "And there'll be phone calls and letters from Nik and the kids. You'll still be connected. Geez, last year I got over two hundred pieces of mail!"

"Two hundred?" Dolly was wide-eyed.

"Yep."

"Hey, let's go in the house and talk to Aunt Anna," I suggested.

"Do we have to tell her *everything*?" Dolly sounded a little anxious.

"No, Doll. Not everything. It'll be okay."

Once again the three of us were walking up the front porch steps and there was Aunt Anna putting the finishing touches on the beautiful afghan she'd been knitting. We all sat on the floor around her.

"Well, what's all this?" she questioned with a smile.

"Aunt Anna? Doll's having some problems at home and…" I took a deep breath. "And she'd like to stay here and feel safe and happy until she has to leave for school next month. Nik's okay with it if you are."

My aunt looked sympathetically toward Dolly. "Are you all right, Dear?"

"I'm better now, thanks."

"Well, since it's okay with your family, it's certainly all right with me and John."

Dolly jumped right up and gave Aunt Anna such a big hug she almost knocked the wind out of the poor woman! "Thank you a *million* times over, Mrs. Turner!"

My Aunt smiled. "It'll be our pleasure to have you here with us."

Dolly was relieved and excited. "Can I get my stuff now?!... Or some of it?"

"Sure you can. Would you like to use that wagon we have out back in the shed? It can hold a lot of stuff!"

"I sure would, thanks!"

"We'll clean it out, Aunt Anna," I said as I left my seat on the floor.

My Aunt stood and once again Dolly hugged her.

"I can't thank you enough. I'll clean, I'll do laundry... I'll..."

"You just get to Shellum's every day and take care of that wonderful new college life you have coming up next month... the rest will *all* fall into place."

Dolly smiled.
Brenda smiled.
And I smiled.
...Another silver lining for Miss Dollio.

* * * * * *

By the time the three of us reached Dolly's house, Mack and Apry were already visiting a nearby neighbor's house - a friend of Nikki's to give her a break for the day. Sometimes Nik and her friend, Charlotte would do that - you know, the kids would have company their own age, and the one mom could catch up on other things that she never seemed to get to with two young children around 24/7.

Today was Nikki's turn for a break, and I knew she needed it.

Forget about the kids. Being Married to Mr. Dollio? *That's* why she needed a break!

"Wait out here for just a bit while I break the news to Nik, okay?"

"Sure."

Brenda and I paced back and forth, pulled each other around in the old Radio Flyer wagon, sang a few songs, just anything to keep busy while waiting for a sign from Dolly. I wish I could have been a fly on the wall to hear what was going on inside that house. But I knew I'd have to wait to find out... and so would Brenda.

"NIK!!! I'M HOME!!!!"

Nikki walked down the staircase. "Hi! How are you?"

"I'm okay. How are *you*?"

"Well, I guess I'm getting used to the kids not being here. Normally Mack is in his walker and Ap is coloring on the table, making me a new picture for the fridge. But I need a little time off."

"Yeah, I know the feeling."

Nikki put her hand on Dolly's shoulder. "Listen, I know you don't want to talk about this, but you *really* need to make amends with your father."

"Not gonna happen."

"Why?"

"I already saw him this morning."

"Where?"

"He drove over to Pattie's, he said he was gonna take me out to breakfast but instead he pulled over by Jake's old crab pier, and he started to yell at me."

"Yell?"

"Yeah. Long story short - He got angry, I got angry. I just want out, Nik."

"Oh, my God, Dolly. No."

"I want to move into Turner's 'til I leave for school."

Nik started to cry. "This is really about me, isn't it?"

"Huh?"

"Did I make it too hard on you here… you know with the kids and…?"

"No, Nik. I love the kids."

"Well, I know it was a little rough at first, but…"

"Listen, it's not about *you*! It's about Dad and his outdated ideas for women."

Nikki nodded her head.

Dolly continued, "Of course, his standards for men are borderline bohemian! Do as I say not as I do. Know what I mean?"

"All too well," Nik answered softly.

"I just hafta go, Nikki. I gotta get outta here."

"The kids will miss you somethin' awful!"

"I'll come over when Dad's gone and you can stop by Shellum's. I'll treat you guys to a sundae or a burger or somethin'."

Nikki dried her eyes on a small tissue she pulled from inside her pocket. "Did all this start over a bikini? Be honest with me, Dolly."

Dolly looked Nik straight in the eye. "Yes, Nik. It honestly started because of a green and white bikini."

"That's so ridiculous."

"Well, it was even crazier than you can imagine, but I'm not accepting certain behaviors from my father anymore."

"Well, Sweetheart," Nik hugged her close, "If this is what will make you happy, then you do it. I'm on your side all the way."

Dolly smiled.

"I'll help you pack some stuff, okay?"

"Thanks, Nik. And, umm... Pattie and Brenda are outside; can they come in and help?"

"Why didn't you invite them in?"

"Well, I just wanted to make sure this was okay with you, that's all. I wanted to tell it to you personally, not in front of anyone."

Nikki smiled at Dolly.

No sooner had the two hugged again when Brenda and I were waved into the house to help collect Dolly's shoes and dresses and peddle pushers, makeup, etc. She didn't have a lot of stuff, but it was more than enough to fill that little wagon. We stacked paper bag upon paper bag, and added one little navy blue suitcase on top of the pile and we were on our way.

"Bye, Nik! Stop over the store later when the kids get back! We're there from Noon to 6:00 today!"

"Will do," she smiled. "Bye, Dolly! Take good care of yourself!"

"I will. See ya!"

"See ya!"

* * * * * *

Dolly, Brenda, and I wheeled that old Radio Flyer wagon over to the Turner household, unpacked, showered, got dressed for work, and clocked in at Shellum's with four minutes to spare!

"What a morning, huh, Pat?" Dolly said as she quickly buttoned up her Shellum's- by-the-sea smock.

"You can say that again!"

I was a bit leery about the noon to six shift, but I actually enjoyed it. The lunch crowd was ready and waiting, and the locals stopped in just to chat or pick up a stray item for dinner. By the time the afternoon deliveries were priced, shelved, and put away it was almost four o'clock!

Just as I was about to say that the store crowd had died down for the day, in walked Nikki, Apry, and Mack.

"Dolly! Pattie!" Apry sang out as soon as the door swung open.

"Hi, Ap!" I smiled.

"Hi, Pat! Where's my sister?"

"Right here, puddin'!" Dolly grinned from her work station at the soda fountain. "Care for an ice cream sundae, anyone?"

"Now that sounds good to me," Nikki said as she pushed Mack's stroller in her direction.

I got back to work and let Dolly take care of her family. I figured they needed some time alone, you know, with Doll just moving out and everything.

I heard giggles and laughter and happy talk coming from the soda fountain so it made me feel good. Dolly might not have a great relationship, or any relationship for that matter with her father, but she sure had one with Nikki and the kids! Just as I had finished stacking a fresh supply of Cheerios I heard Nikki say goodbye to Dolly, and Mr. and Mrs. Shellum.

"Hey, you forgot about me!"

"Oh, Pattie, there you are!" Nikki craned her neck toward my side of the store. "Have a great day and thanks for taking good care of our girl. My love to your Aunt and Uncle. I'll give them a call to thank them when I get home."

"Our pleasure, Nik! Bye, Ap! Bye, Mack!"

Nikki waved, Apry waved, and Mack just smiled and gurgled - as always.

They sure were a nice family. The only thing wrong with them was… well, Mr. Dollio.

* * * * * *

Dolly and I finished work at six on the dot, we signed out, and then started our usual walk home. Doll chuckled as she turned back toward me. "See? Neither of us noticed! I was walking back to my old house! I don't live there anymore! I live with you guys!"

"We're conditioned, Dolly. It'll take a few days and we'll be in the swing of things."

"I wonder how things are swinging back at my old house? I hope Nikki and the kids are doin' okay."

"Doll, Nikki seems a little too easy going sometimes, but I honestly believe she can hold her own against your Dad."

"Really?"

"Yes, really."

"She has those kids to think about. She won't let your Dad jeopardize their future, you can count on that!"

Dolly nodded. "Yup, I think you're right. Nik'll have what it takes when she needs it."

"Like you, Doll." I smiled. "Like you."

Just as our conversation had ended we were home! And, a BIG official 'Welcome to your new home' dinner was waiting for the newest member of our family!

We walked into the kitchen and it looked like a summer feast fit for a king.

Dolly started to cry as she read the little makeshift banner that hung right above the table.

Welcome to your new home Miss Dolly!
And God Bless you, always!

What a wonderful family, I thought to myself. *Dolly and I are two lucky young ladies!*

On the other side of town was another wonderful family, that is, if you didn't include Sean Dollio.

Nikki made dinner for everyone, but her husband had called and said he'd be a little late, so she wasn't to bother cooking his dinner. Sean told her he'd get a bite somewhere else.

I bet.

Apry was sad that her Daddy wasn't home, but Nik handled everything. Dinner was cooked and eaten, the dishes were washed, dried, and put away, the kids were bathed, Mack was put to bed for the night, and then came story time for Apry.

"Read me the one about Cinderella again, please."

"Sure." Her mother smiled. Nik walked to her daughter's pink and white book case and took out the Little Golden Book that had the beautiful Princess on the cover.

Apry settled in next to her mother, and listened to every word. "Once upon a time there was..." She managed to stay awake up to the part where Cinderella was dancing with the Prince, she always seemed to fall asleep at that part. Nikki would joke with her that she would have to start reading the book from the back to the front one of these days just so she could hear the ending. That always made Apry laugh. Nik tucked her daughter in, and then went back to Mack's room to check on him.

He sleeps like a baby, she chuckled to herself.

With her work all done for the day, Nikki decided to go downstairs for a nice cold 7-Up and look over the latest Reader's Digest. No sooner had she started to read an article on the Kennedy home in Hyannis Port, her husband walked in the door.

The clock read 9:30.

"Gee, honey, I thought you'd be home around 7:00! I mean, when you said later, I didn't think you meant *this* much later. Are you hungry? Can I get you anything?"

"Grab me a beer," he garbled.

Nikki got up from her comfy chair and brought Sean in an ice cold bottle of Ortlieb's and poured it into his favorite glass.

"I saw Dolly today," she said offhandedly.

"Yeah?"

"She came over here with Pattie and Brenda."

"I figured she would."

"She took everything, Sean. She's not coming back."

"That was her choice."

"It wasn't *her* choice. You forced her hand and you know it."

Sean took a big gulp of his beer. "Why do you say that?"

"You know *why*. She *told* me why."

"She *told* you?!"

"I don't know what to say to you, Sean. I'm just…"

"She said she wouldn't tell you!"

"Well, too late. She did."

"Listen, baby…"

"A green and white bikini… was it worth it, Sean? Was it? What's wrong with you, for God's sake?!!"

Now *here* is where that thing called Karma comes into play. Here is where those words Dolly said are about to ring true.

"Your past'll catch up to you soon enough. You reap what you sow, Dad."

"Baby, listen to me. Valerie and I just went out that one time."

All of a sudden Nikki's innocence made an about face. "Valerie?"

"It was just a stupid fling and…"

"Valerie Aleardi?"

"Yeah, baby, but…"

"A fling? You said a *fling*?!!"

"Well…"

"What's that got to do with Val?!"

Sean's face reddened. "Well…"

"You mean *Valerie* was with you and *she* was the one wearing a green and white bikini?"

"Whoa, wait a minute, wait a minute…"

"That dancer from my Dad's club?! You mean this isn't about Dolly wanting that two-piece?"

All of a sudden Sean knew he was in the middle of something that he couldn't get out of.

"Why are you so shocked?! You *said* Dolly told you!"

"I *said*, a green and white bikini… was it worth it? That's what I *said!* I thought I was talking about you and Dolly arguing over that two piece suit she's been begging for since she was fifteen! Dolly never said *anything* to me about Valerie Aleardi!"

Sean guzzled the rest of his beer.

"And she *never* said anything about you having a *fling* with her! You son of a bitch! YOU did! YOU said it!!!!"

"Baby, let me…"

"Let you *explain*?! And *don't* call me, Baby! Where were you tonight? Or maybe I should call Valerie and ask!"

"It didn't mean *anything*. I was going to end it, we were out in my boat and…"

"You were OUT in *your* boat?! That is OUR boat, for your information and we've never even been for a ride in it yet! You said it needed engine work! You lying son of a…"

Nikki headed to the closet and started to tear through the clothes.

"Baby, listen… just don't get crazy!"

Nik stopped and turned with a calm and serene air about her. "Don't get *crazy*?! You think I'm going through this closet to take out something of *mine*? *Your* ass is outta here! Sleep in the car." Nik tossed him an old beach blanket. "And don't bother to come back! The rest of your stuff'll be out in the driveway in the morning."

"YOU CAN'T DO THIS TO ME!!!" he screamed.

"Can't I? I just did!"

Sean cooled down fast and stammered, "Listen, I… I can work this out with…"

"WORK WHAT OUT?!!! I'M GETTING A LAWYER!! SCREW YOU!! IT'S OVER!! You filthy, lying, cheating, BASTARD! GET OUTTA HERE!!!!"

Sean's old anger reared its ugly head. "Who are *you* to tell *me* to get out?! This is *my* home, and don't you EVER forget it!"

"NO! THIS home was your first wife's *family* home, and, when Marcia died, 99% of it went to Dolly. So, I think it's *safe* to say that the person who holds 99% interest in this house will be in full agreement with the woman who held 100% interest in her marriage to you. So, get out and STAY OUT!!!"

Sean grabbed a pack of cigarettes from the table as he was leaving. "I'll be back! YOU and the kids will be outta here, not *me*!" Sean slammed the door so hard it almost came off the hinges.

Immediately Nikki walked to the kitchen telephone and dialed, Sea Isle 71468. "Hello, Daddy?" her voice trembled, "I… I need a *really* good lawyer. And I want to see him… tomorrow."

* * * * * *

Dolly, Brenda and I didn't hear about the fiasco between Nikki and her husband until after work the following day. Not that Nikki was hiding anything from Dolly, but she didn't want to call her after her father left because it was way too late, and then the next day we worked from 8:00 to 5:00. Right around 7:00 PM Dolly got the call that straightened everything out for all of us.

Nikki saw a lawyer earlier that morning and had started divorce proceedings. It seems that not only was her husband having an affair with Valerie Aleardi, but with Valerie's roommate, and *cousin*, Joan Petrini as well! What a slug this guy was.

Sean Dollio was ordered to remove all of his worldly possessions by 9:00 AM on Saturday, July 8th. Nik told Dolly that wouldn't be a problem, she'd have everything he owned bagged up and sitting in the driveway on the 7th!

Apry and especially Mack were way too young to understand what was going on and that was a good thing. Their Dad wasn't around all that much anyway, and he'd actually get to see them more during visitations than when he lived there - if he even bothered, that is.

Mr. Dollio's cover was now blown wide open and for sure he wouldn't be living in the quaint little village of Townsends Inlet any longer. We all figured he'd hit a big city like New York or Philadelphia. But, where ever he was going, no one really seemed to care.

The man dug his own grave, and now it was time for him to climb into it.

Adios, Sean Dollio.

Chapter One Hundred and Three

The rest of the week went by pretty fast - the usual work and fun routine. Every now and then Dolly's dad's name would come up between us, but for the most part, we knew the loose ends had been tied up, and we were all moving forward, letting the sleeping dogs lie. Dolly and I also started to notice that we were seeing less and less of Dale and Barb and Brenda. Well, I guess that was to be expected. For one, they were all down in Townsends Inlet for vacation, they didn't have to work, so that freed up a lot of the time Dolly and I didn't have. And, secondly, all three girls were seriously dating - especially, Brenda. Yup, Luke Cramer was her dream guy and she was his dream girl. That's the stuff happy endings are made of, and we could all see that one coming a mile away.

The dances on Friday night were terrific; in fact, they seemed to get better every week. Uncle John would always ask me and Dolly to run up to Dalrymple's for the latest releases so the music was always as up to date as possible. I thought it was great to watch my uncle enjoy himself like that! In fact, he even brought Aunt Anna along one night to be a guest DJ. How sweet is that!

It was pretty funny and pretty cute all at the same time to hear a woman in her mid-seventies announce, "Here's a really great song to get out on the floor and dance to; Little Richard's, Long Tall Sally!!!"

At one point during the evening I asked Aunt Anna to come downstairs and dance with us, but, she said the only dance she ever did well was 'The Charleston' back in the 1920s, so she politely passed on the invitation.

Days moved on faster than any of us wanted them to. We'd always spend time together as a group at the dances, and even on a few Saturdays we'd all be down on the beach together, but as I said, our friends were moving on with their lives, taking new boyfriends, surrounding themselves with different sights and different people. It was sad to see it happen. We knew we'd always be friends, but we also knew that the circumstances around our friendship would be different - that's just the way it works out… just a part of growing up.

Before we knew it, it was July 23rd. It was the last Friday night dance before Dale and Barb would attend before they left for home on the 25th. Dale's all-time favorite record was, 'Stagger Lee' by Lloyd Price, and Barb's was, 'Johnny B. Goode', by Chuck Berry. Uncle John dedicated both songs to the girls and they were absolutely thrilled to be in the rock and roll spotlight. The girls also loved 'Tonite Tonite' by the Mello Kings, a beautiful sweet love song from back in 1957. When my Uncle announced that it was the last slow song of the night before The Spaniels sang, 'Goodnight Sweetheart.' Dale and Billy, and Barb and Bobby quickly took the floor, but all the rest of the kids there that night, including us, stood back and gave our four friends their own space. No one wanted to take away that last real special moment from the four of them.

So, there they were, Dale and Bill, Bobby and Barb, dancing underneath that beautiful sparkling globe in their own little world.

A few of us started to sing along with the music, then a few more, and then a few more, until every one of us on the sidelines of The Civic Center was joined in song.

Tonite, tonite may it never reach an end…
I'll mi-i-iss you so till you're in my arms again…
With all of my heart I declare with all my might…
I'll love you forever as I lo-o-o-ve you tonite.

As the song ended we all applauded.

There were tears in my eyes and Dolly's too.

Our four friends kinda kidded with all of us and took a little bow, but they were touched by the sentiment, I can tell you that.

What a perfect way to end a summer.

Magical memories to last a lifetime.

It was one of the sweetest things I had ever seen.

Then, the evening was over. 'Goodnight Sweetheart' had played, and our friends went their separate ways.

That left just me and George and Dolly and Clark. We waved goodbye to everyone and then walked over to VanSant's for an ice cream cone before heading back to the house.

"I told you it would be a great summer, didn't I, Pattie?" George smiled at me.

"Yes, and you also said, 'It'll go by fast.' Remember that?" I sighed. "It's just all over too soon. New kids will start to come by and the old crowd will…"

"But no one can take away our memories, Pat," Dolly said.

"It is what it is," Clark stated.

George put his arm over my shoulder and hugged me close. "Yeah, it is. But, listen to this, Pattie." George then recited some of the most beautiful words I had ever heard:

"The roses under my window make no reference to former roses or better ones.

They are what they are.

There is no time to them.

There is simply… the rose."

"Why, George Ludlam, I didn't know you wrote poetry." Again my eyes filled.

"I don't. That was Emerson," he smiled. "But it's true, Pattie. There's no time to us, to what's happened."

"You mean…"

"What, Pat?"
"That we're the roses?"
"Exactly."
July 25th came and we knew it was time to say our goodbyes to Dale and Barb. We all gathered at their house right after dinner, and although we wanted to stay to wave them a final farewell, we knew it was best to go early so the girls had time to spend with Bob and Billy.
"See you next summer!" they shouted as we were leaving.
"1961, here we come!" I smiled.
"BYE!"
"See ya!"
Yeah... see ya.

* * * * * *

As it was the preceding year, so it was in 1960. In the order our friends came to the shore, was the exact order in which they left us.
July 27th took Clark away.
We all decided that right after Dolly and I left work that day, we'd all meet over at The Charcoal House. There were actually times when it seemed like we were all just out for another fun night, and then there were times when we all would look at each other, knowing that Clark would be on his way back to Philadelphia in just a few hours.
"We are the roses," George whispered to me during one of my melancholy-filled moments.
"I remember." I smiled.
After dinner we all walked over to Clark's house and did what we could to help his family pack up the car and get organized. Before we knew it another goodbye was upon us.
"I'll call you when I get into Philly," George said shaking his friend's hand.
"Okay," Clark nodded. "Sounds good."
Luke and Brenda shared their goodbyes and well wishes, I gave Clark a huge hug and handed him a small bag with a few of his favorite butterscotch Tastykake Krimpets inside of it.
"See you next year, Mr. Lowen." I tried on a smile.
"See you next year, Miss Pattie."
Dolly was the last to say goodbye. "I'll miss you, Clark. You always gave me faith that something good comes along just when you need it the most."
Clark hugged her tightly. "Do real well this year, Doll. No one deserves genuine happiness more than you do. And keep singing!"
"I will."
"Time to leave, son!" his father called.
Clark turned toward us and started to say something, but the words

never left his mouth. Somehow I knew exactly what he wanted to say to us.

I think we all did.

We stood on the sidewalk as his father's new Chevrolet pulled out of the driveway.

"Bye, Clark!" Dolly and I waved.

"See ya later, Buddy!"

"So long, everyone! So long!"

One last wave from the back of that beautiful blue and white Chevrolet and Clark Lowen was gone.

* * * * * *

Dolly and I woke up the next morning at 7:00 AM and Brenda was already in the shower.

"What's with her?" Dolly said. "Brenda wouldn't get up until noon if someone didn't wake her!"

"I dunno. Maybe she's got a breakfast date with Luke or something."

"Mmm, could be. I never thought about that."

"Breakfast date?" Brenda echoed entering the room.

"Yeah, what's with you? Bren, it's 7:00 AM not 7:00 PM!" I laughed.

All of a sudden her face appeared sullen.

"What's the matter?"

"Well, I wanted to tell you yesterday, but Luke and I figured you were upset enough about Clark leaving and…"

"What are you talkin' about? Tell me what yesterday?"

"We're leaving today, Pattie. We're taking the 11:00 bus into Philly."

"YOU'RE WHAT?!"

"It came up fast between us when we were talking. I want him to meet my family, we both have to get ready for school, I want to meet the rest of his family and we're flying out to California together. If we wait another two weeks, we won't be able to fit every thing in. You're not mad at me are you?"

Dolly and I both flopped down on the side of the bed.

"Eleven o'clock?"

"Yeah."

"Do Aunt Anna and Uncle John know?"

"We told them yesterday."

"You're leaving here… today… at 11:00?"

"I'm sorry, Pattie."

Dolly got up off the bed. She said she was heading to the bathroom for a shower. But I honestly think she left to give me a few private moments with my old friend.

Brenda sat down next to me. Again, she said, "I'm sorry, Pat. I didn't mean to lay all of this on you so fast."

I looked at her and sighed. "That's okay. Who am I to stand in the way of true love, a bus ride to Philadelphia, and sophomore year at UCLA?"

She smiled and gave me a hug. "And, I'll be seeing you next month, remember? In California! Think how cool that'll be!"

"Any time I spend with you is cool, Bren. You know that."

"So you're not mad at me, then?"

"Nope. I'm happy for you."

"Cross your heart?"

"Yep. Cross my heart."

* * * * * *

Brenda, Dolly, Aunt Anna and I had one last Summer of 1960 breakfast together. In fact, even Uncle John decided to curtail his early morning fishing jaunt so all of us could be together.

And what a spectacular breakfast it was! Belgian Waffles with Spiced Apples and whipped Cream, a scrumptious sharp cheese omelet complete with home fries and toast, a tray of bacon, scrapple, pork roll and sausage, *And* the best Danishes in Southern New Jersey courtesy of the Sea Isle Bakery: cherry, raspberry and coconut. There was also a new pot of coffee perking on the stove, and frosted glasses filled to the top with freshly squeezed orange juice.

"Take your pick ladies!" Aunt Anna smiled.

"Wow! I'm telling you, there's nothing even close to this kind of eating out in California," Brenda said. "I'm gonna miss this. They wanna put alfalfa sprouts on everything. It's all about nutrition... so they say."

"Alfalfa sprouts?" Uncle John winced. "That stuff's for cows not people. Gimme some good old Philadelphia scrapple any day of the week!"

"Hear, Hear!" we all applauded.

Just then I took my frosted juice glass in hand, stood, and faced my dear friend, Brenda Ethel Mayberry. "A toast to you as you move on your way to a happy new year at school and to a happy new life with Luke Cramer."

"I'll second that!" Dolly smiled.

We sat at that table longer than we ever had before. Aunt Anna put on another pot of coffee and we reminisced about our wonderful, albeit all too brief summer: our trips to the beach, shopping at Pfeiffer's, The Trading Post, Dalrymple's, dinners at The Charcoal House and Bush's Seafood House, VanSant's ice cream, the best boardwalk pizza in America, the great hoagies at Shellum's, the fabulous dances at The Civic Center, and of course, the day Brenda met Luke. Just as the third pot of coffee was about to be perked, there was a knock on the front door.

It was Luke.

"My God," I said, looking at the wall clock! "It's 10:30!"

Brenda rushed to the door to greet her sweetheart. I ran upstairs to pack the last of her clean clothes that Aunt Anna had taken off the line, and Dolly, Uncle John, and Aunt Anna were on dish patrol. In nothing flat it seemed that we were all ready to make that walk to Landis and 85th Street to wait for the 11:00 AM Greyhound.

"Geez, George doesn't even know you're going," I said as we walked toward the front door.

"He does," Luke said. "I called him this morning. He should be at the corner by the time we get there."

Brenda smiled as she turned toward my Aunt and Uncle. "I can't tell you how great it was to be here again… to see you and spend time with you. Thank you both so very, very much!"

"John and I thoroughly enjoyed your company." Aunt Anna smiled. "We'll see you next year, I hope?"

"Wild horses couldn't drag me away," Brenda said as she hugged Aunt Anna. "And *you*, Mr. Disc-jockey!" she said hugging Uncle John. "*You* are the best! Thanks for having me here, Mr. Turner."

"You're quite welcome, Brenda. Come back again."

I looked at the wall clock, it said 10:50. "We better leave."

Aunt Anna and Uncle John stood on the top step of their cozy little cottage and waved goodbye to Luke and Brenda. "See you next year!" They waved.

Brenda kept turning back and waving until the leaves from a huge maple tree in front of Mrs. Bitner's house blocked the way.

Just then we saw George sprinting up Landis Avenue with a Greyhound Bus in full view just a few blocks behind him.

"I was afraid I'd be late," he said totally winded, "but I made it!"

We barely had time to start saying our goodbyes to each other when that big blue and silver bus was pulling up at its usual pick up spot on 85th Street. The doors made a whooshing sound as they opened and the driver smiled at all of us. "How many are comin' aboard?"

"Just the two of us," Luke answered.

"Well, come on in! Next stop Sea Isle City and then, Philadelphia!"

Luke handed his suitcase to the driver and then Brenda's. "We gotta go, Bren," he said softly.

Luke quickly gave me and Dolly a hug, and then shook George's hand. "Take care, guys!"

"And *you*… take good care of our girl!" I smiled.

"You can count on it, Pattie."

"Come on, Bren… the driver wants to leave."

Brenda turned to the three of us and started to cry. "This has been the most wonderful summer of my life. And the best part about meeting Luke was that I had all of you to share the happiness with me."

"All aboard!" the driver called.

I handed Brenda the handkerchief Aunt Anna had made for me. "Don't cry. I'll see you *real* soon. Have a wonderful trip back home, Bren. See you in LA! I'll call you with my arrival time, okay?"

"Okay," she sniffled.

"All *aboard*!!!" the driver called out once more.

Quickly Brenda threw her arms around George and then Dolly. "I'm gonna miss you guys. Write to me, okay?!"

"Last call!"

George and Dolly said their own personal goodbyes to Miss Mayberry, and, in less than the wink of an eye, the doors whooshed closed, taking our Brenda away from us. As the bus started to leave, Brenda stuck her head out of the back window and hollered, "Bye, Guys! I love you!"

"I LOVE YOU, TOO!" I shouted over the roaring bus engine.

Dolly, George and I waved until the bus turned the corner at the old Coast Guard Station.

We walked back down 85th Street in silence.

The pain of missing Brenda was too fresh to start thinking about George leaving us in less than three days.

But somehow…

I was thinking about it anyway.

Chapter One Hundred and Four

In the footsteps of those who had just gone before us, Dolly and I passed the time by working and readying ourselves for school too. We filled out the last of any forms our universities had sent to us, and we were packing and making sure that no stone was left unturned.

As a gift to us, Aunt Anna and Uncle John, God bless them, bought me and Dolly our airplane tickets! Mine to Los Angeles via Chicago, and Dolly, a direct flight into Denver! How sweet was that?!

George was also college bound and I know he was excited about it, too. It was a whole new world for all of us and although we knew we would miss each other, we were more than ready to take that leap of faith.

It was easier to think of George attending college in the fall than saying goodbye to him. But, as time does, it moves on no matter how you feel about it, and the dreaded day came when the Ludlam family was heading back to Philadelphia.

I called George first thing in the morning. "Hi."

"Hi, yourself."

"What time are you leaving?"

"Dad said 11:00. When are you guys going to work today?"

"We don't have to be in until 12:00."

"Perfect."

"Is it?" I sighed.

"You know what I meant, Pat."

"Yeah, I know. So, see you about 10:30? We won't be in the way or anything will we?"

"10:30 is fine. See you and Dolly then, okay?"

"Okay."

"Bye, Pattie."

"Bye, George."

I ran downstairs and poured myself another cup of coffee – as if I wasn't already filled with enough nervous energy.

"PAT?!" Dolly called "When are we leaving?"

"TWO MINUTES! If you hurry we can be late!"

Dolly quickly ran down the staircase. "How do I look?"

"You look like you're gonna miss George an awful lot... same as I look."

She hung her head and sighed. "This is *so* sad."

"You can say that again."

"This is *so*..."

"Let's just get goin'."

Dolly and I took the shortcut through the back bay and were in front of the Ludlam house in less than those two minutes I thought it would take.

George walked down the steps with the largest piece of luggage I had ever seen in my life.

"Good thing you're big and strong." I smiled.

"That's what they tell me."

Dolly and I helped George tie the black Samsonite suitcase on top of the family car.

"Well, that looks like it!" his father called from the porch. "We'll be right down; your mother's just checking the stove to make sure it's off and all the lights are out."

"Okay, Dad!"

"Well, Sport," I tried on my best smile, "I guess this is goodbye for a while."

"Just for a while, Pat."

"Yeah." My voice was soft and sounded very unlike me.

"Hey! Where'd that smile go I just saw?"

"Oh, you mean the one I was faking?"

"Yeah, that one."

"Well, I guess I *could* find it again. How's this?" Again I showed him a nice, big toothy grin.

"It's beautiful, Pat… just like you."

I smiled again, this time, for real.

Before we knew it the Ludlams were all seated in their car just waiting for George to say his final goodbyes.

"Time to go, huh?" Dolly said sadly.

"Looks that way, Doll."

"Bye, George," she said as tears filled her eyes. "Have a great year and write and tell me all about it, okay? And, well… thank you for… for everything."

I could see George's eyes start to mist over. I guess I just never realized how difficult this was for him, too. "You take good care of yourself, and I expect to hear that you're the smartest student the University of Colorado has ever had!"

"You give me more credit than I deserve, George, but I'll do my best."

As Dolly left his kind embrace, I knew it was my turn to say goodbye. "Here we go again, Mr. Scarecrow…" I tried hard to hold back the tears, "I think… I think I'll miss you most of all."

He gave me a quick hug and then looked right into my eyes. "I love you, Pat. Take real good care of yourself."

"I love you too, Mr. Ludlam."

George turned and walked toward the car and then turned back to me once again. "Gimme another one of those great fake smiles, okay? I could use one."

I jokingly gave him a silly grin.

I waved…
He waved…
…and then he was gone.

The two of us stood there until the Ludlam car had turned onto Landis Avenue and then out of sight.

"Doll? Remember what you said when we did this last year?"

"What I said?"

"Yeah… when George left."

"Oh," she sighed once again. "I remember."

"Well?"

"And then there were two."

* * * * * *

Dolly and I decided that rather than go back home for a half an hour we'd be better off going straight to work. Mrs. Shellum greeted us with a big smile and a nod toward the soda fountain.

I immediately turned in that direction and saw a rather large tissue wrapped package of some kind. "It's for you, Pattie." She smiled again.

"What is it?" Dolly followed right behind me.

I quickly tore at the frail paper, revealing inside of it, ten beautiful long stemmed red roses.

"George," I whispered.

"Why would he send you *ten* roses, Pattie? Isn't the standard a dozen?"

"Nothing is standard for George Ludlam," I smiled. "Think!"

Dolly stood there for a minute and then I saw the light bulb go on inside her head. "Ooooooh, I get it! One for each of us. Me, you, Brenda, Luke, Clark, Dale and…"

"That's right. *We* are the roses. Remember?"

"I *love* that guy, Pattie."

"Me too, Doll."

Chapter One Hundred and Five

Not only did that day mark a lovely reminder from Mr. Ludlam of who we all were as friends, the day that George left town also marked exactly one week left for me and Dolly to work as employees at Shellum's by-the-Sea. We had given notice to leave just four days before we were scheduled to fly out to our respective universities. The Shellum family was very proud of us and even took out an ad of Congratulations in the local Sea Isle News Paper. What nice people!

To say the week flew by would be the ultimate in understatements. Work was busy, busy, busy, Dolly made regular nightly visits to see Nik and the kids, we both made our rounds to our friends and neighbors and Dolly sang her last solo with the church choir the Sunday before we left.

When our last work day ended and each of us was handed our final paycheck, there was an extra envelope there for both of us. And, inside of those extra envelopes, was a crisp brand new one hundred dollar bill for each of us! I'd never seen a hundred dollar bill before in my entire life!

"We wish it could be more," Millie said wiping tears away from her eyes. "You've been like family to us."

What thoughtful and kind people!

The Shellums, sweethearts that they were, also packed a goodie bag for each of us to take on the plane, filled with: a half a dozen Tastykakes, five packs of Juicy Fruit gum, three boxes of Goobers, two Lunch Bars, a Nestles Crunch, and a half a pound of pistachio nuts. Ya had to love these people!

The night before we were leaving, Dolly and I went over to see Nik and the kids right after dinner. Although Nikki now was in possession of that 1959 Red and White Chevy Impala, she thought it best if she didn't drive to the Philadelphia Airport with Apry and Mack to see Dolly on her way. One, it was a four hour drive, and two, she was extremely nervous about the late night drive back home by herself with two sleepy, fussy kids at her side. We told her not to worry, and that Aunt Anna and Uncle John would be driving us there in their huge tank of a car and we'd all be just fine. Nikki was greatly relieved.

"Are you gonna be smarter when you come home from college?" Apry asked in all sincerity.

"Well, I hope so," Dolly smiled.

"We're gonna miss you," Nikki said hugging her step daughter goodbye.

"I'm gonna miss all of you, too, but I'll write you all the time, I'll call when I can, and I'll be back as soon as school lets out for the summer."

"Are you gonna sing in the choir when you come back? I'm going to join, you know," Apry said with pride.

"Ap, I wouldn't miss it for the world."

Our goodbyes were said to Nik, Apry, and sweet little Mack, and, as Dolly and I left the home she had known all of her life, oddly enough we didn't feel sad. We seemed rejuvenated and alive! We had tied up all of our loose ends, said a fond farewell to all of our friends and loved ones, and we were reeling with joy about our new lives... the new adventures that were out there waiting for us.

* * * * * *

For the last time, well... at least until next year, Dolly and I woke up to the aroma of one of Anna Turner's scrumptiously delicious breakfasts.

"You know, this is enough to make me waylay my Freshman year 'til 1961!"

My Aunt smiled. "Well, you can't do that, but I can always send you two some gift packages. A nice little chocolate cake here and there, some cookies, cupcakes..."

"Aunt Anna, *you* are theeeee best!"

"I second that!" Dolly cheered.

"What time should we leave, Anna?" Uncle John asked as he replaced the name tag on my suitcase.

"Well, Dolly's plane leaves at 4:03, and Pattie's leaves at 4:43, so we have to scoot from Pan American for Dolly and then over to TWA for Pattie."

"Are we stopping at Olga's Diner on the way?"

"Well, I hadn't thought of it but it might be a nice place for some coffee and pie or a Danish or something. Their pastries are delicious! What do you say, girls?"

"Olga's is great! Sounds good to us!"

"So again, Anna, what time are we leaving?"

"Well, I would think 10:00 AM."

"It's almost 8:30 now, we'd better check and make sure we didn't forget anything." I quickly ran up the stairs and Dolly followed me.

"You put all your winter stuff in the basement, right?"

"Yup. I did that yesterday."

"Me, too."

"Got all your makeup?"

"I'd rather die than be without my supply of Coty and Helena Rubenstein, you know that!" I smiled.

"Yeah... I know that."

"Doll?"

"Yeah?"

"I packed the picture you gave me for Christmas, you know, that really pretty one with your Mom. It was too precious to me to leave here."

Dolly then unzipped her carry-on bag, and there, wrapped in a soft sweater was the photo that I had given her for last Christmas. "It's something I'll treasure all of my life, Pattie."

"I feel the same way about the one you gave me, Doll."

We smiled at each other.

"Well, looks like with the exception of a HUGE Elvis poster up here on the wall, we've got everything we need."

Dolly took one final sweeping glance around the room. "Yup, I think we've got it all."

"Ready?"

"Yup, I'm ready."

We both turned to look over the room one last time.

"So long, Elvis. See ya next summer!" Dolly blew him a kiss and then we closed the bedroom door and headed down the back staircase for the very last time that year.

I could hear the roar of Uncle John's car engine so I knew he was warming it up for the four hour ride to Philadelphia Airport. I watched as Aunt Anna packed a little picnic basket full of goodies for us to eat on the way.

My dearest and darling ever thoughtful Aunt Anna Turner.

The huge trunk in the Turner's 1956 Buick Roadmaster 2 Door Hardtop could almost fit a small rowboat, so Dolly and I had no trouble at all-fitting our two suitcases and two small pieces of carry-on luggage inside of it.

Jake and Carrie Robinson waved from an open porch window. "Do well, girls! We'll miss you! Come back soon and learn a lot!"

"We will!" Dolly and I smiled.

Uncle John had barely closed the hood of his car when eighty-three-year old Jake called out, "Race you into Sea Isle, Turner! My Electra versus your Roadmaster! Twenty bucks says I win!"

Before my Uncle could even answer him, Carrie quickly closed the window, obviously embarrassed by her husband's juvenile behavior. We could see her still scolding Jake as she walked him away from the front porch.

Some kids never grow up, huh?

Aunt Anna waved a fast goodbye to Carrie and then turned toward me and Dolly. "Well, girls, all ready to go?" she said through tear-filled eyes.

I nodded.

"Got your tickets?" Uncle John added.

Dolly nodded. "We're all set, Mr. Turner."

"Then let's get this show in the road!" He smiled.

My Uncle opened the door for his lovely wife and then Dolly and I piled into the back of the car. As we started to leave Aunt Anna adjusted the dials on the radio and tuned in something that sounded like Bing Crosby. Uncle John, who had now acclimated himself to the finer side of the radio dial, said, "Anna, put on WIBG! It plays all the latest Rock and Roll! The kids will love it!"

"Oh…" she smiled slyly, "the *kids* will love it… I see, okay."

Dolly and I chuckled.

Just then, out of the static, a song by Johnny Mathis played. I remembered dancing with George to it just a few Fridays earlier. As we pulled slowly down the street, Uncle John remembered it too, and sang every word of it to his 'best girl.'

"Sometimes we walk hand in hand by the sea
And we breathe in the cool salty air
You turn to me with a kiss in your eyes
And my heart feels a thrill beyond compare…"

I leaned into Dolly, "Now *that's* the way love should be."

"You ain't kiddin', sister!"

As quickly as the songs changed, so did the scenery.

We drove up Landis, passed Garrity's, VanSant's, and the Coast Guard Tower, and then into Sea Isle and over the little bridge that overlooked the bay area.

Soon all those quaint little Jersey towns and farms started to surface: Pleasantville, Egg Harbor, Hammonton, Glassboro… it was really a beautiful ride. Dolly and I waved at the farmers and their kids; moo'd at the cows, sang along with Uncle John, and just had a grand old time.

Before we knew it we were just about to enter a cute little town called Marlton - the home of Olga's Diner! Uncle John pulled up out front of the shiny silver eatery and opened the car doors for us. "All ashore who's goin' ashore!" he smiled.

"I love this place!" Uncle John said. "Ever been here Dolly?"

"Once, with my Mom. We had tea and banana cream pie. It was delicious!"

"Mmmmm, pie." My uncle said rubbing his tummy. "How does that sound to you, Anna?"

"It sounds to me like you're having pie!" She smiled.

The moment we entered the Diner, a hostess came over and seated us, and in less than a wink of an eye a waitress was there to take our order.

"A piece of apple pie and coffee for me, please," Aunt Anna said.

"Make that two," Uncle John chimed in.

"Make that *three*," I smiled.

"What are you having, Doll?" I asked. She looked the menu over one last time and then said, "I'd like some tea please… and some banana cream pie."

Chapter One Hundred and Six

Before we knew it our mid-trip snack time treat was over and we were driving through the larger towns of southern New Jersey: Cherry Hill, Merchantville, and Pennsauken. Soon the Tacony-Palmyra Bridge was in sight and Philadelphia was just a short ride away from us.

"That'll be a five cent toll, please," The uniformed booth person smiled. "And remember to drive safely!"

"We sure will. And you have yourself a mighty fine day!" Uncle John said handing her over a nice shiny buffalo nickel.

Even though we were now in Philadelphia, it would still be a pretty long ride out to the airport - Delaware Avenue was the route and it was a long and bumpy one. I thought Philly was pretty cool. Not because I was raised there all of my life, but because they had real neighborhoods. People looked out for each other, they went to church together, they sent their kids to the same local school. I loved the place! I sat with my face pressed up against the window as we drove through: Tacony, Mayfair, Frankford, Port Richmond, Kensington, Fishtown - right in to South Philly.

"Look! There's the Billy Penn statue!" Dolly said as we drove down Delaware Avenue with Center City in full view.

"You know," Aunt Anna told us, "since William Penn is the city's Founder, there's a law of some kind that says no other building will ever be taller than Billy's Hat on top of City Hall!"

"That's a good law," Uncle John said as he turned the radio down just a bit.

"You don't think there'll ever be a building taller than that in Philly?" Dolly questioned.

"Not as long as that's the city's die hard rule!"

"*I* can see taller buildings there someday. Politicians will call it progress and poor old Billy's hat will be nowhere to be found."

"Pattie," my uncle smiled. "No one is ever gonna do that to Philadelphia. Mark my words, Sweetheart!"

I smiled back at him.

The ride down Delaware Avenue was bumpy. Riding parallel just twenty feet from all of the city's docks, on all those old railroad tracks was not a ride for anyone with a full stomach, I can tell you that! Just then Uncle John spied a pretzel vendor, waving a bag of soft pretzels over his head and shouting, "Hot pretzels here! Getcher hot pretzels! Five pretzels for a quarter! Twelve for fifty cents! Hot pretzels here! *Hot* pretzels!"

"We'll have the fifty cent bag, please," my uncle said, handing him a crisp new dollar bill. "And keep the change!"

In less than the time it took for a fast South Philly light to change, one brand new dollar bill was exchanged for a dozen soft pretzels and all of us were happy!

As Delaware Avenue got a little less bumpy we rode by factories and huge warehouses and then, we knew the airport was close-by because two planes flew right over us, heading in the same direction we were.

"Well, girls, it won't be long now!" Uncle John said.

"Yeah, it won't be long now," I said to Dolly.

"I know," she said quietly. "I know."

As we drove closer into the outskirts of the City of Brotherly Love more and more planes were making their landings or departures into Philadelphia Airport. I could see the tower where the air controllers worked, and the smaller privately owned single prop planes all lined up near the larger TWA hangers, I took one more look at my surroundings and suddenly noticed we were driving under a HUGE green and white sign that read:

WELCOME TO PHILADELPHIA AIRPORT

Well, here we are, I thought to myself.

The Pan AM and TWA departure signs soon caught our eye.

Well, here we are, Dolly thought to herself.

Dolly's Pan American Flight to Denver would be taking off only two gates away from my TWA flight to California. It couldn't have worked out better if we had tried.

Uncle John let us out on the sidewalk right in-between both major airlines, while he drove around looking for a place to park. "Be back in a few!" he smiled as he drove away.

Several airport helpers were immediately at our side, tagging our bags, putting them on these sturdy little push carts, and then off we all went to the ticket office for our boarding passes.

We walked Dolly to the Pan Am station, she checked in her luggage, and received her boarding pass. She would be boarding gate D14 starting at 3:45 for her 4:03 departure.

"Well, that was easy enough," Dolly smiled. "You're next Miss Pattie."

The same routine applied to me. My luggage was checked and then sent off on its merry way down a black conveyer belt. My TWA representative then handed me my boarding pass and wished me a pleasant flight.

"Thank you." I nodded.

I looked at my pretty blue and white pass. According to the paperwork, I would be boarding at 4:25 from gate D16 for a 4:43 departure. Dolly and I would be flying right about the same time and in planes right next to each other! That was so cool! This meant that I could stay with Aunt Anna and Uncle John and watch Dolly's plane take off!

All three of us stood at the entrance to the Gate 'D' area, waiting for Uncle John.

I was a bit nervous and fidgety.

"You okay, Pat? You've flown before, right?"

"To Disneyland, twice."

"Lucky duck."

"You've flown before, haven't you, Doll?"

"Mom took me to the Grand Canyon before she started to get sick. It was a wonderful trip. I've loved plane rides ever since."

Just them Uncle John appeared. "Where to, girls?"

"Up thatta way," I pointed toward the Gate 'D' area.

Aunt Anna and Uncle John took the escalator but Dolly and I opted to use of some of our nervous energy by racing up the steps.

I glanced at my watch. It read: 3:20. Just five minutes until Dolly boarded her plane.

"Not much time to say goodbye is there?"

"There's time for whatever needs to be said," Aunt Anna smiled, gently patting Dolly on her shoulder.

"Mrs. Turner, I can't thank you enough for opening your home to me. The last time I ever really felt like I had a home was with my Mom. It made such a difference in my life... even for the short time I was there."

"Well, Dear," Aunt Anna said sweetly, "Our home will always welcome you as if it's your home. Come back and visit whenever you like."

Dolly hugged my Aunt tightly. "I love you, Mrs. T. You're the best."

"Well, we love you too, Dear. And we wish you well in school. We'll have a big backyard party next year for when you and Pattie are home. We'll invite *everyone*!"

"And I'll be the disc-jockey!" my Uncle smiled.

Dolly and I laughed.

Just then we heard an announcement, "Ladies and Gentlemen we are now boarding Pam American's Non-Stop Flight 826 to Denver, please line up for your flight. Rows 80 to 89, please board now, and..."

"What row are you on, Doll?"

"Sixty-Four."

"Geez, you're gonna be called soon!"

Again the announcements continued. "Rows 68 to 79, please board now..."

"Oh, my God! They're gonna call you next!"

Dolly threw her arms around me. "Oh, Pattie. I'm just gonna miss you so much."

I started to cry...

Then Dolly started to cry...

Then Aunt Anna started to cry!

And Uncle John? Well, he just 'had something in his eye', that was all.

"Promise you'll write to me, let me know how you're doing. We have to stay connected, Dolly."

"You know I will."

"I'm not only lucky and happy to have you as my friend, Doll... I'm proud of it! You're amazing! And you'll continue to do wonderful things. You'll see. Hey, I wouldn't be surprised if you started to change lives before you even got off the plane."

She laughed at me. "There you go, seein' into the future again."

"Well," I smiled, "anything's possible."

Then Dolly's announcement came, "Rows 48 to 64, please board now."

"Oh, God! That's really me! I'm so excited!"

Dolly and I were a mess. One minute we were laughing, the next minute we were crying. Believe me, it's not easy being seventeen!

"Final call for those seated in rows 48 to 64! Please board immediately."

Quickly Dolly turned and gave Aunt Anna a hug and then one for Uncle John. "I love you both! I'll write as soon as I can and thank you again for all you've done for me!"

"Our pleasure, Dear."

Then Dolly turned toward me. "You know, I think I'm gonna steal one of your lines," she said, giving me the best smile she could muster.

"And what's that?"

"I think I'll miss you most of all."

We both hugged each other and cried, then we laughed and then we cried some more.

"You take care of yourself, Miss Dolly."

"And you take good care of yourself too, Miss Pattie."

With that said, Dolly and thirty other passengers walked down the staircase and out onto the tarmac to start their walk up into the beautiful blue and white 707.

I rushed over to the window and waved to her just as she was just about to climb the steps into the plane that would take her away to her new life in Colorado. Aunt Anna, Uncle John, and I stood there, constantly waving and smiling. Soon Dolly stepped onto the last rung before she entered the plane, she turned to us, gave us a huge wave and a big Hollywood kiss, like the ones Marilyn Monroe would give right before one of her planes would take off. It made me smile.

Then...

Well, then... she was gone.

We waited for the other rows to be called, watched as the large portable staircase was removed from the side of the aircraft and then the plane started to taxi down the runway.

"Good luck, Miss Dolly." I said quietly. "See you next year, my friend."

The plane made a left, then a right, then another left until it was sitting on the runway ready to take off. It started out slowly, and then it got faster and faster until finally it picked up enough speed to lift itself up into the sky, like a huge silver bird. Aunt Anna and Uncle John were slowly walking toward gate D16, where I would be leaving from, but my eyes were still glued on Dolly's plane. I watched until it was just a tiny black dot in the sky, and then… even the dot was gone.

Aunt Anna patted me on the shoulder. "We have to go, Dear, they're calling your boarding numbers."

"Are they?" I sighed.

Just as those words had left my mouth I heard, "Those in rows 70 to 90, please board now."

"Holy Cow! I'm next! Mine says 65!"

Aunt Anna and Uncle John wrapped their arms around me.

"We'll miss you very, very much." My Aunt's eyes started to fill. "But I know you'll be a shining star out there and, well, I'm just *so* proud of you!"

Uncle John who was never one for any flowery moments with me gave me quite a surprise. "Pat, we're gonna miss you like crazy. You were a wonderful kid who grew up and became an even more wonderful young lady." Tears started to fill my eyes as he continued, "And, well… if Anna and I could have had a child we… we would have been blessed if she'd even been half the beautiful soul that you are." He reached for his handkerchief.

I gave him a HUGE hug. I heard him sniffle. "Something in your eye again, Uncle John?"

He smiled at me. "Yeah."

"Rows 43 to 65, please board now."

"That's me!"

"It sure is," Aunt Anna sighed. "God Bless you, Dear and have a safe flight!"

"Call us as soon as you're near a phone," Uncle John chimed in. "And I don't care if it costs a hundred bucks! Just call us!"

"Cross my heart." I smiled.

"Last call for rows 43 to 65, please."

It seemed as if everyone was better at following orders than I was, and as I turned around, I noticed there was no one else left to board rows 43 to 65 but me.

I smiled, waved, said, "I love you," and then I blew a big kiss to each of them!

And then…

Well, and then I was gone too, I guess.

That left just the Turners.

Or, as Dolly would say, "And then there were two."

Chapter One Hundred and Seven

As my plane was taxiing down the runway Dolly was already in full flight.

A young girl, our age, situated herself in the seat right beside her.

"Man, am I ever glad I got to sit next to *you*," the girl smiled.

"Yeah?"

"Yeah, I figured I'd be stuck on this five hour flight next to a priest, a shrink, or a seventy-eight year old virgin who hates teenagers."

Dolly chuckled. "Well, you lucked out, I'm definitely none of the above."

"Looks that way." She smiled again.

"So, what's your name?"

"Chris. Actually it's Christine, but I prefer Chris."

"Really? That's *my* name! Well, everyone calls me Dolly 'cause my last name is Dollio, but I was born a Christine, too! You from Philly?"

"Originally."

"Originally?"

"Yeah… it's kinda a screwed up story."

"Well, if you wanna talk, I'll listen."

"Really?"

"Sure. I mean where am *I* goin' for the next five hours?" Dolly smiled.

Chris smiled back and easily settled into a comfortable feeling – knowing she had a captive *and* willing audience. "Well, I had to live with my Aunt and Uncle for a while in Northeast Philly, and then I lived with my mother's parents up in New Hope, then with my… who was that… oh, yeah my cousin, Trish in Yardley, then with another aunt way up in Catawissa, then with my *father's* parents in South Philly, and then back with my Aunt and Uncle and *now* I'm going to Denver so I can live with my Dad, *who*, I might add, hasn't seen me since I was seven!"

"That's a lot of movin' around. How old are you?"

"Seventeen."

"You didn't mention your mom in that long list. Didn't you ever live with her?"

"Well, I had some problems when I was born, you know, one kidney, a slight heart murmur, so, the story goes, she didn't want to be stuck with a sick kid, and she split."

"That's a shame, you okay now?"

"Yeah. Just a little asthma, no big deal."

"And your Mom?"

"I never give her a second thought."

"Oh, *really*?" Dolly said suspiciously.

"Nope, like I said… I never give her a second thought."

"And you've adjusted to all this chaos?"

"Sure. Well, my family doesn't think so, but they don't live inside my head."

"What do they say?"

"They just say I don't have a… wait, it's something my aunt says to me all the time… that I don't have a… oh, yeah, that I don't have a *foothold* in reality."

"How come she said that?"

"I dunno."

"Sure you do."

"Well…" Chris hesitated.

"Well what?"

"She says I tell *stories*."

"What kind of stories?"

"You know… to make my situation look better, to feel better about myself, to fit in."

Dolly nodded.

"But did any one of them try to get me any help? Noooooooo. They just bitched on me."

Dolly sighed.

"And, my Aunt Laura *never* fails to remind me that it'll all catch up to me if I don't straighten myself out."

"That *can* happen, Chris. Believe me."

Christine never acknowledged Dolly's statement, she just went on and on about her life, *all* of her boyfriends - real or imagined - the unfairness of life, the pressures that come with being seventeen… you name it, and Chris was talking about it. The kid was in obvious pain and distress, but she always put a positive twist to all of it – apparently for Dolly's sake.

"And I don't *really* lie…" Chris continued "I'm just…"

"A fact reconstructionist?" Dolly smiled.

Chris rolled her eyes and then looked out the 707's sun-filled window quickly changing the subject. "Geez, I bet we've flown over three states already and I've done all the talkin'."

"So, are you done now?" Dolly chuckled.

"Yeah, I guess so." Chris settled herself back into her seat. "That's my story and I'm stickin' to it." She rolled her neck from side to side as if to adjust the tension. "So, how 'bout you?!" Without even waiting for Dolly's answer, Chris continued, "Can you top that? Yeah, well, none of my friends could either. They always say, 'You gotta get outta this rut!', 'You're headin' for trouble!', 'Chrissy, you're so smart, if *anyone* can change, *you* can change!' Blah, blah, blah."

Dolly nodded, "Change."

"Yeah, change. It should be so easy," Chris started to sulk, "What do they know anyway?"

"Maybe more than you do."

"Are you kiddin' me? No one else in my family's ever been in my situation. They don't have a clue what I feel like."

"Have you…"

"What? Talked to them? Given them the 'honesty' routine? A lotta good that would do."

"But…"

"No buts. I feel like I don't fit in anywhere. My head's never on straight 'cause my feelings are… well, meaningless. I hate it."

Dolly sighed while Chris continued to ramble.

"It makes the lines blur all the time. Know what I mean?"

Again Dolly nodded.

"And, if you can't think straight enough to *see* your way out, and you have no one who really wants to deal with you… *how* can you get out?!"

Chris' eyes shifted downward.

"So what you're sayin' is…"

"What I'm *saying* is…" Chris stopped herself in mid-sentence and sighed.

"Is what?"

"Is that…" She sighed deeper this time.

"What, Chris? Just keep talkin'."

"It's that… that no one gets it. You know, what I've… what I've been through and all that. How it makes me feel inside and…" Chris' voice started to crack. "And now…"

"And now?"

"And now they're throwin' me to the wolves again!"

Dolly's mind made a quick flashback over her last two years: to Pattie, to Aunt Anna and Uncle John, to Brenda, George, Clark, Jack Dawkins, and her own personal metamorphosis.

"Chris…"

"Yeah?" She sniffled.

"Did you ever hear the one that goes: Just when the caterpillar thought the world was over, it became a butterfly?"

"No…" she sniffled again, "But I'd like to."

"You would?"

"Yeah. I really would."

Dolly turned toward her world-weary flight partner and gave her a gentle and understanding smile. "Well then… you just sit back and relax for a while, Miss Chrissy.

"…Have *I* got a story for you!"

Personal note from the author

On March 6th, 1962, Townsends Inlet and Sea Isle City were hit by a massive hurricane.

My favorite boardwalk ride of all time, a huge carousel, was totally destroyed by the storm; and, my favorite carousel animal, a lion I named "Big Kitty" when I was barely three, was swept out into the ocean, never to be seen again.

Aunt Anna and Uncle John's house was saved because it was built on stilts, so, even when the ocean met the bay in the middle of their street; the house itself was high and dry - although the stilts were left standing in almost seven feet of water.

Thankfully, Aunt Anna and Uncle John were transported out safely by helicopter. The only thing my aunt took was a honeymoon photo of her and Uncle John taken in one of those pretty wicker push chairs that used to ride along the boards in Atlantic City.

Such was their love.

The tiny village of Townsends Inlet that was once dotted with only about 100 simple little screened-in-porch houses is now a bustling sea side resort. Huge condos line the beach front and the bay area.

Yet, even now, in the Summer of 2005, as I sit on what used to be John's Pier I can look over toward the old Coast Guard Station and still see a few of those sweet screened-in-porch houses, looking exactly as they did when I was a child.

It's comforting to me.

Just this morning I took a brief walk up to the beach, and then back down to Landis Avenue, passed Busch's Seafood House, a 5th generation restaurant that has been in operation since 1882! Just about a block away from Busch's I walked by a building named Blitz's Market that once housed my favorite store in the entire world, that charming, quaint little grocery store known as Shellum's. I also walked by a huge state of the art condo where The Charcoal House once stood, passed the little church on the corner, and, of course, I walked into The Civic Center. (I could almost hear Elvis singing 'Heartbreak Hotel.') As I continued my walk along 85th Street, I found myself ignoring the beautiful new "Luxury Town homes" that now line the block. My mind could only focus on the few old ones that remained, the ones of my childhood...my teenage life... well, the ones I had known for *all* of my life. To the new summer visitors of Townsends Inlet those cottages just weren't very modern and up to date, and a lot of people wondered why anyone would even let them stay the way they were: you know, that old-fashioned, takin' it slow and easy, Jersey shore look.

Well, *I* knew why.

Those comfortable screened-in back porches were the perfect place to sit at night and watch a glorious summer sunset, a place to rest and read a good book, a quiet place to sit and rock your child gently to sleep. And those 'small kitchens'? I had to laugh when I'd hear someone talk about the size of the kitchens in cozy homes like Aunt Anna's and Uncle John's. Some of the best meals I ever ate, in fact, some of the best meals that were ever cooked in the entire state of New Jersey came out of that 11X8 foot kitchen - courtesy of my Aunt Anna, and one well-used 1939 green and white porcelain claw foot stove.

That little cottage on 85th Street had character.

It had history.

It withstood hurricanes, record snow falls, and the chopping block from die hard, "I wanna buy this place and turn it into a palace" contractors.

Thank God!

Now call it my writers imagination or whatever, but as I watch those million dollar yachts ride down the bay, along with the magnificent cabin cruisers, and the glorious sail boats... somehow they disappear from my sight, and all I can see out there on the water is a happy little nine year-old girl and her favorite uncle fishing for flounder in a tiny, green and white wooden rowboat.

I hear her laugh as she makes the first catch of the day.

I sense the pride her Uncle has for his favorite fishing buddy.

A sweet voice calls and says, "There's a nice piece of fresh strawberry shortcake waiting for you, Dear."

My head fills with wonderful memories and my heart overflows with happiness.

And, once again...

I am... home.

Judith Kristen
Townsends Inlet, New Jersey
July 14, 2005

John and Anna Turner

Honeymoon Photo

Atlantic City, New Jersey

Circa 1909

John and Anna Turner
Outside their happy home on 85th Street
Townsends Inlet, New Jersey
Circa 1959

The Light and Dark Side of Seventeen is sure to be Judith Kristen's third best-selling Young Adult book! Ms. Kristen lives happily ever after in Southern New Jersey with her husband, Andrew, four cats: Cynthia, Miss Rose, Mookie, Ned, and a sweet old sheepdog named Henley

Part of the royalties from this book will be donated to:

The Frankford High School Library
Oxford Avenue at Wakeling Street
Philadelphia, Pennsylvania
and
The Sea Isle City Historical Museum
4208 Landis Avenue
Sea Isle City, New Jersey